CALIFORNIA BRIDES

Love Is Given a Fresh Chance in Three Historical Novels

CATHY MARIE HAKE

BARBOUR PUBLISHING

ISBN 978-1-59789-848-5

All scripture quotations are taken from the King James Version of the Bible.

Published by Barbour Publishing, Inc., P.O. Box 719, Uhrichsville, Ohio 44683

Our mission is to publish and distribute inspirational products offering exceptional value and biblical encouragement to the masses.

Printed in the United States of America.

Dear Reader,

Fair weather, Pacific Ocean, Rocky Mountains, and Yosemite. . .California has it all. A song says there's no place like home. For me, home has always been California, and I agree—there's no place like this sunshine-blessed part of America. I'm thrilled to be able to share "my" state with you.

Sometimes love slips in softly and takes us by surprise. Then there are the rest of us—who have to overcome obstacles, seek God's will, and discover what the future holds.

This collection of stories is the next generation of the Chance family. If you haven't read *California Chances* or *Kentucky Chances*, that's okay. I've written these so they stand alone. These stories came about because of readers like you who enjoyed the rugged Chance men and the women who tamed them. Those readers asked for more—so here are the Chance daughters. I hope you enjoy meeting these four girls and fall in love along with them.

Thank you for sharing your precious reading time with me.

God bless you,
Cathy Marie Hake

Handful of Flowers

Dedication

To nurses and doctors everywhere,
whose dedication transcends long hours and lousy pay.
So many of them reach out their hands in the name of the Lord
and minister with loving care. God bless you one and all.
Also to Elvera Smith, my mama—a nurse
who brought up both of her daughters to be nurses.

Prologue

1889
Chance Ranch, just outside San Francisco

Heart pounding, Polly Chance lay stock still as the door whispered open and shut. From her bed in the loft, she couldn't see who'd let himself in. Midnight darkness shrouded the cabin. Whoever it was, he moved silently as a coyote.

She slid her fingers under her pillow to grasp the knife she kept there. Mama Lovejoy had given her that knife the day she turned nine. She'd taught Polly how to use it for gathering plants, but Daddy took her aside and told her to keep it beneath her pillow each night for safety's sake. Her fingers curled around the bone handle.

"Polly!" a whisper sounded from down by the door.

She bolted upright in bed and hissed, "April, you near scared me out of my mind! Why are you sneaking around at this time of the night?"

Laurel grumbled from the other side of the bed, "What does time have to do with it? A lady never sneaks anywhere."

Polly lit a lantern and stared down at her cousin, who had moved to the center of the small cabin. April stood there dressed in her deep blue robe. Frills from her pale pink flannel nightgown peeped from the neck and hem, but the satchel by her bare feet captured Polly's attention.

"I'm running away." April fussed with her robe's belt until she tied it into an absurdly huge knot. "Either you let me stay with you, or I'm going to mount up and ride over to the MacPhersons'. They'll take me in."

"Couldn't you wait till morning?" Laurel yawned. "Things always are better in the daylight."

"They'll be worse in the daylight!" April burst into tears. "I got up to visit the outhouse and found Cole at the table, reading my diary."

Laurel vaulted over Polly, scrambled down the ladder, and enveloped April in a hug. "You poor girl!"

"If I don't move in with Polly," April said tearfully, "I'll never have any privacy."

Polly slipped the knife back under her pillow. The unsettled rhythm of her heart no longer came from fright; it came from the knowledge that her well-ordered, comfortable existence had just slipped out the door when her cousin came in. Climbing out of bed, she realized the wisdom behind one of Daddy's sayings. *Nothing ever stays the same, but changes are always for the better if given to God.* She took hold of the lantern, handed it down to Laurel, and lifted the hem of her buttercup flannel gown. As her instep found the next rung to the ladder, she said, "Let's have some tea and talk this over."

It didn't take any time whatsoever for Polly to decide what type of tea to brew. Though she kept an appreciable array of teas from the times she went gathering with her mother, only one tea would do under these circumstances: chamomile. It soothed.

Huddled across the table, hands curled around her teacup, April asked, "Will you let me move in?"

"If she moves in," Laurel said, "so do I."

"Can't we worry about you some other day?" April sniffled. "Come morning, Cole is going to blab to everyone what I wrote!"

"Whatever did you write?" Laurel asked.

Polly wondered, too—but she tamped down her curiosity. "That's none of our business. Diaries are personal. Don't you worry about Cole. He owes me a favor. I'll take care of him."

"Cole owes you a favor?" Laurel and April said in unison.

Polly pressed her lips together and shrugged. From an early age, she'd learned the value of discretion.

"Well, that takes care of that." Laurel giggled.

"I'm still not living under the same roof with him. I can't bear it!" April took a gulp of tea, made a face, and dumped in more sugar. She stirred it with such agitation, the tea sloshed over the brim and formed a puddle in the saucer. "The older boys are in the bunkhouse. It's only fair for us girls to have a cabin."

Polly sat in silence. Laurel often spent the night with her already. If April moved in, Kate would, too. Literally overnight, Polly would be assuming responsibility for three younger, sometimes flighty girls. *Lord, You gave me fair warning this was going to happen. I figured it would be another year or so, but we'll just put it in Your hands.*

"It's Polly's cabin, really." Laurel cast a look up at the loft where she'd been sharing Polly's bed. "I mean, well—"

"Everyone calls it my cabin," Polly said slowly, "but the Chance family shares. We always have. Maybe this needs to be the girls' cabin. The only problem I see is, it seems unfair to leave Kate out."

"You're right," Laurel agreed.

April's eyes filled with tears. "This isn't fair. You know Uncle Titus won't ever let Kate live here."

Pouring more tea, Polly chose her words and modulated her tone just as Mama had taught her to. Often the lessons on healing folks applied just as well to dealing with them. "Once you move in with us, April, Kate's bound to want to be here, too."

"I can't blame her," Laurel admitted. "The odds around this place are abysmal. We girls are outnumbered something awful."

Polly nodded. "I'll tiptoe over and have a little talk with Cole." On her part, the decision was already made—if only her aunts and uncles would agree with the plan, this would become the girls' cabin. The Chance families all lived in a large rectangle of cabins so their daughters would be close by—but the Chance men lost their famed logic when it came to protecting their daughters. *The last thing we need is to rile them from the start.* "April, did you leave a note for your folks to let them know where you are?"

"No."

Laurel let out a squeak. "Aunt Miriam will be devastated!"

Polly snorted. "Uncle Gideon's the one who's going to have a fit and fall in it. First off, we're going to put a note on the table for them. We need Uncle Gideon's help to reason with Uncle Titus, or Kate is doomed."

"We ought to pray," Laurel said.

April let out a short, teary laugh. "All I can think of is that saddle tramp who came through here last summer. Remember how he'd shake his head and say, 'God help us all'? Well, that's how I'm feeling."

"I like that. It's heartfelt, and we're praying it with respect." Polly put down her cup, reached across the table, and clasped both of her cousins' hands. She bowed her head. "Lord, we're blessed with a big family, but there are times it's hard to put up with them. Give us patience and humor. We'd like to ask You to make straight the path with the family so they can let us unite together here in this cabin. Thank You for all You do for us, and help us to be Your servants. In Jesus' name. Amen."

She looked up at her cousins. In unison, they said, "God help us all."

Chapter 1

A week later

We gotta make tracks. Eunice drops her young'uns faster each time." Uncle Mike shuffled nervously in the doorway. "Last one didn't take from dinner to supper."

Polly didn't respond. Mama Lovejoy had taught her to hold her tongue when her comments might cause anxiety.

"Do you"—Laurel's voice went shaky and high—"need me to come along and help?"

Polly cast a quick glance at her cousin. In the days since they'd joined her in the cabin, Laurel, April, and Kate had all offered to assist her on sick calls. They'd certainly taken to heart their pledge to stick together and help one another out, but Laurel blanched to the color of dandelion fluff at the mere mention of anything medical. She'd be in the way. "Thanks for the offer, but Aunt Tempy will be there to help. Maybe you could. . ." She thought hard to concoct some other task.

"She can finish sewing the blanket whilst April and I make lunch," Kate cut in.

"We'll be praying for you," April tacked on as she gave Polly a push. A second later, mounted atop Blossom, Polly clutched her brown leather healer's satchel and did some praying herself. Riding fast as the wind alongside Uncle Mike, Polly followed the prayer with a mental rehearsal of the necessary steps to follow for safe delivery.

They reached the MacPherson ranch, and one of the men swiped her from her mount. "We was scart you might not make it in time." He didn't even bother to set her down. Instead, the hulking man carried her straight to the doorstep and shoved her inside.

Aunt Tempy met her with a quick hug and whispered, "Lovejoy's not coming?"

"Daddy said he'd bring her soon as she got home from seeing someone who's ailing."

Tempy grinned and nodded. "You know what to do. I've boiled water aplenty for ye. Lois'll be watching the other young'uns whilst we welcome this one."

Polly appreciated Aunt Tempy's confidence in her. A prayer she'd heard her mama say ran through her mind, and the words rang deep and true. *Lord, use my hands. You created this little life—now help me bring it safely into the world.* She set down her satchel, then rolled up her sleeves as she approached the rocking chair. "So how far apart are your pains, Aunt Eunice?"

"Middlin' far. I—ooohhh."

From the outside of the house, a deep male groan sounded.

After having been through other births here, Polly knew the MacPherson men made it a habit to stand directly under the window and "share" their wives' travail. At the moment, Aunt Eunice arched her head back against the pressed-wood oak rocker as the pain washed over her. When it ended, she mopped her brow with the edge of her shawl. "Guess I'd best change that to middlin' close. These pains got a fearsome grip on me when they come."

Polly nodded. Aunt Eunice didn't complain unless she had cause. "Did Uncle Hezzy bring in the ax yet?"

Her aunt let out a weary puff of air. "I been a-keepin' it under my bed, but that knothead took it out to chop wood, and now he cain't 'member where he left it!"

Supposedly, the ax cut the pain of childbirth—not that Polly believed it much after seeing women in their travail—but Aunt Eunice certainly put store by that tale. Thinking quickly, Polly pasted a smile on her face. "Well then, it's a good thing I just sharpened my gathering knife. You never saw such an edge on a blade. I don't aim to be boastful, but it could shave a gnat's whiskers. It'll do the trick." She pulled the knife from her sheath, held it up for show, then went over and slid it under the bed.

"I don't have me much time to ponder on whether that'll do," Aunt Eunice choked out before she started to moan again.

Polly splashed some whiskey onto the table and wiped it down. The pungent odor made her nose twitch, but she'd read all about Lister and knew the value of ridding her working surface of bacteria. From the looks of things, she had no time to scrub the table with lye soap.

As Aunt Tempy laid out a little blanket, diapers, a gown, and a tiny cap for the baby, she whispered, "Good thinkin' on that knife. You know how stubborn Eunice is when she catches 'old of a notion. She refused to get into bed till Hezzy found the ax. I was a-feared she'd birth the babe in the chair and drop him on his head!"

Polly flashed her an understanding smile, then opened her satchel. The MacPherson men and women stayed true to their culture from back in Hawk's Fall and Salt Lick Holler. Their more-mythical-and-magical-than-medical notions might have made sense thousands of miles away in the secluded mountains and hills, but here they amounted to amusement at best and danger at worst. No use trying to argue with a laboring woman, so Polly simply honored their traditions and went ahead with the more important preparations. She knew full well once she got Aunt Eunice upright, the baby would arrive, so she wanted everything ready first. . .if the baby cooperated.

A small vial of precious ergot came first. She carefully measured a few purplish-black scrapings onto a tiny china plate. After the delivery, she'd rub that on Aunt Eunice's gums and inside her cheek to keep her from bleeding too badly. Next, she took out the pale yellow towel she'd boiled and spread it on the table, then unrolled the necessary instruments.

"Reckon that knife'll have to do." Aunt Eunice twisted her shawl in one hand as she gripped the arm of the rocking chair with the other. "This babe ain't gonna wait for nuthin'."

"Have you decided on names yet?" Polly helped Eunice from the rocking chair and walked her toward the bed.

"No. I'm too old for this nonsense," Eunice panted. "Thirty-eight. My oldest ought to be carryin' on the line 'stead of me goin' through this."

"In the Bible, Sarah had baby Isaac, and she was much older than thirty-eight." Polly rubbed her aunt's back when the woman stopped for the next pain.

Aunt Eunice let out a gusty sigh after the contraction passed. "Ain't no questionin' the Almighty's plan. You ken how much I love every one o' the babes He give me."

"Yes, I do." Polly helped her into the bed.

Grabbing Polly's arm, Aunt Eunice whispered, "But I got me a dreadful feelin'. Thirteen's a rare bad number."

"I told her to go ahead and have another to make it fourteen, but she didn't appreciate that one bit," Aunt Tempy said as she fluffed the pillow.

"Mercy!" Aunt Eunice curled up and clenched harder on Polly's arm. A lifetime of kneading bread lent her bone-crushing strength. "Oh, Lord a merrrcyyy!"

"Dear God in heaven!" Uncle Hezzy prayed loudly from outside the cabin, "Holp my Eunice. Don't let her be a-hurtin' so bad."

Aunt Eunice's eyes narrowed as she chuffed air. When she finally relaxed, she hollered, "Hezekiah MacPherson, don't you go askin' the Almighty to do His side of a bargain when you shirked your own. Git yerself out there and find me that ax!"

Polly doubted Uncle Hezzy would leave the vicinity. Then again, everyone else in the entire clan would search high and low on his behalf. Judging from the exam she did, Polly figured they'd better hurry, because Aunt Eunice was right. This baby wasn't going to wait.

"I done decided onct this here babe comes, I'll—ohhh, hit's too hard on me," Aunt Eunice whimpered. She sucked in a deep breath and hollered, "I cain't do it 'less I got me that ax."

"Ever'body's lookin' for it, lambkins!"

Rolling her head to the side, Aunt Eunice muttered, "Ain't that jest like a man—letting his woman labor and his young'uns work, and there he stands, pretendin' a few fancy words'll—ahhh, mercyyy!"

Fifteen minutes later, Polly laid a just-wiped-clean newborn into her aunt's arms. "A girl, Aunt Eunice! A pretty little redhead."

"Now praise the Lord!" Aunt Eunice smiled wearily. "Leastwise, I got me another daughter. Reckon 'twas worth it, after all."

"You would have said that about a son, too," Aunt Tempy said.

"Gotta set your mind to bein' satisfied with whate'er the dear Lord give ya." Aunt Eunice put the babe to breast. "Kickin' 'gainst what is don't make it no different; jest gives you sore toes."

"She takes after you," Aunt Tempy said. "Lookie at that hair."

"I prayed for mercy. That's why she looks like me," Aunt Eunice said. "A girl-child who took after Hezzy would grow up to be a lonely old spinster."

"Uncle Hezzy is handsome on the inside—that's what counts most." Polly tended to matters.

"Yore mama got herself a good man, and you got yoreself a good daddy," Aunt Eunice crooned to the baby. A tired smile chased across her face, and she whispered, "And I hollered an extry bit so's Hezekiah will let me stick with the name I had my heart settled on 'stead of the one he wanted."

Aunt Tempy and Polly muffled their laughter.

"My girl-child's gonna be called Elvera. Did you ever hear a more beautiful name?"

"Elvera," Polly repeated. She'd been prepared for something unusual. Aunt Eunice and Uncle Hezzy argued over names and managed to have created some doozies. Elvera rated as one of the nicer ones. "We could shorten it to Elvie or Vera, too."

"Nope. Nobody's gonna cut down a perfectly fine name. Couldn't take an ax to the pain, and they ain't a-gonna take an ax to her name." Aunt Eunice bobbed her head emphatically. "My mind's made up."

"I got one! I got one!" The shout sounded over the thunder of horses' hooves. "Here. Take this in with you." A second later, the door opened, then shut, and someone cleared his throat.

Polly hastily flipped the sheet over Eunice and turned around. She frowned at the handsome stranger standing there. "Thank you for the ax, but we're about done here."

The tall, dark-haired stranger shoved the ax off to the side and rumbled, "Axes don't belong at a delivery. Someone handed it to me, but it's not needed." He peeled out of his coat, then stopped cold when the baby started to whimper. "He's here?"

"Yes, she is." Polly tried not to laugh at the man's horrified expression. "All ten fingers and toes."

"Only because you didn't have the ax," the stranger muttered. Instead of looking relieved and making a quick getaway, he rolled up the sleeves of his snowy shirt, baring muscular forearms. "Now then, let's make sure everything else is—"

"Hold it right there, mister." Aunt Tempy parked herself in front of him and glowered. "You don't belong in here."

"I'm Dr. Walcott."

"We're pleased to make your acquaintance," Polly said crisply, "but a man doesn't belong at a birthing."

Aunt Tempy folded her arms across her chest. "Everything's swimmin' along, right as a tadpole in a water hole."

"I'm gratified to hear that." He pushed past Aunt Tempy. "I'll just have a look—"

"No, you won't." Polly couldn't fathom the arrogance he displayed. "Mother and child are both in my hands, and—"

"And if someone competent doesn't see to matters, they'll just as likely be in God's hands within the week."

"I got me my niece and my sister-in-law here. I'm farin' better than after any of my other birthings."

"And we're glad they were here to help you," the doctor said smoothly. Stubborn as could be, he reached the bedside. "However, a woman who's had several children and is your advanced age—"

"You a-callin' me old?" Aunt Eunice nearly shouted, "I'm only thirty-seven! I got plenty of years left in me and pr'bly two or three more babes, too."

"Right now, I need to be concerned with Aunt Eunice and this baby." Polly pivoted to the side to block him. Under any other circumstances, she'd find it entertaining that her aunt had just shaved a year off her age, but right now, other matters were more pressing.

Aunt Eunice shot her a look of relief. "Doc, you cain step back outside till after my Hezzy sees his young'un. 'Tis fittin' for a man to see the child he fathered afore anyone else does."

"The father can come in and see the babe. I'll tend you," the doctor announced.

Polly looked over her shoulder at him. "Doctor, we don't know you from Adam. Now's not a good time for introductions. You need to honor Aunt Eunice's wishes."

"He's upsetting me. If my milk a-curdles, I'll know who to blame!"

The doctor frowned at the collection of instruments on the table, then looked at Aunt Tempy. "You must have some basic knowledge; else you'd not possess these things. The multiparous woman is likely to hemorrhage. Ergot—"

"Whoa. You're talking to the wrong woman." Aunt Tempy pointed at Polly.

The doctor's gray eyes widened in frank disbelief.

Polly sought to assure him she'd anticipated the need to administer ergot. "I have scrapings from rusty rye."

"Hit come from Hattie back home in Salt Lick Holler," Aunt Eunice said. "None better. Now you scat."

The doctor's jaw clamped shut. He nodded curtly, turned, and left.

Chapter 2

Eric Walcott left the cabin and practically got mobbed.

"What're you doin' out here?"

"Git back in there and holp my Eunice!"

"Is sommat a-wrong?"

Plenty's wrong. That woman in there could be bleeding to death, and all she has is a few well-meaning, backward family members who don't understand the danger and are too steeped in ignorant folklore to accept help. Only Eric couldn't face these worried men and children and tell them those harsh truths. To add to the mind-boggling peculiarity of the whole incident, he noticed everyone happened to be dressed in some shade of gold.

"Doc, my Eunice—she didn't. . ."

He forced a smile and tried to give what reassurance he could honestly offer. "The babe's already made her appearance."

"Boy or girl?" one of the large, hairy men asked.

"A girl, you dolt!" The other smacked him with a battered hat. "He said 'her,' so it's gotta be a girl!"

"And my Eunice? She's farin' well?"

Well, he'd tried to avoid this. But he couldn't very well lie. "I can't say. My offer of help was refused." The admission galled him—a little because of his pride but mostly because he genuinely worried about that woman. Her niece wanted to treat her with—of all things—rust and bootleg rye whiskey.

"We'll see 'bout that!" The father shouldered through the crowd of children who spanned everything from diapered to desirable and opened the door. "Eunice, you let this here sawbones come see to you and little Elsiebelle."

"It ain't been half an hour yet, so you jest turn tail and wait till me and Elvera are ready!"

Someone slammed the door, and Eric watched in disbelief as the other two men burst out laughing. "Shoulda knowed that'd happen," one said.

"You broke the rule," the other short, wiry one agreed.

A school-age, barefoot boy scratched a bony elbow and scrunched his sunburned nose. "Pa, what's a vera?"

The father glowered at them. "She done went and named my baby girl Elvera!"

"I swan that name's sorta pretty, Pa."

The scowl melted, and the huge man sat down on the porch step. He opened his arms, and a whole bunch of children pressed into him for a tangled hug. "Iff'n she's half as pretty as y'all, my heart's gonna bust."

Another redheaded woman rounded the far side of the barn and came toward them. From the looks of her, she'd be having a child in four or five months. The way she waddled at this early point of her carrying months told Eric this child had to have several brothers and sisters ahead of it. For now, that redhead had a knot of young children skipping at her heels and clinging to her skirt. "Did Eunice make me an aunt?"

A hundred times or so, I'd say, Eric thought.

"Aunt Lois! She had a Vera!"

Lois grinned and nodded. "Now ain't that the finest thang you ever heared? Johnna, yore old 'nuff to come on inside with me. The rest of you young'uns pay heed to what your pas tell you."

Things continued in that bizarre vein. The crowd parted to allow them access, then the door shut yet again—with both the doctor and father still left outside!

Eric marveled that this clan endured. They must be exceptionally hearty stock to survive the appalling medical "practices" he'd witnessed. The cabin had been tidy, and a quick glance around showed the farm to be well kept. Surely that ought to be counted as a good sign. These folks wanted to succeed. They might kick a little, but when he demonstrated the advantages of the scientific advances, they'd progress into the modern age.

"Thanks for coming anyway, Doc." The young man he'd seen in town—Peter—extended a callused hand.

Eric shook it. "I'm glad no one used the ax."

Peter shook his head. "Uncle Hezzy'll never hear the end of that."

"I saw a perfectly good pair of scissors in there."

Confusion furrowed Peter's brow. "What do scissors have to do with anything? They're too puny to cut much pain."

"The ax was supposed to cut the pain," Eric deduced. He didn't know whether to be astonished by that nonsense or glad they hadn't used it to cut the cord.

Unaware of the doctor's thoughts, Peter nodded. "Only Uncle Hezzy lost the ax, and Aunt Eunice has a long memory when it comes to things like that. Bet he'll even let her name the next baby, too."

The door opened. Lois came back out. "Hezzy, go say howdy to yore new babe. The rest of you, take your turn, then come on over for supper. Got a big ol' mess of chicken an' dumplin's ready."

As the others crowded to go see the latest member of this enormous family, Polly exited the cabin. "Doctor, let's talk."

"Yeah, Doc." Lois beamed at him. "We'll fatten you up a mite and get to know you."

Eric shouldered through the throng and made it to Polly's side. They'd mentioned Polly was a niece. No use insulting her—and especially not in front of family. He'd ruffled feathers, and as soon as he calmed her, they'd review Eunice's delivery. In the meantime, he refused to budge. "This little lady and I need to compare medical notes. I'm sure you all understand."

"We'll sit here on the porch." Polly lowered herself onto a bench. "That way, we'll be close to Eunice and Elvera."

Eric sat on the other end of the bench. "Absolutely."

"Then I'll jest send out some vittles for ye." Lois turned and headed into another cabin.

Eric's stomach rumbled. He figured he might as well have a quick supper and turn Polly into an ally. Then he'd go make sure Eunice and Elvera hadn't suffered any complications. A mouth-watering aroma filled the air, and he nodded his head as a young woman handed him a sizable bowl. "Thank you."

"Welcome." She blushed.

Polly accepted the other bowl and murmured her thanks. He'd said a quick prayer, but he waited until she finished her silent grace before taking a taste from his bowl. "This is excellent!"

"Lois would be pleased to send you home with a jar."

His sense of humor kicked in, so he muttered, "Eunice was ready to send me home in a jar."

Polly didn't bother to muffle her peal of laughter. "You caught her at a bad moment."

Her reaction pleased him. This young woman might be misguided, but she wasn't malicious. That boded well. "Soon as I'm done with this"—he lifted the spoon to his mouth and chose his words with exceeding care—"I'll go in and make sure matters are resolved."

Polly looked him directly in the eye. "Matters between you and Eunice, or medical ones?"

"Both," he answered succinctly. Several more MacPhersons ambled out of the cabin, but he stayed focused on her. "I took an oath—"

"I lernt 'bout that at school," a wiggly boy boasted. "It's the hip. . .the hip. . ." He strained, then jumped up and down. "The hippopotamus oath!"

"Nah, silly." One of the other older boys poked him. "It's the hypocrite's oath."

Amused, Eric said nothing.

Polly laughed again. The woman's laugh was light and free—sweet and nothing like the practiced giggles of the debutantes back East. "You're close, boys. It's the Hippocratic oath. Hippocrates was the father of medicine."

"Don't tell that to Hezzy," a beefy man moaned from the doorway. "He'll take a mind to name his next 'un 'Medicine' iff'n you do."

Though that observation set off a round of hoots, Eric knew better than to express an opinion. He lifted his bowl. "Good supper."

"Always welcome to come back for more, Doc." The man and children all ambled over to the supper cabin.

Eric then turned back to finish his explanation. "Polly, I meant every last word of the oath. It would be remiss of me to fail to render care."

"It would be remiss of you to fail to offer care. You did that." She took a bite of a dumpling, chewed it thoughtfully, then swallowed. "You're wearing what my mama calls a 'dig-in-the-heels look.' I suppose I could tell you everything's fine, but you're still going to march back in there."

He shrugged. "I won't pretend otherwise."

"Eunice is sure her milk will curdle if you upset her again." Nicely enough, Polly didn't even react when he choked on that little piece of information. Instead, she merely continued, "Perhaps it would be best if I eased you in and out real quick."

He gulped the last bite as he thumped his bowl onto the bench between them. "Good. Good."

She set aside her own half-eaten bowl and rose. Eric winced. In his urgency, he'd rushed her. It was all for a good cause. Only the dear Lord knew just what was happening with that mother in there.

"Stop scowling. I've had plenty." She tapped on the door, then opened it. "Aunt Tempy, Uncle Hezzy? Why don't you go eat supper? Doc and I will come sit with Eunice and the baby. I'm sure they'll be keeping you up all night."

"I don't need no doctorin'." Eunice lifted her head from the pillow and glowered at him.

"Doc wanted to see Elvera." Polly kept her tone light. "Let's let him estimate her weight." She slipped the baby from father to physician.

"Well, now!" Eric gently bounced the baby in his arms as a sense of awe swept over him. "Nice-sized. I'll have to take away a few ounces for this blanket, though. Someone quilted a fine one—warm."

"Eunice makes ev'ry young'un one whilst she's a-carryin'," her husband boasted.

"Well, I'd say she makes a fine blanket, but she makes an even prettier daughter. This one's eight pounds even. Let's take a look at those little fingers and toes." He needed to examine the babe, so he laid her on the bed next to her mama and opened the wrap.

"She's got long fingers. I'm thinkin' with our passel of young'uns, mayhap we should get a piany."

"Hmm. With those fingers, that would be possible. Wasn't that a mandolin I saw in the corner?" He lifted the gown and continued to confirm Elvera's health rated as superior.

" 'Tis mine," Tempy said. "And many of the children play it passingly well."

"If I don't put a stop to this, the next music is going to be you singing the praises of the MacPherson children." Polly plumped Eunice's pillow. "Aunt Tempy, Uncle Hezzy, go enjoy your supper."

"I reckon we will. You'll be jest fine here, lambkin. Doc agrees with our Polly that Elvera's eight pounds, so he must know what he's about."

That had to be the most backhanded, ridiculous endorsement Eric had ever received. He didn't let on. Instead, he nodded. That action, he'd found, often rescued him.

He tucked the baby into Eunice's arms as the others departed, then deftly drew back the covers.

"Polly, if that there doc dares ta lift my hem, I aim to clobber him. Should you be a-holding my little Elvera?"

"The doctor can speak for himself." Polly's calm blue gaze rested on him.

"I'm able to assess the womb like this." He placed his hand over Eunice's gown. "It's firm, and that's good. Very good." Satisfied she couldn't be hemorrhaging, he covered her once again. "Mrs. MacPherson, I'm pleased you and your daughter are in the pink of health. Having thirteen children is quite an accomplishment."

"Yore a-tellin' me." She let out a raspy laugh. "All of us together got twenty-four. Lois and Obie got 'leven—soon to be twelve—but no need to mention that since you pr'bly took note on that fact. Tempy and Mike have nine."

The woman must not have had any schooling. Her arithmetic was faulty.

She lovingly traced the tiny whorls of the baby's hair. "We done lost five when the diphtheria hit, and a few others jest winnowed away back to the bosom of Jesus when He took a mind to call 'em home."

"My condolences."

"He talks pretty, Polly." Eunice gave her niece a weary look.

"I venture it's more owed to him having a good heart than a glib tongue." Polly gave Eunice a sip of something. "Now you sleep. We'll be here."

We'll be here. Not I'll be here. Eric pulled up a chair and sat by the bed. Things were looking up. When he first got here, Polly told him a man had no place at a birthing. Now she'd accepted him.

Surely this little MacPherson woman had opened the door for him. If her loving but misguided family allowed him to treat them, then the rest of Reliable ought to follow suit. It was all working out so well—he'd asked the Lord to send him somewhere where he was needed. Now, more than ever, Eric knew he was in the center of God's will.

Chapter 3

"Wake up, sleepyheads." Polly woke her cousins the next morning as she put down her gathering sack. She and Mama Lovejoy went gathering almost every morning—as much for the quiet time together as for the opportunity to harvest essential plants. Even though Uncle Mike had brought Polly home late last night, she hadn't been able to sleep in. As soon as the first rays of sun crept into the sky, her eyes always popped open.

"Polly," Laurel said from their bed up in the loft, "must you sound so cheerful this early?"

" 'This is the day which the Lord hath made; we will rejoice and be glad in it.' "

April and Kate crawled out of the bed they shared and shimmied down the ladder in their ruffled nightgowns. Kate waggled a finger at her. "It's a good thing the Bible doesn't say anything about being jolly at night, because you'd use that as an excuse to wake us up, too!"

"It's our turn to make breakfast," April said. "Stop teasing her."

Laurel stayed in bed and began unwinding the rags from her hair. She managed to make rolling and unrolling those long tresses look so easy. It took her just a few minutes to accomplish it.

Polly unraveled her night braid, brushed her hair, and twisted it several times to form a bun at the back of her head. No matter where she stabbed in the hairpins, they didn't tame the wisps or keep the arrangement orderly. One last glance at Laurel made her give up. "I'm hopeless," she muttered.

April turned backward so Polly would help her with her stays. "Not too tight."

Polly tugged and tied, then gave her back a pat. Sweet April. She could cook, and her waistline tattled on all of the little tastes she took. "How about if I make coffee cake this morning?"

"I'll help you." April whirled around. "We'll bake bread, too."

Polly arched a brow. "Are you doing that for my sake or yours?"

Her cousins all laughed. Polly could follow instructions to formulate any elixir, unguent, or salve, but she couldn't follow a recipe if her life depended on it.

Yanking on a stocking, Kate mused, "I think it's because April wants to hear more about that new doctor."

"So what if I do?"

"April!" Polly gawked at her. "You're only sixteen."

"Plenty of girls marry when they're sixteen." April's chin lifted. "And—"

"And it's because they either don't have family to help them or the brains to know better." Polly shook her head. "Your daddy hasn't given you leave to even walk with a boy. What makes you think he'd let a doctor half again your age pay you court?"

Laurel stood at the mirror and neatly tied a bow at her throat. "You're simply too young and unsophisticated."

"And you aren't?" April half-shouted.

Polly held up a hand. "Whoa. We're all together here in this cabin. Remember our motto? 'God help us all.' I won't stand for squabbles. We're here to love and care for one another."

April's chin shook. "Sorry."

Laurel came over and settled her hand on April's arm. "I'm not setting my cap for the doctor. Don't think I'm trying to steal your man." Laurel sighed. "Truly, April, I'm eighteen and barely old enough myself, but I couldn't abide marrying a doctor."

"She couldn't wash the blood from his sleeves," Polly said succinctly. She then turned and glowered. "Kathryn Anne, don't you dare." In the midst of the conversation, Kate tried to wiggle into her dress without wearing her stays. Kate made a face, but she reached for the garment she hated.

"Let's go get breakfast," April muttered.

"I thought maybe I'd try Mrs. Dorsey's casserole recipe for lunch today," Laurel said as she headed toward the door. She waited until Kate was decent before opening it. "I want to perfect it for the next church supper. After all, the way to a man's heart is through his stomach."

"Then I'm going to be a spinster." Polly tugged Kate along. At the moment, being a spinster didn't seem like such a dreadful fate. Trying to keep track of her cousins and sidetrack their wild plans had become a nonstop job. But a husband like that tall, handsome, growly voiced Dr. Walcott would make handling children more than worthwhile.

Eric wiped the last dot of lather from his face, then cleaned his razor. A knock sounded.

"Breakfast in five minutes, Doctor."

"Thank you." He shrugged into his shirt and inhaled deeply to detect what the boardinghouse featured for breakfast. His cabin with the downstairs office wasn't available until the end of the month. Until then, he'd stay here. His bag and a crate of essential medicaments lay against the far wall, and it was awkward not to have an examining room. *It's just temporary. I chose to arrive early.*

HANDFUL OF FLOWERS

What an arrival. He'd no more than stepped foot into the mercantile when a young man barreled through the door, shouting about a woman in labor and needing an ax. Eric mounted up and rode along to the MacPhersons. He'd returned late last evening and hadn't met any townsfolk yet. How many of Reliable Township's inhabitants were hillbillies? Would they all cling to the misguided ways and silly notions he'd seen Polly employ yesterday?

The advertisement he'd responded to stated the town was a "thriving place near a metropolis." Well, San Francisco was a day away, but Eric wondered if their concept of thriving matched Polly's notion of medicine.

He didn't smell any particular aroma until he opened his door. "Mmm. Coffee."

A man exiting the room next to his chuckled. "Makes waking up worth it. I'm Bob Timpton." They shook hands.

"Eric Walcott."

As they tromped downstairs, Bob said, "No one was expecting you here yet."

"It took less time than expected to close matters back East." They sat at the table and waited until a gentleman at the head of the table said grace. As soon as folks started passing the platters and bowls, Eric asked, "Any recommendations on where I can buy a decent horse?"

"Chance Ranch," someone across the table and another two seats down said in unison.

"Fine horseflesh," Bob attested. "They'll give you a fair price. Livery can board your mount."

The owner of the boardinghouse leaned over his shoulder to fill his mug. "Dr. Walcott, I'm sure you aimed to pay a professional visit to the Chances, anyway."

"Is someone ill?"

"No, no." She continued to round the table, filling cups. "Lovejoy and Polly Chance live there. I'm sure you'll all be working together."

"Polly?" The bacon scraped his throat as he swallowed it too quickly. "She's not a MacPherson?"

"She's a Chance. They're loosely related. Not even kissing cousins." Last cup filled, the woman whisked off to the kitchen.

"So Polly wasn't merely helping out her aunt yesterday." Coffee churning in his stomach, Eric tried to digest this news. He didn't have to coax Polly into stepping aside to treat her family; he had to completely take away the business she and her mother ran. Quite literally, only God knew what they'd done to patients in the name of medicine. This was going to take finesse. Tact. Prayer. But Eric knew then and there he couldn't sit back and permit backwoods myths and folklore to be the basis for curing people in the modern age.

Times were changing. These people would, too—even if he had to nudge them. It was his duty, because he'd taken an oath. Nothing—and no one—would stop Eric Walcott from keeping that pledge. Not even some pretty little wheat-haired, wide-eyed, whiskey-dispensing girl.

"Oh. Look at him!" April whispered to Polly at the water pump.

Polly cast a glance over her shoulder, then straightened up. "Hello, Doctor."

"Hello." He cast a keen glance toward the main house, and for good cause. Perry kept letting out bloodcurdling screams. "Is everything okay?"

"Mama's fixing up Perry," Polly said. "He took a fall."

"I see." The doctor scanned toward the barn. "Are your men around?"

"Which ones?" April hefted a bucket.

Dr. Walcott dismounted from a sorry-looking old nag. "Whoever is in charge of the horses."

"Uncle Gideon's in the main house." Polly lifted another bucket. "This way, please."

The doctor silently took both buckets from the girls and followed. Polly appreciated his manners. He'd not made a big deal out of helping with such an ordinary task, but simple things like that tattled about a man's character.

April scurried ahead and flung open the door. "We have a caller. It's the doctor."

"I don't want the doctor," Perry cried. "I want Auntie Lovejoy!"

Polly turned to the doctor. "Please don't take offense. Perry's a tad riled."

The doctor set down the buckets just inside the door and headed toward the noise. "What seems to be the problem?"

Mama turned to him, but she also held Perry's hand. "Nothing a few stitches won't solve. This little feller took a leap into the hayloft and didn't aim true."

Uncle Gideon held Perry on his lap and kept the towel wrapped about him so he couldn't squirm much. "Look at what Laurel has, Perry. You get to pick whatever color stitches you want."

Laurel held out a fistful of silk embroidery floss. "I brought lots of colors so you could choose whatever you like best."

"What are you putting on him?" Dr. Walcott's eyes narrowed as he watched Mama.

"Toothache plant." Mama stopped pressing ice to the gash and started to rub the flower against the edges. When Perry whimpered, she said in a loud whisper, "You're brave as a buccaneer, so I'm a-thinkin' mayhap black's the color for you."

"Ben had black." Even though Perry's lower lip trembled, it now stuck out in a pout. "It looked like a big, fat woolly worm."

"Iff'n I make the X to mark the spot dead center, we'll all know 'tis like a treasure map."

Polly watched as Mama finished applying the toothache plant. The ice began numbing the cut; toothache would finish numbing it and act as an antiseptic. With so many children around, the family had the whole technique down to an art by now. Polly or Mama numbed and treated the wound while another adult kept hold of the child and others distracted him. Polly headed for the stove and brought over a pot of boiling water.

"I wanna treasure map," Perry sniffled.

"I'll make a fine one. No fair lookin' till I'm done, though. It's the rule."

Uncle Gideon pulled the towel tighter to hold his nephew immobile and cupped his hand around Perry's head. "Close your eyes. Kate will tell you a story, so you listen real good."

Kate started in with a swashbuckling story as Mama threaded the needle and dipped it and the floss into the boiling water. Dr. Walcott hovered close. Though Polly would normally assist, she could tell the doctor itched to help out. All in all, it was probably a good idea for him to see up close just how skilled Mama was. That way, when he did surgery, he'd have the assurance that capable assistants were on hand. Polly took him over to the washstand. "If you scrub, you can clip for Mama."

He scrubbed thoroughly but with almost blinding speed, then went back to assist. His brows rose as he realized Mama was already half done with the sutures, but he picked up the scissors and started clipping the thread after the knot so Mama could continue on with the next stitch. He stepped back when it was all done.

"And so he sailed off toward the sunset," Kate finished.

Perry sniffled. "Can I look now?"

"Shore 'nuff cain," Mama said. "Lookie there at yore treasure map. 'Tis a cryin' shame to have to cover it up with a bandage, but we'll have to."

The little boy inspected the gash. "That's a map?"

"Here." Dr. Walcott dipped the blunt end of a probe into a bottle of iodine. He painted along the suture line, then drew another streak perpendicular to the sutures. "We don't want anyone but our crew to know you have the treasure map, so here's what we're going to do. . . . North, south, east, and west. See? We made it a compass." He drew an odd shape around the boy's arm. It didn't escape Polly's notice that he managed to trace over the deeper scratches. "That's Hazard Island."

"Is it, Auntie Lovejoy?" Perry asked.

"Niver seen better." Mama smiled.

"Do I gotta have a bandage?"

"Absolutely." Dr. Walcott smiled. "I'll put it on."

Perry stared at the doctor, then slowly shook his head. "Auntie Lovejoy and Polly take care of us when we get sick or hurted."

"I see." Eric nodded sagely. "Well, I came to see about buying a horse, so I'm glad the trip was still useful."

"We gotta lotta horses."

"Good." Eric smiled at Uncle Gideon. "Word has it you sell the best horses around."

"Daddy, he needs a horse badly," April said. She managed to sidle next to the doctor. "You should see what he rode in on!"

"My grandfather's horse isn't suited to this terrain. I hadn't realized there'd be such heavy riding, and she's too old. I'd like to turn her out to pasture. She served well, but the time has come to move ahead." Eric's explanation showed sense and compassion. Both fine qualities.

"What do you have in mind?" Uncle Gideon waited until Mama finished tying the bandage; then he ruffled Perry's hair and set him down. "We've horses aplenty."

"If possible, I'd like to get a young, even-tempered mount and pay lodging for the old mare to live out her days here."

"That must be hard to do," April cooed.

Polly wondered what had come over her cousin. Then again, she didn't. April was trying to flirt, and she was making a ninny of herself.

Eric shrugged. "Things serve a purpose. In life, new things come along. No reason not to trade up to something better."

Polly got a funny sensation in the pit of her stomach as he spoke. Then again, it might not be the words he used. Sometimes when she had a headache brewing, she got that same sick feeling. As soon as the men went outside to look at horses, Polly slipped away and took some feverfew, then returned to the kitchen and started making sandwiches. Soon the happy chatter around her made her wince. Pain streaked from her right temple to behind her ear. Within minutes, she set aside the knife and whispered to Mama, "I'm going to go lie down."

Mama frowned. "Yore pale as a new moon. You getting a sick headache again?"

"I took some feverfew."

"Aww, my Pollywog." Mama slid an arm around her waist and guided her toward the door. "Jest close yore eyes and cover them. Sun's bright as cain be. I'll lead you."

Polly stumbled along, and seconds later Mama stopped.

"Not again." Uncle Titus spoke in a low whisper. "C'mere." He lifted Polly and carried her to her cabin.

Chapter 4

Eric exited the barn and surveyed the layout of the ranch. Several cabins formed three sides of a rectangle. Lush gardens abounded, and half a dozen picnic tables took up part of the yard. Clearly, several branches of the family tree still lived and worked together here.

Movement off to one side captured his attention. A dark-haired man carried Polly into a cabin. Her head rested on his shoulder—a rather romantic scene, especially at midday in the middle of a big family barnyard.

Maybe I haven't quite gotten things straight. Maybe she's married to one of these men. Good. She'll be too wrapped up in family matters to tromp around and play doctor much longer.

He tried to convince himself of that. After all, he'd just seen Lovejoy Chance rub a fresh flower all over a gaping wound. If it didn't fester, it would be due only to heavenly intervention and the iodine Eric had painted on after the sutures. These people were practicing medieval medicine in the modern age.

"Your saddle and tack look to be in good shape," Gideon said.

"Yes, they are. I'll just switch it over to that gelding."

"One of the boys'll do it after lunch." Gideon headed toward the picnic tables in the yard. "Come have a seat. We eat lunch in shifts. That way, work doesn't have to grind to a halt."

The man he'd seen carrying Polly just moments before approached them. Up close, he looked far older. *That could be good—he'll have a stabilizing influence on Polly.*

"Doc, Lovejoy asked if you could take a peek at Polly."

"Oh?"

"Yeah. My niece gets these rip-roarin' headaches. Come on of a sudden and lie her low for days."

"I see." Eric headed toward the cabin into which he'd seen the man carry Polly. Headaches were symptoms of several maladies, but from what the man just described, Polly probably suffered from migraines. Unfortunately, modern science hadn't yet found the cure for that dreadful malady.

Concerned for her, Eric almost reached the small porch before the words sank in. That man had called Polly his niece. They weren't lovebirds—they were just close kin. *If I want to see her married off, then why am I not sad at that news?*

Eric didn't dwell on that question. For now, he had a patient to treat. The second he stepped foot on the porch, the door opened and someone grabbed him and yanked him inside. The door whispered shut.

By way of excuse for the abrupt action, Lovejoy murmured, "Light troubles her."

He nodded as his eyes adjusted to the dim cabin. The place definitely belonged to women. It smelled of flowers and held white-painted furniture. A loft increased the space significantly, but his eyes narrowed as he realized no stairs led up to it. Surely no one in the clutches of a migraine ought to be climbing the slender ladder propped against the rail. Spotting something in the corner, Eric headed there.

"I made her a pallet." Lovejoy brushed past him and knelt. Stroking the cloth over Polly's forehead, she whispered, "Honey, Doc's here to see you."

Other than the fact that the corners of her mouth tightened, Polly gave no response. She made for a huddled ball of misery.

Eric knelt down and began by pushing a hairpin from the pillow. Pesky, stupid things. If she had any more hiding in that bun she wore at her crown, they'd skewer her. Cradling the nape of her neck in one hand, he reached under her head and searched for more of the offending items. Masses of soft curls filled his hand.

"Thankee." Lovejoy took the pins from him. "I hadn't got 'round to that yet."

"Which side hurts?" he whispered.

Polly's lips moved silently. *Right.*

He turned her head that way. It seemed paradoxical that the pressure in the head caused this agony, but contact lessened the pain for many.

"Light and sound are troubling you. Are you nauseated?"

Yes, she mouthed.

Silently, he performed an examination. Pain darkened the blue of her eyes when he checked her pupils. He ruled out this being a sinus headache or allergy attack. Her hands shook and were cold when he checked her grip and pulse.

"She took feverfew," Lovejoy said.

"Good." That fact surprised him. He'd have prescribed that selfsame remedy. "How long ago?"

" 'Bout fifteen minutes or so. Often as not, it doesn't make a difference."

"Exceptionally strong coffee sometimes works."

"No," Polly moaned.

From the sick way she swallowed, Eric surmised Polly had tried coffee to cure the headache before and hadn't managed to keep it down. "Laudanum." He doubted it would do more than help her sleep through the pain, but that would count as a blessing.

"Makes her sick as cain be." Lovejoy shook her head. "Niver give her that stuff. It makes things worse 'stead of better."

Eric filed that piece of information away in the back of his mind. Those facts mattered, and he figured he'd treat Polly for various reasons in the coming years. In the past, he knew some doctors who carried their bags no matter where they went. He'd considered it overkill. Now he rethought his stance as he hit the end of his possible treatments. Careful to pitch his voice low, he asked Lovejoy, "Do you have oil of peppermint?"

"Shorely do." She slipped off.

Eric folded the cold compress and replaced it over Polly's eyes. Just yesterday, she'd been a tigress. Now she'd become helpless as a kitten. The tigress would inevitably cause him many annoyances, but he'd rather have her back.

Lovejoy handed him a small glass jar. "Niver used this for the headache. Hit's good for stomach ailments." Other than her colorfully archaic hill-country words, she spoke much like Polly. Their tone carried confidence and comfort. Last evening, after Eunice had fallen asleep, Polly's volume dropped to this same hushed whisper that barely stirred the air.

I've never used it to treat a headache, either. I recall my grandmother borrowing it for a maid, but I'm not about to confess that. They need to have confidence in this. Sometimes it's not the treatment but just the belief that it will work. Eric nodded to Lovejoy. "Oil of peppermint is known to work for both stomach ache and headache."

"You got a fine touch. The carin' shows."

The candy-sweet fragrance of peppermint filled the air as he uncapped the bottle. Eric removed the compress only long enough to rub oil on Polly's temples and forehead. The texture of her skin was soft as her hair, but tension pulled it taut. He could literally feel the ache. Eric capped the bottle, set it aside, and murmured, "Do you want anything, Polly?"

No.

"Precious Lord Jesus, hold my Polly." Lovejoy smoothed the blankets and continued to pray under her breath.

Prayer. On that, they agreed.

Polly closed her Bible and took another sip of tea. Though the migraine finally eased off last night, her stomach still felt tipsy. Oftentimes after a headache, her stomach stayed unsettled for a day or so—but she secretly wondered if part of it might be butterflies. After all, Dr. Walcott hadn't just checked in on her the day he was here buying a horse. He'd also come back again late this morning.

"So now that you're done with devotions, tell me," Kate said as she sat down beside Polly and leaned close, "wasn't it thrilling to have the doctor come pay you a visit?"

"It was a medical call, not a visit," Polly replied.

"Of course it was," Laurel agreed, far too fast. Her huge smile and the tightness at the corners of that smile labeled her as a patent liar. "I'm sure if it were any of the boys who complained of a sick headache, Dr. Walcott would have been just as concerned and would have taken their hand in his for minutes on end."

"He was taking Polly's pulse," April snapped.

He had taken her pulse for a long while. Just the memory set those butterflies into flurries again. Steadying herself with a deep breath, Polly warned herself, *Don't be a fool and imagine something stupid. It was merely professional concern.* Long ago Mama taught her to be careful about this very issue—folks felt grateful and vulnerable when sick and newly healed. Sometimes they mixed up the appreciation with attraction. *He came for my headache, not for me,* Polly told herself firmly. Then she looked at her cousins and said that very thing.

"Are you coming to supper?" Laurel stood by the stove, exchanging the sadirons so she could press their Sunday dresses.

"I think I'll stay here." The notion of some quiet time felt good. Polly had a lot of thinking and praying to do.

"I'm thinking perhaps I ought to skip supper myself," Laurel confessed. "I want to be able to cinch in my waist tomorrow."

"You don't need to," Polly said. "A man could span your waist with his hands."

"I have to keep it that way."

"Oh, stop being so vain," April moped. "Every man in the county is after you. It's not as if you can't capture whomever you set out to attract."

"I already know who I want." Laurel giggled. "I'm trying to keep his attention."

"You won't see him till tomorrow at church," April said. She handed the hairbrush off to Kate and started to towel her wet hair. "And if you help me put my hair up in rags tonight, I'll even polish your shoes."

"I'd help you curl your hair anyway." Laurel leaned forward and whispered loudly to Polly, "I think she's still hoping to have the new doctor take notice of her."

April headed out the door. "So what if I am?" She shut the door before her cousins could react.

"What got into her?" Kate set down the hairbrush and took up her mending. Awkwardly mending a hole in her petticoat, she said, "We're both sixteen, and I'm smart enough to know a woman doesn't chase a man. Why doesn't she? Polly, you'd better sit her down and talk sense into her."

"That's Aunt Miriam's place. I'll give April my opinion if she asks, and when we're around the doctor, I'll try to help her so she doesn't make a ninny of herself."

"Oh, she's sure to do that. Ouch!" Kate jerked back her hand, dropped the mending, and popped her finger into her mouth.

Polly sighed. "If she brings up the topic, we need to be direct but gentle. Her feelings are running high. Honesty is essential, and we'd be failing her if we pretended it would be a sound match, but I don't want either of you teasing her. If you do, she'll dig in her heels, and it'll be a mess."

Laurel swept the iron back and forth, navigating ruffles with great skill. "Polly, why don't you set your cap for the doctor? You'd make a fine pair, I'm sure."

"I agree!" Kate bravely picked up the needle once again. "Think of all the help you could give one another."

"When the time comes for me to marry, I want a man who loves me as a wife—not someone who's looking to get a nurse for free."

"Of course you do," Laurel said. "I was just trying to point out that the two of you have a lot in common. That always makes for a happy home."

"We barely know each other. Snap judgments like that are bound to be fraught with danger. To my way of thinking, the home we need to concern ourselves with is this one. One of us chasing after a man is one too many."

"Well, I'm just saying you need to keep your eyes open to the men God puts in your life." Laurel set down the iron, lifted her midnight blue gown from the ironing board, and gave it a pleased shake. As she pretended to waltz across the plank floor, she shot Polly a coy glance. "I don't intend to be mean, but you're getting old."

"Old?" Polly gave her cousin an offended look.

"Now don't get all fussy on me. I'm trying hard to make sure you'll be happy in the future."

"Pastor Abe always tells us not to worry about tomorrow."

Laurel hung her dress in the wardrobe. "All right. So let's look at that entire verse in Philippians 4: 'Be careful for nothing; but in every thing by prayer and supplication with thanksgiving let your requests be made known unto God.' I'm saying we need to be praying about a husband for you."

"Oh no," Polly heaved an impatient breath. "Keep going. Verse 7: 'And the peace of God, which passeth all understanding, shall keep your hearts and minds through Christ Jesus.' I've a peace about this. When the time comes, the man will come."

"I agree." Laurel gave her a sweet smile, then singsonged, "Verse 8: 'Finally, brethren, whatsoever things are true, whatsoever things are honest, whatsoever things are just, whatsoever things are pure, whatsoever things are lovely, whatsoever things are of good report; if there be any virtue, and if there be any praise, think on these things.' I'm telling you it's time for you to think on those things."

"What I'm thinking about is we're going to have a bunch of hungry Chances banging on our door if we don't go to supper!"

"Oh, so you're going now?" Kate hopped up.

Polly rubbed her forehead. "Why not?"

Polly thought she'd managed to hold her own with Laurel's matchmaking conversation until they cleaned up after supper. Laurel dropped a handful of silverware into the sink. "Aunt Lovejoy, it occurs to me that we ought to invite the new doctor to Sunday supper."

"There's a right fine notion." Mama Lovejoy bobbed her head. "Poor feller's on his lonesome. Hope he'll come to worship. Mayhap Dan'l can give him the invite."

"Yes. That's a wonderful idea," Laurel enthused. She shot Polly a sideways glance and grinned.

"Man likely doesn't know a soul. He jest moved here."

"That's true." Laurel's tone set Polly's nerves jangling. "It's the way of the world for all of us to grow up and move on. Why, one of these days, Polly will marry and move away. Most of us will—though not as soon."

Polly tamped down the urge to serve Laurel a secret little kick.

Mama turned to her. "You got yore eye on somebody, Polly-mine?"

"When I fall in love, you'll be the first to know."

Dread snaked through Polly. She knew that look in Mama's eyes. It said, *This topic isn't over yet.* Just as soon as dishes were finished, Mama walked outside and steered her off to the side. "So what's this 'bout you marryin' up and movin' on?"

"Laurel's being silly. She's wanting someone to pay court to her, and I think she's afraid I'm supposed to be married first."

Mama nodded sagely. She peeled bark from an oak with economical movements for a few seconds, then cast away the shreds. "What do you think?"

"The bark was too damp."

"I'm not askin' 'bout the bark, and well you know it."

Polly smiled. "I'm in no hurry to get married. All three of the girls could marry before me, and I wouldn't be upset. You always told me to wait for the man who set my heart afire. Until he comes along and kindles the flame, I'm content to wait."

Chapter 5

Hey, Doc?" A slick-looking man strode into the boardinghouse. "How 'bout you grab your bag and follow me?"

"Jake's got trouble at the saloon again," one of the men muttered. He gave Eric a telling look.

"Go on ahead," Bob said. "I'll ask them to keep some supper in the warmer for you."

"Thanks." Eric hastened upstairs, grabbed his bag, and followed the saloon keeper. "What sort of difficulty will I be treating?"

"You'll see."

The brightness of the street gave way to the dank atmosphere of the saloon. Eric followed Jake up the crimson-carpeted stairs. Jake motioned him into a room, then shut the door. A painted woman sat by an iron bed, murmuring softly to a sweat-soaked younger girl who was curled up tightly on her side. She looked up at him, spied his bag, and sighed.

"Jake found out she was carryin'. He gave her something, and now she's crampin' something fierce. No doubt, she'll lose the babe, but she's in a bad way. I told Jake to fetch your help, or we'd lose her, too."

Everything within Eric revolted. Just yesterday, he'd wanted to try to pull a mother and child through, and he'd been rebuffed. Now his first case was to salvage the life of a soiled dove whose child was not to be. *Lord, why?*

He set down his bag and rolled up his sleeves.

"Gideon, I thought you invited the doctor to church," Aunt Miriam said after the service.

"I did." Uncle Gideon helped Aunt Miriam into the buckboard, then lifted in their youngest sons.

"I heard him," Polly heard Daddy say as he lifted Mama Lovejoy in. He then swiped little Troy from Alisa, gave him to Mama, and lifted Alisa in.

Mama gave Aunt Daisy a look that bordered on frazzled. "But neither of them thought to ask the man to supper."

Daddy and Uncle Gideon didn't look the least bit chastened. Uncle Gideon leaned over and kissed Aunt Miriam's temple. "Everyone for miles around knows they're always welcome at our table."

"Everyone for miles around," Aunt Alisa pointed out, "has lived here for years. The doctor is new."

"Supper or not, it still woulda been nice for him to show up and let us know if he's happy with that new gelding," Calvin grumbled. "He's had it a few days now. I spent a lot of time taming and training that mount."

"It would have been nice to have the doctor come for worship," Aunt Miriam corrected her son.

"There was a time I didn't want to worship, either," Aunt Delilah confessed.

As the family chattered and loaded the smaller children into the buckboard, Kate, Laurel, and April all piled into the MacPhersons' rig. Polly still hadn't decided where she'd spend her Sunday afternoon. The notion of having the cabin to herself held some appeal. She didn't regret inviting the girls to move in with her, but the continual chatter when she was accustomed to silence and precious solitude did wear on her some of the time—especially when she suffered the aftermath of a migraine.

Complicating the matter even more, Kate and Laurel managed to pair her up with the doctor in their conversations. April bristled over that fact until Polly finally sat up in bed last night and told them all to stop acting like a flock of gossipy, pecky hens. They'd apologized to one another, said a bedtime prayer, and slipped off to sleep.

Only Polly hadn't slept. *If I go home, I can be alone—even take a nap—without anyone bothering me.*

Uncle Bryce mounted his sorrel gelding and nosed him toward Polly. He reached a hand toward her. "Ride with me."

She rode pillion. None of the other girls did—they always rode ahead of a man on his horse, but Mama Lovejoy always rode pillion with Daddy, and Polly followed her example.

The older cousins and men rode horses to and from worship; the women and smaller children took two buckboards. Only now Bryce didn't take the usual path back to the ranch. He turned south and rode along the fence.

"Gotta talk," he finally said.

"What's on your mind?"

He squinted ahead and cleared his throat. "If you plan to meet with the doc or work with him, make sure your ma's with you."

"Is there a problem?"

"Might be."

Polly poked him. "Stop being so cryptic."

"I don't ask you 'bout the calls you pay on folks and what ails them."

"That's because they deserve their dignity and privacy. What does that have to do with the doctor?"

Uncle Bryce heaved a sigh. "Do you have to be so difficult?"

She laughed. "When haven't I been difficult?"

He chuckled. "You got a point there."

Polly waited. He didn't say anything more, so she prodded, "Well?"

"Can't tell you how I know what I know. I just know it."

"Okay, Uncle Bryce, so what do you know?"

"Doc spent half the night at the Nugget." He paused and tacked on, "He wasn't downstairs."

"I see."

Her uncle turned in the saddle and gave her a sour look. "I don't want you around that man."

"This isn't like you, Uncle Bryce. You don't make snap judgments."

"I'm not leaping to any conclusions. I know what I know, and I've told you as much as you need to know. I'm keepin' this just 'tween the both of us because I won't go blackening a man's name—but I'm not going to have your reputation sullied by association."

Polly took a deep breath and let it out slowly. "I'll do my best."

He nodded, then turned toward home.

They'd traveled about fifty yards when she tugged on his shirt. "Stop here. I'll gather some of this lupine as an excuse for us to have come by this way."

"We just left church—do I have to remind you that it's Sunday?"

Polly wasn't sure if he meant that she'd be walking a fine line in regard to being truthful or if he referred to the fact that unless a dire need for a particular herb existed, gathering on Sunday simply wasn't done. "I won't get in trouble. We need fresh flowers on the tables."

"Next thing you'll tell me is that you have your bag with you."

She laughed. Polly rarely went anywhere without her gathering knife or a bag to collect the plants, bark, or twigs that caught her fancy.

"That sounded like a guilty laugh."

Polly slid off the horse. "Turn your head." He muttered something under his breath, but he dismounted and complied. Polly yanked up the right side of her skirts and bent down to take the knife from the small sheath she'd buckled atop her ankle boots.

"Are you going to take all day? I'm hungry."

"You could help me."

Uncle Bryce turned around and let out a snort.

"Then make yourself useful and hang on to this." Polly handed him the bag, which he held open. In a few short minutes, she cut checkerbloom, lupine, and hound's-tongue. "There. That ought to do."

"Good. Let's go."

"Wait." Polly impulsively gave her uncle a hug. He was the youngest of her uncles and the last to get married. Aunt Miriam said he'd taken a special shine to Polly from way back, but the year diphtheria took his little stepson Jamie and her sister Ginny Mae, they'd mourned and comforted one another. Often she thought of him as being more like a cousin than an uncle. More than once, he'd stood up for her when the boys didn't understand why she was different. Bringing her out here for this conversation was another example of how he cared. "Thank you. I'll be mindful of what you told me."

He nodded. "You do that."

Much to Eric's regret, he'd slept straight through the church bells chiming. He'd been up late into the night tending that soiled dove and nearly lost her. It wasn't until the wee hours of the morning that she stabilized.

During his hours at the bordello, he'd managed to pass the word to the older painted woman that he had connections. In the future, if one of the "girls" found herself "in trouble," he could send her away where she'd be placed with a family and leave the baby for adoption. To his relief, she'd promised to whisper that possibility to everyone.

But his heart still weighed heavy. Wanting time alone with the Lord this morning, he'd grabbed his Bible and walked out of town. This spot seemed perfect for devotions—serene, beautiful, private. Unfortunately, he'd barely opened the Word when the couple rode by. He recognized Polly at once. He'd not yet seen the man before.

Unwilling to be present at a tryst, Eric closed his Bible and rose to leave. For some reason, he couldn't quite set his feet in motion. To his surprise, the couple didn't linger at all. Less than five minutes after they rode up, they rode off again. Judging from the hug, they were probably courting.

A smile chased across Eric's face. The day he'd bought his horse, he'd determined if Polly married, she'd have her hands full with helping her husband and rearing children. An older husband would be especially good for her—settle her down. And she'd looked at that man with a lot of tenderness.

In the short time he'd spent with her, Eric determined Polly was generous, gentle, and exceedingly kind. The man who married her would be getting a gem. Never before had he felt the emotion, but Eric diagnosed it immediately: He felt jealous of whoever that man was.

That's ridiculous. I'm glad. He and Polly will court, marry, and she'll be too busy to give me any grief. In the meantime, I'm going to have to cope with her trying to dally with my patients. He had a feeling that interim would be fraught with tension.

"Tincture of time," he said to himself. In medical school, one of his professors had said many ailments required little intervention but rather the "tincture of time" to be resolved. Well, in this situation, a short, sweet courtship and a trip to the altar would be his prescription for that young lady.

Eric sat down, opened his Bible again, and read Psalm 133: *"Behold, how good and how pleasant it is for brethren to dwell together in unity! It is like the precious ointment upon the head, that ran down upon the beard, even Aaron's beard: that went down to the skirts of his garments; as the dew of Hermon, and as the dew that descended upon the mountains of Zion: for there the Lord commanded the blessing, even life for evermore."*

Such a short chapter—but those three verses spoke volumes to him. Eric scanned them again and thought about how the Lord was faithful to speak through His Word.

Eric wanted to live in unity here—to be part of this place and help his brothers and sisters in Christ. The Chance men had already invited him to church and sold him a horse for a more than fair price. The folks at the boardinghouse welcomed him warmly. Mrs. White at the mercantile seemed pleasant enough. "The only fly in my ointment is that girl. God willing and tincture of time..."

Eric rose. Though he'd missed worshiping at church today, he'd still met with God. He ambled back toward the road. When he reached it, he looked in the direction opposite the town. A white clapboard building stood a ways off. He'd passed it that day he'd ridden out to the MacPherson place to offer his assistance with the birthing. The large size of the church had astonished him that day—but after he'd witnessed the size of the MacPherson clan, it made sense. The mayor hadn't been exaggerating when he wrote that the town was "thriving."

Eric walked back to town, dropped off his Bible, then went to see Kitty. He'd told the older woman to send for him if any complications arose during the night. Though no one came, Eric wanted to be sure the girl was all right. He gave a fleeting thought to slipping into the Nugget from the back door. Then again, that would give the appearance that he had something to hide. Instead, he walked through the bat-wing doors and headed straight up the stairs. The medical bag in his hand should provide answers to any questions the good folks of town might have about him frequenting such a place.

"Outstanding medical supplies," Eric complimented Mrs. White two days later as he paid for Vaseline and five yards of soft, snowy cotton.

"I'm happy to order whatever you require." Mrs. White wrapped his purchase in brown paper. "Though from all the supplies I saw them unloading at your new place, it challenges me to think you might need anything more."

"My research showed the town didn't have a pharmacy. It seemed prudent to stock up on essentials. I thought it silly to pack material for bandages and slings when the mercantile would undoubtedly have a supply."

"I keep this particular bolt just for medical purposes." She ran her hand across the fabric to smooth it, then rolled unbleached muslin around it a few times to keep it sanitary.

Eric took note of how she minded such an important detail. "You can be sure I'll buy more."

She smiled. "Whenever you need it, let me know. I keep it in the back room."

"Excellent." He tucked the package under his arm and left. It was just a short walk down the street to his office. He'd officially take possession of the place today, but when his freight wagon pulled up late last evening, the town lawyer permitted the bullwhacker to dump all of the doctor's possessions in the just-vacated cabin. Even then, the lawyer declared that at 10:00 a.m. sharp, he'd give Eric the keys—and not a breath before.

Eric didn't desperately need the cotton or Vaseline. He'd restlessly walked down the boardwalk and ended up in the mercantile. Buying those paltry items gave him an excuse to waste time.

From what he'd seen last night, the building he'd occupy and turn into his office and abode left much to be desired. A single large room made up the entire downstairs, and the sink at the rear had no pump for running water. A pair of support beams stood at awkward places in the middle of the room. The upstairs consisted of two modest-sized rooms.

His priority had to be simply getting things arranged in such a way that he could practice medicine. All other aspects of the move would fall into place in the passage of time.

Thump. "Ouch!"

Eric frowned at the sound coming from his place. He pushed open the already ajar door.

Chapter 6

Mornin', Doc." Daniel Chance stood by the closest boxes. He jerked his chin toward the hook on the wall to his right. "Your keys are over yonder."

"I see. Is everyone all right? Did you need assistance?"

Daniel chortled. "Doc, we're all right as rain. From the looks of it, you're the one who needs help."

"I do have a lot of work ahead of me."

"Hey, Uncle Dan," someone called from the head of the stairs, "want us to bring anything else up?"

Dan gave Eric a questioning look.

Eric looked around. "Perhaps my books. I can't have the boxes lying around down here, but I use my references heavily."

"Couple of shelves would be handy."

Three strapping Chance boys stomped down the stairs. Eric took one look and felt a flash of inspiration. "Would you mind carrying over a bookshelf if I buy one over at the mercantile?"

"Dan," someone said from the doorway, "I bought that metal mesh for the women. Got extra—looks good for keeping flies out the windows!"

"Titus, come meet the doc. Doc, this is one of my brothers, Titus. Titus, Doc Walcott."

Eric shook the man's hand. "Pleased to meet you. Back East, they've been stretching the mesh in frames and using them as doors. Nice ventilation in the heat of the summer."

Daniel chortled. "Titus, you'd better track back over to the mercantile and buy up whatever Mrs. White has."

"Not until I buy some first," Eric claimed. He looked around and winced. "Forget that. Take it all. I have plenty of other projects to do first to bring this place up to snuff."

"Like what?" one of the boys asked.

"A wall over there at that post." Eric waved toward the back. "And another perpendicular to it to divide the room up to this other post. A big T-shape will chop it into three sections. Shelves, cabinets, a pump at the sink. . ."

"Caleb and Calvin, did you hear that?" Daniel asked.

"Yes, sir."

Titus and Daniel exchanged a look. Titus looked to the tallest boy. "Tanner, you go fetch Peter, Matt, and Mark. I'm sure the MacPhersons'll spare them. Swing by home and get the tools. We'll have them ready."

"Sure, Dad!" Tanner took off.

Feeling as if they'd committed him to something but not knowing exactly what it entailed or what it would cost, Eric held up a hand. "Hang on here." In the light of day, seeing the true condition of the place, Eric knew he desperately needed this help. On the other hand, he didn't want these men to feel he—or they—betrayed their women when Eric divested them of their "healing" careers.

"No need to thank us, Doc. We're just being neighborly." Titus nodded his head and walked straight out the door.

Daniel smacked his thigh and looked at his nephews. "Two hours. By then, you'd better have it framed." He strode out.

Caleb—or was it Calvin?—asked, "You got a yardstick 'round here somewhere?"

"Probably."

"Never mind," the other said. "I'll just pace if off." He walked heel to toe between the posts and counted his steps. "Doc, I need paper or a slate. Which walls did you want shelves on, and how deep do you want 'em?"

Eric dug out a pencil and a sheet of foolscap. He quickly drew an outline of the room. "Here's what I had in mind. This area back here will be for washing and sterilizing."

"You gonna cook any meals on the stove?"

"Not many." Eric made a face. "I'll end up having to doctor myself if I do."

The young men found his admission hilarious.

He tapped the left side of the remaining rectangle. "This will be my treatment room."

"So you'll need that big old table there to do examinations."

"Exactly." Eric felt a surge of energy. He'd planned on it taking awhile to establish himself and whip this place into shape. All of a sudden, God had provided an opportunity. Enthusiastically drawing a line between the posts to form a T-shape of walls in the room, he said, "Putting a wall here will create a waiting room and my office."

The boys looked around. "Is there a desk in here somewhere?"

"Back in that far corner, behind the crates." Eric looked at the two young men. "Let's set out a plan and budget."

"We got the plan now, Doc. Tanner's impatient, and we have framing to do. Cal and I'll go get the lumber from the feed store. Details will have to wait."

Chances never do things by halves. Once we get going, we always go overboard, Polly thought as Tanner lifted her into the buckboard. The family tradition started when Uncle Gideon held a cabin raising for Aunt Miriam when she came to help rear Polly and her little sister. What was supposed to be one cabin turned into three that day.

Daddy and Uncle Titus had taken three of the boys to town this morning to help the doctor move in his furniture. The project sort of mushroomed from there. Uncle Titus came home and said the doctor needed more help. Fifteen minutes later when Tanner came by, tools weren't all that filled the buckboard.

"Wait! I want to come, too!" April galloped up.

Polly winced. It wasn't her place to say no, but having April there would complicate matters. The girl had stars in her eyes over the doctor and couldn't see reason.

"Aw, April." Mama Lovejoy slipped her arm around April's shoulders. "My heart's set on pie tonight, and my back's painin' me too much to make crust. Nobody makes a finer pie than you. Won't you stay and holp?"

April's smile wobbled, then lifted. She slid her arm around Mama's waist and rubbed her back. "Of course I will."

Dear, sweet April. Polly knew this qualified as a huge sacrifice for her, but she didn't hesitate. She put Mama ahead of herself. Mama had been kicked by a horse last year and still suffered from it. The whole family pitched in to take over the heavy things whenever Mama took a mind to do too much. It was rare for Mama to ever admit weakness.

Polly smiled at her cousin. "Thank you, April. Thank you so much."

April continued to rub Mama's back. "Without all of you underfoot, we'll turn this place into a bakery."

"We'll be sure to come back for that," Aunt Delilah declared. "I guess we're off, then."

Once the buckboard traveled far enough from April to keep her from overhearing the conversation, Aunt Delilah turned to Polly. "Don't for one moment think we haven't noticed April mooning over the doctor. Nearly every girl fancies herself in love with a man and makes a nuisance of herself until she comes to her senses. We're counting on you girls to talk sense into her in that cabin of yours."

"We're doing our best," Polly said.

"Not that it shows," Laurel tacked on. "Honestly, Mama, I wouldn't blame the doctor if he got annoyed and told her to go play in the schoolyard."

"He's a gentleman. A gentleman wouldn't do such a thing. If he's got any common sense, he simply ignores the situation until the young lady decides to cast her affection elsewhere."

"If she doesn't cast it somewhere soon, I'm going to be tempted to cast her out the window," Kate said. "There I am, trying to sleep, and she swipes my pillow and asks me if I think she ought to take up embroidery so she can put her initials and his on a pair of pillow slips!"

Aunt Delilah hid her laugh with a cough. "This is far more serious than I thought if April is considering picking up a needle. The girl does magic with a rolling pin, but she's deadly with a needle!"

"Maybe you could have Aunt Miriam speak with her," Polly suggested. She couldn't be sure whether her aunt nodded in agreement or if it was just the bumpy road that made Aunt Delilah's head bounce up and down.

Oh, and the road did need work after all the spring rains. The women, tools, and supplies rattled in the buckboard on the way to town. Uncle Titus said the doctor's place looked filthy as a pigpen, so buckets, rags, and plenty of lye soap rested in a crate next to a good supply of food.

Aunt Delilah jostled against Polly and decided, "First off, you girls go on upstairs and scour it while I tend the kitchen. We're not taking a morsel of food into the place until it's spic and span. Then, Polly, while you unload the food, Laurel and Kate can measure the windows. I'll go to the mercantile and decide on paint and material for curtains."

Tanner called over, "Doc might want Polly to help him decide on where to put the medical supplies. He has crates of them."

"It'll be a pleasure to help him. I'd like to see what's new, and I can offer him some of our herbs." As soon as the doctor set up his office, folks would feel comfortable about seeking his help—maybe not at birthings but for other matters. That would be wonderful.

"Polly," Kate asked, "are you worried about Doc taking away patients?"

"Not at all. Mama and I are excited he's come. There's so much we haven't been able to do. Having him here for surgery and such will be a blessing. There's far too much for us to handle, and Mama's happier doing gathering and helping children than anything else. She just doesn't like me treating the men."

"None of us do." Aunt Delilah jounced along with them. "It's one thing for an older, married woman to work on men, but you're still a young lady."

"I'm sure some of those patients will seek out Dr. Walcott's care. You know me—I'm happiest delivering babies, and there isn't a man in the world who's going to need me to midwife him!"

Jars and bowls rattled. "Peter MacPherson, you'd better drive more smoothly," Aunt Delilah warned, "or lunch will be ruined."

"Took you long enough," Calvin greeted them as he swept Laurel from the buckboard.

"Don't complain, or you won't eat." She moved to the side.

Polly winked at Laurel. Only she could say something that bossy and still sound charming.

"No eating until the job's done," Aunt Delilah declared as Tanner helped her down from the back of the buckboard.

"What job?" Bob Timpton asked from the boardwalk.

"We're just helping the doc set up," Tanner said.

"I'd offer to help, but—"

"Thanks," Calvin said as he looked at the family ganged around him, "but we have it handled."

While the men spoke, Polly rummaged through the cleaning supplies. She couldn't recall having brought any stove polish.

"Let me help you down."

The doctor's deep voice startled her. Her head jerked up. "Oh. Yes, well, thank you."

He'd rolled up his shirtsleeves, and the muscles in his forearms flexed as he curled his hands around her waist. The sight made her go breathless. *Dear me, I'm going giddy over nothing. I'm worse than April.*

"Here we go." He had her on the ground in just a second.

"Thank you," she said again. Realizing she'd thanked him twice, Polly blurted out something—anything—to divert his attention from that stupidity. "Your shirt is white. It's going to get dirty."

"All my shirts are white." He released his hold on her. "And I daresay dirt washes out more easily than blood."

"True."

"What can I carry in?"

Minutes later Laurel, Kate, and Polly all had kerchiefs over their hair, smudges on their faces, and dirt on their skirts. Polly missed April. The four of them always worked as a team, and it felt odd to have her gone. She'd stayed behind willingly, and Polly strained to think of a way she could show April her special appreciation for why she hadn't come today. Perhaps she could press flowers to make her a little toilette water or scent some glycerin soap. April loved lavender and lemon verbena. Either would be a nice little thank-you.

"I declare." Laurel's moan jarred Polly from her musings. "I can't imagine how anyone could live in such squalor."

Kate vigorously brushed grime from the window frame. "At least the men had the presence of mind to leave most of the stuff downstairs. I can't imagine trying to wash down all of this with a bed in the middle of the muddle."

"Middle of the muddle," Laurel singsonged back. "I like that. It's fun to say."

"I've never been in here before." Polly continued to wipe down the wall. "I'm glad it's plastered. It ought to clean up well."

"What color do you think we ought to paint it?" Kate nudged a clump of dusty old draperies.

"I don't know," the doctor said from the doorway. "I hadn't thought that far ahead. My planning went only so far as setting up my surgery."

"Since the walls will be clean and nothing's in here, it's an ideal time to go ahead and paint." Polly looked at him. "So do you have any preferences?"

"Do you?" he echoed back.

"Her favorite color is green," Laurel said.

"Green sounds like a fine color. Your aunt is downstairs attacking my oven."

Laurel let out a peal of laughter. "Take my advice and don't go near her. You're liable to be conscripted into doing some of the dirty work."

"It's my place. I ought to." He shook his head. "The army needs to hire her. In less than three minutes, she had seven grown men dusting down the ceiling."

The window screeched as Polly finally forced it open. "Do you think it's funny that they cooperate, or are you amused because we'll have sawdust all over by the end of the day?"

"The former shows family spirit. I'm impressed. It's the latter." He bent down to take the draperies from Polly.

Polly watched as he looked down before tossing the dusty bundle out of the room. When he turned around, she informed him, "The dirt is old. Sawdust is fresh."

He gave her a wary look. "I see."

Polly nodded sagely, but she couldn't hide the laughter in her voice. "That's what my uncle Paul told Aunt Delilah when they added onto their cabin."

Eric chortled. "That explains why he was the first one to start cleaning."

Kate tossed down her scrub brush. "I, for one, am going downstairs. This is a sight never to be missed—Chance men doing housework!"

Laurel and Kate ran downstairs. Eric lifted a brow in silent query.

"My first memories are of Daddy and my uncles doing housework."

"Is that so?"

"Mother died soon after the birth of my sister." Polly turned to the side and resumed work. "Aunt Miriam is the first woman I remember, and from all accounts, the. . .um. . .housekeeping the Chance men had been doing wasn't exactly to standard."

"I see. So which of the girls is your sister?"

Her hand halted. "Ginny Mae passed on from diphtheria when she was ten."

"My condolences."

"Hey, Doc!" someone shouted from down below.

Eric gave her a look filled with compassion and apology, then turned and headed downstairs. "Yes?"

A moment later, hearty guffaws filled the air. Polly could pick out Dr. Walcott's laughter.

Food overflowed Eric's desktop, and everyone sat on the floor with a full plate. "You folks can't imagine how much I appreciate—"

"Got anymore deviled eggs?" Polly's father interrupted.

"Yeah," one of the boys said. "Caleb, pass 'em this way. I want one before they reach Uncle Dan, else I won't get another."

Eric started anew. "Your help has—"

"Someone toss me a roll, will ya?"

"Here you go." Kate pitched it across the room with stunning accuracy.

"I'd like to—"

"Don't suppose you saw any salt in the kitchen, did you, dear?" Paul hitched a shoulder.

Delilah shook her head. "Not a lick." Everyone laughed at her choice of words.

Originally, Eric didn't think Daniel had interrupted him intentionally. With the second interruption, he figured it was simple youthful lack of manners. After the third interruption, he got the message loud and clear. He'd find some way to thank them, though. He opened his mouth.

"So what color did you think about painting the surgery?" Polly gave him an oh-so-innocent look.

"Green." He bit into a carrot. A couple of quick chomps, and he swallowed; then he used the remainder of the carrot like a pointer. "I thought to place my desk back parallel to that wall."

"Do you still want your books upstairs?" Daniel asked.

"Tomorrow I'll purchase a bookcase and fill it. No use hauling the boxes for one night."

"Why don't you use that big old cabinet over there for your books?" Kate tilted her head toward the piece one of the boys was using as a backrest.

"I use that for my medications and instruments. The glass front protects them."

Lunch was over quickly. Polly and her aunt cleaned up as the other girls measured windows and doorways and chattered like a pair of magpies. While the sounds of hammers and saws filled the air, Eric went outside, dipped a brush in wood stain, and started working alongside Daniel.

"Anybody know if the doctor's around?"

"Back here!"

"Get going." Daniel didn't even bother to look up. "Somebody needs you."

Polly appeared in the kitchen doorway. She held a cake of soap and a towel.

"I'm sorry—"

"Your calling comes first." Pouring water into the sink, she added, "I—we understand."

Chapter 7

Weary, Eric opened the door to his new place and stopped cold. The smell of fresh paint hit him. For a moment, he had the odd sensation that he'd entered the wrong residence, but the moon cast a weak glow through the window and illuminated his desk.

He blinked in disbelief. He'd forgotten about the Chance men offering to "help out." They'd done far more than just erecting the walls. He stepped inside and lit a lantern.

It didn't take long to walk around the downstairs, but each step brought a small revelation. The walls were complete. Sanded smooth. All of the walls in his examination room had been painted a pale green that looked fresh and calming. Shelves lined one entire wall and the top portion of another.

The old walls in his office were painted: one a buttery yellow, and the other a deeper green. The new walls were stained, and the wood grain gave a dignified feel to the place. Dark green curtains hung in the windows and also across rods in the open doorways. They'd been pulled to the center of the rods and knotted up in order not to brush against the fresh stain and paint.

A glass-fronted, oak bookshelf he'd seen at the store now rested against a wall and contained his precious texts. They'd even been arranged almost in the exact order he would have put them. Polly must've done that. A pair of benches rested against a wall, and brass hooks gleamed in wait for patients' coats and hats.

The place looked. . .professional. It would have taken him weeks to accomplish this. Thanks to the industrious Chances, he'd be able to concentrate fully on his chosen profession right away.

Though the smell of paint still permeated the room, the note he'd seen on the counter reminded him he hadn't eaten in hours. Eric took the plate from the icebox and peeked at what lay beneath the napkin—a mammoth roast beef sandwich and a mound of potato salad. He opened the drawer where he'd plopped his silverware and discovered that a dish towel now lined the bottom and bore a few strategic folds that kept the knives, forks, and spoons separate. After snagging a fork and bumping the drawer shut with his hip, he sat at his desk to eat the supper.

A note rested beneath a jar of flowers. *No pumps at the store. Glad to put one in when it arrives.* Eric leaned back and let that thought settle in his mind. Running water. He'd have the ability to wash things down quite easily and control contagion. Others thought of water as being life-giving because it quenched thirst; to Eric, boiled water meant lives would be saved because it prevented infection.

" 'My God will supply all your needs. . .' " He quoted the scripture softly. *Thank You, Lord, for supplying all of this.*

His grandparents had given him a beautiful leather treatment register when he'd begun to see patients. Not only did he keep a separate file on each family, but the treatment register allowed him a quick overview of the practice and finances. Skipping a page between his eastern clients and the new ones here in Reliable Township made sense. Eric opened the register, took another bite, and wrote on the blank intersecting page, "RELIABLE, 1889."

Dipping his pen into the inkwell again, Eric planned what he'd chart about his first case here. Suddenly, the wonderful taste of roast beef turned to sawdust in his mouth.

Facts. A patient chart contained the specific facts and no emotion. Just the patient information, diagnosis, treatment, and prognosis—but the cold, hard truths in last night's and tonight's cases knotted Eric's gut. A physician wasn't supposed to be emotionally involved. But how could a Christian man—any man—close his heart and soul to such travesty?

He'd just spent hours treating a drunken father and son who shot at one another during an argument. The father didn't survive; the son now lay bandaged on a cot over at the blacksmith's since there was no jail. When he sobered up, he'd have to grapple with what he'd done.

Boiling his medical care down to a few brief, stark sentences, Eric penned the information, then waited for the ink to dry. His desk had a deep drawer in which he locked his patients' records. Though everyone would be aware of tonight's murder, last night's travesty at the saloon was recorded in the same book. Eric carefully turned the brass key in the lock.

Mounting the stairs, Eric noticed the rich glow and satiny feel of the just beeswaxed handrail. The room to his left had been painted the same buttery color as downstairs and filled with miscellaneous boxes and crates. As the lamp cast its light in his own room, Eric inhaled deeply.

Deep green paint coated the walls, and insubstantial pale curtains fluttered by the open windows. His wardrobe, washstand, and bed each rested against different walls—all familiar items that made this feel like home. He'd tossed open the trunk lid downstairs to yank out a clean shirt to wear on his call. That trunk now lay at the foot of his bed.

Though the turned-down bed looked inviting, Eric suffered a restless spirit. He took the lantern into the treatment room and lit a second lamp, then opened a box. Unpacking and setting everything in order might help.

"You have a shipment, Polly," Mrs. White called as the bell at the mercantile door dinged.

"Wonderful!"

Eric turned at the sound of Polly Chance's cheery voice. Every time he saw her, the woman had that same bright-eyed, everybody's-best-friend look. The corners of her mouth tilted up naturally, but her lips stayed together. In the last few weeks, he'd seen her weigh her words before she spoke and hold confidences—both admirable traits. If only she weren't so. . .misguided.

"Mama made you some of her blueberry jam, Mrs. White." Polly drew a jar from the basket she carried, set it on the counter, then added another. "And I brought you some tea. I reckoned you'd be running low on it."

Watching them, Eric presumed Polly was bartering. He'd seen the same thing done by every ranch woman in town.

Mrs. White picked up the first jar and held it close to her bosom. "Oh, isn't that just like Lovejoy. You Chances just spoil me."

"We love you. Will you be coming to the bee this week?"

"I don't know. . . ." Mrs. White looked around the mercantile, and her voice trembled. "Without Mr. White. . ."

"We have that covered. You get your choice of a Chance and a MacPherson. Just tell me which ones, and they'll come mind the place so you can get away."

Mrs. White sighed and wiped the edge of her eyes with the corner of her apron, making Eric wonder how long she'd been a widow. Though he'd planned to buy a stamp and send away for more medications to round out his pharmacy, he turned away and secretly pulled the list from the envelope. It might cost a bit more, but he decided to help out the widow by placing the order through her store.

"As I said, you and your mother have a shipment. It's from Salt Lick Holler."

"It must be from Hattie. My brothers have a box out in the wagon to ship to her."

Mrs. White laughed. "I can't figure out how that happens. There's no rhyme or reason to when you trade herbs, but whenever one sends a box, the other does, too!"

"It makes perfect sense. You see, Widow Hendricks taught both Mama Lovejoy and Hattie Thales, so they both follow the same seasonal calendar and phases of the moon."

Eric crouched down to examine a tin of honey just to hide his reaction. The sheer ignorance of what this girl believed was enough to choke him.

"So did you want to order another instrument from the Claflin Company back East with the funds in your account, or did you need something else?"

Claflin? Eric nearly dropped the honey. This woman mail-ordered equipment from the premier medical company?

"I believe I'll wait on that. What I need is some cheesecloth so I can make more tea balls and infusions—and six yards of the bandaging cotton."

The bell over the door dinged again. A young man stuck his head into the shop. Unless Eric missed his guess, this was fifteen-year-old Calvin. Then again, all of the Chance boys looked alike. "Polly, get bullets."

"Okay. Do you need anything else, Cal?"

"Nope." He ducked back out.

Eric felt a flare of satisfaction. He'd recognized the boy, after all.

"Pardon him for being so unsociable," Polly said. "He's not been his best for the last few days."

Mrs. White nodded. "Ulysses MacPherson mentioned he'd tangled with a porcupine."

"I just can't tell you how much we appreciate the way you keep the bandaging cloth wrapped up to keep it clean."

Eric's brows rose. Polly Chance just changed the subject without confirming or denying anything about her cousin's injury. She'd done it so tactfully, Mrs. White probably hadn't even noticed it.

"Six yards." Mrs. White scurried off to the back room.

Eric took the honey to the counter along with a cake of Pears' Shaving Soap. When Mrs. White reappeared, he smiled. "I'd like some of that, too, please. Eight yards."

"Very well." She took off the muslin outer wrap and started to measure. "One, two, three, four. . ." She stopped. "Oh, dear. Six for Polly and eight for the doctor—I don't believe I have fourteen yards here."

Eric waited for Polly to demure. Surely she'd allow that a physician ought to have first call on all medical goods.

She didn't. Instead, she rested her basket on the counter. "How much do you have, Mrs. White?"

Mrs. White continued to measure it out. "Seven yards, give or take a few inches. I'll order more right away. It'll be here in just two days. Polly did ask first. . . ."

"Why don't we share it?" Polly suggested. "Three and a half yards apiece."

Eric had already solved the issue mathematically: If Polly offered to take three yards and he took four, they'd each have half of what they requested. But that was inconsequential. A half yard wouldn't make any difference. Then again, neither would three. "Just sell it all to Miss Chance. I'll have you order me a full bolt so we don't run into this difficulty again."

Mrs. White gaped at him, then stammered, "The factory usually sends thirty-yard half-bolts. Do you want sixty yards?"

He shrugged. "Go ahead and order a half-bolt for me and another for the store. I don't like to be without."

"Those special plasters you ordered came in." Mrs. White gave him a conciliatory smile. "Maybe they'll fill in, in the meantime."

"Good, good."

"Plasters?" Polly asked.

"Oh, they're astonishing," Mrs. White declared. "Dr. Walcott sent off for them—they're the latest thing."

Polly's head tilted to the right. The action made the feather in her hat sway slightly. Under other circumstances, it would be a very charming sight. "What kind of plasters, Doctor? Onion? Mustard?"

"No." He watched Mrs. White fold the cotton. "A company back East makes individual bandages and wraps them separately. They contain healthful powders. I'm able to use them both wet and dry."

"Imagine!" Polly beamed at him. "Would you show me one?"

Eric knew he'd run into these touchy situations. This woman wasn't a peer, and if he treated her as one, he'd implicitly be endorsing her practice. On the other hand, if he failed to use these moments to open her eyes to modern medicine, he could scarcely blame her for her backward ways. If she used old techniques to treat someone when he might have educated her to practice something medically sound, ethically Eric bore the responsibility for that patient's lack of recovery.

Lord, what would You have me do?

Chapter 8

Of course the doctor will show you." Mrs. White lifted a box from behind the counter with a little flourish.

"Johnson & Johnson," Polly read on one of the wrappers. "How very clever of them to come up with such a product! It would be a waste just to open one for the sake of idle curiosity."

Eric swooped in on the opportunity. "Let's put it on your cousin's leg." He snatched the box, took her by the arm, and escorted her out the door. "Where did he go?"

"He's supposed to buy chicken feed." Of all things, Polly laughed. "I hope for his sake, he remembered to buy it in the yellow-and-blue-striped sacks. Aunt Daisy has plans for them."

"So you have chickens? I haven't seen any of the Chances bring eggs to town."

"No small wonder. There are the ten adults, four girls, and fourteen boys, plus a few hands on the ranch!"

"I didn't realize there were that many of you."

"Might be because the church is holding Sunday school for the children. Between my aunts and uncles playing the piano, teaching Sunday school, and ushering, we don't all sit or stay together. Are you from a large family?"

"No." He helped her cross the street. "I'm an only child."

"How sad!" She stopped. "Don't your parents miss you terribly?"

"My mother died in childbirth when I was five. My father sent me back East to my grandparents."

"How dreadful for you and for him." She blinked. "Where is your father now?"

"He's no longer living." Her stricken expression made him soften his voice. "Don't pity me. My grandparents were exceptional people."

"But you have no one now!"

"Which is why I was able to come back to California—I had no one to tie me down." He supported her elbow as she stepped up onto the boardwalk. Now that they were out of earshot, he asked, "Have you had any more headaches?"

"No. I get one or two a month." She blushed but still looked him in the eye. "It was nice of you to check in on me."

"Not that I was able to do much. Feverfew's the best treatment." From his examination, he'd detected nothing abnormal—no evidence of disease or tumors—

but other than feverfew and tincture of time, no remedy existed. "I've written back to Boston to see if a neurologist there has any suggestions."

"Mama always said two heads are better than one." Polly wrinkled her nose. "But there are days when one's more than enough for me."

"I imagine so." The stage pulled up, and several folks spilled from it. Discretion demanded he change the topic. He spotted a youngster carrying a huge feed sack on each shoulder. Just the top of his deep brown hair showed. "Is that your cousin coming toward us?"

She stood on tiptoe and craned her neck to see past other folks. "Yes, and he bought the right feed sacks!"

Concerned that if they didn't snag Calvin on his way down the street now, he'd refuse to come into the clinic, Eric said, "Have him set down the bags here at the door. No one will bother them."

"Oh, he'll just dump them into the buckboard." Polly smiled at him. "Something you'll learn about the Chances—once they set their mind or hands to something, they don't stop."

I was afraid of that. Eric didn't voice his opinion. Instead, he reached out as Calvin drew near. "Here. I'll get this one."

"I'm managing just fine, Doc."

Polly raised both hands in a what-did-I-say gesture. "I warned you that we're a stubborn lot."

Realizing he might have given offense by making it seem as if Calvin couldn't handle the heavy load, Eric chuckled. "At least your cousin has a strong back to match his strong mind."

Calvin shot him a cocky grin, then turned to Polly. "Did you get everything at the mercantile?"

"Not exactly," she confessed. "After you drop off the chicken feed, come here; then I'll finish up."

Her cousin jolted. "Is something wrong? You ailing? Want me to fetch your ma?"

"No, no. Doc has some new plastering bandages."

"From the looks of things when we put up those walls, he's got half the world in there."

"These just arrived," Eric declared. "They're the latest in fine medicine."

Calvin glowered at Polly. "If you lollygag, we'll miss out on April's berry strudel."

"I promise you won't go hungry. I'll make you something—"

"Oh, no!" Calvin backed up.

Color flooded Polly's face. "Hey, my cooking isn't that bad."

"No, it's worse." Cal turned to Eric. "Doc, take my word for it—when the church does box socials or there's a gathering, be sure to avoid Polly's stuff. Otherwise, you'll gnaw your way through half of that pharmacy of yours before you're not breathing fire."

"There's nothing wrong with spicy food. I enjoy it."

Calvin shook his head. "You've got my warning. The woman's a risk to public health."

Eric chuckled. "Why don't you go unload those sacks and come back? After we're done here, you'll be my guests for lunch at the diner."

"Nope." Calvin shook his head.

Eric's heart skipped a beat. He hadn't realized how much he wanted to show Polly the new bandaging plaster. "Why not?"

"Because you keep glancing down. My boots aren't all that interesting, so I'm assuming something"—he glowered at Polly—"got said about my mishap."

"I did overhear something, but Polly didn't breathe a word." His sense of fairness had him vouching for her—the whole situation was taking more twists than a tornado.

"Well, Polly—what do you think?"

"I think even with your strong back, the chicken feed has to be getting heavy. Go dump it and come back. You'll be doing me a favor since I want to see this new plaster."

"Oh, all right." His brow puckered. "But if Doc treats my leg, then we'll treat him to lunch."

Polly nodded. "It's only right." As soon as her cousin clomped off the boardwalk and across the street, Polly gave Eric a rueful smile. "Honesty demands I confess Calvin wasn't wrong. I'm an abysmal cook."

"Then how do you make your curatives?"

A purely feminine shrug lifted her shoulders. "I can follow formulas but not a recipe. It's rather embarrassing, but with seven other women on the ranch, it hasn't been a problem. So I take it you're capable in the kitchen?"

"Not in the least." He couldn't help chuckling. He'd thought that a fault in her—but she'd just held up a mirror and shown his hypocrisy.

"I'd like to pretend it's a trade-off, but Mama's a wonderful cook." Polly smiled at him. "Enough of our shortcomings. I want to thank you for being mindful of Calvin's pride. He's taken quite a ribbing the last few days."

"Family, I've noticed, is allowed to tease. Outsiders aren't."

"That's honest as a robin on a springtime windowsill." She saw his puzzled reaction. "Mama Lovejoy married Daddy when I was five. She's been wonderful to me. I've learned healing, cooking, sewing, and even some colorful 'hill' phrases from her."

"The MacPhersons are from. . ."

She nodded. "Kentucky Hill country. Temperance MacPherson—Tempy, for short, is Lovejoy's youngest sister. Eunice and Lois are sisters, though I'm sure you noticed the resemblance already. Lovejoy brought the three of them out as mail-order brides."

"I see."

"In all, when both families get together, we make a swarm of locusts look downright pitiful."

"Locusts?" Cal approached. "I'm hungry as a swarm of 'em. How long is it gonna take to make a fuss over nothing?"

"Not long." Eric clapped his hand around Calvin's shoulder and led him inside. "I've never seen a porcupine. Did you save any of the quills? I'd like to examine one under my microscope."

"You've got a microscope?" Polly's voice held nothing short of awe.

"The microscope assists me in making definitive diagnoses in several cases." The doctor headed into his examination room.

Polly stayed at the doorway.

Eric turned and gave her a quizzical look. "Is there a problem?"

"I'll wait out here until Cal's on the table with a blanket over him." Why did heat rush to her face? Oh, she'd done that the first few times she helped Mama treat patients, but that embarrassment was long past. With a few simple measures, modesty could be preserved in nearly every case—and in the few where men needed more frank assistance, Mama cured them. Polly tried to cover for her discomfiture by walking toward the other side of the partitioning wall. "Shout when you're ready."

"Let's get this over with," Cal called out a minute later.

Polly entered the room and went straight for the washbowl. The smell of lye soap filled the air and lent a much-needed sense of familiarity to these impressive surroundings. She looked about. Jars with fancy Latin names lined a whole bank of shelves. On another wall, he'd added glass-fronted doors to the shelves her family had erected. Medical instruments, bandaging supplies, towels, and blankets filled it. "My, you've set up a wondrous surgery here!"

"Thank you." Eric scanned the room. "Your father, uncles, brothers, and cousins couldn't have done a more remarkable job of putting up shelves—and in functional places."

"They were all cousins. I don't have any brothers."

"If the both of you are done gawking at this place and discussing the family tree," her cousin said in a wry tone, "maybe you can see to my leg so I can finally fill my belly."

Polly started unwinding the bandage she'd applied to her cousin's leg early that morning.

"So tell me what treatment you've given," the doctor commanded.

"Porcupine quills have odd little backward barbs that make them hard to get out," Polly began.

"You're telling me," Cal muttered.

"I mixed a cup of vinegar and two teaspoons of baking soda together, then soaked the needles."

"The vinegar burned like anything," Cal tacked on.

"After applying a few doses, it softens the quills," Polly said as if her cousin hadn't complained. "Using hemostats, you grab as close to the skin as you can and pull them out."

"You have hemostats," the doctor said in an even tone.

Polly nodded. "They grab better than tweezers. Quills are anywhere from half an inch to four inches, so you have to be careful not to miss some of the shorter ones." She unwound the last bit of the bandage, baring Cal's leg.

"She got twenty-nine outta me. Stupid critter made me a pincushion."

"After I got them out, I used stinging nettle juice and lemon balm on him to stop the swelling and itch. On the spots that are looking red now, I'm using arnica."

"Arnica," the doctor repeated. He stepped closer and examined the puncture marks. "Why are they all just on this one leg?"

"I stepped over a log. Dumb thing was on the other side."

"I see." The doctor continued to examine the punctures. "That could happen to anyone. I presume your boots protected you to some degree."

"Too bad that stupid critter got away. I would have skinned it and made me new boots from its hide."

"They aren't thick enough or big enough," Polly said.

"Yeah, but Obie and Hezzy said he would have made a fair stew."

"They're welcome to it," the doctor said under his breath. He glanced at Polly and winked. When he straightened, he became businesslike. "Let me apply that plaster now."

From what Polly could see, Dr. Walcott wasn't afraid of pitching in and getting his hands dirty. He'd jumped in and pulled his weight on construction day. Judging from the fact that he'd been willing to carry feed sacks, she figured he didn't shy away from carrying heavy loads, either. Then again, she ought to have gathered that just from the fact that his muscular frame proved he was in excellent physical condition. His hands bore no calluses, but the tan line at his wrist told her he conscientiously wore work gloves. It was prudent—a healer had to guard the sensitivity of his or her fingertips.

His hands were wonderful—long fingered, large, and strong, yet he possessed remarkable deftness. Polly watched as he demonstrated step-by-step with exacting moves and words. He would have made a good teacher, and his competence was undeniable. Afterward, he looked at her. "Do you have any questions?"

"Yeah," Cal said. "Can you stop talking so I can pull on my britches and let us go eat? No use in the two of you trying to heal me at the same time you let me starve to death."

The doctor led Polly into the other room. He sat at his desk, and she sat on one of the new benches. "Once you remove that plaster in two days, I recommend using the arnica," the doctor said.

Polly nodded. "That Johnson company is very clever to have invented those."

"Yes. Medicine has come a long way. There are many inventions and discoveries." Eric ran his knuckles across the smooth surface of his desk in a long, slow arc. "Old ways are phasing out as we learn improved methods of treatment and care."

"I'm ready." The green curtains parted, and her cousin came in. "Bet we're not home five minutes before you have Aunt Lovejoy gawking at this newfangled bandaging."

"There are always new things to learn." Polly cast a smile at the doctor. She had the feeling she'd learn a lot from him.

~

Later that week, furious pounding and a holler, "Doc!" made Eric race for the door. He needn't have bothered. John Dorsey threw open the door, nearly tearing it off the hinges. "My wife's in labor!"

Delighted to be called out for a maternity case, Eric quickly grabbed his bag. "Congratulations. How far apart are the contractions?"

"I don't know."

Since so many folks didn't own timepieces, that answer didn't surprise Eric. He simply closed the door, mounted his gelding, and asked, "Are they far apart or close together?"

"Couldn't rightly say."

"Then did her water break?"

"How would I know?" John rode out of town at a demented pace.

After riding up abreast of the man, Eric said, "Last I saw Beulah, she looked full term."

"I hope to shout. The carryin's been hard on her."

Now that he'd managed to get John to calm down a bit, Eric went back to gathering information. "So how long was her last labor?"

"Don't know."

Eric couldn't recall ever having a less informative father-to-be.

"How many children has she had?"

"This'll be her fourth in six years." John sat a bit straighter in the saddle. "My first."

That explained a lot. "Congratulations. Tell me, when did her pains start?"

"Honest, Doc—I don't know!" John shot him an irritated look. "Can't talk sense into her. She and her mother took the little ones off to a quilting bee over at Chance Ranch. Tanner rode over to tell me I'm due to be a papa."

"So where is Beulah now?"

"At the bee."

Chapter 9

Visions of rust, rye whiskey, and an ax loomed in Eric's mind. He nudged his mount to go faster. When they reached Chance Ranch, thirty or so children were racing around, climbing trees, and playing on rope swings. If that wasn't enough activity, most of the Chance men were fitting logs together in order to expand one of the stables. At the edge of that utter pandemonium, a dozen and a half women sat around a pair of quilting frames.

"Beulah!" John roared. "What're you doin' sittin' there?"

"I'm stitching," she answered back. "What're you doing here?"

"I fetched Doc. You're supposed to be havin' our baby."

"I am." She poked her needle into the quilt, curled her hands in a white-knuckled grip around the frame, and moaned.

Polly sat on one side of her. She set to rubbing the small of Beulah's back. Lovejoy wafted a silk fan toward Beulah.

Eric dismounted and headed toward them. "How far apart are the contractions?"

"Middlin' close," Eunice MacPherson volunteered.

Eric couldn't imagine what business she had, sitting out here with her new babe. She ought to still be lying in her childbed. He chalked that up as yet another example of poor judgment on the part of these self-proclaimed midwives.

Looking over his shoulder, Eric addressed John: "How long will it take for us to transport her back to your place?"

"The only place I'm going," Beulah said, "is inside. You don't mind, do you, Lovejoy?"

"Not a lick." Lovejoy stood, as did Polly. Polly dragged Beulah's chair back.

"I was hoping to finish this quilt afore I birthed this babe," Beulah said in a mournful tone. "With four little ones, I'm not going to have time to do much quilting for a while."

"We'll finish it for you," several of the women said.

John tried to pick up his wife to carry her inside.

Polly stopped him. "Your wife needs to walk. It's good for her."

"How long was your last labor, and how long have you been contracting?" Eric nudged his way between Lovejoy and Beulah.

The laboring woman took two more steps, then stopped. "Three hours." She started to moan again.

John braced her arm; Polly stepped in front of the woman and started swaying her as if they were going to waltz. He didn't criticize her. These little things—odd as they were—could be ignored. He'd save his objections for things that really mattered. No doubt existed in his mind that several important issues would come up during this delivery. Then, too, he'd have more success in having Polly see the errors of her ways if he spoke with her privately instead of in front of half the women in Reliable.

Polly's eyes met his. "In case you're not sure which question Beulah answered, it was both. The last labor lasted three hours, and she's been at this for just about three hours."

When the pain eased, Beulah let go of her death grip on Polly and started to shuffle ahead. "I don't have a gown or blanket here for my baby."

"You know how our Laurel loves to sew," Lovejoy said. "I got me a whole stack of baby clothes jest in case, and Alisa crochets more baby shawls than I can keep count of."

Eric made a mental note of that fact. He had all of the medical supplies, but he assumed mothers kept the essentials on hand. In a situation like this, he supposed he'd have wrapped a baby in that soft white bandaging cotton, but women cared about minor details like that. He'd ask Mrs. White to order a few infant blankets and gowns for him to use in emergency situations.

"I don't think I can do this," Beulah whimpered.

"You're doing beautifully," Polly praised as she continued to assist the laboring woman toward the cabin. "We'll help you."

John walked backward in front of his wife. "I got Doc for you. He'll know what to do."

I certainly do, and I'll be sure to deliver this child with the best of medical technique.

Beulah stopped again. Eric thought it was for a pain, but Beulah straightened up. "I want Lovejoy and Polly."

"But—"

Lovejoy let out a crack of a laugh. "Ain't nobody pushing t'other away. Doc and us—we'll all work together."

"I want my mama, too."

Eric knew better than to argue with a laboring woman—especially one asking for her mother. "Of course your mother is welcome."

"And—" Beulah's eyes opened wide, then narrowed into a squint as she began to let out a guttural moan of a woman bearing down.

Polly jerked Beulah's face toward hers. "Blow. Blow. Come on. Blow."

Deciding this had gone on far too long, Eric swept Beulah up and strode into the cabin. Someone had already folded back the blankets and covered the bed with oilcloth. Left to their own timetable, these women would have Beulah standing in a barnyard, dropping the newborn on his head in the dirt as chickens pecked the ground around him.

As he laid Beulah down, Polly quickly robbed the woman of her shoes and stockings. John called from the doorway, "You take good care of my wife!"

Beulah's mother hobbled up and shoved the toddler she was carrying into John's hands. "You see to this one for a while." She shut the door in his face. "Doc, you turn away. It's not fittin' for you to stand there whilst we peel off her gown."

Eric couldn't care less about those issues at the moment. He needed to set out his equipment and scrub. A towel covered a small table by the bed. He swept it off, only to reveal an array of hemostats, scissors, and gauze—all things he'd have chosen for the case.

"They've all been sterilized in boilin' water," Lovejoy said from over at the washbasin. "C'mon o'er here and scrub up."

Beulah's mother smoothed a sheet over her as Polly hung the dress up on a peg. From the sound of logs thumping loudly into place and hammering, the men weren't in the least bit concerned about the goings-on. Eric had to admit to himself that so far, their confidence appeared to be well placed. These women seemed to have everything under control.

Then Polly went to a door and opened it.

Narrow shelves lined the wall of the dank room she'd revealed. Bottles, jars, and jugs filled them, and bunches of leaves hung from the ceiling. Until now, he hadn't realized the full extent of the "medical practice" these "healers" exercised. It was a marvel they hadn't killed off all of Reliable with their quackery.

Grim determination swept over him. He had to protect this mother and baby. "Shut that door!"

Polly looked at the cabin door, thinking John might have burst in to check on his wife, but it was closed. She gave the doctor a startled look.

"I said, shut that door." Using swipes as harsh as his voice, he dried his hands and headed toward Beulah.

"I need to get the rust—"

"I have ergot in my bag."

Mama shrugged. "I'm shore it'll work jest fine. Beulah, we need to—"

"Mrs. Dorsey," Doc said as he shoved a hand beneath the sheet. "I'm going to examine you."

Polly dug through the doctor's bag and found a vial of ergot. "How much do you want me to measure out?"

"Zero point two milligrams. It will be exactly one level scoop of the smallest spoon in the adjoining pocket."

"Okay." Polly efficiently measured out the drug and said nothing about how abrupt Dr. Walcott had become. Maybe it was his way of handling the awkwardness of such an intimate situation. Maybe he felt a tad nervous. She tossed out the used water, refilled the pitcher with freshly boiled water, and began to scrub.

"Breech," Eric announced.

"Last two were, too." Mama patted Beulah's arm. "You done fine with them. Wanna do the same as we did t'other times?"

Beulah nodded.

Doc straightened up. "We're not doing anything. The precept with breech deliveries is to allow the child to descend on its own."

"Hands off a breech," Polly recited Mama's ironclad rule.

"Exactly."

Beulah didn't care about their conversation. She'd started bearing down again. When the contraction ended, her mother bathed her face with a cool rag and murmured encouragement.

Polly stepped up beside the doctor. "Ready?"

Mama nodded, and Beulah weakly said, "Yes." They turned her onto her side, then helped her up on her knees. As she gripped the headboard, she moaned. "Jesus better give me a boy. John's wanting his firstborn to be a son."

"Son or daughter, he'll love 'em," Mama reassured.

Eric glowered at Polly and yanked her aside. "What are you doing?"

"Kneeling widens her hips. Beulah has big babies."

"We'll discuss this later." He headed back toward the bed.

Things happened fast after that. Just another two pushes, and the baby spilled out onto the bed. Mama dried it off, and Eric made sure it could breathe. They each grabbed a hemostat to clamp the cord, but the doctor cut it. While Eric handed the baby to Beulah's mother, Polly helped Mama lie Beulah back down.

Eric's jaw dropped in astonishment when he pivoted toward the bed. He didn't say a word. Polly supposed since he wasn't accustomed to a woman kneeling, he hadn't taken the next logical step of realizing the simplest thing to do would be to lay the woman down so her feet were at the headboard.

Twenty minutes later, Polly stood at the footboard next to Eric and grinned at Beulah. They'd gotten her all cleaned up and turned around, and the doctor had given her his special ergot powder. Since Eric was present, they'd covered Beulah with a shawl when the babe started suckling.

"I heard a cry—what's going on in there?" John Dorsey shouted.

A chorus of giggles from the quilters filled the air. "Thirty minutes," several of them called out.

"Thirty minutes?" Eric gave Polly a wary look.

"It's the rule. A new daddy tends to get underfoot, so Mama makes them all wait half an hour to come in."

Mama nodded. "'Tis reasonable. Lets a babe eat well and a mama have a chance to remember 'twas love, not pain, that brung the child."

Eric shoved the vial into his medical bag and latched it shut. Ten minutes later, satisfied Beulah and the babe looked fine, he opened the door. "Congratulations, John. You have a healthy son."

John plowed into the cabin. The doctor grabbed Polly by the wrist and yanked her out the door. The man made a charging bull seem tame.

Kate, April, and Laurel all popped up from the quilting frame and dashed toward Polly in a flurry of calico and petticoats. The last thing she needed was them to get an earful of the doctor's opinion. She felt certain whatever he had to say, it wasn't going to be mild or kind. Emphatically waving them off, Polly stumbled alongside the fuming man.

He towed her around the cabin, away from everyone. Finally, he stopped and faced her. "This can't go on."

Chapter 10

"What are you talking about?" Polly gave him an exasperated look.

"That!" The doctor waved his arm toward Mama and Daddy's cabin. "It was unbelievable."

"I thought it was beautiful."

Air gusted from his lungs in a loud huff. "You had no business being there. You're untrained and unmarried."

Quite literally, Polly dug her heels into the earth. She planted her hands on her hips and leaned forward as she hissed, "I've assisted with over four dozen deliveries and performed eleven on my own." Straightening, she tacked on, "As for unmarried—you are unmarried, too!"

He scowled at her. "We are not discussing my status. I'm a licensed physician. You, on the other hand, think a handful of flowers and a headful of wild notions are all it takes to effect a cure."

Never once had anyone faulted her for following her calling. Patients were thankful, and her family did all they could to help her. Thoroughly shocked by his accusation, Polly stared at him. Behind her, her friends chattered at the quilt and her cousins enlarged their cabin. They were all building things up; all Dr. Walcott wanted to do was tear down.

He shook his head. "I'm sure you mean well, but medicine is a science."

"Healing is an art. It's a gift from God."

His jaw hardened. "I agree it is a gift, but God expects us to develop our talents so we use them wisely and well."

"Let me get this straight." Polly stared at him. "You've decided you're the only person qualified to help the sick and injured of Reliable."

He gave her a curt nod. "You're able to treat minor injuries, but—"

"And you're turning up your nose at flowers and such because you send away to a pharmacy back East for fancy prescriptions."

"Patients deserve the best we can give them."

"Oh, I see. According to that logic, the herbs God made aren't as good as something a pharmacist sticks in a bottle."

"Now wait a minute—"

"No, you wait. We were happy when you answered the ad to come to Reliable. Mama ran herself half-ragged until I grew old enough to assist her. Between the two of us, we've stayed more than busy, caring for our neighbors and kin. Some things, we couldn't treat—and we knew it full well. We've sent folks to San Francisco for surgery."

"That won't be necessary anymore."

"I know. That was one of the reasons I was glad you responded. Mama's not saying much, but I can see how her back's bothering her. I've tried to take over more, but I can't handle everything on my own, either."

"That won't be necessary anymore."

"You're welcome to think whatever you want, but believing something doesn't make it true. You yourself said earlier that God expects His children to use their talents wisely. I'm not boasting when I say I'm called to heal. It's not me—it's God working through me. His herbs, flowers, and roots bring relief to folks. Just because you suddenly come here and decide you're the only king of the hill doesn't mean everyone else has to get off the mountain!"

"There's a right way and a wrong way to do things—"

"Those are the first words you've said I can agree with," she interrupted hotly. "And you messed up horribly back there. What gave you the right to announce Beulah's news to everyone?"

Dr. Walcott gave her an icy stare.

"Everyone knows it's the new mother's joy to tell her husband what God gave them. You went and spoiled her fun after all her pain." Polly shook her head. "Back East, they might do things differently, but that doesn't make it any better or any more right. You're here now."

"And I aim to stay and do my best for everyone."

"Well, I aim to stay and do my best, too."

"The road to hell is paved with good intentions," Eric muttered to himself as he rode back to town. He already knew that adage. Well, today proved it—and he'd seen firsthand that weeds-, leaves-, and berries-lined road. Those Chance women merrily dished out whatever concoctions suited their fancies as treatments for the supposed diagnoses they made.

And how did they make reasonable, rational diagnoses? They had no microscope. They had no medical training. Granted, he'd seen Polly employ some of the more standard treatments such as camphor, but that didn't endorse her skill. It merely proved the law of averages that occasionally she accidentally stumbled across a correct remedy. All he had to do was remember Lovejoy rubbing Perry's open wound with a plant she called "toothache" to remind himself that, left to their own devices, Polly and her mother could very well kill or maim patients with the simplest of maladies.

He wondered how so many women had survived their birthing techniques.

Rust and rye whiskey. Kneeling on a bed and lying upside down on it. Putting an ax under the bed to cut the pain! Mothers announcing the gender of the baby—it was utter nonsense in the least. At worst, it was life-threatening.

Not only had he seen Lovejoy rub a flower over an open wound, but Polly had volunteered how she'd applied vinegar and baking soda to porcupine needles. The former was unsanitary; the latter made no sense whatsoever. Vinegar was acidic; baking soda was alkaline. By mixing the two, she'd canceled out the effectiveness of either. On a scientific level, the women defied every rule. Only by the compassion and mercy of God had this community survived.

He'd held his opinion for long enough. Instead of barreling into town and declaring himself the only one able to help the ill, he'd given Polly a chance to prove herself. In his practice back East, he'd met a few women who quietly, efficiently worked alongside physicians and gave excellent, practical bedside care. Never once before coming here had he imagined he would have to wade through rivers of nonsense—however well-intentioned the women might be.

Eric didn't regret for one minute the fact that he'd finally taken a stance. He didn't even regret the fact that he had pulled Polly aside and put her on notice. After all, the Good Book taught that when a Christian had a problem with another, he should take that person aside and try to reason with him or her in private.

But she'd looked so. . .shocked, then angry. He'd have never guessed beneath her calm facade, Polly could turn into such a virago. *Then again, I could have chosen my words more carefully. I didn't use much tact.*

Fretting over what he'd set in motion wouldn't accomplish anything. Eric tried to formulate a plan of attack. First, he'd continue to practice superlative medicine so his patients and their families would understand the level of his knowledge and ability. Second, he'd behave civilly toward Polly—but he'd not mentor her as he'd originally planned. Third, he'd need to think of another woman who might be a good surgical assistant and nurse for him on the occasions when he required an associate. Finally—and most importantly—he'd go to the pastor.

Yes. He liked Pastor Abe. The man exerted a calming influence on his flock. Seeking wise counsel and having the minister mediate with the Chances would be biblical. It would also remain confidential. That way, Polly and her mother wouldn't be open to public censure.

Satisfied with his plan, Eric reached town. He hitched his gelding to the rail and went into his office. Once there, he opened his patient register and smiled as he wrote, "Delivered Beulah Dorsey of her fourth living child. Breech. Male, seven and one-half pounds. Mother and child fine."

He locked away the book, then noted a small piece of paper on the far bench. Eric strode across the floor and picked up the scrap. It had been folded several times. As he opened it, several black needles rolled into his hand. Loopy letters in pencil formed uneven lines across the paper: *You said you wanted to see porkypine needles. Plaster itched. Took it off. Cal.*

Eric sat on the bench and let his head thump against the wall. The Chance clan was a good bunch. Salt of the earth. They'd welcomed him and fixed up his place, and he'd even discovered they and the MacPhersons donated the land, lumber, and labor for the church. How could they have reared Polly to be such a good-hearted, wrongheaded, strong-willed woman?

The grating sound of boots on the boardwalk made Eric shoot to his feet. It wasn't seemly for him to be loafing about. He had no more than tucked the porcupine needles back into the paper when an older woman rapped on the screen. "Dr. Walcott?"

"Come on in."

"I just wanted to get a recommendation for a cough elixir."

"Please come in, Mrs. . ." His brows rose in invitation.

"Greene. Violet Greene." She gave him a weak smile.

"Please, have a seat. Tell me how long you've had the cough."

"Oh no." She let out a trill of laughter. "I'm in the pink. It's my grandchildren. Davy's children. They're fine all day long, but come nightfall, they'll be croupy again. Mrs. White at the mercantile said you might have a suggestion."

Mrs. White. God bless her soul, she's been a voice of reason since the day I arrived. "There are a few elixirs I recommend or blend, but it depends on the patient. I'd have to examine the children when they're in distress."

"Sounds sensible to me." Mrs. Greene pleated the material beneath her fingers in an unconscious show of nerves.

"Do the children worsen at night, then improve during the day?"

"Yes. That's exactly it! My Davy never did that, but all three of their children do. It's positively nerve-racking."

"Would you like me to come by after dark to see it firsthand?"

"Yes. Oh, please. That would be wonderful. Thank you for offering. We live in that cottage back behind the smithy."

Eric gave her a reassuring smile. "Fine. Come nightfall, I'll drop in. We'll see if we can't get everyone squared away."

Mrs. Greene scurried away, and Eric stayed busy for the afternoon. He enjoyed a plate of pot roast for supper at the diner, dallied over a fine slice of apple pie, then returned to his office. He read up on children's respiratory ailments before packing additional medicaments specific to croup in his bag and walking down the street. By the time he drew abreast of the smithy, seal-like barking filled the air.

Eric knocked on the cottage door, and the moment David Greene opened it, the smell of eucalyptus and berries assailed him. A woman in a huge cape stood by the stove with a baby on her hip. She spooned something into his mouth. Eric didn't need her to turn around. He knew just from the unique tone of her murmur that Polly Chance was interfering with his patients.

Chapter 11

Doctor?"

Polly tensed at the sound of Davy Greene's one-word greeting. *What is the doctor doing here?*

"Oh, it's the doctor." Violet Greene let out a nervous laugh. "I asked him to come see the children."

"Well, I asked Polly to come while I was at the quilting bee," Davy's wife said in a sharp tone.

Polly intentionally kept her silence. Everyone in Reliable knew Davy's mother and his wife didn't get along. Violet hadn't exactly approved of Marie as a prospective daughter-in-law, and when Marie suddenly inherited a niece and nephew, Violet announced the engagement was off. Davy and Marie went behind her back and visited the pastor. Since then, strife had filled the household.

Davy shuffled into the room, took stock of the situation, and did his best to make peace. "With four youngsters, it doesn't seem unreasonable for us to have Polly and Doc both here."

Polly set down the spoon and used her right hand to unfasten the ties of her cape. That action would let the doctor know she had no intention of leaving. Hanging it on a hook on the brass hall tree, she stated, "I've already dosed this one with my elixir."

"Then you go ahead and see to him; I'll treat the other three." Eric set his bag on the table and reached for the closest child.

Teddy scooted between the chairs, ducked under the table, and raced over to cling to Polly's skirt. Just that exertion set him wheezing.

Polly stooped down and wrapped her arm around him. "Remember my rule? When you sound like your daddy's accordion, no running."

"Here, Doc." Violet shoved the little four-year-old toward Dr. Walcott. "This is Madeline. Maddy, Doc'll fix you up."

"Hello, Madeline."

Madeline tilted her head back and measured how tall he was, then burst into noisy tears. The baby in Marie's arms started crying, too.

"Look what you've done. It's worse now," Marie snapped at her mother-in-law.

"I was just trying to help!"

"Let's all settle down." Eric scooped the baby from his mother. "I need it quiet in here so I can determine where the constriction is."

"It's never quiet around here," Davy muttered.

Teddy's blue-tinged lips sent Polly into motion. "Violet, you hold Eddy. I need to get some medicine into Teddy."

"What are you giving him?" the doctor demanded.

Polly resisted the temptation to simply state, "An elixir." Instead, she listed the contents of the herbal combination. It was the first medicine Mama Lovejoy ever gave her, and just the scent of it brought back memories. If Dr. Walcott dared to say one bad thing about it, he'd regret it.

He gave her a stern look. "I prefer to treat this with camphor inhalation."

"Camphor's what I use on the baby, too. The older ones have runny noses and watery eyes, so they need more than just that." She waved toward her satchel on the table. "I've got a tin of camphorated salve in there."

"I brought some, thank you."

So much for trying to cooperate. Polly spooned elixir into Teddy and put him on the settee. Maddy clung to her like a limpet.

"My turn."

"Go ahead." Eric's begrudging tone made it clear he was making the best of a bad situation. His look told her she was the bad situation.

Whatever he thought, however he acted—that wasn't important. The patient always came first. Polly clung to that precept and concentrated on the children. She gave Marie a reassuring smile. "Dressing the children in these flannel vests was a good idea."

"I sewed them for the children," Violet boasted.

Polly nodded sagely as she rubbed her hand up and down Maddy's back to calm her cry so she'd be able to swallow the medication. "I'm low on red flannel, Violet. Do you have any left over?"

"I'll go check." Violet bustled out of the room.

Eric opened his bag and took out a hornlike wooden stethoscope. Pressing it to the baby's back, he closed his eyes and listened.

He closes his eyes—just as I do. The realization irritated Polly. Why did something that minor make a difference? But it did. She'd discovered shutting her eyes helped her concentrate more fully on the sounds.

Polly turned away and picked up a clean spoon. She set Maddy on the table, measured out the elixir, and coaxed the little girl to take it.

Sticking two fingers in the air, Maddy bargained, "Two spoons and no stinky."

Polly tucked Maddy's braids behind her. "One spoon of the medicine is just right for a girl your size."

Maddy's wheeze accelerated. "No stinky!"

They'd been through this on other occasions. Maddy hated the onion and mustard poultices. Polly didn't fault her for it—though effective, they reeked. She'd anticipated this. "I brought something special, Maddy. Could you please open my satchel?"

With tears in her eyes and her lower lip protruding, Maddy fumbled with the clasp. When she opened it, Polly urged, "Look inside."

Maddy's eyes grew huge. She yanked out the surprise. "Dolly!"

"A special dolly." Polly had asked Laurel to embroider a face and hair on pink flannel. It buttoned onto a triangular red flannel "dress" with little hands and feet sticking off it. "This silly dolly likes to eat smelly onions and mustard! We're going to fill her tummy with them, then you get to hug her close."

While Maddy played with the doll, and Teddy and Eddy held mice Polly had made from a handkerchief, she chopped onions and started butter melting to make poultices. In no time at all, she wrapped the poultices in Violet's red flannel. After having done this so many times, she automatically made a fourth one.

Eric swiped the teakettle from the stove and thumped it down on the corner of the table. It made considerable racket, and he mumbled an apology. Camphor fumes radiated from the baby in his other arm. "Mrs. Greene, why don't you sit beneath a steam tent here with the baby?"

When both of the Mrs. Greenes moved toward him, Polly grabbed Violet. "Could you please refill the reservoir on the stove and fill a pot to boil? We'll need to steam all the children."

Polly caught the silvery glint in Dr. Walcott's gray eyes and didn't know how to read it. Was he angry she interfered, or was he glad she'd just averted another squabble? The hot poultices wouldn't allow her time to ruminate over that. She handed one to Davy. "If you'll pop this under Teddy's vest, I'll get Eddy."

"I'll examine Eddy first." Eric's declaration came in a rare silence among all the children's coughs.

Unwilling to argue, Polly simply grabbed a poultice and wiggled her forefinger to beckon Maddy.

"Is that for my dolly?"

"Sure is. See how it makes her tummy all happy and full?" Polly stuffed the poultice inside. "You need to cuddle the dolly and make her feel at home."

The doll worked. Maddy gleefully allowed the reeking poultice to rest against her chest. She wrapped her arms around it. "Rocky-bye, baby," she crooned to the doll.

"Yes, that would be wonderful. You go ahead and sit in the rocking chair. I'll cover you and the dolly with your favorite blanket."

Dr. Walcott opened his jar of camphorated salve. Polly cleared her throat. "Teddy can inhale that, but he breaks out in a rash if you put it on him."

"Now there's a fact," Davy agreed. "Gets the same rash from playing with cats, too."

Eric capped his jar. "Croupy children are more prone to such sensitivities. We'll steam treat him. The eucalyptus I'm smelling in here ought to serve."

The children all started to breathe better. The harsh coughs softened and lessened. Marie reappeared from beneath the towel with the baby fast asleep. Polly took the two unused poultices and put them in the warming section of the stove. Marie winked at her, signaling she'd seen where they were and would use them if necessary.

Polly took the poultice out of the dolly and let Maddy continue to hold it while Teddy and Eddy still clung to their little hanky mice. Mama Lovejoy had done that, too—given Polly and her little sister something soft to hold and love when they were sick and scared. From the day Polly had received her own healing satchel, she'd made it a habit to include handkerchiefs or bandanas so she could create instant "loveys" for her young patients.

"Davy, if you warm their bed, we'll bathe them—"

"You're not tubbing croupy children!" Eric glowered at Polly.

"The water's warm," Polly reasoned. "The room's warm. The bed will be warm. They won't chill, and it gets the fragrance off of them. Besides, a little extra steam would probably be a good idea."

"I'm all stinky." Maddy wrinkled her nose.

Dr. Walcott leaned down and cajoled, "You don't want your dolly to catch a chill, do you?"

"The water's not cold." Maddy gave him an angelic smile. "Dolly won't get her hair wet."

Eric threw back his head and laughed. He tugged on one of Maddy's braids. "You're a charming little minx." He looked to Marie. "If you heat the towels in the oven so we keep the children warm afterward, I'll approve of a quick steam bath."

Polly drew a little flowered dimity "sack" from her satchel. "This is your dolly's dress for when she feels all better. Mama or Grandma will wash the other one."

"How clever!" Marie happily unbuttoned the red poultice.

"Good thing," Violet muttered. "I didn't want that thing reeking up my bed."

"I thought that Maddy and the boys all slept together." Polly frowned.

"It's too crowded." Marie lifted her chin. "But someone"—she cast a dark look at her mother-in-law—"keeps tucking them back in the same bed."

"When did you start this new arrangement?" Eric strode toward the small, rumpled bed in the corner.

"A week or so ago." Davy's voice held a weariness that made it clear he'd been stuck in the middle of another ongoing battle.

Eric pushed aside the quilt and sheet, then shoved one pillow toward the foot of the bed. As he reached for the next one, Polly groaned. "Don't tell me that's a down pillow."

"It is." Eric held it up and scowled.

"Polly told us not to have feather pillows." Marie gave her mother-in-law a look that would scald water.

"I concur." Facing Violet, the doctor dropped the pillow and folded his arms in an unmistakably stubborn stance. "You asked me to come treat the children. I will not be responsible for patients when they or their families fail to follow explicit instructions. This was dangerous. It's no wonder the children are in distress."

Violet burst into tears, snatched the pillow, and stuffed it in the fireplace. "I never meant to hurt them. I love my grandbabies. Truly, I do!"

" 'Course you love us," Maddy said as she wound her arms around Violet's legs. She stood on tiptoe and whispered loudly, "Don't be mad at me, Gramma. I'll sleep with you now."

"Madeline Marie Dorsey." Davy's voice took on an ominous tone. "Have you been—"

"She just missed Teddy and Eddy." Violet petted Maddy's hair. "When she's a little older, she'll want to sleep in my big bed."

Marie collapsed into the rocking chair. "You mean—"

"I think the children will be fine once you square them away in bed," Eric cut in. He looked at Polly. "Surely you won't be going back to the ranch tonight."

Normally, she spent the night here in the rocking chair, minding the children when they took ill. She clasped her satchel shut. "Actually, Mrs. White's been terribly lonely. I think I'll keep her company tonight."

After saying their good-byes, Eric swept Polly out of there fast as could be. As they walked toward the mercantile, he cleared his throat. "I've found children who rash and wheeze are more sensitive to apprehensions and nervousness within the home."

Polly didn't abide gossip, but she conversed with Mama about cases. It made sense she and Dr. Walcott would also discuss situations. She chose her words carefully. "Perhaps this will be an opportunity for them to. . .um. . .clear the air. It would be nice for everyone to breathe a little easier."

He nodded. "Thanks for warning me about applying camphor on that little boy."

Polly stopped. "You and I might not see eye to eye, but I promise you, I always put my patients first."

Eric studied her in silence. He gave no reply and started walking again. Silence hovered between them as he saw her to Mrs. White's. Polly thanked him for walking her in the dark, then slipped inside.

"My, my. The doctor taking you on a walk," Mrs. White cooed once the door shut.

Polly gave her a stern look. "We were treating patients. There was nothing in the least bit personal about him seeing me safely to your door."

"Oh. Well." Mrs. White's starry eyes made it clear she didn't believe Polly for one second. She headed upstairs. "Come on. I'll brew a pot of tea. Could you please close the windows? It's getting nippy."

Polly made it upstairs and put down her satchel. Drawing back the edge of a drapery so she could reach the window more easily, she spied the doctor down the street. He was talking to one of the soiled doves on the corner by the Nugget.

Chapter 12

House call on David Greene family. Baby's distress from croup alleviated with camphorated rub and steam tent. Other three children suffering from respiratory affliction. Eddy inhaled camphor; reportedly allergic to contact of same. Teddy and Maddy treated by lay healer with elixir of unsubstantiated contents, mustard and onion poultices, and steam bath. Feather pillow and family strain exacerbating the children's health.

Eric waited for the ink to dry, then turned to the next page and dipped his pen in the inkwell. *Kitty recovering from her ordeal. Still anemic. Recommended she ingest liver thrice weekly and take to sipping beef broth.*

Again, he allowed time for the ink to dry, then locked up his book. Hungry, he headed toward his kitchen shelves. Underwood's deviled ham spread on a handful of Dr. Graham's crackers would provide him with a pleasant snack as he studied the porcupine needles under his microscope.

Indeed, his shelves boasted the finest in healthy fare. An abysmal cook, he normally depended on the local diner. Physicians didn't have the luxury of living by a clock, though. That being the case, Eric made it a habit to keep modern, convenient foodstuffs in his kitchen. Quaker Oats, Joseph Campbell's beefsteak tomato in a can, Libby's Vegetables. . .yes, he'd managed to make do on many occasions.

The next morning, he set oats boiling. Eric rather liked his morning schedule—he'd awaken, use water from the reservoir to start breakfast, then do calisthenics. He'd wash and shave, then dish up the oatmeal. Allowing the oatmeal to cool slightly, he'd finish dressing. A bowl of oatmeal, a piece of fruit, then quiet time with the Lord. By seven fifteen, he'd take a morning constitutional, then return and see patients.

Today he'd taken his bag along on his walk with the intent of checking in on the Greene children. Polly was slipping out of the cottage as he arrived. He inclined his head. "Miss Chance."

"Good morning, Doctor." Her smile could have coaxed out the sun. "The children are ever so much better."

"Wonderful." He still planned to check in on them himself.

She stepped to the side, pulled a knife from a leather sheath at her waist, and proceeded to neatly slice several leaves from a plant. The scent of mint filled the air.

"What are those for?"

Tucking the leaves into the pocket of her apron, she shrugged.

"You just chop up leaves for the sake of it?"

She concentrated on fastidiously wiping her knife on a strip of cotton cloth she'd produced from a different pocket. "I didn't chop them up. I merely harvested them."

"Why?"

"Because." She slid the knife back into the sheath and looked at him. "It's wise to take advantage of the supplies God sets before us."

"And what will you use that for—or should I ask whom?"

"I can't say."

"Can't," he gritted, "or won't?"

Polly's face puckered in frustration. "Both. I don't discuss the persons or maladies I treat because patients deserve privacy."

"Under other circumstances, that would be admirable, but I've already pointed out this cannot continue. Interactions are known to occur between different medications. If you give someone an herbal remedy before or after I prescribe something, it could be disastrous."

"Then you have two choices: you can either ask the patient, or you can tell me whom you treat and why."

"We both know I'd not break my patients' confidentiality." He glowered at her.

"Then you'll simply have to make it a point to question your patients about what remedies they've attempted before seeing you." She gave him an innocent smile. "I always do. It's astonishing what they'll try before seeking competent assistance." With that galling comment, she pivoted and let herself back into the cottage. "David, the doctor's come."

Well, at least she hadn't left him standing out there. Eric stepped up to the threshold. "Good morning. I came to see how the children are."

"Everyone's just fine," David said.

Eric would have been delighted with that news if it hadn't been for Polly and Violet standing over by the stove, whispering as Marie lifted the lid of a teapot that let out an unmistakably herbal aroma.

"Nothing," Mama Lovejoy said as she lifted her face to the sky, "showers a body with joy better than the rays of the sun."

Polly laughed. "Mama, you said that selfsame thing about last week's rain."

"I reckon I might have, but that's no matter. Joy's a fleeting thing—you gotta snatch it up with both hands every chance you get."

They dismounted and put their gathering bags on one of the picnic tables out in the yard. Mama said she'd spotted flowering currant over on the border of the Dorseys' when she'd gone to pay a visit to Beulah. Though Mama still liked to walk and gather each morning, Polly suggested they ride over and collect some of the shallow roots in order to preserve the integrity of the plants they had in their own patch. If they cut into their patch, the supply wouldn't flourish or be available in an emergency.

"Need some help?" Kate and April traipsed over. Kate pulled string from her pocket. "I figured you'd want to hang leaves to dry."

"Surely do." Mama started separating things from her bag—roots at one end of the table, leaves toward Kate, and strig heavy with black currants in the middle.

"Black currants!" April perked up. "You know how I love black currant jam!"

Polly and Mama exchanged a fleeting glance. They'd actually collected the fruit in order to extract the juice to use as a diuretic. Then again, they'd decided to go gather more in a day or two. By boiling down the juice, a special sugar called rob could be extracted—and nothing worked better on sore throats. Polly winked at Mama.

"April," Mama said as she held up some of the currants, "my mouth starts to waterin' jest at the thought of the jelly you and yore mama're gonna make of these."

"I'll go get a bowl."

Laurel joined them. "For being so pretty, why do those have to smell so awful?" She handled the currants by the strigs and avoided the leaves.

"You like horses and cattle, and they smell pretty bad, too," April teased as she set a huge red glass bowl on the table.

"I keep my distance from the cattle and ride in a buggy or buckboard whenever I can," Laurel answered with a giggle.

"Dear Lord above made us all different," Mama said. "Yet look how we live in harmony."

"I don't know about that harmony, Aunt Lovejoy." April leaned forward. "I heard Dad tell Uncle Daniel that Pastor asked them to bring you and Polly in for a meeting tomorrow. Tanner thinks the doc's behind it."

"No reason for ever'body to get het up." Continuing to sort through her gathering bag, Mama didn't even trouble to look up. "We all want what's best. Sometimes, folks jest need to have a meetin' of the minds."

Mama's wise words usually gave Polly a sense of serenity, but this was different. Dr. Walcott didn't think she or Mama had any ability. In fact, he'd intimated they posed a danger to those they treated. Folks in Reliable Township and the outlying area had depended on the Chances for medical care for sixteen years—but would they suddenly side with the doctor, now that he had arrived with an office full of fancy stuff and a medical degree hanging on his wall?

Laurel, Kate, and April all wanted to be wives and mothers. Polly—well, she wanted those things, too, but being a healer was her calling. She'd never once imagined anyone would try to take that from her. The community had grown enormously. It stood to reason that there were more than enough folks needing help that the doctor wouldn't be able to handle them all on his own.

"Mercy me, how many currants did you pick?" April asked as Mama headed toward her horse. She raced over and helped untie Mama's other bag from the saddle horn. "I've got it for you. You're better at tying leaves. Go ahead whilst I sort through this."

Polly flashed April a look of thanks.

"You gals are such a blessing." Mama stretched gingerly. "If it grows much hotter, them currants might droop. Cain't take the sun, you know. Mayhap we oughta think on goin' back today—"

"What a good idea." Polly nudged Kate's foot. "Kate and I can go do that while you remove Perry's stitches. Uncle Bryce and Tanner could come along and scout around for the hive."

"Hive?" Laurel shivered. "I'll stay here and help with the jam."

By midday, Polly plopped down on a log next to Uncle Bryce and surveyed the full buckets with a sense of satisfaction. "When we get home, we'll start pressing the juice right away."

Tanner chuckled. "May as well. You're already stained clear up to your elbows."

"You have no room to speak," Kate countered.

"Yeah, well, Uncle Bryce set me to digging up those roots, so you can complain to him."

Bryce shook his finger at Tanner. "Lovejoy taught me to make a paste from them to cure cattle. You'll be glad we have it one of these days."

"We ought to make you scrub the dirt and honey out of your shirt." Kate eyed their shirts with obvious dismay. "I don't think it'll come clean in a month of Sundays."

"You'll scrub however long it takes so I'll give you some of the beeswax for candles," Tanner shot back.

"Brothers are an affliction." Kate sighed. She gave Polly a resigned look. "Do you have a cure for that?"

Polly looked at the siblings and smiled. "Mama says love and time cure a lot."

Uncle Bryce brought the lunch bucket from the buckboard. He pulled an apple from it and handed it to Polly. "Here's the cure you need most."

"Oh?" She accepted it.

"An apple a day keeps the doctor away," he recited in a voice that held a slight edge.

Chapter 13

"Then she can have mine," April said, offering her apple.

"You're only saying that because you want my share of the cheese."

Polly tried her best to change the topic. The whole thing had snarled into a huge mess. April was still interested in the doctor. Polly realized she was, too—but that only made this whole betrayal worse. He'd turned out to be arrogant and condescending.

Times like this, she almost let down her guard—but Mama drilled into her the necessity of minding her tongue. Things were already brewing—the last thing she needed to do was turn up the heat. "Nobody makes better cheese than Aunt Tempy, and I aim to eat my fill."

Tanner scowled. "I used my knife to get those roots for you. Is it okay to use it on the cheese?"

"The roots are for the cattle, not for me to use as curatives." Polly grabbed for the bucket. "Even so, I don't think there's a problem, because if I don't miss my guess, Laurel and Aunt Delilah already cut the cheese into wedges. We won't have to slice it at all."

The cheese tasted great. The apple—well, the first bite reminded Polly of Tanner's words. An apple a day. . .yes, she'd like to keep the doctor away. She took a second, savage bite and chomped on it. By the fourth crunch, though, the flavor turned. Polly took yet another taste, then rotated the apple and spied a bruise on it. Without hesitation, she pitched the fruit as far as she could.

That night, back in her cabin, she snuggled under the quilts and tried to go to sleep. She'd been fighting a sick headache all evening. Laurel squirmed closer and half-whispered, "Are you going to be okay tomorrow?"

Polly moaned. She hadn't realized Laurel suspected she had a headache.

Laurel poked her. "Need me to come along?"

"What good would you do?" April asked.

Laurel sat up. "I'd sit beside her and glower at the doctor while I prayed."

Polly groaned—more from the loud pronouncement than the fact that Laurel stole all of the blankets when she sat up.

"I'll go, too," Kate promised loyally. "We all promised to stick together, and this is one of those times when unity counts most."

"That's right." April sat up and immediately unraveled her night braid.

Within seconds, it was undone and she'd started to wrap her tresses with rags.

Oh, this is a mess. Laurel's ability to glower is nonexistent. April will bat her lashes and flirt, and Kate can't sit still, so she'll squirm the whole time. I've got to put an end to this right away. Trying to ignore the pounding in her head, Polly said, "Hold on a moment. I appreciate your support—"

"No need to thank us, Polly. You'd do the same if any of us was in a fix." Kate sat up and swiped the rags from April. "We're going to back you up, so we'll be somber as judges."

"And we'll wear our black dresses," Laurel tacked on.

"We're not mourning!" April cried.

"We're protecting our Polly." Laurel dragged Polly upright and wrapped her in a surprisingly fierce embrace. "How dare that man call her before the pastor as if she were morally flawed."

Morally flawed? Polly spluttered at that assessment. "Now just—I—"

"Don't you worry, Polly." Kate wrestled the hair rags from April again. "We'll vouch for your character."

"I'm not worried. Well, at least, not about my character," Polly amended honestly as she managed to peel herself from Laurel's clinging embrace.

"But you are worried, and we'll be there. I'll talk to Eric—"

"April," Polly said in her firmest voice, "You will not—"

"Call the doctor by his first name. It's simply far too forward," Laurel cut in. "You'll be silent. We all will. Uncle Daniel and Uncle Gideon will do the speaking, and when it comes up, I'll be the spokeswoman for our cabin since I'm the eldest of us."

"Polly's older," April muttered.

"You can't expect her to stand there and proclaim her innocence," Laurel pointed out.

Polly couldn't believe the speed at which her cousins chattered. This conversation was moving faster than a locomotive in full steam. "Everyone quiet down and listen to me."

The girls all hushed.

"I appreciate your support, but you're not going. Mama is attending the meeting with me, and it's best to keep matters like this discreet."

"Discretion is important," Laurel said slowly. "But then maybe just I ought to go along."

"Not fair!" April protested.

"We are more like sisters than cousins, and we're sisters in Christ." Polly took a deep breath. "But there are times each of us is going to need some privacy."

"Privacy, around this ranch?" Kate snorted.

"I've been accustomed to having a measure of solitude," Polly said slowly.

"Don't get me wrong—I love you all being here with me now. It's just that with my healing, I still have times when I must handle confidential matters. I've resolved that tomorrow will be such a time."

"You can't go alone," Laurel gasped.

"Daddy, Mama, and Uncle Gideon are accompanying me. I don't want the doctor to feel as if the whole Chance family is ganging up on him. As much as I appreciate your caring sentiments, you're all staying home." Polly looked around the loft and met her cousins' gazes. "That's the way it's going to be."

Laurel pursed her lips for a moment, then nodded. "Then we'll fast for breakfast and lunch and support you in prayer."

"We don't have to fast to pray," April objected.

"And it's our turn to cook tomorrow," Kate pointed out.

"The Bible says, 'Where two or three are gathered. . . ,'" Laurel began.

"Well, we're four here. We'll storm heaven's gate with prayers." Kate bounded out of her bed.

Polly gave in to the need to bury her head in her hands as the headache exploded.

"Don't despair, honey." Laurel stroked her arm. "God will help you."

"I have faith, but I'm also fighting a headache," Polly whispered tightly.

"Then you just lie back down. Kate, get her a cool compress. I'll get the feverfew. April, you track down where the oil of peppermint is that the doctor used. We'll take care of Polly and pray downstairs all night long on her behalf."

"No sleep?" Kate moaned.

"It's better than fasting," April said.

Polly scrunched down in the bed and pulled the blankets over her head. She couldn't even handle her cousins. How would she ever deal with the doctor tomorrow?

When Eric heard the Chances arrive, he stepped back deep into the parlor. He'd intentionally arrived a little early. Since he'd requested this meeting, it was only fitting that he be here first. Through the window, he could see they'd come not on horses or in a buckboard, but in a buggy he'd not seen before.

"Hello, Mrs. Abrams." Polly gave the pastor's wife a hug.

"Hey there," Mama said as she smiled and gave Mrs. Abram's tummy a loving pat. "Ain't you jest fat and sassy-lookin' today?"

Joyous laughter trilled out of the pregnant woman. "Isn't it wonderful? God has blessed us, indeed."

Pastor Abe shook hands with Gideon and Daniel Chance, then motioned toward the parlor. "Come on in."

Eric remained standing and solemnly shook hands with the men. Though this would be awkward, he'd found that civility often mediated in such situations. It didn't escape his notice that Daniel Chance had his arm about his wife's waist and Gideon kept a proprietary hand on Polly's arm. These men were protective, and one look made it clear they didn't appreciate being brought before the minister. *The matter is even touchier than I thought it would be.*

"Why don't we all sit down." The pastor's words rang out as a command, not a suggestion. Good. He didn't kowtow to the Chances simply because they were major benefactors of the church.

"Lovejoy, you sit in the rocker. It's easiest on your back," Mrs. Abrams trilled.

Daniel seated his wife and remained standing by her. Eric sensed the man would turn to stone ere he ever left her side in this situation. Thankfully, the pastor shoved a chair behind the stubborn-looking man, and Daniel grudgingly forced himself to sit down. Gideon steered Polly to the settee and sat beside her. He slid his left arm across the back of the settee and curled it around Polly's shoulders in a move that nearly shouted, *Watch yourself, mister. This is my niece you're calling on the carpet.*

Lovejoy's face looked open and guileless as it always did; Polly's features looked strained and pale.

Maybe she's coming to realize things have to change.

"It's so nice to have you all come pay us a visit." The pastor's wife perched on the piano stool. "Would you all care for some lemonade, tea, or coffee? I have strawberry pie, if that influences your decision."

The pastor cleared his throat. "Sweetheart, this isn't a social visit."

She popped up. "Oh, dear. I'm so sorry."

"Oh, you go ahead and sit yoreself back down—but someplace more comfortable," Lovejoy said. "Ain't nothin' being said that needs to be kept secret, and I cain't abide the thought of pushing a woman outta her own parlor."

Eric would have preferred the matter to be handled without an audience. Then again, after this got settled, someone would need to subtly spread the word that he'd be handling all of the community's medical needs. He eased into the one empty chair—an ornate rosewood piece built low to the ground and suited to a woman. His knees folded up ridiculously, so he eased them out until the toes of his just-polished shoes missed the hem of Polly's gown by a mere inch.

It didn't escape his notice that Polly kept her face averted.

"I'd like to start with a word of prayer," Pastor said. "Heavenly Father, Thou art all-wise and all-knowing. We implore Thee, be among us and grant us wisdom and grace. In Jesus' precious name. Amen."

Well, that was a fine prayer. A great opening to this. With God going before me, surely the road will be smoother and straighter.

"Doc Walcott came to me with some concerns," the pastor started in. "Apparently he's discussed the issue with Polly already, but they didn't reach a satisfactory agreement."

"He's spoken with you, Polly?" Her father's tone carried astonishment.

She nodded but gave no details.

"Actually, we've spoken twice." Eric cleared his throat. "The matter is rather delicate—"

"What?" Daniel Chance bolted to his feet. His hands knotted into fists, but to his credit, they stayed at his sides. "My daughter is not that kind of woman. There's no way she'd be—"

"Oh, dear me," Mrs. Abrams said, her voice fluttering.

"No. No!" Eric held up his hand. "You mistake my meaning."

Daniel glowered at him. "Choose your words better. I'll not have you slur my daughter's reputation."

"Dan'l, he misspoke. Ain't a one of us who hasn't done the same." Lovejoy slipped her hand into her husband's. "Jest go on ahead and speak your piece, Doc." Humor glinted in her eyes. " 'Tis plain you got our attention."

"Thank you." He nodded his head in gratitude and respect. He'd not spent much time with Lovejoy, but she exuded warmth and kindness. If anything, that made him feel worse about the whole matter. "What I meant to say is that the topic I'm broaching is sticky."

"Get on with it," Gideon said. He took up more than his half of the settee, and he'd wrapped his arm more tightly around his niece.

"In the past, Mrs. and Miss Chance have done their best to care for the people of Reliable."

"And they've done a wonderful job of it, too!" Mrs. Abrams chirped.

Eric wouldn't stand for many more interruptions. He forged on ahead as if nothing had been said. "But now that I've come, they can relinquish their responsibilities in that arena."

There. He'd said it diplomatically, but the issue was out in the open now.

"Me and Polly're happy as a sparrow with two worms that you come to our town, Doc." Lovejoy tugged on her husband's hand. "I told Dan'l it'll be a blessing to have someone hereabouts to handle surgery and such."

"He wants us to stop everything, Mama." Polly's words hung in the air.

Gideon and Daniel exchanged a grim look. The pastor's wife burst out, "But you promised you'd deliver my baby!"

"Yes, well—" Eric began.

"And we will." Polly's voice held quiet resolve.

"I mean no disrespect, Doctor, but I can't imagine. . ." Mrs. Abrams blushed to the roots of her hair. "Well, I just. . .you know. Besides, this baby wouldn't have ever come into being if it weren't for Polly and her mama."

Eric folded his arms across his chest. "That baby, Mrs. Abrams, came into being because God willed it and due to the—"

"Watch it," Gideon cut in.

Eric stared at the head of the Chance clan. "You've just underscored part of the problem. Lovejoy and Polly are ladies. There is no denying that medical practice necessitates dealing with intimate and personal issues."

"Precisely." The pastor's wife finally relaxed. "I'm so glad you understand, Doctor. I just couldn't ever have a man attend me when my time comes."

"I assure you, Mrs. Abrams, I've delivered many children. Maintaining modesty is quite simple by the application of a few draping sheets. Medical training prepares a physician to attend a woman with the latest in scientific advances."

"Far as I know, babies have always come the same way," Polly said tightly.

"Now let's jest calm down. Doc, Polly and me, we're happy to serve folks however best we cain. There's more than enough to keep us all busier than a fly at a hop-toad party. Nothin's a-wrong with us partnerin' up."

Everyone else in the room—the pastor included—smiled as if the matter had been settled amicably. Eric heaved a sigh. They simply didn't understand. He was going to have to be blunt. "There may be sufficient work, but knowledge is lacking."

"We'll teach you what you need to know about folks. I recollect from when I moved here how it takes time to figger out the peculiarities. Folks all have some odd little kinks and pet remedies or notions you have to work 'round."

"Mama, that's not what he's saying."

Eric looked at Polly. She remained tucked into her uncle's side and couldn't even bear to face the room. . .or him. He'd known she enjoyed dabbling with her herbs, but the depth of her sadness cut at him.

But I have to do the right thing.

"A handful of flowers and a few medical instruments amount to medieval medicine." Eric looked at Daniel. "In the past, you didn't have anything more than that. I don't doubt that your wife and daughter did the best they could with what they had. It's just that the time has come for change. Medical science has made astonishing discoveries and advances. We've abandoned treatments that were once standard and turned to superior methods in their place."

"Seems to me, folks can decide who they want to give them care," Daniel said in an all too reasonable tone. His hand slid over Lovejoy's in a move that said he'd far rather entrust his life to her care than any doctor's.

"They can't make wise decisions when they still think the world is flat, because Polly and Lovejoy navigate by the same principles that were used centuries ago!"

"The world is round, Doc. Ain't nobody gonna fall off." Lovejoy gave him an earnest look. "But you got my solemn promise that iff'n I got me a patient who's close to the edge, I'll send 'em yore way."

She tried to rise, but her husband had to assist her. Pain flickered across her face, and Eric wanted to offer his help—but knew it would be ill-advised at the moment. Lovejoy gave him a long look. "Now that we've got things settled, I'm taking my girl home."

Polly rose, but she didn't do so with her usual grace. The way she'd spoken so little and used muted tones suddenly took on a completely different significance. When she instinctively averted her face from a stream of sunlight, Eric gritted his teeth and demanded of Daniel in a low tone, "Why did you bring your daughter if she's fighting a migraine?"

"The family respected her choice. Fools that we were, we hoped this meeting would resolve the strain so she could rest."

Gideon's brow furrowed. "Polly, go on out with your mama. We'll be on momentarily."

Lovejoy reached up and pulled Polly's head onto her shoulder. Polly tenderly wrapped her arm about her mother's waist and stroked a few times before bracing Lovejoy's back. Slowly, silently, they shuffled from the room. The sight of them wrenched Eric's heart—mother and daughter both in pain, each trying to be mindful of the other's infirmity. More than ever, he wanted to relieve them of trying to care for the people of Reliable. They had their hands full with one another.

Mrs. Abrams toddled out behind mother and daughter, fussing over them.

Once they were out of earshot, Eric appealed to Daniel to be reasonable. "They're struggling."

"They're just having a bad day," the pastor said.

Eric shook his head. "The problem's existed a long time. It's why your township advertised for a physician. I'll relieve them of the burdens of caring for the town. In the end, we all have to admit that it's the best thing for them as well as for the folks of Reliable."

Daniel's feet widened in an aggressive stance. "I give folks the benefit of the doubt. There was a time I wouldn't have, but Lovejoy changed that about me. Right about now, Doc, you're skating on mighty thin ice. We want you here. We need you here. But I won't stand for you insulting my wife and daughter."

"I meant no offense. It is a matter of patients deserving the best of care. I truly regret the fact that such a concern casts a shadow on them. They've given their best; it's just not good enough anymore."

"There's a line between confidence and pride, Doc." Gideon strode toward the door. "You just crossed it."

The Chances all left then, and the pastor walked Eric out to the hitching post. "Thanks for trying, Pastor." Eric swung up into the saddle.

"It'll take awhile, but I believe you'll all iron this out."

Eric looked down and nodded. "In medicine, that's called tincture of time, but I'm not sure that's all it'll take in this situation."

"Have faith. In my profession, I've seen God work miracles."

"Well, Pastor, I'll gladly treat you for free if you develop knee problems from kneeling and seeking heavenly intervention."

Chapter 14

"Miss Chance."

At the sound of Dr. Walcott's voice, Polly's three cousins immediately spun in a swirl of their Sunday-best dresses. She hesitated.

"Now I suppose that was predictable." The doctor's tone held wry amusement.

Ashamed of her attitude toward him, Polly turned.

Eric smiled—an easygoing, lopsided grin that made him look downright neighborly. "At least the Chances only had a handful of girls instead of a bumper crop of them like they do boys. If I called Mr. Chance, I'd be mobbed."

"Doctor," April cooed, "the Chances and MacPhersons have given leave for people in Reliable to call us by our Christian names. With such large families, going by our surname becomes confusing."

Polly watched as Kate reached back and pinched April's arm to hush her. Reasoning with April hadn't done any good, because she considered the doctor to be exceedingly handsome and imminently eligible. If she didn't stop acting like a henwit, she'd embarrass herself and the doctor.

"Very well." Dr. Walcott focused in on Polly. "Miss Polly, I'd like a word with you."

"We're in charge of Sunday school today, Doctor."

"All of you? How is it that all the Chance gals are doing the Sunday school together? I thought you usually split up two by two."

"Like the creatures on Noah's ark?" Kate teased.

Eric chortled. Polly wished he hadn't. At the moment, she didn't want to like him, and he was being impossibly charming.

"I've noticed the parishioners all take turns." He drew closer. "Why don't I come along?"

"Do you like children?" If April perked up anymore, she'd be on tiptoe.

"Definitely." Eric deftly stepped to Polly's side. "What is today's lesson for Sunday school?"

"Ephesians 4:32." Polly felt more than a slight twinge when she answered the question. " 'Be ye kind one to another. . .' "

" 'Tenderhearted,' " the doctor joined in, " 'forgiving one another, even as God for Christ's sake hath forgiven you.' " He spoke the words softly, solemnly. Polly couldn't interpret the look in his eyes.

Soon they sat in a big circle out on the grass. Kate led the singing, and Polly couldn't help enjoying the doctor's bass voice amid the childish sopranos.

April read the Bible verse; then Laurel gave a short lesson.

"Why don't we take time to share how someone was kind to us this week?" Polly's suggestion resulted in a sea of waving hands. "Birdie, hand me Judy, and you share; then you may pick whose turn it is next."

Birdie handed over the soggy toddler, then popped to her feet and yanked a small tin item from around her neck. "Pa bought me a chewin' gum locket at White's."

"And she shart the gum with me. 'Twas hardly e'en chewed yet!"

Birdie scowled at her sister. "I didn't pick you to share next, Vinetta."

"How wonderful that she couldn't wait to tell us all what a grand sister you are," Polly said.

"You are a grand sister, Birdella. Iff'n God let me pick a sister, I'd pick you."

"Now that showed tenderheartedness, just as today's verse said." Eric gave the sisters an approving nod. His quick thinking impressed Polly. He'd managed to praise the children and keep their focus on the lesson.

"Let's have Octavius take a turn," Vinetta suggested, and Birdella nodded.

Eric followed Polly over to a table, where she started to change Judy's diaper. Her cousins hated that task, so she handled it as a matter of course. They'd continue to monitor the children.

Eric leaned against the table and fleetingly touched the puffed sleeve of Judy's little dress. He said quietly, "Is there something special about gold and the MacPhersons? It's the only color I see them in."

Polly smiled. "The MacPhersons hail from Hawks Fall and Salt Lick Holler, where they could barely eke out a living."

"I recall you saying Lovejoy brought the women out for arranged marriages."

Polly nodded. "Uncle Obie wanted his children to know they weren't growing up poor, so he bought a whole bolt of fabric. By using flour and feed sacks for collars, bodices, and pockets, my aunts managed to dress the entire clan, but then they realized they'd have a problem with hand-me-downs if they changed color."

"Why?"

"The younger children would be dressed in golden yellow, and the older ones would be in other colors—so the littler ones would always feel as if they were left out of getting anything new."

"That could pose a problem."

Polly nodded. "Hezzy thinks gold looks fine with Lois and Eunice's red hair, so the family decided they'd stick with gold. That way, they look like a family, and hand-me-downs aren't apparent. The manager at the feed store is smart enough to always have a selection of yellow-toned bags just for them." She shot Eric an amused look. "I'm so accustomed to the gold, I forgot about it until you just pointed it out!"

"I suppose I have no room to speak." He glanced down at his chest and tacked on, "I always wear white shirts."

Thankful they were keeping the conversation light, Polly smiled. "You mentioned that the day we worked on your office. My cousin Cole said he can't decide whether you're trying to look like a pastor or a penguin."

"To whom does Cole belong?"

"Miriam and Gideon. It's easy to tell by how the children are named."

"Enlighten me."

"The girls are named whatever the mother fancies, but the boys' names are chosen by letter. Miriam and Gideon's sons all have C names."

"Caleb, Calvin, Cole. . ."

"Yes, and Cory and Craig are over by April. She's their sister. Then the boys belonging to Alisa and Titus begin with T: Tobias, Tanner, Terrance, and Troy. Kate is their daughter."

"So that leaves Delilah and Paul with the *P*s," he deduced. "I've met Parker and Perry."

"Patrick, Paxton, and Packard are in the sanctuary."

"And. . ." He thought for a moment. "Lauren is their daughter?"

"Laurel." The fact that he hadn't gotten Laurel's name correct surprised Polly. Feminine and soft-spoken, she managed to catch the attention of every other man in the county.

"I suppose the MacPhersons all wearing gold is my only clue for them. It'll probably take me months to sort out that clan."

"Just listen for names. Tempy and Mike love to read, so their children have Greek or Roman names. Lois and Obie named all their tribe after the disciples—but they made allowances for Johnna, Jamie, and little Judy here."

"Very clever."

Polly then muffled a laugh. "If it's an odd name, you can be certain the child is Eunice and Hezzy's. We do our best to tag a nickname onto each of the children so they won't be teased mercilessly."

"Birdella is Birdie." His brow rose in a silent invitation to provide more.

"Meldona is Melly. Register is Reggie. Benefit is Benny. . ." His gray eyes reflected growing astonishment as she mentioned each name. She let out a sigh, "No one's come up with anything for poor Lastun."

The doctor's eyes twinkled with mirth. "Let me guess. That must have been the one before Elvera."

Polly nodded. "Eunice declared he was the last one she'd have. I guess it's proof God gets the final word on everything."

"Indeed, He does." He swiped Judy from her and obligingly made a funny face when the toddler poked him on the nose.

Polly washed up at the bucket, then helped Craig with the fastener on his overalls.

"Your father and Lovejoy didn't have children?"

Polly willed him to understand. "She couldn't have any of her own, but Lovejoy's children are all around you. Her hands catch, soothe, and cherish them."

He didn't look away or pretend to misunderstand. Instead, the doctor gently shifted Judy to his other side, cupped her head to his shoulder, and swayed from side to side as if he'd fathered half a dozen children himself. His thumb absently played with a wispy auburn baby curl at Judy's temple. "They're blessed to have the love she gives."

"Then why are you trying to stop her? Why are you trying to stop us?"

The corners of his mouth tightened, but he kept his voice gentle. "Polly, I couldn't ever stop you from loving your family and neighbors. I'm just freeing you from the responsibility for their health so you can help them in a thousand other ways."

Judy stuck her middle and fourth fingers into her mouth and started sucking on them. Her eyes drooped, and Eric cradled her as she fell asleep. He absently rubbed his jaw along her carroty curls, then said, "I heard back from the neurologist. Unfortunately, there's no specific cure yet, but he suggested your headaches might be caused by something you ingest. The list he sent included red wine—"

"I don't partake of alcohol."

"So you've said. But I wondered about oranges. He mentioned with California shipping oranges back East in abundance, he's noticing a connection there."

"No, I love oranges."

"Nuts?"

She shook her head.

"Aged cheese." The doctor looked at her steadily.

Thunderstruck, Polly stared back at him. She enjoyed those other foods without any trouble, but. . . "Tempy's cheese," she said. "I love it. I never connected that, but before the last two—no, three—headaches, I'd eaten a wedge."

"Well, then, let's hope you have far fewer migraines now." Instead of sounding smug as he might have, his tone carried sincerity. He turned when someone called for him. "Yes?"

Perry pointed at his arm. "I told 'em how you came to buy a horse, but you drew a pitcher on my owie 'cuz I got hurt."

A girl giggled. "That's a funny way to heal somebody."

"It worked. I'm all better," Perry insisted.

"And we praise God that you're strong and healthy now." Eric wandered around the edge of the clump of children. "Don't you all think the way God makes us better is proof of His kindness?"

"Maybe forgiveness, too." Perry's face puckered. "I wasn't 'posed to be jumpin' outta the hayloft when I got hurt."

"God doesn't always heal us when we're sick, but He is always faithful to forgive us." Eric continued to hold Judy's sleep-lax little body as he imparted those wise words. "We have to tell Him we're sorry for the wrong things we've done. The Bible verse today talked about being kind, tenderhearted, and forgiving. God is all of those things. Because we are His children, we want to be like Him."

"You're not a children," little Craig hollered.

"Sure I am." Eric stood there, tall as Gulliver in the Land of Lilliput. "God is my Father. No matter how old I get, I'll always be His child."

"Like Mama is all growed up, but she's Grampa's little girl?"

"Exactly."

Polly leaned against the small table and tried to clear her mind. Dr. Walcott confused and confounded her. He loved children, was called to heal, and seemed to be a strong believer—all things they held in common. They weren't trivial things—they were soul-deep values. If it weren't for his absurd notions about who could care for the sick, they'd undoubtedly get along very comfortably. She and her family had done everything they could to welcome him. Why couldn't he get past his selfish pride and accept her help?

April came back toward Polly. From the awkward way she carried Lastun and crinkled her nose, Polly assumed he needed his diaper changed. April laid him on the table and whispered, "Dr. Walcott really does adore kids, doesn't he?"

"Yes."

"He'll make a good father," April said in a dreamy tone.

"You're too young," Polly hissed.

"It's not like you want him for yourself," April snapped back.

Polly didn't respond. Then again, she couldn't. She wasn't sure whether it was the truth or a lie.

Chapter 15

Eric straightened up from his microscope and reached for the mug. By habit, he raised it toward his mouth, but the pungent smell of vinegar caused him to set it back down. A cup of coffee would taste great, but he wanted to finish this experiment.

Deftly, he removed the porcupine needle from beneath the microscope. Indeed, the end bore nasty little barbs as Polly had told him it did. Each of the ten he'd inspected were the same in that regard—though they varied in thickness and length. He'd mixed vinegar and soda in the exact proportions Polly mentioned, and now he would dip three of the needles in it to see how they reacted. Three, he'd grind up and see if he could determine what minerals they were comprised of. The other four—well, they'd be interesting things to add to his collection of oddities.

Someone knocked on his screen.

"Come in." He stopped dipping the quills and set them aside on the corner of a towel.

One of the workers from the feed store tromped in. "Doc, I'm just fine, other than, well. . ." He shifted from one foot to the other. "My guts are all bound up."

Eric took him into the treatment room, asked several questions, palpated the man's belly, and took down the jar of *cascara sagrada* to measure out a dose. "This ought to do the trick."

"Oh, good." His patient paid a nickel for the exam and medication, then wandered back out.

As Eric put the jar away, he mentally translated the Latin name. *Cascara sagrada. Sacred bark.* His hand stilled for a moment. Setting the jar farther back on the shelf, he stood eye-level to feverfew. Bark and flowers. Two of the common cures he dispensed were simply dried from nature and pulverized into a fine powder.

But I base my prescriptions on years of training, sound medical examinations, and scientific knowledge. Who knows what possesses Polly to dispense herbs or her mother to employ her odd treatments? Besides, my pharmaceuticals are of standardized strength and produced in a sterile environment.

He went back to his experiment. When he lifted the porcupine quill from the soggy towel's edge, Eric stared in disbelief. The vinegar solution had actually softened it! How had Polly learned such a trick?

And what else does she know? Is it possible I could experiment on some of her herbal compounds and discover if there's any scientific basis to her remedies?

Even Hippocrates advised using willows' yellow leaves or bark to help with aches and pains. From back during the Revolutionary War days, a doctor had distilled digitalis from purple foxglove to help certain heart problems. But Eric's supply of those medicaments was, again, standardized and reliable.

Oil of cloves, magnesia, bromide of potash, boric acid crystals and powder, zinc carbonate, ether, and morphine—his shelves and cabinets contained almost the complete pharmacopoeia. Each compound filling the vials and bottles could be vouched for in purity and efficacy. The memory of that dingy room off Lovejoy's cabin that held the jugs and jars of the Chance women's homemade apothecary renewed his doubts.

To be sure, a fraction of their so-called treatments would probably be effective, but that didn't make those women safe practitioners. Modern medical science demanded proof—experiments that rendered the same results when repeated. Those women practiced by trial and error, by folklore and fanciful thinking.

He eased back. Perhaps he could meet Polly and her mother halfway. He'd inspect their apothecary and approve of certain substances, then convince them to agree to limit their practice to treating cases of croup, mending sprains, and stitching up minor wounds. Surely those maladies comprised a large part of their practice anyway. He'd "review" proper technique with them and update their practices so they'd not indulge in dangerous oddities like rubbing a flower near an open wound.

Then he'd take care of the rest of Reliable's medical needs.

It all seemed so easy...but the longer Eric stood there, the less comfortable he felt. Gideon Chance had told him flat out he'd been prideful. Indeed, he had. In fact, he'd hoped Polly would understand when he spent time with her at Sunday school that he was trying to make peace.

It wasn't that he was wrong. It was just that he needed to be sure he framed matters carefully so no one's feelings were hurt and Polly and Lovejoy still felt useful. Confident in his stance, he'd failed to weigh the human factor—a mistake he'd not repeat. Surely if he overtly showed approval of the things the women did well, he could either teach them better methods for what they did wrong or simply convince them to refer such cases to him. Yes, Lovejoy was right—this could become a partnership of sorts.

Partnership means both parties bring something to the table. Polly knows the community well. In fact, Lovejoy offered to guide me past some of the "peculiarities." That would be a terrific help, he mused as he continued to look at his supplies.

Oil of cloves. . .oil of eucalyptus. . .morphine—they were all plant-based.

Zinc and magnesia were minerals. For that matter, lye soap came from leaching acid from ashes. Perhaps what he needed to do was view Polly's collection as a source of something that might add to medical science. Much of it might be nonsense, but a few gems might well shine in the darkness of that closet.

Excited by that prospect, Eric grabbed his coat and hat. He'd pay a call on Miss Polly Chance. Maybe they could be partners, after all.

"Polly." Uncle Bryce stepped into her cabin and shut the door behind himself. "That doctor is out here. Wants to see you."

"Dr. Walcott?" She gave her uncle a startled look.

"Ain't no other doctor roundabout here. I'm sticking to my guns." Uncle Bryce gave her a stern look. "I don't like you keepin' company with him."

"I'm not 'keeping company' with him." Polly set aside the herbs she'd been grinding and stood.

"Hmpf. My brothers all said the same thing 'bout women who showed up here; then they up and married 'em. This guy might be rich and smart and handsome"—he waggled his finger at her—"but you remember what I told you."

Polly patted him on the center of his chest. "You don't need to worry."

"My Daisy's in town, or I'd send her out to keep watch over you. Where are your cousins? Most always, they're a gaggle around you. Now, when you need 'em most, they're nowhere to be seen."

"They're visiting Beulah and the baby, and a good thing, too! If they heard you liken them to geese, they'd be offended."

"Truth is truth." He squinted at her.

"Oh, honestly, Uncle Bryce! I understand why you all send the kids along with Caleb for his courtship with Greta. They're young and foolish. I'm twenty-one, and I'd like to repeat. This is undoubtedly a professional consultation."

Uncle Bryce snorted. "I don't believe that for a second. The man's already said you're dangerous. He couldn't care less what you think about medicine; he cares what you think about him. I'd still feel a heap better if at least one of the girls was here to vex you and that man. That'd make him keep his distance and stop any stupid notions or designs he might be concocting."

Polly decided not to argue the point. Mulishly stubborn, Uncle Bryce wouldn't let go of a notion any sooner than a coyote would yield a meaty bone. She straightened up and waved a hand downward to call his attention to her attire. "Look—I'm not even taking off my work apron to go meet him."

He held her back. "Hang on a minute and tie the belt looser. Cinched in so snug, it makes you look like a girl."

"I am a girl." Laughing, Polly opened the door and walked across the yard. More than a few men in the area knew she was a girl—they'd asked Daddy permission to pay her court—but not a one of them managed to pull it off. Simply put, they were nice—but for some other woman. None of them ever made her heart sing. Then there was the doctor. Polly wondered if he even thought of her as a woman instead of as a pain in the neck.

"Hello, Doctor."

"Miss Polly." Eric doffed his hat. "Since you're interested in botanicals, I thought perhaps we ought to compare notes."

Taken by surprise, she stammered, "What kind of botanicals?"

"Healing ones. Your garden is quite impressive. Perhaps we could start there."

"Oh. Okay." She took a few steps toward the pump and rinsed out a bucket. "If you don't mind, I need to gather a few things."

"I don't mind at all." He sidestepped when Cory, Packard, and Terrance ran past.

Perry skidded to a halt. "Wanna come with us? Caleb's taking Greta on a picnic. We're going along to fish."

"Does Caleb know you're joining them?" Polly gave her little cousin an amused look.

"My daddy and Uncle Giddy said we could!" He raced away.

Trying hard not to laugh, Polly pressed her lips together.

"Why"—the doctor swiped the bucket from her hand—"do I have the feeling Caleb's not going to be thrilled with this development?"

Losing the battle, Polly laughed aloud. "If I don't miss my guess, Greta's mother is probably packing enough food for an army and will send her two youngest along, too. Greta and Caleb are both eighteen. Both families feel it's a good match, but it wouldn't hurt for them to wait a few years before meeting at the altar."

"Being an only child suddenly is far more appealing to me. When I decide to woo a young woman, I won't have tagalongs."

Is he thinking of courting someone? Polly felt a twinge at the thought, then got angry at herself. *Well, Uncle Bryce couldn't be more wrong—it's certainly not me. He'll want a meek, mild woman who stays home. We'd never suit.* Reaching around, she pulled her apron strings and retied them looser.

Chapter 16

"I'll have to ask you to be careful to stay on the path, Doctor." Polly set out at a brisk pace. "It's pretty narrow, but we rely on each plant."

"Sure." His stride matched hers until he stepped ahead to open the garden gate.

Polly walked into the garden and caught sight of Uncle Bryce glowering from the barn. She'd reassure him later that the doctor had come for professional reasons. "The garden is divided into two sections." She headed toward the right. "Though most of these herbs can be medicinal, their major use is in cooking."

"Interesting."

Walking along, Polly named the plants aloud: "Rosemary, thyme, sage, basil, sweet and wild marjoram, chives, lovage, lemon balm, parsley, borage, mint, fennel—"

"Fennel is effective for dyspepsia."

Polly nodded and started using her knife to cut small bits of fennel. "True, but I'm harvesting it because I'm making a brine for pickles. Dill, fennel, a little onion, and mustard make for tasty pickles."

"You don't have any mustard here."

She looked around the patch. "No need to. It grows wild all around the area. I used mustard in the poultices for the Greene children."

He nodded. "I keep a fair supply of dried mustard on hand."

Well, that was nice. He just admitted that we sometimes use the same curative. Maybe we'll find other things we can agree upon.

She dropped more fennel into the pail. "Let's go to the other half. It holds the medicinals. Mama and Aunt Delilah put in a lot of work to plant things that were scarce or foreign to this region."

"So am I to presume you keep cuttings from plants that are out of season in that room over there?" He gestured toward the hallway between her cabin and her parents' abode.

"Those are the things we've harvested and keep on hand. Mama and I gather almost daily."

"I haven't found the people of Reliable to be of such poor health." He followed her steps with caution along the narrow path between patches of plants as he continued to discuss the citizenry. "On average, I think they're actually rather hale."

Polly glanced back and noted how his footsteps literally overlaid hers. He'd been walking precisely where she had—a mark of his respect for her precious garden. Gratitude filled her heart.

"Do you disagree? Have you considered your neighbors to be sickly?"

"No, no. Not at all. It's that you never know when you'll need something, so Mama and I have been diligent to keep stock on hand. I noticed your shelves when we put that plaster on Cal. At the time, I remember thinking your supply rivaled one of the pharmacies in San Francisco."

"The mayor told me Reliable didn't have a pharmacy, so I planned on having to dispense whatever I prescribed."

"That'll be handy. In the past, if we didn't have something, we sent to San Francisco. Waiting is hard—that's why the garden here keeps growing. We've added something nearly every year."

He scanned the collection. "I recognize the feverfew."

"Tansy's on this side of it. St. John's wort is on the other side. Then we have comfrey, herb Robert, self-heal, valerian—"

"Did you try valerian for your headaches?"

"Yes, but to no avail." She gave him a sideways look. "My headaches are not from nerves."

"I didn't mean to imply they were. Valerian can be effective for a variety of problems."

"It's putting down good roots—roots are what we harvest. But you only dig them up in September." She felt her nose wrinkle. "They don't smell bad fresh, but once they're dried, they reek."

"So how can you keep them in that shed by your cabin?"

"We dry them in the barn. After grinding them up and putting them in a tightly stoppered jar, the smell is contained. It's useful for insomnia and women's complaints." The minute the words slipped out of her mouth, Polly wanted to spin around and flee.

Eric didn't bat an eye. "Lydia Pinkham's Vegetable Compound contains cohosh and more than twenty percent alcohol." He leaned over and examined wood betony as he added, "Several women partake of it."

"Mama says cohosh is good, but we don't add any spirits to our elixirs."

The doctor nodded. "Good, good."

She didn't want to continue the discussion of women's complaints. As healers, they both dealt with such issues, and the Bible even spoke about Christ healing a woman with a female complaint, but it didn't seem like a proper subject of conversation. Grabbing the opportunity he'd opened, Polly said, "That plant you're inspecting is wood betony. It can be helpful with mouth sores and throat irritations."

"Fascinating. Do you mind if I take samples?"

Extending her gathering knife to him, she said, "Not at all."

They spent time going from plant to plant. The doctor asked several questions and made interesting observations. As it became awkward for him to harvest, label the small papers in which he folded the sample, and tuck them into his pocket, Polly took back her knife and assisted him. She used the techniques Mama taught her.

The doctor questioned her every action. "I use the petals that are darkest because they are richest in the healing properties. . . ." "The leaves are best when harvested in morning shade, so we won't take any today. . . ." "These must be rinsed thrice before drying upside down. . . ."

He scribbled notes to himself and asked dozens and dozens of questions. Polly surprised herself with just how much Mama had taught her. The teaching had been so gradual, she never fully appreciated the lore Mama shared so generously.

At one point, the doctor frowned. "Why aren't you wearing a bonnet out here?"

She lifted a hand and touched her hair. *Oh, dear me. It's probably a horrible mess.* Self-conscious laughter bubbled out of her.

"I didn't mean to embarrass you. My only thought was that sunlight might trigger headaches."

"I love the sunshine."

"Hey there, Doc." Mama leaned over the fence. Try as she might, she didn't manage to disguise the grimace of pain that came with the action. "Nice of you to drop by. Why don't you stay to lunch?"

"I'd be honored." He sidestepped between a few plants very carefully and lowered his voice. "I'd also be honored if you'd allow me to examine your back. Something must be done."

Mama let out a chortle. "Oh, Doc, now if that wasn't smooth as rain off a winderpane. I've done my share of bargainin' folks into accepting care. Suppose it's justice someone turned the tables on me."

Eric dusted off his hands. "How long till lunch?"

"We have time for you to check on her now," Polly said. She didn't want to give Mama an opportunity to come up with an excuse and wiggle out of an examination. Knowing Mama, Polly figured that's exactly what she'd do, too.

She couldn't fault the doctor's bedside manner. He'd washed his hands outside while she helped Mama change into a lawn nightdress. Once he came in, Eric performed a deft examination of Mama's back, asked several pertinent questions, and managed to be both professional and personable.

"The hot and cold packs and the liniment are all fine. Continue on with those and the massages," he told Polly. "I'd like to try traction—a series of ropes and weights to stretch the spine." He held his fists together, side to side, then slowly drew them apart. "Slow, gentle force could straighten the kink and allow the nerves and disc to slip into a natural position again."

"Mama, that ought to work!"

Mama sighed. "Hope so. You jest tell us what to do, Doc."

"I'll step out and talk to your husband about rigging up the traction apparatus."

He left, and Lovejoy tugged on Polly's hand. "Help me get dressed. I wanna soak up some sunshine this noon afore he and yore Daddy strap me to the bed."

Slender and sprightly, Mama had never needed to resort to stays, but since her back started paining her, Polly had made her a back binding with boning in it to render some support. She laced it up, then knelt to help Mama with her shoes while Mama buttoned up her day gown. Once they were done, Polly opened the door, and Mama gingerly stepped outside.

Lord, let Dr. Walcott's treatment work. Mama's hurting. I just want her to be well again.

Eric stood over by Daddy and some of the boys. Daddy's brows were furrowed.

"Yore daddy and uncles are good men," Mama whispered to Polly as they headed toward the tables. "Don't you be troublin' yourself o'er how things'll work out. They're not gonna give Doc a hard time or carry a grudge. Feelin' ran high t'other day, but I know 'em—they'll be examples. A shining example is a better lesson than a lot of gusty words."

Polly wasn't quite so sure. Then again, since Mama let Dr. Walcott examine her, that ought to mean a lot to Daddy. Then, too, the doctor had accepted the lunch invitation, so they'd be breaking bread together.

A few moments later, Eric, Daddy, and Uncle Paul strode up with an odd assortment of ropes, leather, and—"That can't be the pulley from the hayloft!" Polly couldn't hide her astonishment.

"I scrubbed it," Uncle Paul confirmed.

"Let's go," Daddy said to Mama.

Mama's jaw jutted forward in a stubborn tilt. "I'm aimin' to eat first."

"That'll be fine." Eric nodded. "It's not healthy for you to lie in one place for days on end. I want you to be up for half an hour, four times a day." He then tacked on, "But no working during that time. It's just for eating and essentials."

Mama gave him an exasperated look.

Polly laughed. "Mama, your face has the same expression as the Greene children when I tell them they need those stinky mustard and onion poultices!"

"I'd rather wear a poultice and still be upright," Mama muttered. She glanced at the doctor. "Don't you fret yoreself none. I git het up when a patient doesn't mind me. I'll be good and foller yore instructions."

"Thank you," he said in a tone that sounded mildly amused.

At lunch, the doctor sat at the lunch table by Polly's side. That was saying plenty since there were six tables and he could have plopped down wherever he wanted. Maybe he was avoiding April, though. The girls had come back from visiting Beulah and gone in to prepare lunch. April got news that Dr. Walcott was there, dashed out of the kitchen, and immediately started making a pest of herself.

Uncle Gideon stood at a table and clapped his hands once. Everyone fell silent for the prayer. "Our Lord of abundance and grace, we give thanks for Your providence. Bless and keep us as we seek to do Your will, and we ask a special touch of healing for our Lovejoy. Amen."

Every second or third day for the next two weeks, Dr. Walcott came out to check on Mama, go on a gathering walk with Polly, and sit beside her at the lunch table. Mama's improvement pleased them all, and Polly looked forward to his visits.

They wandered along the back path toward a stand of trees. Polly gently tugged on Eric's shirtsleeve. "Beware of that plant hanging off the far tree. It's poison oak."

"It doesn't look like any poison oak I've ever seen. Are you sure?"

"Aunt Miriam found out the hard way." Polly stood on tiptoe to peel off a little bark from a neighboring tree.

"What is that for?"

"Kate wants to tan a little leather. This'll do the trick, and if she adds a little iron salt, the leather will go black." She stuffed the bark into her gathering bag. "But don't tell Uncle Titus. She's making him a belt as a surprise for his birthday."

"Why doesn't she just buy stain?"

"Then he'd find out about it. With such a big family, it's hard to keep secrets. We help one another out."

He peeled off more bark. "How much do you need?"

"Just a little more." . . . *Of the bark. But a lot more of you.*

Eric thoroughly enjoyed Polly's companionship. Such a bright woman! Clever, cheerful, hardworking. He'd never met anyone with such a capacity to love. Her family, neighbors, folks in town—even the animals on the ranch—they all adored her.

And I do, too. Eric halted midmotion at that realization. He'd told himself he was interested in Polly because of her abilities, her knowledge, even her slightly quirky ways. But the truth stared back at him. He'd come to make peace with her and explore her knowledge of plants, but somewhere on one of their walks, she'd gathered his heart just as surely as anything else she collected.

Chapter 17

Lovejoy's back improved almost daily. In a matter of another week or so, she wouldn't require traction at all. Eric had been collecting botanical specimens with Polly out of interest—but that interest was every bit as much personal as it was scientific. The time had come to test the waters to see if she returned any feelings for him. He'd couch it carefully in such a way that they'd still be able to bump into one another if she tactfully indicated her affections lay elsewhere.

He'd never seen her walking or riding with anyone. She never sat at church with a young man or appeared at the mercantile with anyone other than family—unless he counted the MacPherson boys, and they were distant kin. The fact that no man had yet managed to capture her heart both puzzled and pleased Eric. Lord willing, he'd be that man.

I'll offer to bring my microscope and equipment here to Chance Ranch. Flushed with excitement over that idea, he said, "I've been conducting experiments on the plants you and I have been gathering together. Perhaps I could do some of the experiments here at your ranch as the season starts to change. The last few days, you've mentioned autumn harvesting will begin. Maybe I could accompany you, and then we could prepare powders and slides."

"Aunt Delilah doodles with her colored pencils every chance she has. If you'd like, she'd probably illustrate your notes."

"Great!" Delilah's talent would be an asset, but she also stuck close to her smaller son and the house. That meant her sketching wouldn't involve her tagging along while he conducted his wooing. He still remembered how the Chances sent a few of the younger boys along on Caleb's picnic as chaperones. A few times, April or Kate had come along on the gathering walks, but neither seemed especially thrilled with all of the botanical conversation. Thereafter, they found excuses not to tag along—which pleased Eric to no end.

Heading back toward the ranch house, feeling confident in all he and Polly had accomplished, Eric continued, "I'd like to work with you more, train you with some of my things."

"Like the special Johnson & Johnson plaster?"

"Yes. . ." He paused, then dared to push on, "and like childbirth." *If you become my wife, we'll tend women together.*

Polly stopped and gave him an entertained look. "In eighteen years, Mama's lost only two women in this township within the first ten days of their deliveries. Can you boast the same statistic?"

"We both know I haven't practiced for eighteen years, Polly. I do have modern scientific techniques." Though confident in his own medical ability, his assurance of Polly's faith in his talent flagged. Perhaps she wasn't attracted to him, either. He'd come too far to back out, though. "The pastor's wife is due any day now, and—"

"She's been clear about her desires, Doctor. Mama and I will be attending her."

"Your mother oughtn't do that. It's too hard for her yet. I thought you and I—"

Polly's eyes widened. "How could you suggest that? Mrs. Abrams already told you how she feels. I'm not going to plow over her feelings."

"She's older—far older—than most first-time mothers. Complications are more common in such circumstances." He could see he wasn't getting anywhere. Eric heaved a sigh. "Then promise me two things, Polly: that you'll summon me if there are any problems whatsoever, and that you'll use my ergot."

"You insisted on your ergot at Beulah's delivery, too. Why?"

"Because. . ." He looked at Polly and hated to crush her confidence, but the folklore she used was still dangerous. He needed to convince her to use sound medicinals, even if he couldn't win her heart. "Because ergot is scientifically proven to prevent postpartum hemorrhage. The rust scrapings and rye whiskey you use are hazardous to the patient."

"Rust scrapings and rye whiskey," Polly echoed. Her blue eyes grew huge, and her mouth dropped open. Laughter bubbled out of her. "Rust scrapings and rye whiskey? Oh, Doctor. The whiskey on the table was to sterilize it. By the time I arrived, Eunice was ready to deliver. I didn't have time to do a lye soap scrub. As for rust—you misunderstood. We have Hattie send us scrapings of rusty rye."

"And my ergot is from rye," he said. He chortled in disbelief and relief.

"Oh, my." She laughed merrily. "Between that and the ax at a birthing, no wonder you felt Mama and I were quacks!"

"When I was just five, my mother died in childbirth, Polly. It's one of the reasons I became a physician. Attending Reliable's women during that dangerous time is important—for them and to me."

Polly looked him in the eye and slowly shook her head. "I love delivering babies and helping the mamas, too, but that's not the issue. The fact is, women have the right to decide who's going to help them. I'm not going to sway a woman to come see me if she seeks you out; you oughtn't do the reverse."

Stubborn woman. Eric looked at her in silence.

"You suggested partnering. If a woman wants the both of us there, I'm fine with that. Mama always said another pair of skilled hands isn't ever wasted."

Eric couldn't deny that fact. Nonetheless, he didn't want Polly carrying on the misguided notion that she could cure the collective ills of Reliable's citizens. "As I mentioned, it would be a good thing for me to train you in modern medical practices."

"The traction you set up for Mama works beautifully. Those kinds of things fascinate me. I'd enjoy learning whatever you're willing to teach me."

"Good." Maybe things could work out, after all. *Why does she have to be so confusing?*

She slanted him a look. "I'm willing to assist you, too—in regular cases, emergencies, and during surgical procedures. Please feel free to send for me."

He studied her. Something about the attentiveness in her posture—the slight forward tilt of her head and the ever-so-subtle narrowing of her eyes—made him take notice. "Are you referring to a specific case, Polly?"

"Might be."

Eric frowned.

She shifted subtly. If it weren't for the way her skirt scuffed a tiny mark in the earth, he would have missed it entirely. "Oh, dear." She winced. "This is difficult. With Mama, I'm free to discuss the neighbors to whom we render care. On the other hand, it's not right for me to reveal things to you about them. I'm afraid it's going to be problematic."

"There are bound to be difficulties. You and I agree on something, though: The patient's welfare is always foremost."

Her eyes pled with him for confirmation. "I referred someone to you yesterday."

"Is that so? No one's sent for me or come to the clinic." The pleasure that she'd sent a case to him couldn't offset the concern he felt. Polly still felt competent treating simple cases; this one must be exceptionally involved or difficult.

Polly started toward the barnyard. Eric strode alongside her, matching her rapid pace. The resolute set of her jaw warned him something was wrong. "What is it?"

"I suppose that partnership's going to be trial by fire." She dropped the gathering sack onto a table and called, "Hey, in the barn!"

Someone stuck out his head. Eric thought it might be Tanner.

"Saddle up Blossom right away!"

"Where're you going?"

"The Big G." Polly looked at Eric. "I'll grab my satchel. Did you bring your doctor's bag?"

"Yes."

"Good." She headed into her parents' cabin. Eric stood in the doorway and overheard her whisper, "Mama, I'm taking Doc over to the Big G. Mr. Garcia didn't go get checked."

"Mmm. Best you shake a leg. I didn't like the way he looked."

Polly headed into the odd closetlike place. Eric invited himself to go see what she was gathering from the shelves.

To his surprise, the shelves weren't dusty—they were all painted a grayish brown. The jars, jugs, and bottles were all sparkling clean and bore labels. Sure, bunches of leaves and roots hanging from pegs pounded into the roof looked strange. He suspected there was some order or method to the arrangement, but this wasn't the time to ascertain those details.

"What are you getting?"

"Essentials. If it's what I think it is, we'll take him to your office for surgery; if it's worsened, you might have to operate at his place." Metal pieces chinked together as she lifted a tightly wrapped towel and stuffed it into her satchel. "I'll bring my instruments just in case."

"Fine." He grabbed a bar of lye soap.

She took a bottle of carbolic acid and the accompanying mister, a container of tincture of iodine, then one last bottle and slipped them all into her satchel.

He couldn't believe what he'd seen on the label. "You have ether?"

"Yes." Right beside where that bottle had rested on the shelf sat paper-and-cotton cones in which to drip the ether. That surprised him; most often, folks saturated a sponge with it, but many didn't awaken after the surgery because the anesthesia went too deep.

"A doctor in San Francisco trained Mama and me about it. He suggested the cone because he's seen too many people harmed with an ether sponge."

"Polly, why don't you tell me what you've diagnosed?"

She stopped for a moment and gave him a grave look. "I suspect appendicitis."

Grabbing her wrist in one hand and the satchel in the other, he plowed toward the door. His voice vibrated with concern and supplication as he prayed, "God help us all."

Chapter 18

The sickly sweet smell of ether lingered in the kitchen as Polly carefully washed the instruments. As Eric came back into the room, she asked, "How is he?"

"I got him settled in bed. Pulse is strong, breathing is steady. He's in God's hands now."

Polly nodded. When they'd arrived, they'd found Mr. Garcia in his stable. He lay doubled up beside his saddle, barely conscious. Eric hefted him, carried him into the two-room shack, and gave the shambled place a look of despair.

Polly hastily swept everything off the table, and in a moment of tension, Eric still managed some mirth. "No time for a lye scrub. Do you think he has any of that medicinal whiskey for sterilizing the table?"

Polly located a bottle and doused the table thoroughly, and that was where they operated. The water in the stove reservoir was still scalding, so she'd been able to give the instruments a cursory dip for better sterility. They'd worked furiously but well together. Polly paused from washing those instruments now, glanced up at the doctor, and nodded. "Yes, it's up to the Lord now."

He watched her as she washed the handles of a pair of hemostats. Suddenly, Polly felt unaccountably shy. She concentrated on making sure the little metal ridges on the other end of the instrument came sparkling clean.

"You did the right thing, Polly. If we hadn't arrived when we did, that appendix would have ruptured and Mr. Garcia would have died. It would have been a lonely, painful death."

She nodded. "Healing is a matter of asking God's guidance and doing your best. I'm glad you were here. I couldn't have operated."

"We work exceptionally well together." Eric dipped each of the just-washed instruments into boiling water, then set them on a clean towel. "I'm not sure what's yours and what's mine."

Polly stared at the shiny collection of scissors, probes, retractors, hemostats, scalpels, and needles. "Yours are the experienced ones. Most of mine don't see much use. Other than births and doing sutures, I don't even take them from their sterile wraps."

"Your plants are your tools."

His words left her feeling lightheaded with pleasure. Polly leaned against the sink. "Yes, they are."

Eric frowned, wrapped his hand around her elbow, and dragged her toward a chair. "Here. Sit down." As soon as he'd deposited her in the seat, he opened the door and muttered to himself, "I was an idiot not to air out the room."

"Really, I'm fine."

He came over, tilted her face to his, and shook his head. "Ether is harsh. You're—"

"If you dare call me fragile, I might never forgive you." Even though she didn't feel weak, she didn't mind his touch. It made her feel. . .cared for.

His brows hiked upward, and he let out a short laugh. "The fresh air is giving you back your sass. As for you not forgiving me. . ." He stroked his thumb slowly across her jaw. "You don't carry grudges. If you did, I wouldn't be standing here."

"Why are you standing there?" Uncle Bryce's voice made them both turn toward the door. A thunderous scowl darkened his face. "I thought somebody was supposed to be sick. And you"—he shook his forefinger at her—"Polly Chance, you know better. You're not to go gallivanting off without one of us comin' along."

"It was an emergency, and I was with Polly." Eric stood beside her.

Uncle Bryce didn't respond verbally. He gave Polly a we'll-talk-about-this-later look.

"Mr. Garcia's going to need help for a while here." Polly tried to steer the conversation into safer territory. "Could you please go to the MacPhersons and see if they can spare Peter and Matt? I'll ask Cal and Tanner to come, too."

"From the looks of things, it'll take the four of them weeks to whip this place into shape." Uncle Bryce folded his arms and continued to wear a stubborn expression. "You can tell plenty about a man from his animals. Garcia's stable is full of beasts he's ignored."

"He's been sick, Uncle Bryce. Really sick." She refused to divulge the nature of the malady, and her uncle knew better than to ask particulars, but Polly did impart, "We just operated. How about if you and I go water and feed those animals while Dr. Walcott checks in on Mr. Garcia?"

"So you're done here?"

"Not yet."

"I aim to toss you back on Blossom and send you home. Ain't fittin' for a young woman to be all on her own out in the wilds with two men."

Heat flashed from her bosom to her hairline. Polly wanted to let out a squawk of outrage. Uncle Bryce had no call to be embarrassing her like this. "Mama knew Dr. Walcott and I were paying a medical call. No one will give it another thought."

"Your mama couldn't concoct a bad thought about anybody," Uncle Bryce grumbled. "Don't hold her up as a sample on how others think."

"More's the pity," the doctor said. "I've found Lovejoy to be a wonderful Christian example."

Uncle Bryce shook his finger at Eric. "An example. Yes, a Christian example. There you have it." He paused a moment, then blurted out, "Actually, you don't, and that's the problem."

Eric's lips parted. He waited a heartbeat, then asked solemnly, "Have I offended you or someone?"

"You wander off, missy." Uncle Bryce shot Polly a "mind-me" look.

She lifted her chin. "The doctor asked a question. You made an accusation in front of me, and he deserves the opportunity to clear his name."

Folding his arms across his chest, Uncle Bryce glowered at Dr. Walcott. "You've been to the Nugget." He paused meaningfully and cast a quick glance at Polly. "Now you walk off, missy."

"There's no need," the doctor said.

Uncle Bryce shook his head. "I tried to handle this best as I could. Neither of you is making it easy. Fact is, Doc, it's known you've been upstairs at the Nugget."

"Yes, I have," Doc said mildly. He looked from Polly to Uncle Bryce and back again. He didn't sound in the least bit offended or defensive. "I treat anyone in need. Where they live or what they do for a living isn't an issue for me."

"Folks get the wrong impression," Uncle Bryce grumbled.

"I suppose that could be true. But Jesus didn't ask what people did for a living; He reached out and healed them. I won't do any different. If folks make false judgments about me, that's their business. I'm accountable to the Lord."

"You're right," Polly murmured.

"Reckon so," Uncle Bryce agreed in a surly tone.

Eric asked, "Is there anything else?"

"Not at all," she said swiftly before Uncle Bryce set in for a repeat of his opinion. He tended to do that. Stubborn as a mule, he'd likely prod the doctor just to be sure he'd gotten the whole truth. Polly felt certain in her heart the doctor had been completely, wholly honest.

"Then I'll go check on our patient, Polly." Eric headed across the cabin.

Polly accompanied her uncle out to the stable. She half-stomped out there, then turned on him once they were out of earshot from the cabin. "What got into you?"

"I oughta be asking you that selfsame question. I told you right from the start to beware of that man and not go off alone with him. That first time he came to wander 'round and gawk at your plants, I warned you not to keep company with him. The man keeps turning up like a plague of flies."

"He's not a pest; he's a professional. Not one single thing's passed between us that is in the least bit questionable."

"Keep it thataway." Bryce started watering the animals. "Soon as we feed these critters, I want you to go back home. He don't care what folks think, but you need to. What he does still reflects on you if you keep company together."

Polly thrust the scoop into the oats and yanked it back out. Uncle Bryce tended to be an easygoing man, but when he dug in his heels, he could teach stubborn to a mule. She'd have to talk to Daddy and have him set his little brother straight.

Pastor Abe stood at the pulpit and beamed at the congregation. "I'd like to open the service with a special praise. The Lord blessed my wife and me with a healthy little boy late last evening. Given the fact that we've waited for him for so long, he's to be called Isaac."

The rest of the parishioners laughed and murmured at the wonderful news and clever name. Eric forced a smile. He'd been home last night, but no one sought his assistance. The woman he loved essentially had stolen away the part of medical practice he most enjoyed.

Daniel Chance scooted into the pew beside Eric. He gave him a curt nod, then paid attention to the pastor. Well, he tried to. The man fidgeted. He curled his hands around the seat on each side of his thighs in a death grip, then eased back and drummed his fingers on the edge. A moment later, he twisted and leaned closer. "Meet me outside."

Chapter 19

Eric rose and followed him out to the churchyard. "Is there a problem?"

"Lovejoy's back is bad again. She went to help the pastor's wife last night. Polly gave her something to stop the spasms and help her sleep, but I don't like this one bit. The traction—I rigged it up the way you showed me, but all it did was make Lovejoy hurt worse."

"I'll go check on her. Why don't you ask the congregation to pray?" Eric didn't wait for a response. He unhitched his gelding and swung up into the saddle. The road to Chance Ranch would take half an hour—far longer than he'd accept. Eric cut across a patch of land, jumped the fence, and took the most direct route.

Polly opened the cabin door as his horse skidded to a halt. "Dr. Walcott!"

"Your father sent me." He dismounted and headed into the cabin. "He said your mother's in a bad way."

Polly shut the door behind him, and a vile odor permeated the cabin. "I just rubbed her down with liniment."

"I'm tellin' you, Doc," Lovejoy said from the bed, "hit's a case of wonderin' if the cure's worse'n the affliction. McCleans Volcanic Liniment reeks to high heaven, don't it?"

"Does it make you feel better?" He bent over the bed and noticed the lines of pain bracketing her mouth.

"Reckon I couldn't feel any worse." She sighed. " 'Tis my own fault, too. I been fightin' the direction God's leadin' me. He knocked me on my back so's I'd be forced to look up."

"Then I'm going to tie you up to the traction and keep you here until you and God get that matter ironed out." He assessed her, then looked at Polly. "I need to apply traction higher on the back than we did before. Instead of the waist belt, we'll need to devise something that straps just beneath her arms."

Polly looked around the cabin.

Lovejoy winced from a spasm. "Cain't we jest use a belt?"

"If we rigged cloth into a suspenderlike arrangement in the back, that would work." Eric headed for the open door to the apothecary. "Don't you keep the cotton bandaging material in here?"

"Grosgrain ribbon would be stronger and flatter. I'm sure Laurel has yards of it in her sewing basket." Polly slipped past him and opened the door that led to the adjoining cabin.

The only time he'd been inside her cabin was when she had the migraine. Other than a vague memory of the floral scent and white furniture, Eric didn't remember anything about the place since he'd been focused on Polly's headache. Curious about where Polly lived with her cousins, Eric craned his neck and took in the yellow gingham curtains, the bright rag rug, and the far wall that bore a large wreath of dried flowers and a picture. The place looked like it belonged to Polly—cheery and practical.

She called over her shoulder, "The boys' cabin is next door. There's a box under the bunk bed on the left that holds clothes they've outgrown and can pass on. Could you please go see if there's a belt?"

"Sure." Eric walked into the cabin she specified and headed toward the box. He had to step over discarded socks, a book, and a shirt and push aside a saddle frame. They'd added on to the cabin in order to accommodate what looked to be another set of bunk beds, and the sheer disorder of a bunch of young men gave the cabin an air of rowdy acceptance.

For a moment, Eric looked about and felt a pang. He'd missed out on all of this—the sense of belonging, of having a brother as a confidant, of scuffling and arguing and teasing with someone. He envied the Chance men for having brothers and sons so they'd never sit alone at a table and eat in deafening silence.

Setting aside those thoughts, Eric yanked a crate from beneath the bed and rummaged through it. He found a belt he thought might work and jogged back to join Polly at Lovejoy's bedside.

It took a few tries before they devised a setup Eric felt would work. He bent over Lovejoy. "I'm going to lift you so Polly can slip the strap beneath you."

"How's about I wind my arms 'bout your neck and pull myself up?"

"Mama, you're going to hurt Dr. Walcott's feelings. He'll get the impression you don't think he's strong enough."

Eric flashed Polly a smile. She'd kept him from having to argue with Lovejoy and managed to hint that she found his physique manly.

"Okay. Let's get on with it."

A ragged moan tore through Lovejoy's throat as Eric lifted her. He murmured wordless sounds of comfort, then carefully laid her back down once Polly arranged the apparatus. Quickly, he buckled the belt, then attached the weights to form the traction. "Her muscles are already in spasm. I want to go ahead and get this done so she won't have to endure another jolt," he said to Polly.

Her hands shook, but she hastily tied the weights as he'd shown her the last time. Once done, she darted to the other side of the bed and wiped away Lovejoy's tears. "I'm sorry, Mama. It'll be better soon. Jesus loves you and cares about your pain. You know He does."

Eric watched Polly. Her hands were beautiful—caring, gentle, soothing. She moved with grace that never hinted that there was any urgency in her actions. Tiny things—pushing back a wisp of hair, fluffing a pillow, speaking in a soft, confident tone—everything she did exuded love. She gave her heart to each patient. He'd seen her this way with Beulah, Perry, the Greene children, and during the surgery. Her herbs, teas, and poultices might well have medicinal effects, but the real secret behind her healing was that she simply opened her heart to the Lord and let Him pour His love through her.

After ten agonizing minutes, Lovejoy's body relaxed. She closed her eyes as her head sank deeper into the pillow. "Confession's good for the soul. I need to make a confession. My pride's gotten in the way of my common sense."

"Mama, you don't need to—"

"Child, I do. 'Member how I told you healin' ain't just flesh and bone? When somethin' ails a body, a heavy soul makes it worse. I gotta speak my piece here."

"All right, Mama." Polly curled her hand around her mother's.

Eric wondered if he ought to leave. Was this a mother-daughter moment? He didn't do well with these family things—the nuances escaped him.

"Doc, stop bein' antsy as a turkey at Thanksgivin'. Ain't nothin' sweeter than God's children sharin' their joys and woes. I seen you plenty these last months. God claims you as one of His own. I ain't feelin' shy 'bout openin' my heart in front of you."

"I'm honored."

Polly glanced up at him. He couldn't read the look in her eyes.

Lovejoy let out a long, choppy breath. "Of all the things I like, catchin' babies always pleases me most. 'Tis a miracle, and the both of you know what I mean. Mayhap, on account I couldn't have me babes of my own, I came to think of midwivin' as being God's way of lettin' me have a snippet of that joy.

"I niver thought I'd have me a man who cherished me or little girls who called me their ma. God ended up givin' me my Dan'l and Polly and Ginny Mae. But sometimes God gives us things for a season. Ginny Mae was here just awhile; then the dear Lord called her home."

Eric watched as the two women's touch altered—the hold tightened in remembered grief. They'd shared that loss together. *What would it be like to have someone to bear the burden of sorrow with you?* His father had sent him away when his mother died. His grandparents had passed on at the same time. He'd never known the solace of mourning along with others who'd felt that deep wound of loss.

"You were the only mama Ginny Mae ever knew, and she adored you. God blessed us the day you marched onto the ranch."

Lovejoy managed a weak laugh. "Yore papa shore didn't think so at the start. But that all worked out. Our love is one of God's gifts. He's been generous to me.

I enjoyed bein' a healer; then I even got to share that with my Pollywog. All those times, they fill my heart like a treasure box. Any smart woman would count herself blessed and let it be. Only I ain't been so smart.

"After that horse kicked me last year, I knew I couldn't keep on doin' everything. Dan'l and me—we talked it over, and he's the one who told the mayor to put that ad out for a town doctor. We prayed o'er the man God would send. Yup, Doc, afore you come, my Dan'l and me done covered you in 'nuff prayers to keep a whole passel of angels busy."

"I'm humbled." *Oh, am I humbled. These people saw a need, provided a job for me, and set up my clinic. I thought I had to prove myself, and they'd already accepted me. I stood on my pride and challenged them.*

"But you got here, and 'stead of me letting go, I didn't. I held on. Oh, I reasoned it through—but that's not what God asked of me. He told me to let go and trust Him to use the both of you to do His healin' works. Me? I figured I could sorta help and partner and dabble. Not a soul knew it—but I did. Deep in my heart, I did."

You're not the only one who's been guilty of that. I was so sure of myself, I didn't seek God's guidance as I should have.

"So here I am, flat on my back, and it's time for me to come clean. Dan'l learned a hard lesson early in his life, and he favors a sayin' that's fitting. Nothin' ever stays the same, but the changes are always for better if we give 'em to God."

"Daddy is fond of saying that, isn't he?"

"Yup. Hit's time I stopped tryin' to force God into seein' things my way and I look at things through His eyes. My season of bein' a healer is over. I 'spect it ain't gonna be easy for me to turn loose, but now that you heard me out, you cain hold me accountable."

Silence and the pungent smell of liniment hovered in the air.

"Mama, I'll do my best to trust the Lord and care for folks." Polly laced her fingers with her mother's. Such a simple move—but it connected them, twined them together in an unconscious move that bespoke the intimacy of their bond. "I think you're right. God sent Doc here, and we can handle things. From now on, you can concentrate on getting better and spoiling Daddy."

Longing to be a part of Polly's world where caring came so easily, Eric dared to rest his right hand on her shoulder. She didn't pull away. Instead, she looked up at him and gave him that smile that made his heart skip a beat.

He'd wondered if he'd ever find a time and way to apologize for how he'd acted toward Polly and her mother. Polly acted as if he'd never once overstepped himself, but that was a tribute to her character. Lovejoy was right—nothing was better than honesty among believers.

Eric cleared his throat. "Since humble pie is on the menu, I'm going to have to eat a slice, too—a big slice."

Chapter 20

Grab you a fork, son." Lovejoy gave him an unsteady grin. "We won't make it taste too bad."

"I came here thinking book knowledge and scientific treatments were what it took to heal. As a Christian, I knew God is the Great Physician, but I let pride get ahead of wisdom. Daniel is an astute man. He nailed me on it, and I've had to do a lot of thinking and praying. My only pride ought to be in Christ's works."

"Iff'n my back weren't so nasty, I'd be standin' and shoutin' glory, 'cuz God is faithful to meet us at our honest needs."

"I haven't had a very meek spirit," Polly said.

"Never did," Lovejoy shot back. "But your vine bears fruit of other kinds."

"It does, indeed." Eric looked at Polly and recited, "Love, joy, peace, longsuffering, gentleness—"

Polly and her mother started laughing.

Baffled, Eric demanded, "What's so funny?"

A look of tenderness crossed Lovejoy's face. "My mama loved that verse in Ephesians."

"In fact, she named her daughters after it," Polly tacked on.

"Lovejoy," Eric said slowly, "and your sister is Temperance."

"Mama used all but Longsuffering and Meekness."

"I've been sitting in church worrying about you, woman." Daniel Chance strode in. "And here you are, reciting your family tree."

"Betwixt Polly rubbing me down and dosing me up and the doc roping me like this, I'm tolerable."

Daniel knelt by the bed and kissed her. "Listening to that, you sound like a seasoned roast on a spit!"

Polly moved out of the way and laughed.

"We prayed for you this morning," Daniel said.

"Thankee, Dan'l. We've had us our own time with Jesus here."

"I'll go rustle up some Sunday supper." Polly headed for the door.

"No, no." Her father shook his head.

Eric wondered if Daniel would make any reference to his daughter's lack of culinary skill. He'd been understandably protective of her in other matters.

"It's family picnic day," Daniel went on to say. "I'll slap together sandwiches for your mama and me. You go on ahead."

"I was so worried about Mama, I forgot."

Eric couldn't recall any announcement at church about a picnic. Had he been out on a call?

Lovejoy called, "Doc, I'm shore you oughta go, too. Us and the MacPhersons git together for Sunday picnic 'bout once a month. Since we both got our boys up at Mr. Garcia's place, Eunice sent word that we'd hold the picnic up there. That-away, the boys cain all show off their hard work, and Mr. Garcia'll git up and walk outside and eat more. You've been payin' calls on him since you done surgery—'tis 'bout time you broke bread with the man to show him you think he's hale again."

Daniel came out onto the porch, and Eric discussed how often Lovejoy's traction could be removed. Polly disappeared and returned with Blossom saddled.

"Thanks for coming, Doc. That traction had me puzzled. It made Lovejoy a heap better last time," Daniel said.

"It'll help again, but she needs to be careful. No more lifting or straining for her."

"We'll find other things to keep her busy." Dan grinned at him. "Things have worked out better than I thought with you." Daniel shook his hand. "Glad you came."

"Thanks. I'm glad I'm here." He stepped off the porch, wrapped his hands around Polly's waist, and lifted her into the saddle. For the few minutes when he had hold of her, everything felt so right. *More than anything, she's why I'm glad I'm here.*

Showing up at the family picnic with the doctor earned Polly plenty of sly smiles and assessing looks. Her cousins sometimes brought along the folks they fancied. Caleb and Greta walked by, then Johnna and Trevor. No one was giving either pair a second glance.

Polly couldn't decide what she wanted. *Well, yes, I can. I want Doc to court me. But until I clear things with April and he makes a move, it's going to be downright embarrassing for everyone to keep gawking. I never should have come.*

Eric dismounted, and Polly decided to scramble down before he might feel obligated to help her. With his fine manners, he was always doing chivalrous things—but that would fan speculation among the family.

"I need to go fetch something." Eric smiled. "Please go ahead and eat. I'll be back later."

April scurried up. "Doctor!"

"Miss April." He flashed her a smile. "Might I have a word with you?"

"Why, yes!"

Polly wandered off a few feet. She didn't know what to think.

"Polly, cain you come help me? I'm needin' someone to spell me with Elvera whilst I git me a dollop more of the tater salad."

"Sure, Aunt Eunice." Polly took possession of the baby and sat in the grass. A few minutes later, April came up. She brought an overflowing plate and put it on the blanket. "I brought enough to share with you, Polly."

Her bright eyes and flushed cheeks made Polly take note. "What did the doctor have to say?"

"He's so nice, Polly."

"Yes, he is." Polly didn't have much of an appetite. It seemed the courtship she wanted was going to happen—but for April instead of herself.

"Haven't you noticed how he loves children?"

"Yes."

"And he's gentle. You can see it in his eyes and hear it in his voice."

Polly nodded.

"And sincere—he speaks from the heart. And his heart is in the right place."

Unable to speak, Polly nodded. *But my heart is in the wrong place. If he really prefers April, and April obviously cares for him, I should be happy for them. I don't understand, Jesus, how I misread this. I don't understand how You could let someone come into my life and win my respect and affection—even my love, only to intend him for some other woman.*

It felt like an eternity, April chattering all about what a wonderful man Dr. Eric Walcott was. Others sitting on nearby blankets chimed in to attest to his good qualities. Unable to hide her distress much longer, Polly slipped Elvera onto the blanket. "Excuse me."

She rushed off to the outhouse. It was the only place she'd get any privacy. A couple of minutes alone, and she scolded herself into composure. For years, Mama had taught her to keep her feelings hidden. Those lessons now served a completely different purpose.

Polly slipped from the outhouse and wandered off past a line of trees. She hoped for a little time and space of her own. Ever since her cousins had all moved in, she missed her privacy and times of solitude. If ever she needed them, it was now. Leaning against the trunk of a tree, she closed her stinging eyes.

Changes are always for the better if given to God. Daddy's wisdom filtered through her mind.

Lord, I have to give this to You.

"Polly?"

It was the doctor. She stiffened and didn't open her eyes.

"Aw, honey, not another headache," he said in a whisper-quiet voice. He moved close. His fingertips skimmed across her forehead.

How easy it would be to lie! It would let her save face. Someone would take her home and leave her alone in the dark where she could weep in utter privacy.

"Here. Sit down."

Her watery knees just gave way. Against her will, she opened her eyes. Eric knelt beside her, concern creasing his forehead. An armful of wildflowers lay strewn across her hem and at their feet.

He was gathering those for April. Her breath caught on that painful realization. Straining to maintain the slender thread of her composure, she whispered, "I really don't have a headache. I just wanted to be alone."

He sat back on his heels as a slow, low chuckle rumbled out of him. "With both clans together? You must believe in miracles."

She managed a wan smile.

"I hold a lot of faith, and I believe in miracles, Polly." He leaned to the side and scooped up several flowers. "Healing and loving are acts of faith."

She stared at the mariposa lilies, mustard, poppies, and shooting star in his strong, large hand.

"I once told you a handful of flowers didn't make a healer. You've taught me it's not the flowers—it's the hands God puts them in and blesses that makes the difference."

"Thank you."

He placed the flowers in her lap—all but one bunch of white buckwheat blossoms. "But today, I'm hoping for a different kind of miracle. I love you, Polly Chance."

Her heart leapt.

"Will you marry me?"

He'd just asked what she most wanted—and she'd given it to God. Polly looked at him in stunned silence.

His eyes sparkled. "I have your parents' blessing—I let you go saddle Blossom today just so I could be alone with them. If that's not enough, April's promised to bake us a spectacular wedding cake. I figured if I was going to be part of the family, I'd better get them on my side from the very beginning."

"My family loves you. . . ." She slid her hand up to his and took the flower. It looked like a simple, sweet bridal bouquet. "But not as much as I do."

"Well?" a voice prodded from not far away.

They both turned. Everyone stood around them. Polly and he had been so intent upon one another, they hadn't heard a thing.

"Polly's consented to be my wife."

"Well, then, what're ya waitin' on?" Uncle Obie asked. "Kiss the gal!"

Eric cupped her face and smiled. "Don't mind if I do."

Polly didn't mind, either.

Epilogue

"You're going to be late," Aunt Delilah called through the door.

"It can't be helped," Polly called back as her gaze met Eric's.

"They can't do it without us," he said in a practical tone.

"I cain't do it without you, neither," Aunt Lois moaned. "I'm powerful sorrowed by that. Truly, I am."

"We aren't. We're glad to be with you." Polly wiped her aunt's face.

"Awww, merrrcyyy!" Lois curled up, grabbed Polly's hand, and bore down.

"Lord, help my Lois in her travail!" Uncle Obie groaned from beneath the window outside.

After that contraction, Eric went to the window and called out, "You keep praying, Obie. I'm glad you found the ax. Lois is grateful to have it under your bed today."

"And we're more'n grateful to the both of you fer bein' here with us today," Obie hollered back.

Polly smiled at her fiancé. He winked back. He'd learned to understand the oddities, rituals, and special ways of doing things for the people of Reliable, and now he didn't balk at mixing them with "sound medicine." He'd come a long way, and she loved him all the more for it.

"Merrrcyyy!"

"Oh no!" Obie moaned from outside. He waited until his wife's contraction ended; then he cleared his throat. "Lois, we've got ourselves a problem. There was twelve disciples, but I don't want no child of mine named Judas Iscariot."

Lois's beet-red face blanched. "This babe is our twelfth," she whispered to Eric.

"That's not a problem whatsoever," he soothed. "Acts chapter one speaks of the apostles deciding on a replacement for Judas. The choice was between Barsabbas, who was also called Justus, and Matthias. They cast lots, so Matthias won."

"Matthias'll do if hit's a man-child. What'll I do iff'n hit's a girl?"

"Matilda," Polly suggested.

"Merrrcyyy!" Lois bore down, then caught her breath. As Polly mopped her brow, Lois caught her hand. "Don't you dare go a-tellin' Obie 'bout those other two names. He'll want me to have two more children, and I'm plumb wore out."

"It'll be our secret," Polly said.

"Patients deserve privacy, after all." Eric's voice stayed low, but he wore a conspiratorial grin.

By the time they'd delivered baby Matilda and made sure mother and child were both stable, it was obvious Polly and Eric would arrive at the church thirty minutes late. He strode up to the altar, leaving Kate and April to keep guard in front of the door to the coatroom. Five aunts and Laurel all bumped around, dressing the bride.

"I just can't imagine this," Laurel fretted. "Bad enough, you're late to your own wedding, but don't you know it's bad luck for the groom to see the bride on their wedding day?"

"We don't need luck. We have love, and we have God." Polly felt her bun slipping.

"That you do," Mama said as she calmly reached up and tamed Polly's hair into submission and pinned the veil in place.

Her aunts and Mama all took their seats. Dressed in new lavender dresses, Kate and April walked down the aisle. Just before Laurel took her walk, she kissed Polly. "I'll mind them. Don't worry. And by the way—throw the bouquet to me!"

Step-by-step, holding Daddy's arm, Polly walked to the handsome doctor, to the love God had given her, and into her future.

Bridal Veil

Chapter 1

1891
Chance Ranch, just outside of San Francisco

"It'll be such an adventure!" Paxton Chance could barely sit still. He looked across the table. "I've been reading all about Yosemite."

"I'm going, too," Caleb declared.

"Me, three." Calvin didn't even swallow his bite of ham before inviting himself along.

Laurel Chance didn't think for a single moment that this trip was a spur-of-the-moment whim. For weeks, ever since the local paper had featured an article about the newly created national park, her brothers and cousins had been hatching the plan.

"What about your responsibilities around here?" Laurel's dad asked.

"We've got it all worked out. Half of us Chances will go and so will half of the MacPhersons. Then we'll come back and trade off with the ones who stayed here."

"I wanna go with the first group," eleven-year-old Percy declared as he grabbed the bowl of mashed potatoes and thwapped a huge dollop onto his plate.

The older Chance boys exchanged a pained glance.

"Now hold on a second." Her uncle Gideon looked at his younger son. "According to my thinking, you have something else you're to do this summer."

Percy jolted, and his scrawny chest puffed out.

Uncle Gideon nodded sagely. "Your mother and I discussed it last night. Time's come for you to train your horse, son."

"What about me?"

"And me?"

Laurel stiffened. One of the things she loved most about home was the reliability of life on Chance Ranch. Year in and year out, life went according to the same timetable, the same ebb and flow. Suddenly, that had changed. The older boys wanted to hie off, and the younger ones were being promised horses now instead of having to wait until they reached the age of twelve. *What's happening here?*

Uncle Bryce thumped his hand on the table. "Listen up. We took a vote last night."

"You took a vote?" Caleb looked thunderstruck. "Without me?"

Uncle Gideon stood to speak. Everyone fell silent.

"You kids have done us all proud. It'd be nice for you to all have a grand adventure to look back on later in life, and Yosemite sounds like just the place. We did a lot of thinking and praying, so here's what we've decided."

Laurel watched her cousins all lean forward. It wasn't until she glanced to the side that she realized Kate and April were holding their breaths, too. *They want to go!* The very idea stunned her.

All of this talk about adventure made no sense to Laurel. She didn't desire to take a big journey and felt no need to have exploits to recall in her dotage. Ordinary life pleased her; she found contentment in the everydayness of Chance Ranch. The very thought of her cousins wanting to do this—well, she could chalk that up to what Aunt Lovejoy termed, "Male sap flowing through young veins." But for the girls to go? Ridiculous!

"Now this plan comes with a commitment." Uncle Gideon stared directly at Caleb.

Caleb's eyes narrowed. "I'm twenty-one, and you left me out of the vote. Now I see why."

Uncle Gideon continued as if his son hadn't said a thing. "It's a two-year plan. This year, the eight oldest boys all go for seven weeks. Yes, all of you. While you're gone, the rest of us will hold down the ranch. The next four boys in line are getting horses."

"Me, too?" Cory croaked.

Uncle Gideon nodded. "We're expecting you juniors to become men a little early, and you'll have to prove yourselves. Any slacking or whining, and you'll forfeit the horse and have to wait two more years.

"We've designed the plan so when summer rolls around in 1892, those of you who go this year will stay behind and let the rest of us go explore."

Caleb's jaw hardened. "What all this boils down to is you're asking me not to make any promises to Greta."

"Not exactly. If you and Greta pray about it and find you're ready to marry, we'll grant you our blessing to become betrothed. No marrying up until the autumn after we return."

"I want to go this year," April said.

Tobias and Tanner both groaned.

Kate folded her arms across her chest. "Just what do you think you guys are going to do about eating if we girls don't come?"

"You and April, maybe." Calvin shot a look at Laurel. His scowl darkened. "But Miss Priss? No thanks."

Ouch! His attitude stung. Laurel gave him an outraged look.

He motioned for her to pass the corn bread.

Looking down at her plate, Laurel pretended she hadn't seen him gesture. *He has a lot of nerve, asking for the corn bread I made after insulting me like that!*

"No kidding," Caleb tacked on. "The last thing we want is to have Laurel fussing about getting freckles or shrieking when she spies a snake."

"All the girls go together," Aunt Alisa declared.

"Only if they all want to go, right?" Tanner's voice still held hope.

"Only if they want to go," Uncle Titus agreed.

Kate looked at her parents, then at April and Laurel. "We're not letting this opportunity slip past us, are we?"

"Absolutely not! Count me in." April slathered honey on a chunk of corn bread. To Laurel's dismay, April then caught Cal's gesture and passed him the platter of corn bread.

It would serve him right to choke on it. Laurel stunned herself with that uncharitable thought. But still, the way the boys were talking about her hurt. Everyone on Chance Ranch was accepted and teased; nevertheless, this teasing was sharp as barbed wire. The boys truly didn't want her to go along, and they weren't sparing her feelings in the least.

"Just a minute." Caleb rapped his knuckles on the tabletop. "We're not staying at one of those log cabins or fancy hotels. This is tent camping. It'll be rough"—he gave Laurel a piercing look and tacked on—"*real* rough."

"They have hotels?" Laurel asked. Maybe they could compromise.

"We're going to be miles from them," one of her cousins informed her in a tone tinged with victory.

April shrugged. "Who cares? We want to go do something different. A tent sounds fun. I'll take care of packing up all the kitchen gear and determining a menu and food supplies."

"Then it's settled." Kate grinned at Laurel. "I know you wouldn't hold us back. It's all for one and one for all."

"Oh, man." Tanner slapped his hand on his forehead. "They're just like the Three Musketeers in petticoats."

Male snickers and guffaws resonated in the yard.

"The other two girls can go." Mom patted Laurel's hand. "Sweetheart, if you'd rather not make the trip, you're under no obligation."

"She wouldn't dare go," one of the boys muttered. "It'll ruin it for us all."

Thoroughly nettled by that attitude, Laurel lifted her chin. "Of course, I'm going. I wouldn't miss this trip for all the tea in China."

"Oh, boy, and she'll probably pack all that tea and china," Cal grumbled.

Laurel pasted a smile on her face, batted her lashes, and said, "You'll be invited to eat off that china, so don't complain." Deep inside, though, she cringed. *I just let my temper lead me into folly.*

Gabriel Rutlidge halted a foot from the ledge and scanned the vista before him. A crisp breeze cut through his shirtsleeves and leather vest, cooling him after the exertion of the climb. The air smelled of a heady mix of pine, but an updraft carried hints of cedar and sequoia. A hawk rode the unseen air stream.

Majestic. No other word described Yosemite. Gabe absorbed the beauty spread before him and knew a sense of satisfaction that this land would be left unspoiled. He'd come here with the sole intent of appreciating nature at its finest and exploring the vast expanses of land now designated as the nation's preserve. Reports hadn't begun to prepare him for what he'd encountered.

"Hey, Rutlidge!"

Gabe shaded his eyes as he turned. He'd heard the horses coming but hoped the riders would turn the other direction and miss him. "What?"

"You didn't check in," one of the soldiers called to him. "Cap'n's hot under the collar."

"Tell the captain I have a mother back in Boston. I don't need anyone else worrying about me."

The three soldiers chortled, but they didn't depart. One kneed his bay and approached.

"We just went through an area south of the big meadow. There's talk of clearing a footpath to some of the rock faces and falls."

Gabe stood silently and shook his head.

"It's going to be done. You know it will. Cap'n said we might as well plot the routes to minimize the impact. You were so opinionated about the last map, he reckoned you might want to weigh in before things get finalized."

"Fine. Where's your camp?"

The soldier shot him a cocky smile. "Found yours. Cap'n's waitin'."

Amused, Gabe lifted his canteen in a silent toast, then took a refreshing gulp of the water he'd fetched from a bubbling stream earlier that day. "Let me guess. The captain's making himself at home, and his cook just raided my supplies."

"Didn't stay long enough to answer that supposition, sir."

Another soldier leaned forward and patted his horse. "It'd please my belly iff'n you'd head back down, Mr. Rutlidge. From the looks of what you had hanging in the branches, I'm shore the cook'll be happy to fix us up something fine."

"Go on ahead. Just save some for me." Gabe sat down. "I want to savor the view awhile."

"Don't wait too long, sir. I don't need to tell you, when night falls, it falls fast up here."

Smiling wryly, Gabe agreed, "You don't need to tell me. Keep fretting like that, Sergeant, and I'll think you're hoping to make captain soon."

The men rode off, and Gabe turned the other way. Though he hadn't said so, he'd welcome some companionship at supper. He and the buffalo soldiers had an unspoken agreement—they informally checked in and shared supplies as necessary. When they—or he—ran short of supplies, they shared so restocking only took place when it became absolutely essential.

In an area this vast and wild, it only made sense to have an emergency plan. Gabe knew he'd been remiss in not checking in. Undoubtedly, the captain would make his displeasure clear by helping himself to something especially toothsome from the supplies. *Fine by me,* he thought. He couldn't claim any great culinary skill. Simply searing meat, eating jerked beef, or opening cans was all Gabe could do. A good, hot meal and camaraderie around the fire would suit him for a night or two—long enough for him to set out plans for the next week or so. Then he'd be on his own again.

Yes, this was why he'd come—to explore, to have time to appreciate nature, and not be bothered by trifling details and petty grievances. He'd left that all behind him five years ago and never once regretted the decision.

This is where I belong. A place as untamed and spirited as I am—and it goes on and on forever. He stretched his arms wide. Wind blew through his hair and left him with the elated feeling of soaring free.

Chapter 2

"Here, honey." Mama handed Laurel a package.

"Thank you, Mama." Laurel shook her head. "You've already been so generous. I can't imagine another thing—"

"Open it up," Daddy urged.

The brown paper rustled as Laurel carefully unwrapped it. She caught her breath. "Oh!"

"Your daddy bought that for you in San Francisco the last time he delivered my paintings to the gallery," Mama said. "Look."

Laurel watched as her mother and father twisted a wooden bar and opened a collapsible easel.

"It's surprisingly sturdy, even though it's compact." Daddy smoothed his big, rough hand over the frame. "I'm looking forward to seeing what you create on it."

"I'll be sure to make a picture especially for you. Thank you so much!" She hugged her parents.

"I think you're taking more art supplies than clothes," Daddy teased.

Laurel grinned. "I wasn't very keen on the idea of this trip at first, but when I realized what beautiful scenery I'd have to paint and draw, we couldn't leave fast enough."

"I helped her pack. She's taking plenty of clothes," Mama declared.

"I'm not sure that'll matter," Laurel said. "After the first day on the trip, anyone will undoubtedly mistake us all for being grubby urchins. The girls and I packed plenty of soap, but I'm not sure we'll be able to bully the boys into using it."

Paxton shot her a grimace. "It's biblical. Adam was made from the dust of the earth. I don't know why you women are always trying to force us to go against our nature. Cowboys out on the trail live in the same set of clothes for weeks on end. Nothing's wrong with just living with the clothes on my back."

"That," Mama said crisply, "is why I insisted on packing for you."

Pax waited until Daddy folded down the easel and pressed it into Laurel's trunk. Once the lid was latched, Pax hefted the huge steamer trunk, let out a theatrical moan, and lugged it out of the girls' cabin. Laurel heard him muttering about it weighing down the wagon so much, they'd never catch up with the others in their group.

"I think he's still sore that you didn't let him go on to the fort to deliver the horses," Laurel whispered.

"You're more precious than a string of horses," Mama said. "Besides, he's made that delivery other times and will again in the future."

"Chances protect their women above all else," Daddy stated firmly. "Tobias, Pax, and Caleb are our strongest. Teaming them along with Peter and Ulysses MacPherson gives me reassurance that our girls will be okay."

"I'm sure we'll all be fine." Laurel didn't want her father to have any last-minute misgivings and keep her from going.

"It did the other boys good to go without the eldest ones leading them," Daddy mused. "This gives Cal and Tanner an opportunity to assert themselves. Our decisions about this whole affair were prayed over—we want this to be fun, but it needs to allow everyone to do some maturing."

Laurel nodded. "Without the adults, everyone is going to have to grow up some. I'll keep watch over them for you all."

Her parents exchanged a look and nodded.

Caleb came lumbering in. "Sis said she forgot something. Can't for the life of me fathom what. She's packed every last thing she owns."

"What was it?"

Caleb scowled. "Something stupid. I forget." He looked around. "What's left?"

Laurel didn't laugh or tease him. It would be stupid. They had to travel together for the next several days.

"Oh." Caleb colored deeply. He glanced up at the sleeping loft.

Laurel guessed at once. "I'll take care of that." She couldn't imagine Caleb scrambling up the ladder and coming back down with his sister's ruffled nightgown.

"Thanks." Caleb beat a hasty retreat. Laurel shimmied up the ladder.

"Check under Kate's pillow, too," Mama called up. "If April forgot her gown, Kate probably did, too."

"You're right," Laurel called down as she found both of them.

"Drop the gowns down. I'll stuff them in a sugar sack so the boys won't gawk at them."

"I had my reservations about allowing you girls to live together here in this cabin." Daddy chuckled. "But times like this, I can see why it was a good idea."

Laurel came back down and gave him a hug. "It was a grand idea. I'll keep careful watch on the girls while we're gone."

"We'll never get there if you won't leave," Ulysses MacPherson grumbled from the doorway.

Laurel laughed at his comment. Ulysses and Peter MacPherson sort of invited themselves along on the trip, and the girls promptly invited Johnna as well. The rest of the MacPherson clan would undoubtedly help out the Chances the next two summers, but that help would be returned in the following two when they planned to go to Yosemite. They weren't just neighbors; they were distant relatives through Aunt Lovejoy. As "kissin' cousins," the children of both families always did things together.

"You're the last one to have her trunk packed," Johnna commented from the doorway. "I've been packed for days."

Mama spread her arms, and Johnna dashed over for a hug. Laurel wrapped her arms around both of them. "I'm so glad you're coming along."

"Me, too!" Johnna said.

As they all separated, Mama nodded. "So am I!"

Eyes sparkling with enthusiasm, Johnna promised, "I'll help Laurel keep tight rein on Kate and April."

Mama grabbed Laurel and gave her one last tight hug, whispering, "You be careful."

"Yes, Mama." Laurel pulled away. "I love you, too."

"Then here are the girl's nightgowns." Mama handed her the sugar sack.

Johnna let out a sound of dismay. "Oh, no!"

"So much for packing early," Laurel teased. "Don't worry. I have an extra." Carefully keeping her back to Ulysses to block his view of her lingerie, she opened a drawer and added one last flannel garment to the sugar sack. "I'm ready. Let's go!"

"We could have been most of the way there by now if you girls weren't intent on totin' along half of your worldly belongings," Ulysses ribbed.

"You'd do well to hope we packed the right half," Laurel said. "And when you see how much food April is taking, you won't grumble another word."

They all walked toward the four wagons. Ulysses took the sack and shoved it into a less-packed spot and informed Laurel, "Food is essential."

She smiled sweetly at him. "And just think: Since our party has four women, we'll be allowed some firearms. Otherwise, as soon as you entered Yosemite, the cavalry would confiscate your sidearms."

Peter steered April and Kate to the nearest wagon. "I, for one, am glad you gals are going." He cupped his hands around April's ample waist and lifted her into the wagon quite easily. Pax hovered by Laurel. He gave her a brotherly glare. "You can still stay home. Last chance, Sis."

"I'm going." She had no difficulty proclaiming that with great assurance. For the next six weeks, she'd have brand new vistas to sketch and paint.

His frown darkened. "I'm not bringing you back partway through the trip if you change your mind."

"There's no danger of that."

"Only," Caleb muttered, "because she's already out of her mind to go."

"Squatters are going to ruin the whole valley," Captain Wood growled as his men tore down yet another sign inviting tourists to stay at a tent-style hotel and eat at the restaurant.

"If it's not the businesses, it's the sheep," Gabe agreed.

"Sheep." One of the cavalrymen swore. "Stupid animals are grazing all the plant life clear down to the roots. Nothing left for the bighorn."

"Well, we ate mighty good mutton last night," another said.

Gabe shrugged. The squatters had received written and verbal notification to remove the sheep. The national preserve was for indigenous flora and fauna; not for flocks of sheep that grazed by cropping the grasses so close to the ground that the plants couldn't renew themselves, destroying the valleys. The cavalry didn't poach on the natural four-legged creatures for food, but sheep had been declared fair game. Since provender never rated as adequate, mutton became part of the menu. Gabe had to agree; the mutton came as a welcome change from the jerked beef he'd been eating for the past several weeks.

As a matter of fact, he'd ridden into Wawona to buy supplies. The proprietor of the store and log hotel there charged relatively reasonable prices, so the cavalry tolerated his business.

Captain Wood ordered his troops, "Pay a visit to that encampment. Confiscate weapons."

"Yes, sir."

Gabe said nothing as the horsemen rode off. Their job demanded much and paid little, but each of them showed admirable diligence. They'd been like children when their cook discovered gumdrops in Gabe's supplies. He resolved to pick up more in Wawona.

"Where are you headed?" Captain Wood inquired.

"Wawona. Supplies. From there, Half Dome."

"Got enough ammunition?"

Gabe crooked a brow. "Same as always. Have yet to spend a single bullet."

The captain grinned. "That's why I allow you to keep arms."

"I'm grateful." With that, Gabe rode off, his packhorse obediently trotting in his wake.

The closer he drew to Wawona, the more tourists Gabe spotted. Some were here to enjoy the beauty, but most irritated him. Groups of men came in hopes of proving to one another who was more masculine by trying daring feats on the rock faces of the majestic formations. More than a few had fallen, but still the challenge drew those with nothing better to do than prove their boasts. The cavalry had to confiscate firearms because those same men couldn't get it through their thick skulls that the animals within the confines of the preserve were to be left alone. Sighting a deer, bighorn, or bear, men automatically grabbed for a rifle. Left to their own devices, those men would hunt the fauna to extinction in just a few years.

His irritation turned to disgust when he rounded a bend and spied a group of wagons. Seated by the man driving the lead wagon was a dark-haired beauty dressed in more frills than most Boston debutantes. Above her head, she held a lacy shade parasol to protect her porcelain complexion. A lady like her had absolutely no business out here. Oh, she'd fit in perfectly with his mother's crowd. He could envision her embroidering pillow slips for the unfortunates while ensconced in a comfortable chair near the fireplace in a well-appointed parlor.

The other three wagons, well, they just reinforced Gabe's opinion. Three women dressed in simple calico, a dozen strapping young men, enough supplies to last the entire U.S. Cavalry for a season—she'd brought all of the comforts of home, including servants, to assure her ease during this grand adventure.

Why did people like her bother to come here at all? Yosemite's beauty was wild; a tame miss like her wouldn't dare soil her kid slippers by hiking up a path. She'd quake in those same slippers at the mere thought of standing on the precipice of one of the cliffs. And the idea of wind blowing through that oh-so-perfect coiffure? Never. She might as well send one of her servants into the store, have him buy some of the stereopticon pictures of the park, and head back home. She could technically say she'd been to Yosemite—even if she hadn't actually seen a bit of it.

Irritated with himself for wasting thoughts on a woman, Gabe kneed his mount toward the store. He swung out of the saddle, hitched the mare, and gave her an appreciative pat before going inside.

"Rutlidge." The proprietor greeted him with a curt nod.

Gabe looked about. "Business is booming, I see."

"Had several big parties come through in the past week. I'm expecting fresh stock in a few days or so."

Neither piece of news pleased Gabe. He wandered about, trying to piece together supplies from what little remained while resolving to create a few caches of supplies the next time he got his hands on decent provisions.

Half a dozen cans of smoked oysters, a gallon-sized rectangular tin of hard tack, five pounds of cornmeal, and matches. He thumped his basket on the counter. "Any gum drops?"

"Nope."

"Lemon drops or peppermints?"

"Nope. Cleaned out. I did get in a nifty new candy. Looky here." The storekeeper pulled a box from beneath the counter and opened it. Lifting out a black shape, he boasted, "Licorice. See?" He held it to his lips. "Shaped like a pipe, no less. I'm betting little boys'll pester their parents to buy 'em. They'll sell like hotcakes."

"No doubt." Gabe thought about the cavalrymen. "I'll take three dozen."

"That's the whole box!"

"Then I proved your point—they'll sell like hotcakes. On the other hand, I don't know why you'd sell something like this to children. Smoking might well be fashionable for men, but I've always considered it a filthy habit. Children don't need to be encouraged toward such vices."

"There's nothing wrong with boys wanting to be like their fathers."

"Agreed." Gabe gave him a bored look. "But fathers need to be good examples."

"And you have children?" The proprietor's voice took on an edge.

"Not a one," Gabe admitted in a pleased tone. "I'm not the type to be tied down." He paid for his order, left the store, and proceeded to pack the odd collection onto his spare horse.

Once done, Gabe looked up just in time to see the princess sweep into the Wawona Hotel.

The sight didn't surprise him in the least.

Chapter 3

"Oh, this is marvelous!" Laurel stretched out on the big iron bedstead. The featherbed billowed around her, then settled enough for her to turn and study the beautiful view out her window.

"Enjoy it while you can." April bounced on the other side of the bed. "Tomorrow we'll be roughing it."

Kate stood over at the window. "Come here, Johnna. Look at this."

Johnna limped across the plank floor. "I got me a blister bigger'n Noah's ark. Any of you bring 'long doctorin' things?"

April laughed. "Are you kidding? Mama Lovejoy put together a box from her herbal room, and Polly and her husband made a whole medical kit. Polly said it's the Dr. Eric Walcott nothing-you-can't-treat crate."

"Now jest you all hold yore horses." Johnna held up a hand. "Ain't puttin' one of them plasters on my blister. I heared they make a body itch sommat fierce."

"Not," Laurel announced, "when you use the special talcum powder that goes along with them." She got off the bed. "Kate, come with me. We'll go to the wagon and get what we need. April, you and Johnna freshen up. We girls are going to have tea this afternoon down in that restaurant. I aim to have us enjoy all the luxuries available before we head deep into this wilderness."

Johnna whirled around. "We're gonna eat in the restaurant? For true?"

"Absolutely." Laurel bobbed her head. "Mama slipped me some extra money for us girls to enjoy ourselves."

Kate giggled. "Mama gave me some money, too."

April twined her arm with Johnna. "Now how do you like that? Laurel's mother is a famous artist, and Kate's mother is an heiress. The two of us are just poor tag-along relations who will have to pity one another."

"Pity's gonna taste right fine at a restaurant tea table," Johnna declared. "I ain't niver gone to a fancy tea afore. S'pose I oughtta fix up my hair, even iff'n it'll all be 'neath my hat."

Laurel swept her shawl about her shoulders. "April will help you with your hair. I've taught her all my tricks, and she's great at making hair look quite fetching. Before she does, though, we're going to get one thing straight: There's never any pity at our table. We always share."

"We most certainly do," Kate agreed. She smoothed up her stocking and tugged her skirts back into order. "So after we have tea, we're going to shop at the store."

"My treat," Laurel inserted.

Kate obligingly nodded and kept right on talking so the others couldn't protest. "I heard they don't have much in the way of food left in the store, but who cares?"

"I packed enough food to feed a shipload of passengers for a month," April declared.

"Exactly. So we're going to look at the other things the proprietor has." Kate spread her hands wide. "What's a trip without a souvenir?"

"What's a souveneer?" Johnna wondered.

"A keepsake," April told her. "Something special you take home from a trip or a visit to remind you of the grand time you had."

"A heartful of memories'll do me just fine," Johnna stated. "I don't need some expensive doodad to remind me of where I've been."

"But think about your brothers and sisters and cousins back home." Kate reached for the doorknob. "You, Peter, and Ulysses are the only ones to come this year. It'll be a couple of years before anyone else from MacPherson Ranch visits Yosemite. Don't you think they'd all like to see a little something from this place?"

"You gotta point," Johnna allowed. "But then I'm gonna cook extry to make up fer it. I don't take no charity. None of the MacPhersons do."

Laurel whipped off her shawl. "You listen to me, Johnna MacPherson. We're family. Oh, I know—maybe not legally, by blood, but by heart we are. We share our family picnics, celebrate things together, and have wept in grief beside one another. After all of that, do you think money matters one whit?"

Johnna winced. "Guess not."

"Good. Then no more nonsense. None from you, either, April Chance. In fact. . ." She grabbed her reticule. "You're each going to have your share of money to spend as you wish so we don't have to go through this absurd conversation again."

"You mean I'll be paying cash money at the restaurant, all by myself?" Johnna gaped at Laurel.

Laurel paused a moment. "No. After all, it was my idea, and I've invited you to be my guest. You'll be shopping in the store." She peeled out two five-dollar bills and gave one to April and the other to Johnna. "No being practical. Mama specified that we were supposed to fritter this money away because vacations are for fun."

"Fritter away five whole dollars?" Johnna looked at April, then back at the bill in her hand. "I ain't niver had one dollar all my own. I cain't 'magine what to do with five!"

"Mama was a gambler's daughter," Laurel reminded Johnna. "She knows what it's like to wish for something and not get it. That's why she wanted us to all have some cash to spend. Money isn't any good if all you do is hoard it. If we go home and haven't spent it, she'll be hurt."

"But five whole dollars," Johnna half squeaked.

"Mama painted a picture specially, just to make the money for us girls to spend. You know how much fun she has painting. It'll make her so happy to know someone's enjoying her art while we're enjoying ourselves."

"Well"—April tugged the pins out of Johnna's hair—"we'll have to hurry to fix ourselves up for tea. Afterward, we'll shop extravagantly to make Aunt Delilah delirious."

"If this ain't the backwardest way of thinkin', I don't ken what is." Johnna flopped down into a chair.

Laurel and Kate slipped out the door, down the hall, and out to the wagon. Kate giggled. "Oh, you did a great job back there."

"You were a wonderful help. I was serious—we're family, and we've always shared. I'd love to see April and Johnna fritter away the money on silly things, but they won't. I bet they fret over every last cent."

"We won't let them." Kate grinned. "Even if they do that today, it's my turn to give them money on the way home. Their pride sure gets in the way of fun, doesn't it?"

"Not today." Laurel winked. "Now let's find that talc and Johnson & Johnson plasters. I hope they have stockings and shoes in the store. Johnna's blister is because she's wearing boots that are too big."

"Oh—is that why she's clomping like a two-ton mule?"

Laurel covered her mouth to keep from laughing. "Oh, Kate! Only you would say it that way."

"It's the truth."

"It's the truth," the storekeeper told Gabe. "I checked the back room. You're welcome to go back and see for yourself."

Gabe groaned. He'd forgotten salt. Of all the necessities, how could he have forgotten that? He'd turned his horses around and come back, only to discover the store was out of it. A man could do without a lot of things, but salt rated as an absolute necessity.

"Restaurant might spare you a bit," a red-haired gal said from across the store. She gave him a guileless smile.

Gabe nodded. "Obliged for the thought, miss." The gal seemed downright pleasant. She'd been practical as could be, trying on sensible boots. Although he wasn't supposed to notice such things, Gabe also spied the stockings she'd draped over the arm of the chair. A man couldn't fault a woman for seeing to such basic necessities.

Then he compared her to the "princess" he'd seen earlier. She stood a row over, looking at a bunch of idiotic little gewgaws that held no value whatsoever. "Excuse me," she called to the proprietor. "Do you have more of these? I'd like... two, no three dozen. They're darling, don't you think, Kate?"

"Huh? Oh, yes. Darling."

"And don't you think Mama will love this cedar wood box?" The princess held up a box far too dinky to hold anything reasonable. "The fragrance is enchanting. It reminds me of the Bible verses about the great temple."

Gabe turned to Mr. Hutchings. "Well, I'm thinking of Lot's wife. All I want is a pillar of salt. Guess I'll head toward the restaurant."

"We just dined there," the princess said. "The food was fabulous."

"I don't know." The young woman next to her shook her head. "April's strudel back home is better, if you ask me."

Gabe headed out as the women continued to chatter about all of the fancy food their cook back home made. He wanted to be away from these tourists. Yes, he reminded himself, the preserve was for everyone to enjoy—especially those who lived in the city and couldn't appreciate nature on a daily basis. But some of these people—they simply didn't get it. They came to nature and dragged the worst parts of civilization along. They represented everything he'd come here to escape.

Mmm-mmm-mmm. The early morning breeze carried the aroma of food—real food. Woman-cooked, mouth-watering, heap-your-plate-full, my-mouth-died-and-went-to-heaven fixings. Gabe closed his eyes and told himself he didn't need it. Didn't want it. Then called himself a liar.

He'd come back late last night and made do with jerked beef, even though he smelled the tempting fragrance of stew. The noise of several young men and the higher, softer voices of women kept him away. If it weren't so dark, he would have packed up and skulked off. He wanted nothing to do with rowdy campers. Tossing off the thick wool blanket he used as a bedroll, Gabe told himself to ignore the smell of bacon. Except his nose forgot to obey, and he sniffed again.

That did it. He wasn't going to stick around here another day. This amounted to torture. Stomping off toward the stream, he tried to decide where he ought to go to avoid the crowds of tourists. Peace, quiet, and a lack of tempting food smells—that wasn't asking so much, was it? He tossed his towel around his neck and twisted the ends in frustration. Once done with washing up, he'd dismantle his simple camp and—

He pulled to a dead halt.

Chapter 4

Sitting on his rock by his stream, a dainty woman in pale pink ruffles with a parasol over her shoulder hummed in a lilting alto.

"What're you doing here?" Gabe demanded.

"Oh!" She twisted about and dropped whatever she'd been holding. The parasol tumbled behind her, revealing abundant black hair all twisted up into some fancy arrangement. Her golden eyes stayed wide with fright as she stared at him.

He tamped back a groan. *The princess! In the back wilderness? I don't believe it.*

She blinked and found her voice. "I'm camping. What are you doing here?"

It didn't escape Gabe's notice that she'd raised her volume a slight bit with each word so the last one came out at respectable volume. Clever little minx hadn't shouted for help, but she'd made certain whomever she was with would hear her. He didn't respond to her question. Instead, he waited in silence for her rescuer.

"Laurel!" Two young men dashed around a stand of trees and skidded to a halt beside her. The taller studied Gabe with no small measure of ire. "Breakfast is ready, Sis. You go on back. You," he ordered, nodding toward Gabe, "leave her be."

"Don't be rude, Pax." The young woman stooped to pick up a sketch pad and charcoal sketch pencil. "Invite the gentleman to join us at the table since you made mention of breakfast."

"Wouldn't do any harm, I suppose," the other young man said.

Pax shifted his weight and moved his right hand in such a way that Gabe could clearly see he wore a sidearm. "We don't want any trouble. You're welcome to eat, but afterward, you leave our gals alone."

Gabe rested his hands on his hips and tilted his head back as he let out a bellow of a laugh. "Believe me, women are a complication I don't want in my life."

"We didn't, either," the shorter man muttered. "But we brought 'em along for cooking and so we could keep arms."

"Well, thank you so much for your complimentary opinions of our companionship," the woman simpered. She turned in a swirl of ruffles and headed away.

"Betcha we pay for that tonight, Ulysses," the one named Pax said with a crooked grin. "Laurel's supposed to make supper."

"What can she do to fish?" Ulysses folded his arms across his broad chest. "I think we're safe."

"You'll go hungry if you plan to fish here," Gabe informed them. "Nothing bites for a good ways up or downstream from this spot."

"You know a good fishin' spot?" Ulysses perked up.

"He can tell us about it over breakfast. If we don't get there, everything'll be gone." Pax tilted his head toward their camp.

Gabe felt torn for a second. He could refuse, go on his way, and be free—or he could eat some of that tempting food, be minimally sociable for half an hour, and then decamp. His stomach growled. "Give me a second."

Ulysses gave him a baffled look.

Having grown up in high society ingrained certain expectations. Gabe shed most of them while alone in the wilderness, but he'd be in the company of ladies. Decency demanded he not appear at their table in his current state. Dipping the end of his towel into the cold stream, he muttered, "I'm wearing half the park."

Pax chortled. "The rest of us are wearing the other half."

By the time they made it to the camp, Gabe had swiped himself fairly clean and combed his wild hair. In retrospect, it amazed him Miss Laurel hadn't taken one look at him and screamed herself hoarse.

Comprised of four wagons and two tents, the campsite looked surprisingly simple—even minimalistic. Surprised at the lack of so-called civilized trappings, Gabe looked around. "Is this everything you brought?"

Ulysses pointed up to several bundles hanging by ropes from high tree limbs. "We've hung the vittles. Bears won't get into it thataway."

"The girls are sleeping in a tent," Pax scoffed.

"Are you going to introduce us to our guest?" a redheaded girl called over to them. Gabe recognized her as the one who'd been trying on boots at the store in Wawona.

"Gabe Rutlidge." Gabe looked at the heavily laden breakfast table and felt his mouth water. "Thank you for inviting me to your meal."

"Grab a plate and have a seat," Pax said. Most of the men already sat around on the ground in clumps with heaps of flapjacks and several rashers of bacon on graniteware plates.

"We already asked a blessing," someone stated.

Pax thumped his chest. "You've gathered I'm Pax. Paxton Chance. That there's Ulysses MacPherson. Peter MacPherson's to your left. He's Ulysses's cousin. Any other P name, that'll be one of my brothers. The T's are all brothers, and so are the C's. I won't bother you with callin' them out. The food'll go cold, and no sane man would remember ten names all at once."

"Obliged." Gabe found himself liking this crew. They bedrolled under the stars, sat on the ground instead of hauling up all sorts of furniture, and showed a practicality sadly lacking in most other groups who came to camp out. He nodded toward the small knot of women. "Breakfast smells wonderful. Thank you."

"You're welcome." Three voices blended like a small chorus in unison. The fourth, Miss Laurel's, waited a beat. "I cannot take any credit for my cousins' cooking, but you're still welcome."

"Laurel uses the early morning light to draw. She makes up for it by cooking supper most often," Pax said as he shoved a plate at Gabe.

Gabe accepted the plate and followed Ulysses down the table. Ulysses forked no less than a half-dozen flapjacks onto his plate, drowned them with syrup, and piled several rashers of bacon atop the meal. Gabe took three of the huge flapjacks, but by the time he lifted the jug of syrup, Pax had dumped two more on his plate.

"No use goin' hungry. We have plenty."

Sitting on the ground with the men, Gabe wolfed down his meal. Every bite tasted as delicious as the first.

"What're you doing here?" someone asked him.

"Exploring. Appreciating."

"Your accent is eastern. Not New York. Boston? Chicago?" Ulysses asked.

Gabe nodded. He didn't want to be specific. Most folks on this coast didn't know of the Boston Rutlidges, but those who did immediately treated him differently. Greed shone in their eyes, and Gabe didn't want money to be an issue when he dealt with others. Part of traveling away from Boston was to know no one pursued him for his money. He'd learned that bitter lesson a million times, but Arabella's scheme was the final straw. And to think he'd been ready to propose to her!

Well, I don't need a woman. I don't need anybody. Sure, he thought as he swallowed the last bite of bacon, *food's much better and companionship is good, but I'm doing fine without those a good portion of the time. I'm better off on my own.*

Then again, watching the brothers and cousins teasing one another hit a soft spot. Gabe missed Stanford. His younger brother viewed their privileged world with a great deal of humor and managed to get along swimmingly. He'd been the voice of sanity on several occasions, and to his credit, when things went wrong with Arabella, Stanford wholeheartedly supported Gabe's decision to get away. Gabe held no doubts whatsoever that Stanford was running the business without a single hitch and actually enjoyed the daily grind. He'd been born and bred to do just that—and Gabe, though capable, never once enjoyed any of it.

A nominal believer in something nebulous called Fate, Gabe figured Stanford was where he belonged—in control of the family fortune. Then, too, Gabe knew he'd landed just where he belonged—free of such encumbrances and alone where he could live without the burdens of society and appreciate nature.

Gabe wondered about this Chance family. Someone said they'd asked a blessing on the food. That meant at least some of them probably trusted in God.

Having grown up in a home where grace was said and everyone attended church, Gabe didn't exactly disbelieve; he just wasn't sure he really did believe. How many of the young people around him still questioned all they'd been told?

His musings left Gabe unsettled. A void opened inside him. *It's just that I'm missing Stanford—that's all.*

"So you were gonna tell us about a good fishin' spot," Ulysses poked at him with a fork.

"Fishin'? Nah. I wanna climb that monstrous rock." Someone else pointed straight ahead.

"Half Dome," Gabe provided the name of the formation. "It's a healthy climb. Great view."

"You've been up there?" Laurel asked. She set down her half-full plate and gave him an enthused look. Intelligence glittered in her golden eyes. "What is the view like? How far can you see, and what details stay in focus?"

"She sounds more like a camera than a girl," Paxton muttered.

Gabe ignored that comment and answered, "The view is stupendous. Close up, massive formations of granite lie all around you. As you look down and out, the stream looks like a silvery blue thread. Trees are blended splotches of green. People are tiny specks, if you see them at all."

"What're we waiting for?" someone across from him said. "Let's go!"

The reaction felt like an interruption. Always deeply moved by the views from the elevated vistas in Yosemite, Gabe enjoyed sharing his observations. He could have gone on to explain so much more, include the interesting details he'd seen. From the eager way Miss Laurel leaned forward, she wanted to hear more, but it wasn't to be. These young men would see it for themselves, and in their zeal, they'd not considered the women wouldn't have that opportunity.

"Best ask what we need to take, Packard," Paxton said.

Packard. He's P, so he's Paxton's brother. Paxton called Laurel Sis. Gabe forgave them their youthful impetuousness and tried to put the pieces together.

"Well, what do you recommend, Gabe?" Packard leaned forward.

Gabe didn't tell the young man his shirt was sopping up syrup from his plate. No use embarrassing the kid. "It's too late to go up today. In fact, we're too far away. Distances are deceiving here. You need to have everything gathered and at the base first thing in the morning. Someone built a wooden ladder to get you to the first level, but from there, you'll require rope—lots of it."

"How much?"

"I recommend fifty yards per man. You're all wearing sensible clothing and boots, so that's good. You'll each need a hat to keep away the glare, and you should take water and nutritious, easy-to-carry food."

"I'll have the food all packed," one of the gals promised.

"You're not going. None of you girls is." One of the black-haired men rose and dumped his plate into a bucket of suds.

"Who's staying behind with them?" another asked.

"Not me," the men all proclaimed at once, then looked around at each other.

"This is why we didn't want girls along," someone said from behind Gabe.

"Tanner Chance, you just said you were glad we came along when you heaped all that food on your plate," a young blond in a blue calico dress insisted.

"How long will you be here?" Gabe asked.

"Six weeks." A redhead with a rowdy-looking beard shook Gabe's hand. "I'm Peter MacPherson. I reckon that's plenty of time. We men can break into teams. One'll explore whilst the other fishes and guards the women."

Gabe nodded.

"You think I'm going to spend half of my trip babysitting the girls?" One of the men smacked his hat against his thigh in disgust.

"What makes you think we want to sit at the campground all the time?" Laurel asked.

"Yeah. We want to go on hikes," said the blond. She flashed Gabe a smile. "And I'm Kate. This is April, and Johnna's standing by Laurel."

"Miss." Gabe nodded in a mannerly fashion as he made a mental note that each had different colored hair: Laurel was raven-haired, Kate was the blond, April had brunette hair, and Johnna unmistakably belonged to the red-haired MacPhersons. "There are pleasant meadows you ladies could walk through."

"I want to climb up to a waterfall and stand in the spray," April confessed as she leaned across the table.

Gabe shook his head. "The waterfalls are at extreme elevations. You'll see them but not stand in one." Seeing the sparkle in her eyes dim, he added on, "Bridal Veil Falls flows into Bridal Veil Creek. You could wade in it. That's all west of here."

"I saw that on the map!" April perked up.

"Perhaps Mr. Rutlidge has some recommendations as to where we ought to go or what we should see," Laurel suggested. "He seems to know the preserve quite well."

"You don't mind, do you?" Paxton yanked a map from his pocket and started unfolding it without waiting for an answer. From the rumpled, much-folded appearance of that map, Gabe surmised the young man had studied it several times.

"Put it on the table so we can all gather 'round and see," Peter demanded.

In a few moments, the nearly empty platters on the table were divested of whatever food remained and tossed into the wash bucket. Paxton spread the map out on the table, and coffee mugs soon held the ends down.

Gabe glanced at the map. He'd seen several—most were poorly drawn. "You have a decent map. The distances on it look to be fairly accurate."

"Tobias and I looked at half a dozen before we settled on this one," Pax said as he poked his forefinger at a spot. "To my reckoning, we're about here."

"Yes. Half Dome is straight ahead. Bridal Veil Falls is here, and the creek flows. . ." Gabe trailed his finger along the path. "Fishing in it is only so-so. The fishing in the Merced River's better."

"Good to know," someone said.

Gabe scanned the intent faces around him. "Fishing is permitted, but this is a preserve. You only catch what you'll eat. No dragging fish out just for the sport of it."

Peter gave him an outraged look. "We ain't stupid. Who kills jest for the sake of it? Then there won't be 'nuff fish for the next year."

"You'd be surprised," Gabe said. "Men come here for the adventure and lose all common sense. None of the streams down here have been supplemented. Three of the lakes northwest of here have additional trout, thanks to Mr. Kibbie."

"Are there plans for stocking the rivers?"

"No. The cavalry is here just for safety and preservation—they're spread mighty thin. No one's available to do it."

A flash of pale pink made Gabe turn. Laurel stood a foot away, holding a huge coffeepot. "Anyone want more coffee?"

Five mugs in heavily callused fists shot toward her. Not a single man said a word. Gabe waited until she filled them all, then extended his mug. "Thank you, I'd appreciate more."

She gave him a stunned look, then smiled. "You're welcome, Mr. Rutlidge."

"The girls wanted to go to Tuolumne Meadows."

"Forget it, Tanner," Paxton growled. "They can see meadows anywhere. We can't waste time on that."

Laurel's lashes dropped, and the corners of her mouth tightened.

Gabe cleared his throat. "Actually, the meadows are worth seeing. They spread out for miles, and wildlife abounds. Take a look at your map. If you start out at the meadows, then travel southwest from there, you'll hit the sites most visitors come for—Clouds Rest, Half Dome—"

"We already saw Sentinel Dome and Glacier Point on the way here," Tobias said.

"So what if we cross the creek and go to North Dome?" Enthusiasm colored Ulysses's voice.

"Hold on. Miss April wanted to see falls. I recommend you spend time seeing Vernal Falls and Nevada Falls. They're on this side and basically on your way. Your map doesn't remark on them, but they're breathtaking. Then you can cross the creek and see North Dome."

"From there," Caleb decided, "we'll hit Yosemite Falls. See, Sis? I'm making sure you'll get your fill of falls. And then us guys'll climb El Capitan. We can cross back over the river someplace."

"Go farther west," Gabe advised, "then double back so you see Bridal Veil Falls. You can trace it through the creek on your way back out."

"You all rushed me through them great big trees on the way in," Johnna said from the washtub. "I want a day to wander 'round them on our way home."

"We got water and trees back home," one of the younger men scoffed. "The rocks are what make this place."

"We've got rocks back home, too—just nowhere near this size," Caleb said. "If we go by Gabe's plan, everyone ought to see something to please them."

"Now about that fishin'." Ulysses jabbed Gabe with his elbow and bent over the map. "How's about you showin' us where a feller cain hope to land him a big old trout?"

Gabe stood in the huddle of men and pored over the map. They asked question after question, and he patiently answered them as he started to pair faces and names.

A platter of sandwiches landed on the table. Gabe's head shot up. He gave Laurel a startled look. "I lost track of time."

She nodded. "I think the time's well spent. You're probably saving us days of backtracking by helping our men figure out where to go."

"Eat up." Calvin shoved a sandwich into Gabe's hand.

Gabe chuckled. He'd never had anyone offer him a meal in such a straightforward way. Back home, there would have been a formal invitation, a well-set table, and servants. Even when his family dined casually, they passed platters. When he ate with the cavalrymen, the cook slopped food onto the plates. Something about the simple slapping of a sandwich into his hand, of skipping plates and diving in appealed to Gabe. "Thanks."

"If you're just ambling along, you're welcome to join us," Paxton said.

Gabe swallowed his bite. The food tempted him. The male companionship appealed to him. But he didn't want women around any more than these men did. Especially not Princess Laurel, who listened to him so intently. The woman was far too easy on the eye, and Gabe refused to stumble into that pitfall again. He shrugged. "The offer's nice, but I prefer to be on my own."

Laurel didn't realize she'd been holding her breath until Gabe turned down the invitation. Then she couldn't decide whether to be glad or disappointed by his refusal.

He'd startled her this morning. She'd been so intent on her sketch that his voice scared her. Luckily, she'd dropped her charcoal pencil instead of making an unsightly streak across her piece. It would have been a shame. She wanted to finish that drawing, add a touch of pastel color to it, and give it to Daddy as a gift.

But Mr. Rutlidge. He scared her in a thrilling way. Oh, men back home thronged around her. She knew they all wanted a pretty woman to squire about. Mama and Daddy never minced words—they told her she was lovely to look at, but beauty was fleeting and proved no accomplishment. God created her as one of His works of art, but it was her responsibility to do all she could to become beautiful on the inside. Any man who wanted her only as a decoration probably wouldn't look for, let alone appreciate, the inward beauty her parents urged her to cultivate. She'd been interested in a few young men from neighboring spreads in a fleeting fashion, but when they treated her like a stupid, helpless woman, her interest waned.

Only Mr. Rutlidge didn't fawn after her; he almost ignored her! He'd sounded outraged that she'd been by the creek. He didn't want her around. In fact, he'd made his opinion of women being a bother quite clear. Then why had he been so polite to the girls? Why had he made a point of including their desires while helping the boys plot out their plan? The man qualified as a bundle of contradictions.

Laurel bit into her sandwich and tried to make sense of it, but she couldn't.

"That there's one fine buck," Johnna whispered.

Brows lifted, Laurel asked, "Which one?"

April tossed an apple into Laurel's lap and giggled. "Ours are all good, but only one of those men over at the table is. . . dreamy."

"Oh no, April." Laurel shook her forefinger at her cousin. "You did this same thing when Eric arrived in Reliable Township. You mooned over him, and all we heard was 'Dr. Walcott this' and 'Dr. Walcott that.' I'm saying here and now, you're not going to make a ninny of yourself just because a handsome man stumbled into our camp."

"So you think he's handsome, do you?" Kate gave Laurel a triumphant look.

"The real beauty of a person is on the inside. We know nothing about him," Laurel said primly, then quickly took another bite so she wouldn't be expected to say anything more.

"I cain tell plenty about him." Johnna settled into a more comfortable spot on the grass. "He talks like a man who's had plenty of book learnin'. His manners are refined. Niver heared a man say thankee as much as he's done."

"He's a good listener. Attentive," April tacked on.

"But he's just wandering around Yosemite—and for a good long while. What kind of man doesn't have a job?" Kate polished her apple on her sleeve.

"None of this matters one whit," Laurel announced. "He's going his way, and we're going ours."

"More's the pity," April sighed.

Laurel shot her a behave-yourself look, then glanced at Johnna. Johnna had a sound head on her shoulders. She could be counted on to say something to bring April to her senses.

Johnna smiled at Laurel. Laurel felt a burst of relief.

"April, ain't nuthin' wrong with settin' yore heart on a buck. Jest be sure he's not all antlers and no muscle."

April's face scrunched up in confusion. "What is that supposed to mean?"

Laurel resisted the urge to bob her head. *I wondered the same thing.*

"Well, he might be real showy, but that don't get no work done." Johnna bobbed her head as if to put exclamation marks after her sage comment.

Laurel wasn't quite sure exactly how much wisdom was behind those words, but she shifted her sandwich to her other hand and patted April. "She's right. We've had plenty of saddle tramps come through Chance Ranch. Some of the best workers have been the homeliest or the scrawniest. You can't make snap judgments."

"I'm not going to have an opportunity to find out, either," April pouted. "He's not going to join us."

"Well, if you ask me, it's just as well," Kate declared. "A man who wears expensive gear like that and doesn't have a job gives me the willies."

He gives me the willies, too—but for entirely different reasons, Laurel thought.

Chapter 5

"One last thing before I go." Gabe looked at the men still milling about him. "Tell your women to stop wearing perfume."

"Hadn't noticed that they did." Paxton scratched his side.

"They do. All of them." *Especially Laurel.* He'd not been around women for months, and the slightest hint of cologne struck him full force. The other three women wore fragrances that were light and pleasant; Laurel favored something outrageously feminine that left a tempting sweetness in its wake something akin to a luscious, ripe berry. "Wasps and bees are more likely to sting a woman if she's wearing a scent."

"They packed half the world to come on the trip," Tanner groused. "We shouldn't be surprised they brought perfume."

"Tell them to leave it in the bottle." Gabe pretended not to notice how abrupt he sounded. "It's for their own good."

"Rather you told 'em," Tobias said. "My sister's far more likely to listen to you than to me."

A rumble of agreements filled the air.

Gabe crooked his brow in disbelief.

"You don't have a sister, do you?" Paxton asked.

"No."

"They have a habit of digging in their heels at the dumbest times," Paxton explained. "Our folks drilled manners into those girls. They'll listen to you far better than they will to us. It's for their own good."

Gabe let out a bark of a laugh and shouldered his way through the men. He walked past a string of some of the finest horseflesh he'd ever seen and paused. "Nice horses."

"Chance horses. Family business." Caleb's chest swelled. "Any time you need a mount, we're the ones to see."

"If these are any sample, I'd agree." Gabe strode on over to the knot of women. They'd cleaned up the lunch gear and were huddled around something. "Ladies."

They all straightened up. Laurel slammed her sketchbook shut. "Hello."

Gabe wanted to know what she'd been drawing, but it would be rude to ask. What was it about this woman that drove him nuts? He wanted to grab her book and flip through it, to have her tell him about what she'd sketched and why. He felt absurd just standing there, so he cleared his throat and resorted to the social conventions that never failed to rescue a man from uncomfortable situations. "I wanted to thank you again for the meals. They were quite tasty."

"You're welcome." April grinned at him.

His gaze swept over them all, then settled back on Laurel. "One other thing. Bees and wasps abound here. They're attracted to scent. Your perfumes are quite appealing, but I'm afraid the only things you'll attract are stings. I suggest you forego wearing those scents while you're in Yosemite."

"It's not perfume," Laurel informed him in her melodious voice. "Polly, our cousin, specially makes each of us our own shampoo and soap."

"Use it, and suffer the consequences."

The other girls nodded. Laurel paled. Her reaction disappointed Gabe. Were the little luxuries so essential to her? *Just like Arabella, the trappings were all-important to her.* He'd pegged Miss Laurel Chance correctly. She acted like a little princess.

"Have an enjoyable stay in Yosemite." He turned and left. The walk back to his own site took no time at all. In a matter of minutes, Gabe rolled up his wool blanket, secured it behind the saddle, and broke camp.

Just as he swung up into his saddle, Paxton rode over. He tossed a bundle into Gabe's lap. "The girls thought you might want supper since you're traveling today."

Whatever rested inside the bundle smelled outstanding. Gabe couldn't imagine that strangers treated him with such hospitality—especially since he'd been so rude to Laurel this morning. "One whiff of this, and I'm ready to eat it now."

Pax chuckled. "They were right—you've been without decent cooking for a while. You know where we're going and about how long we'll be at each spot. You're always welcome to join up with us. Meals are included."

"It's tempting, but I'll pass it up."

"God go with you." Paxton reached over to shake hands.

"How about if He stays with you."

"It's not safe for you to be off on your own like this."

Laurel wheeled around. "Mr. Rutlidge!" He'd ridden away over more than two weeks ago, and she'd resigned herself to the fact that they'd never meet again. "What a pleasant surprise. I heard you coming, but I thought it was one of the men. They're around the bend, swimming and fishing."

His eyes widened and his lips parted in surprise as he stepped closer and studied the watercolor.

Laurel shuffled to the side so he could see the rest of the painting she'd been doing. She hadn't allowed herself much space, but this was the vantage point she wanted. The easel barely fit between her and the tree.

The moment she saw this spot, Laurel had known she had to paint it. Sunlight filtered through a variety of trees, setting a thousand hues of green alight, then glittered on the ripples of the stream. A solitary tree had fallen across the stream at its narrowest point. Roots long since gone, that tree formed a bridge of sorts that promised adventures to places unseen.

After a short while, Gabe's silence unnerved her. Laurel reached out to fuss with a brush, but his big hand manacled her wrist. "Don't touch it."

"Why not?"

"Because it's perfect just as it is. I want it. How much?"

Laurel looked from his suntanned face to the painting. "Thank you for the compliment, but it's not for sale."

"Everything has a price." His hold on her wrist loosened. "It's a wonderful piece, Laurel."

Laurel twisted free of his hold. "My mother is a professional artist. I just dabble. I—"

"Dabble? Woman, this is awe-inspiring. You captured the very essence of this spot."

"It's kind of you to say so, but I already have plans for this. It's for my Aunt Lovejoy."

"Paint her another."

"It doesn't work that way." Laurel gave him an exasperated look. "I could copy this, but it wouldn't be an exact duplicate. The shades and shadows will be different because my lighting will change. I'd be happy to paint you something else if you'd like."

"I'm willing to pay top dollar for this one."

Laurel frowned. "It's not for sale. Contrary to your assertion, everything doesn't have a price."

Gabe folded his arms across his chest. "Then what else do you have? I want to see what you've been painting and drawing—everything you've done since you arrived."

"Everything?" She gave him a shocked look. The man didn't understand how she either had a needle, a pencil, or a paintbrush in her hand all of her waking hours.

The breeze lifted the edge of her painting. He gently smoothed the corner back down and moved to serve as a windbreak. "Is this dry now?"

"Watercolors dry almost instantly."

"Good. I'll carry your easel." He started to bend forward to collapse the legs.

Laurel planned to stay here for some time yet. She'd brought all she needed to paint a few pictures. Then again, Gabe Rutlidge didn't exactly leave room for dissent. The man knew what he wanted and plowed toward it with a single-mindedness she'd not seen in any of the men who came courting.

Not that he's courting me, she quickly reminded herself.

"I don't think you know what you're asking. I've been quite busy with my artwork since we've arrived."

"Then I'm in for a pleasant surprise."

"You flatter me."

He lifted the easel. "Miss Chance, if even one of your other pieces comes close to the beauty of this watercolor, I'll be a happy man."

"Then let's see if you can find something that'll please you." She walked along beside him carrying her brushes in a jar as well as her paint box. "My brothers and cousins have enjoyed your advice regarding rock climbing."

"Good. Did you have a good time at Tuolumne Meadows?"

"Oh, the meadows are magnificent! I could have stayed there forever." She paused a moment as he cupped her elbow to help her over a branch that lay in their path, then murmured, "Thank you. And thank you, too, for talking the boys into going to the meadows. Left to their own devices, we'd probably camp in the shadow of the gigantic rocks and never move!"

"There are always bigger, more interesting rocks. Their collective sense of adventure would drive them to move on." He gave her a boyish grin. "I know whereof I speak."

"How long have you been wandering through Yosemite?"

"Since early spring."

Laurel shook her head. "I can't imagine how lonely that must be. I love my family. It's huge, and I'm always surrounded by noise. There are times when I wish I could have a little time alone, some peace and quiet—but more than a day or two, and I'd be forlorn."

"How many children are in your family?"

"Do you mean, how many children do my parents have, or how many children are on the ranch?"

"You all live together?" He halted and gave her a startled look.

"Daddy and four of his brothers all live on the ranch—each has his own home. The older boys live together in a separate cabin, and we girls have a cabin of our own, too."

"The place must be massive."

"We have plenty of room." She didn't specify the acreage. It seemed boastful. Then again, when they'd gone to Reliable to settle, all six of the brothers and their mother had a right to claim land. Farsighted, they'd grabbed as much as they could and worked hard to improve it. The only one who had moved away was her uncle Logan, but enough land and work remained for all of them. God had blessed their efforts.

"So Paxton and Packard are your brothers. How many more do you have?"

"Three more." She laughed. "We girls have a cabin of our own because we're abysmally outnumbered. Altogether, there are fourteen boys and three of us girls living on Chance Ranch."

He whistled under his breath.

"How many children in your family, Mr. Rutlidge?"

"Just two. I have a younger brother." They arrived back at the campsite. "Where shall I set your easel?"

"Over by the tent, please." Laurel heard voices. "Johnna? April? Are you in the tent?"

"Yes." April stuck her head out of the flap. "We were—oh! Hello, Mr. Rutlidge! Johnna, guess who's here?"

"You just said his name, you silly goose." Johnna exited the tent. "Fancy seein' you again, Mr. Rutlidge. Did we catch up with you, or did you catch up with us?"

He chuckled. "I think we met in the middle."

"April and me—we were just decidin' whether to take a hike or fix something special for supper. Kate's fishin' with the boys, and we'd have to drag someone away from his fishin' pole if we want to wander."

"After Laurel shows me her art, I'd be honored to escort you ladies on a walk."

"Oh, mercy." April laughed. "We won't have that walk for three days. Has she told you how much she's been doing?"

Gabe slanted a smile at Laurel. It made her heart skip a beat, then speed up. "I'm glad to hear it wasn't an exaggeration. The piece she did this morning is stupendous."

"Ain't fittin' for you to go in the tent. Me and April'll drag out the chest for you." Johnna nodded. "Laurel, the both of you go move the chairs to the shade. Sun's moved, and you'll burn worse'n a side of bacon on a griddle iff'n you sit in the bright of the day."

The girls ducked back into the tent, and Laurel busied herself by laying the paint box and brushes on the table. Being compared to a side of bacon somehow made her want to giggle, but she didn't dare. It would be rude.

Gabe leaned a little closer. "I could listen to that gal talk all day. She's as colorful as your painting." He waggled his brows. "It might not have seemed complimentary to you, but men happen to love the smell of bacon."

That did it. Laurel burst out laughing. Gabe's deep laughter mingled with hers as he moved the chairs into a patch of shade.

Laurel noticed he didn't just move two chairs—he moved all four so April and Johnna could join them. Gabe proved himself to be just as thoughtful the second they cleared the tent with her crate of art. He strode over, immediately hefted it away from them, and brought it to the shade. Standing in front of Laurel, he glanced down at the crate, then back at her. "I can see I'm in for a treat."

"The watercolors are in the two tablets on the right."

"And what's in the other tablets?" He set down the crate and surveyed the contents.

"Sketches. Pastels. Oils take too long to dry. I tried one, but it got bugs in it and smeared."

"The bugs were attracted to the scent you're wearing." He gave her a stern look.

Unwilling to tell him she'd broken out in a terrible rash from the lye soap, Laurel changed the subject. "Perhaps I'll make lunch while you leaf through—"

"No." He sat down and gently tugged her wrist to get her to sit beside him.

"Show him your meadows first," April urged.

"No, the one of the butterfly. 'Tis the one I favor most." Johnna settled in next to Laurel.

"I'll see them all." Gabe reached into the box and took out the first tablet. He handled it deftly, but with care. Opening the cover, he stated, "I've always admired folks who could draw. I don't have in it me."

A charcoal pencil sketch of Tuolumne was the first piece. A sea of grass and wildflowers waved across the page, swept by the breeze. Gabe didn't tear his gaze from it as he said in a low tone, "But you certainly have the talent, Miss Laurel. This is wondrous. I can see the blades bending in the wind. That's just how it looks, too."

"Thank you."

He soaked up that picture, then slowly turned to the next. . .and the next. "You captured the bark perfectly. I feel like I could touch this and pick up the rough texture. . . Mule deer step so daintily, don't they? You have her poised exactly the way they do—I don't know how you captured her in motion like that."

"I've always dabbled at home. Here, I can't seem to help myself. Something inside demands I sketch or paint. I can't explain it."

"Hit's a matter of the right seed in the right soil," Johnna declared. "You ken there's places in a garden what'll grow only a few thangs, but when those flower, they're fearsome fine. I 'spect same's true with you. You needed to come here to set your soul abloom."

Gabriel nodded. "Yosemite is like that for some of us. We come here, and it touches us deeply."

"I feel so close to God here," Laurel confessed.

Staring at the next sketch, Gabe murmured, "It shows."

He didn't flip through the books as she'd expected. Instead, he took time over each sketch—even the silly ones she'd done of her cousins and brothers. "Boots, huh?"

She laughed. "Look how scuffed up they are. Climbing is taking a terrible toll on their clothes—and we anticipated that, but I've never seen sorrier looking boots. By the time we make it back home, every last man is going to have to break in a new pair of boots."

"It's only shoe leather," April stated practically. "They've had such a good time, they won't mind a few blisters."

"Kate's mighty good with leather. She's been repairin' the boots regular-like."

"Is that so?" Gabe's chin lifted. "There's a rough spot on my packhorse's girth strap. I've been padding it with a scrap of cloth. Think she could fix it?"

"We'll ask her," Laurel said. "Leatherwork is where Kate's talent shines."

"It's plain to see where your talent lies," Gabe said as he looked at Laurel. He'd set aside a handful of sketches and a pair of watercolors. "We need to discuss these. I want to purchase them."

"I've never sold my work. You're welcome to take them."

"That's generous of you, but I insist on buying them. In fact, I'm hoping to buy a view of Bridal Veil Falls from you once you've been there. My mother would treasure that."

The thought that he wanted to buy something already had her off-balance. Laurel couldn't imagine he wanted to give her art as a gift. The thought stunned her. "I'm not sure what to think."

"Think about doing a watercolor of Bridal Veil," he shot back. "Do you have any pasteboard tubes so I can preserve these? I'd hate to have them get crumpled or dog-eared."

"No, I don't have anything like that."

"Jist use the back o' one of them art pads of yourn," Johnna said. "That ought to work out."

"Good idea." Gabe rummaged through the box. "These two pads are the same size, and you've filled them both. If we take the back of this one but keep them stacked together, the pictures ought to be protected still. What do you say?"

"How do you intend to keep it curled shut?" Laurel wondered aloud.

"Twine. I carry some in my pack. It's handy stuff." Gabe went over to the packs he'd removed from his horses, rummaged for a few minutes, and then reappeared with a decent length of twine in his palm. "This will serve our needs."

"Yes, I think it'll work well." Laurel tore the back off of a pad.

Standing close, Gabe murmured, "Would you rather we spoke privately about the financial arrangements?"

"Honestly, I don't know what to do. I'm not a professional artist. Would a dollar be too much?"

"A dollar!"

Chapter 6

Heat crept from Laurel's bosom to her face. She'd tried to estimate how much the paper, paint, and pastels cost, then add in a tiny bit for her time.

"Woman, that doesn't even begin to cover your costs, let alone remunerate you for your talent!"

Laurel could scarcely hear him for the relief that poured through her.

"I brought one of those Kodak cameras with me. I took all one hundred pictures and sent it back to Rochester. It was twenty-five dollars for the camera, and the developing and reloading of the film was another ten. The sad fact is, I'm no photographer. Scarcely a handful of the pictures turned out at all, and the lighting on them is such that I missed most of what I wanted to show."

"Let's do the arithmetic," April suggested. "You got one hundred photographs for thirty-five dollars. That comes to thirty-five cents per picture."

"No, it doesn't," Laurel protested as she rose. "It included film for one hundred more pictures."

"But not the developing," Gabe hastened to say. "Nor the shipping."

"So charge him thirty-five cents per picture," Johnna suggested. "That's fair, isn't it?"

"No, it's not." Gabe's voice rivaled a thunderclap. "I was attempting to illustrate that for thirty-five dollars, I didn't get a fraction of the value of these beautiful works of art."

Though rarely at a loss for words, Laurel stood in shocked silence. She'd seen others feel this way about Mama's pictures, but no one had ever been so moved over anything she'd done. The magnitude of knowing her art affected someone so profoundly washed over her.

Gabe folded his arms across his chest. "I want to commission a watercolor of Bridal Veil, but I can't if you and I don't come to a reasonable agreement regarding these other pieces. I refuse to cheat you simply because you're an undiscovered talent. Back in Boston or New York, I'd pay a pretty penny for anything like this—and believe me when I tell you it's of the same quality of the drawings and paintings shown in galleries back East."

"What do you think is reasonable?" Laurel half-croaked.

"Sixty dollars."

Her knees nearly buckled. Laurel blindly felt for the seat behind her and promptly folded herself back onto it before she fell. "Impossible!"

He shook his head. "You're a grand artist and a terrible businesswoman, Laurel Chance."

"Whilst she's thinkin' on that, d'you still have that camera?" Johnna grinned. "I've niver seen one. Oh—I seed the big ones them professional photographers cart around, but yourn sounds dreadful nice."

Thankful for the reprieve, Laurel watched as Gabe walked away and pulled the camera from his pack. He returned with not only the camera, but also a small stack of photographs. "These are the ones I kept—you can see they didn't turn out very well."

Laurel slowly shuffled through the pictures. "You're right. The lighting is wrong. These would have done better with early morning or late afternoon light so the shadows would give more depth and definition."

"So that's what it was. I figured I needed the noonday sun to make everything show up more clearly."

She smiled at him. "So now you'll know what to do, and the next batch will turn out better."

"I don't share your faith in my ability." He glanced at Johnna, who reverently turned the camera over in her hands. "I tell you what, Laurel: I'll pay you forty-five dollars and give you my camera for the pieces I selected."

April and Johnna both gasped.

Laurel shook her head. "Just the camera."

"And thirty dollars."

She'd never seen a camera like this one. It intrigued her. "I'll get just as much enjoyment out of the camera as you do from the sketches—probably more."

"Oh, will the both of you stop haggling like horse traders?" Johnna handed the camera to Laurel. "Only horse traders want to cheat one another, and you're bendin' backward and pussyfootin' 'round, trying to be fair."

Gabe chortled. The sound of his merriment made Laurel let out a self-conscious giggle.

"It's about time the two of you came to your senses and agreed on something," April said. "I want to go on that walk, and you're wasting precious time."

"Meet me in the middle." Gabe looked at Laurel. "Twenty-two fifty and the camera."

"Fifteen and the camera," she countered.

"Are you always this stubborn, princess?"

She merely laughed and nodded.

"Hey, what's going on—oh! Rutlidge!" Paxton and a few others strode up. Pax held up a string of fish. "How about you staying for lunch?"

"I don't mind as long as the cook doesn't."

Laurel smiled. "I'm the cook, and I don't mind at all."

I've been wrong about her. Oh, I was right—she's a princess. Regal and beautiful. But she's more than just appearance. The woman can cook, and her artistic abilities are enough to put her in one of the finest European academies.

Gabe ate the last bite of his trout almondine and wondered who thought to pack almonds with the supplies. "Great meal."

"Our table is always open," Laurel told him.

"Don't say that too loudly. The cavalry is poorly provisioned. They might start ghosting alongside you and showing up for meals."

April shrugged. "They're welcome. I expected the men to be more hungry than usual, so I almost doubled my provisions. We're about halfway through the trip, and we've used about a quarter of what I packed."

"I hate thinking that the men who keep this beautiful place safe for all of us might have to do without." Kate looked up from the girth strap she'd been repairing. Gabe hadn't been able to talk her into waiting until after lunch—she'd been adamant about relieving his "poor little horse" at once. "Can we get word to them? How do we reach them?"

"Captain Wood has a way of finding me," Gabe confessed.

He quelled a smile at the memory of their last meeting. The soldiers were disappointed he didn't have any new food after having been to Wawona, but the licorice pipes more than redeemed him in their eyes. They'd been like little boys, relishing that treat around the campfire.

"Captain Wood," Caleb repeated. Gabe noticed he, Paxton, and Tobias tended to assert themselves as leaders in the group.

"Yes. He's a solid man, a good commander," Gabe attested. "If he or his men show up, you can count on them being well-disciplined and helpful."

"Here. This is done." Kate stood.

Gabe rose. "I'm grateful. What do I owe you?"

Kate gave him a disbelieving look. "Mister, it was nothing to fix. We Chances take care of horses."

"So do I. It was my horse, and you provided a valuable service. I can't abide with mistreating a beast. I'd have stopped using him as a packhorse if this couldn't be remedied, and that would have put me in deplorable straits."

"So I helped a fellow traveler." Kate shrugged.

"How about if you take the girls on a walk, and we'll call it even?" Caleb swiped his biscuit across his plate. "They've been wanting to explore, and they're driving us half crazy."

Gabe looked at the women. "Do all of you ride?"

"We've grown up on a horse ranch," Laurel reminded him.

"Why don't I take you on a ride? You'll see more, and we could determine where you'd like to walk tomorrow."

"Laurel, take your camera!" Johnna urged.

"Actually, you'd be better off leaving it here at camp and carrying it on the walk. I found my horse had a bad habit of moving just about the time I hit the shutter."

"Makes sense," Caleb said. "You probably tense up a mite, and horses react to the least little signal."

"Then I'll leave the camera here." Laurel brushed a little speck off of her skirts. "We'll be ready as soon as we do the dishes."

"We'll see to saddling up your mounts," Paxton said.

Gabe watched as some of the men went over and prepared four nice-looking mares. Each of the beasts behaved perfectly. The bay with the special saddle had to be Kate's since she loved to do leatherwork. The stockier mount would be for short, plump April. That left the other two—a dappled gray and a strawberry. He couldn't decide which was Laurel's and which was Johnna's. Laurel would look like a princess on the gray, but the strawberry's walk resembled a dainty march.

Peter sauntered over. "I aim to go along. Promised Pa me or one of the boys'd stay with Sis all the time."

"Fine." Gabe glanced at him. "So Johnna's your sister?"

"Yup. Folks named us all after the apostles. John was the beloved disciple, and it's held true. Our Johnna's something special—ev'rybody latches onto her. On account of that, Ma was downright worried 'bout her comin' so far from home."

Gabe watched the women as they washed and dried the dishes. They chattered like happy little sparrows. "From what I see, all the women in the family are extraordinary."

"Uh-huh. April's a fine gal. Nobody cooks better, and she's got a big heart. Kate—well, a feller couldn't hope to have a gal who's a better listener. Laurel's been the surprise. We all expected her to be a pain on this trip. Finicky and scared. Nary a complaint's come outta her. Fact is, last night she told us we've got bears and snakes back home, so she didn't know what the fuss was all 'bout." He chuckled.

I misjudged her, too. In fact, I'm no good at reading women at all. I was just as wrong about Arabella. "Just about the time a man supposes he's figured out a woman, she changes on him."

"Ain't that the truth!" Peter leaned against a tree. "Contrary creatures, but the dear Lord said it's not good for a man to be alone, so I reckon I'll marry up and have to tame one of 'em someday."

"Are you sure you're the one who'll do the taming?"

Peter tilted his head back and let out a loud hoot. "Now that's a poser, it is.

I'll exercise my mind on it someday. What 'bout you?"

"Me?" Gabe scowled. "The last thing I want is to have to worry about what a woman wants out of me. Being footloose suits me just fine."

"You made 'em all happy with an offer of a ride."

Gabe merely shrugged. A few minutes later, he walked over and untied the tether on his mount. He prized his horse—a Tennessee Walker he'd bought with his hard-earned pay. Though he came from a wealthy family, his father insisted upon his sons having to work in the business and learn the value of a dollar. The lesson wasn't in vain. Then again, Gabe never regretted a single cent he'd paid for Nessie.

"That's one fine beast you've got there," Paxton said.

Gabe nodded in acknowledgment of the praise.

"You ever breed her?"

"No." Gabe gave the mare an affectionate pat. "I've been too selfish to give up riding Nessie for long enough for her to be in foal. If I ever do, her offspring will be sweet-tempered."

"Back home, we have a couple of stallions who would do her justice." Paxton grinned. "I'm not just boasting. Chance Ranch is known for its horseflesh."

Looking over at their rope corral, Gabe commented, "You have a wide variety. You never specialized in any particular breed?"

"We've got everything from bays and blues to mustangs and pintos. Army buys up a couple of sizable strings each season—enough to keep us in business. The rest go to regular folks—farmers, ranchers, travelers."

"Not a one of your mounts has marks."

"You mean a brand?" Paxton clarified.

"No, lash marks—from harsh discipline." Gabe watched Laurel's brother's face cloud over and hastened to add, "I've seen several horses—the wild mustangs that needed taming—that have gotten the spirit whipped out of them."

"Not at our place." Laurel walked up. "Love works miracles. We care for our horses, and they give us their best."

Kate skipped up. "While we're here, four of the younger boys are getting their horses. In our family, everyone is given a horse when they turn twelve."

"A rite of passage?" Gabe marveled aloud.

"Sort of." Paxton winced and theatrically rubbed his back-side. "The boys are given a rough horse and have to break it. If you ask me, the horse makes a man—not the man makes the horse."

"And the girls?"

Laurel smiled. "We're given mares that are already domesticated and saddled."

"Daddy said it's because the Chances protect their women," April chimed in, "but I always said it's because the men would starve if anything happened to the girls."

"I don't blame them. I've tasted your cooking." Gabe grinned. "Are we ready to go now?"

Tobias and Tanner brought over the girls' mares. Gabe managed to be standing by Laurel, so it only made sense that he help her mount up on the dappled gray. "Here you go," he said by way of warning that he'd put his hands on her. The satiny ribbon of her sash felt smooth and cool to the touch, and yards of buttery yellow fabric fluttered as he cinched hold of her waist and lifted.

A gentleman never looked straight ahead or down as he helped a woman into the saddle. Gabe fought the temptation and kept his head tilted back until Laurel gained her seat: then he turned his head to the side and regretfully let go. He heard her fuss with her skirts to be sure her ankles didn't show. He'd forgotten how potent the swishing sounds of petticoats and the fluff of ruffles could be.

"Thank you, Mr. Rutlidge."

"You're welcome, Miss Laurel." He swung up into his saddle and turned to look behind him. "Are you all ready?"

"More than ready!" Kate sang out.

"Please don't hold back on our account," April begged.

"Yeah," Johnna agreed. "Don't mean to sound boastful, but we cain keep up with whate'er pace you set."

Gabe soon discovered they hadn't exaggerated their abilities. He'd originally planned a little half-hour jaunt, but these women wanted far more than anything that simple. They trotted along and called out several questions. Laurel rated as the most curious of them all. She wanted to know what animal different tracks belonged to, commented on the similarities and differences in the flora, and asked for comparisons to other areas of the preserve.

Gabe figured they could have talked nonstop for weeks, but he felt the temperature drop. "We need to turn back."

"Do we have to?" April sounded forlorn.

"We'd better, unless you want to bed down out here in the wilds without fire or a bedroll," Peter responded.

"I've done it afore." Johnna didn't look in the least bit afraid.

"Your brothers will scalp me if I don't have you back soon," Gabe said.

Laurel laughed. "Only because they'll be wanting supper."

"It's best we go back," Kate nudged her mare. "We have to cross that open area, and I want to give Myrene her head. If the sun's setting, I'll be too worried about gopher holes to allow her free rein."

Her mare brushed a low-lying branch, and a few bees took off. Gabe watched them zoom around in angry flight, then circle Laurel. "Don't swat at them!"

"I know better." A moment later, she stiffened and her mare sidestepped skittishly. Air hissed in through Laurel's teeth.

Chapter 7

Sting. The word didn't begin to describe the horrid burning Laurel felt. She'd counted three stings, but it might as well have been a dozen for the fiery feeling.

"Laurel?" Gabe brought his horse alongside hers and dipped his head to get a good look at her.

"Oh no. You're stung," Kate moaned. "I'm so sorry. It's my fault."

"There's prob'ly more where those came from." Peter tilted his head to the side. "Let's move."

Gabe reached over and took Laurel's reins. Thankful, she released them as it allowed her to try to pull the stinger out of her wrist.

"Leave those alone a minute. I'll help you get the stingers out." His voice sounded both firm and calm as he led her horse.

"We have tweezers back at camp," April called back.

Unsure just how far they were from camp since she'd been too busy enjoying the ride to determine whether they'd curved around, Laurel winced. She didn't think she could bear the stingers that long.

"There's a clearing to the right about fifty yards ahead," Gabe directed. "Stop there."

That's not too far. But we won't have tweezers. Laurel clenched her hands together to keep from trying to pull out the stinger.

"Whoa." Her dappled mare obediently stopped at Gabe's command. He dismounted, reached up, and cupped Laurel's waist. "C'mere, princess." He swept her down to earth. "There's a log over here. Let's have you take a seat."

Laurel nodded. Seconds later, Gabe knelt before her. He took a knife from the sheath on his belt. "I'm going to flick the stinger out."

"You'll cut it," Kate objected.

"We always use tweezers back home," April told him.

"I'll use the back of the knife, not the blade." Gabe proceeded to curl his warm, large hand around Laurel's wrist. "Hold still."

" 'Kay."

He pulled the skin taut and did just as he'd promised. The stinger came free, and he brushed it away. "Now where else did they get you?"

"My cheek."

"Oh, lookie. Thar's one on yore throat, too." Johnna sat next to her and took hold of her hand. "Peter, mix up some mud. These gotta smart something dreadful, and hit'll take away that hurt."

Gabe leaned closer and repeated his earlier order, "Hold still."

Laurel barely tilted her head in agreement.

April started to giggle. "I'm sorry. This isn't funny, but it looks like Gabe is shaving you!"

"If you don't hobble your mouth, he can always use that knife to scalp you." Kate plopped down on Laurel's other side. "Pay no mind to her, Laurel."

Laurel closed her eyes and felt cold steel pressed against the burning spot on her cheek. A breath later, the blade was gone.

"Almost done," Gabe said as he tilted her head back and to the side.

Opening her eyes a mere slit, Laurel saw the concentration on his face as he rid her of the last stinger. Once it was out, he gently ran his fingers across her brow, right by her hairline. His touch made her shiver.

"Any more, princess? Do you sting anywhere else?"

"No." Her voice came out in a tight whisper.

"Got that mud here." Peter wedged in.

Gabe dabbed his forefinger into Peter's cupped palm and dabbed splotches on her cheek, neck, and wrist. When Laurel wrinkled her nose, he murmured, "I warned you. I'm not artistic."

"It doesn't look that bad," Johnna declared.

Loyal as could be, April and Kate agreed with vivacious nods.

Gabe rose and again tilted Laurel's face to his. His dark brows knit, and his voice took on an edge. "Now will you stop using that fancy, flowery stuff?"

"She has to." April bumped him out of the way and wrapped her in a hug. "We understand."

"Well, I don't."

"Lye soap makes her rashy," Kate explained.

"Makes her look like a spotted owl," Peter tacked on.

"Sorta like that mud does," Johnna added.

This kept getting more embarrassing. Laurel rested her head on April's shoulder and groaned.

Gabe pried April away. "Are you feeling sick?"

Laurel shook her head.

"Light-headed?"

A gasp escaped her. No gentleman ever posed such a question of a lady. Laurel straightened up and drew in a strangled breath. "I—"

Before she could finish her sentence, he'd swept her into his arms and was striding toward his mount. "We're getting you back to camp. Does anyone know if she's ever been stung before?"

"I don't know about bees. She's been stung by wasps," Kate said as she swung into her own saddle.

Gabe handed her off to Peter, mounted, and took her back. The jut of his jaw screamed grim determination. "Hang on, princess."

The ride from camp had been leisurely, delightful. The ride back amounted to nothing more than a blur and the pounding sound of horses' hooves. Gabe held her tight, and the steady beat of his heart beneath her ear kept her feeling unaccountably safe. The sun was setting as they skidded into camp.

"What's going on?" Pax demanded as Gabe passed Laurel down to him.

"Bees."

Laurel wiggled until her brother set her down. "Really, I'm fine."

"She needs to lie down," Gabe insisted.

"Why?" Pax looked from her to Gabe and back.

"She's sensitive—even lye soap bothers her. She was having trouble breathing." As he spoke, Gabe wrapped his arm about her and started escorting her toward the tent. "You ladies, come tuck her in."

"I'm not sleepy." Laurel dug in her heels. "Other than wearing mud all over, I'm fine."

"Well, if you're fine, can we have supper soon?" Cal patted his stomach. "I'm starving."

"I'll cook," April declared.

"It's my turn," Laurel said.

"They're my fish." Kate headed toward the campfire. "I caught more than the boys did."

"Now there you have it." Johnna grabbed Laurel's hand and dragged her into the tent. "Everything's under control."

Spinning around, Laurel hissed, "You're no help at all. The boys didn't want me to come on this trip because they thought I'd be too much trouble—that I'd fuss and need special attention. The last thing I want is—"

Johnna clapped her hand over Laurel's mouth and whispered in her ear, "Them bucks out there cain think whatever they please. Better they reckon 'twas jest a case of yore stays being cinched a tad too tight than you havin' hysterics or bein' brought low by a couple of bitty bees."

Unable to refute that logic, Laurel nodded.

"So what we're a-gonna do is spend a moment or two in here, then go back outside and pretend nothin' ever happened."

"Nothing did happen!"

Johnna shrugged. "Ma onc't tole me, a man's gotta think he's right. A smart woman lets him think what he will, and she jest keeps doin' what needs to be done."

"That seems like lying to me."

"Nah." Johnna grinned. "Men use their strength to help women. Seems only fair women exercise kindness in return."

"When you put it that way. . ." Laurel reached up to fix her hair.

Johnna slipped behind her. "I aim to loosen you up."

"I don't need you to. I'm fine."

"Ain't about what you need, Laurel. Think on it: Gabe scooped you up and toted you like you was a damsel in distress. He'll be made to feel like a laughing-stock iff'n you sashay outta here."

"Just a minute ago, you said we were going out there and pretending nothing ever happened."

"Shore 'nuff I did. But how're we gonna *pretend* nothin' happened if nothing happened?" Johnna deftly unbuttoned the back of Laurel's gown.

"I could just loosen my sash."

"We'll do that, too."

Gabe stood off a ways from the tent and kept staring at it as he paced. A few of the Chance men had taken the horses and were seeing to them.

Paxton leaned against a tree and folded his arms across his chest as Ulysses turned to Caleb. Entertainment tinged his voice as he drawled, "It's just a bee sting."

"Three." Gabe grimaced as he paused. "And I've seen a man die from being stung."

"No foolin'?" Ulysses gawked at him.

"He swelled up and stopped breathing."

Paxton straightened up. "And Sis was having a hard time breathing."

"No use getting too excited yet," Caleb asserted. "She was talking plenty when Johnna hauled her into the tent."

"Could be," Ulysses mused, " 'twas a matter of her um. . . whalebones."

"Don't you talk about my sister that way," Pax growled.

"Laurel's never been swoony," Caleb said. "Prissy, but not swoony."

"She's not prissy; she's feminine," Gabe snapped. "Enough of this jawing. We need to know how she's fairing."

The tent flap opened. Johnna emerged. Laurel followed right behind. Gabe squinted and studied her. In the lantern light, her coloring qualified as hectic. Her lips. . .if she'd stop chewing on the bottom one, he could see whether they'd swelled at all.

"Sis," Paxton called, "you okay?"

Her hand went to her breastbone, but she nodded.

Gabe stomped toward her. "If you won't lie down, you should at least sit."

"I'm going to help finish supper."

"Not while you're wearing mud." April shook a long-handled fork at her.

"I'll wash it off."

"No, you won't." Gabe glowered at her. "Johnna said it takes away the pain."

Caleb came up on Laurel's other side. "Maybe we ought to trade it for new mud. It might draw off the poison."

"They were bees, not rattlesnakes."

Ignoring Laurel's objection, Gabe nodded. "I'll take her to rest by the fire. You get more mud."

"Is she all swoll up?" Ulysses called over.

Gabe studied Laurel's lips. Since she'd worried them, they'd taken on a deeper tint than usual. They looked okay. No, they looked fine. Real fine. Downright kissable. *What am I thinking?*

"Well?" Ulysses prodded. "Are they?"

"No." Gabe slipped his arm around her waist and started toward the fire. "Grab a wet rag, will you? We need to wash off the old mud pack."

"Sure."

Laurel looked up at him. "This is unnecessary."

Gabe nudged her to sit down. "Let me take a look at those stings." Though she made no complaint, he witnessed how her features tightened as he used the wet cloth to remove the mud.

Paxton whistled under his breath. "Those things've gotta be the size of—"

"Your skin is sensitive, princess," Gabe interrupted. The last thing she needed to know was that the stings had puffed out to the size of a quarter. "But these'll go away in a few days." For the second time, he dabbed mud on her pretty face.

"Don't forget her wrist," Peter reminded.

"Got it." Gabe attended to that one, too. He wished she couldn't glance down and see that huge wheal. Laurel, who loved beauty, would take a good look and worry about being permanently disfigured.

"What are you putting on her?" Kate held a graniteware mug.

"More mud."

She shook her head. "Clean it off. I made a paste of baking soda for her stings."

Laurel grabbed for the cloth. "I'd much rather use the baking soda." As she dabbed at her jaw, her eyes widened.

"Stings swell like that," Gabe reassured her. "It'll go down in a couple of days."

"Days!"

Paxton chortled. "No use kickin' up a fuss, Sis. It's not like we're at home where you'll have suitors knockin' down the door to see you."

Hearing she had suitors shouldn't have come as a surprise. Nonetheless, Gabe didn't like the fact whatsoever. He grabbed the rag. "You missed a spot."

Laurel turned her big amber eyes toward him. "I'm probably wearing mud crumbles all over."

"A little dirt never hurt anybody," Kate declared as she dipped her finger into the mug.

"Cleanliness is next to godliness," Laurel recited.

Johnna walked over with several dinner plates balanced on her arms. "Now's the wrong time to declare such a thang. Ev'rybody here could fill a dustbin with what they shake outta their duds."

"I suppose you're right." Laurel's smile rivaled the lantern for brightness. "I've never felt closer to the Lord than I do here in Yosemite."

Her profession took him off guard. Gabe understood the overwhelming appreciation for the beauty she sensed. *But what does God have to do with it?* No use burdening these people with the perplexing questions he entertained regarding faith. Best he change the topic to something light. Gabe jerked his chin toward Kate and grinned. "Put that baking soda on her and see if she feels closer to the kitchen, too."

Everyone laughed, but deep inside, Gabe felt empty.

Chapter 8

After supper, everyone gathered around the fire. As had become their custom, they conversed. A couple of the boys had brought harmonicas and soughed through them softly. Peter brought his fiddle, and about every other night he'd rosin up his bow. Often as not, they'd all end up singing a few songs. One of the men would finally stand and say a prayer to end the evening.

Gabe and Pax wouldn't leave her side. Sandwiched between the pair of them, Laurel resolved to forget about her stings and relish the evening. Bless his heart, Pax might grouse and growl at times, but he was a fine brother. As for Gabe—well, she'd never met a man like him. He'd been strong yet gentle—but though Daddy, her uncles, and brothers were those things, too, with Gabe it was. . .well, different.

He listened and joined in the conversation now and then—most often to make a suggestion regarding adventures the men could enjoy during the remainder of their trip.

Peter fetched his fiddle and played "June-bugs Dance."

Kate called, "Play 'There are Plenty of Fish in the Sea.'"

"She asked for that because she caught the most fish today," Tanner grumbled.

The rest of the men laughed, then began to sing as Peter started to play.

Laurel leaned toward Gabe and said quietly, "Whenever Kate dangles a hook, fish fight to bite it. It drives the boys daft."

"Does she use the same bait?"

"Yes." Laurel wrinkled her nose.

"So you don't particularly like to hook crickets or worms?"

She pointed ruefully at her wrist. "Insects and I don't get along."

"I'd rather see you with a paintbrush than a fishing pole in your hand any day of the year."

"This little thing will be gone by the time we reach Bridal Veil. I'll be sure to paint that picture for you."

"Good. Thanks."

When the song ended, Tobias started singing, "For the Beauty of the Earth." Laurel joined in.

On the refrain, Gabe finally added his voice. His deep tone rang true. He turned and smiled at her as he sang the next verse, "Hill and vale, and tree and flower, sun and moon, and stars of light. . ."

His love of their surroundings came through with great sincerity. Though she'd always enjoyed the hymn, Laurel hadn't ever found it this expressive. Bee stings aside, this had to be the best day of her life.

After a few more songs, Pax rose. "Suppose we ought to call it a day. Let's pray. Lord, we want to raise our praise to You for so much—for the wonders of Your creation, the love of family and friends, and the mercies You show us. We give special thanks for taking care of my sister today. Keep us and those we love safe through the night we pray, amen."

"Amen," everyone chimed in, but a mere breath delayed Gabe's, and he was looking at Laurel.

She shivered.

"Are you cold?"

It seemed ridiculous to say yes on such a balmy night and when sitting so close to the fire. Laurel shrugged. "I'll be under my quilt in a few minutes."

"Sweet dreams."

Minutes later as she snuggled in the tent, his words echoed in her mind again. *Sweet dreams. . .*

But when she woke the next morning, Laurel couldn't recall having dreamt at all. She quietly dressed, put up her hair, and gathered a tablet and her watercolors.

Johnna sat up and stretched. "D'ya ken whether April had special plans for breakfast? I'm hankerin' after biscuits 'n' gravy."

"It can't be morning yet," Kate mumbled.

"Jist 'cuz we ain't got no rooster to crow here don't mean the sun forgot to make an appearance." Johnna reached over and poked at Kate. "You and me—we got breakfast duty. Rise 'n' shine."

Kate opened one eye. "The Bible says the Lord loves a cheerful giver. It doesn't say He favors a cheerful riser."

"Sleep in. I'll help with breakfast today." Laurel set down her art supplies.

"I'm not ashamed to accept that offer." Kate rolled to her other side and dragged her quilt over her head.

Johnna grabbed her clothes and swiftly dressed. In the dim light of the tent, she squinted at Laurel. "Might be a good notion for you to wear your laces a bit loose today. Yore cinched in within an inch of yore life."

"Nonsense. Look. My dress fits the same as it always does."

Johnna shook her head. "For true, you look bitty as cain be. Plenty of men like that to look at; but when hit comes to gettin' serious, a man wants a woman whose shape says she's a healthy 'un."

"I'm healthy as a horse." Laurel hoped the conversation would end there.

April propped her head up on one hand and whispered loudly, "Did you notice she didn't say anything about a man getting serious? I know her too well, Johnna. She's getting tenderhearted over a certain man."

"I thunk so, too."

"You have no idea what you're talking about." Laurel turned to leave the tent.

"He didn't wish any of the rest of us sweet dreams," Johnna said.

"He was worried about me after the bee stings is all."

"She ain't foolin' us. Think she's foolin' herself, April?"

April's giggles filled the tent. Laurel would have gladly dashed out, but if she did, she'd have to explain why her face was so red.

The sound of a horse leaving camp at a trot came through the canvas tent. Kate sat up and flung off her blankets. "Nobody's letting me sleep. Even the boys are up and rustling around."

"I only heard one horse," Johnna said as she reached for the tent flap. "Hope we don't have us a horse thief."

They bolted out of the tent in time to see Gabe riding away. Johnna shook her head. "Silly man's gonna miss out on biscuits 'n' gravy. Shoulda waited."

Laurel's heart dropped to her knees. *What if he heard what they said in the tent?*

A few minutes later, Laurel dropped the spoon in the gravy as she stirred it. She burned her hand on the coffeepot. How could she ever face Gabriel Rutlidge again after what he'd overheard this morning? After breakfast, she gathered her tablet and charcoals and escaped to the relative privacy of a nearby stand of trees. It didn't help distract her. When the second of her charcoals broke under the pressure she exerted, Laurel slammed the tablet shut and let her head drop back against the trunk of the tree she'd been leaning against.

Lord, I don't know what to do. Back home when boys came to call, it was so easy. I knew them from school and church. But compared to Gabe, they are all such. . .boys. With them, I knew exactly what to expect. Gabe is so different, so wonderful. He understands how I feel about this place. No one else ever looked past the pictures I paint and saw the emotions behind them, but he did. Yesterday, he was so good to me when I got hurt. I didn't want my brother's strength or help; I wanted Gabe's. But Gabe rode off this morning. Did he hear what the girls said in the tent? Will I ever have a chance to get to know him better, or did they scare him off? Was he just being kind yesterday, and I'm making a ninny of myself? I'm so confused, Father.

"Laurel!"

She scrambled to her feet. "Yes?"

Caleb sauntered toward her. "You gals wanted to go for a walk yesterday. You feelin' up to it now, or do you wanna stay here and draw?"

"Oh, I'd love to come along."

"Johnna's hoping you'll take that camera."

She stooped to pick up her supplies. "It's fascinating, isn't it?"

"Yup."

Smothering a smile at the immediacy of his answer, she rose. "Gabe said there are one hundred exposures in the roll. I'm sure we'll all snap a few pictures."

"I'd like that." The light in his eyes tattled that's what he'd been hoping for. "It'd be good to have pictures of the places we've climbed."

"Absolutely. It'll be a nice keepsake, and we can show them to everyone back home so they'll be able to anticipate their trip here next summer."

He bobbed his head affirmatively. "Go shove your stuff in the tent, and we'll get going."

"I made a picnic lunch," April announced as Laurel came into sight.

"How fun!"

Caleb snorted. "We're eating outside for every meal. What difference does it make?"

"We eat outside at home a good deal of the time, too," Paxton tacked on.

"But this will be in a different place," Kate said. "We don't want you boys dragging us back to camp after we've only been out a little while because you've gotten hungry."

"I need someone to hang the food for me." April finished knotting the top of a sack. She looked at Ulysses. "If a bear gets to this, you boys'll have to make your own lunch."

"Whoa. I got it." He snatched the bag and headed for the rope dangling from a high branch.

Laurel tucked her tablet and charcoals into the crate in the tent, then grabbed the camera. Turning the black device over in her hands, she wondered how to operate it. *Gabe was supposed to stay here today and take us on this hike. He would have shown me how to take photographs.*

April ducked into the tent and whispered, "It's getting hot. I'm shucking one of my petticoats."

"You are not, April. That's indecent."

"Mama lets me wear just two at home in the summertime."

Shaking her finger, Laurel whispered, "That's at home. This is out where someone might see you!"

"Like who?" April started to shimmy out of a row of white cotton ruffles.

"Yesterday Mr. Rutlidge showed up."

"He couldn't tear his gaze off of you and your pictures long enough to notice anything else in the world." April opened her trunk and shoved the petticoat inside. "And don't bother to deny it. I'd give up dessert for a month to have a man look at me that way."

Kate romped in. "Did you do it?" She stopped cold as a guilty expression crossed her face.

"Laurel told me not to, but I did anyway. Your skirt is dark. The sun won't shine through it, even if you're only wearing two. Go ahead," April urged.

"Kathryn Louise Chance," Laurel said, "when your mother was your age, she wore all three petticoats and every other proper layer even in the unbearable heat of the tropics."

"She was a missionary's daughter and had to serve as an example. I don't have to be an example. Besides, that was in the olden days."

Johnna tromped into the tent. "What's the hold up? Sun's gonna set afore we ever walk away from this here campsite."

"I don't want these girls out there unless they're decently attired."

Johnna pursed her lips. "I don't see nuthin' wrong."

"Laurel wants us to wear all three petticoats," Kate complained.

"Land o' Goshen." Johnna's eyes widened.

Oh, good. She'll talk sense into April and Kate.

"I've only been wearin' two the whole livelong trip. Ain't nobody seen anythin' wicked 'bout it, so I don't get what the fuss is about. Just shake a leg, else our brothers ain't gonna set aside any more days to take us on hikes!"

Shoulders drooping, Laurel waited for her cousins, then left the tent. *How can everything have gone so topsy-turvy?*

Chapter 9

"Hey, Rutlidge!"

Gabe halted Nessie and turned in the saddle. Dust churned under the hooves of the cavalry horses as the men rode across the distance to join him.

"Where's your packhorse? You camped nearby?"

"Not too far." Gabe hesitated for a moment. He'd already mentioned the cavalry to the Chances. They'd been more than clear about the welcome the men would receive. Then again, Gabe didn't exactly want these men around Laurel. *The girls. I mean the girls,* he quickly corrected himself.

"Thing have been quiet," Captain Wood said. He stretched in the saddle. "I'm going to veer us up toward the pastureland and oust the sheep again. Thousands of those dumb animals, and they're eating all the vegetation the indigenous animals need."

"Shore could tolerate a good mutton roast." One of the soldiers yanked on his uniform coat. "Need somethin' to keep my slats apart."

"I think we can do something about that," Gabe said.

"Oh?" Captain Wood grinned. "Did you go get provisions?"

Gabe shook his head. "Met up with some folks who are camping out here."

"They got extra grub?" The soldier perked up.

Gabe directed his words to the captain. "They're good people. You and your men can count on plenty to eat tonight."

"Lead on," Captain Wood ordered.

An empty campsite lay before them when they arrived. Gabe looked around, and the only signs of life were some squirrels frisking through the branches and pesky blue jays pecking at crumbs beneath the table. All of the horses were gone, and not a soul stirred. Thinking the girls might be in the tent, he called out, "Hello!"

No one answered.

Gabe didn't want to dismount. He'd not think to enter someone's home when they didn't answer the door, and tramping through an empty campsite felt like the same invasion. The fact that he'd brought ten uninvited guests only added to the strain.

"Hey. Ain't just men campin' here," one of the soldiers said. "Men don't bother with clotheslines or fancy stitched dish towels."

"They're ladies," Gabe gritted. "And you'll treat them accordingly."

"My men wouldn't think to do otherwise," Captain Wood said. He then ordered, "Dismount."

In short order, two men set up a rope corral a ways off from the one the Chance men had established. Gabe still hadn't dismounted. "River's that way. I'm going to water my horse."

The cavalrymen were in the process of mounting up when Ulysses came riding up with a long string of horses behind him. "Howdy!"

"Ulysses."

"Fine looking horses. I'm Captain Wood."

"Good to meet you. Ulysses MacPherson. They're Chance horses. None finer."

Gabe dismounted and helped Ulysses get the wet horses into the corral. "Looks like they played as much as they drank."

"That's a fact. Hot as it is, I reckoned they might like a swim in addition to a drink." Ulysses grinned. "Kept me from havin' to haul any water, too."

"Where are the others?"

"Most of 'em went on a hike. They're itchin' to try out that camera. Couple of the boys and me—we lazed around today. I left 'em at the river to swim off some dirt. Johnna told me afore they left this mornin' that iff'n the boys didn't clean up today, they wouldn't get fed tonight."

Gabe nodded. "I can hear her saying that. About dinner tonight. . ."

Ulysses squinted as he surveyed the soldiers. "I reckon these men are ready for decent vittles. Livin' in the saddle don't allow for carryin' any extras."

"You said it," one of the men agreed.

"Why don't y'all unsaddle and take yore horses for a swim?"

Captain Wood didn't crack a smile, but his voice took on an entertained tone, "Are you inviting our horses or us to supper?"

"Horses cain take care of 'emselves." Ulysses folded his arms across his chest. "But I ain't a-gonna account for what my sis'll say 'bout me lettin' scruffy men come to the table when she made that threat afore she left."

Gabe saw to his horse and made good use of a bar of soap. He hurried at the river, not wanting any of the men to get back to camp before he was there to watch out for Laurel and the girls. When he reached camp, Tanner and Paxton were hiking in from the other side. "You're back," he said.

Tanner nodded. "I could say the same thing. You took off early this morning."

"Yeah, I did." Gabe shrugged. He wasn't accustomed to informing others as to his whereabouts. "Where are the girls?"

"Driving Packard, Caleb, and Peter crazy, lollygagging along."

"Are they tired? Do I need to take horses to them?"

"Nah. They've gotta stop every five minutes to gawk." He caught sight of the new rope corral and saddles heaped by it.

"I met up with the cavalry."

"I wondered when we'd cross paths."

Tanner's bland acceptance left Gabe feeling better. If the women took the dinner guests half as well as the men did, things would be fine. *Then again, the men don't have to do the cooking. . .*

Gabe went to the fire pit. The park allowed visitors to chop and use deadwood, and someone had a good-sized stack of wood available. Kindling, logs, and his flint, and he started a fire. "Tanner, where are the coffeepots?"

"Couldn't say. Suppose I could dig 'round for 'em."

Ulysses pointed toward one of the buckboards. "They've been keepin' dishes and such in the crates on the back of that 'un. Tanner, why don't you tote some buckets down to the river. Send the boys back with 'em, and we'll start up a few pots."

A short time later, Kate's voice sounded from a distance. "Oh, I smell coffee!"

The men had been sitting around, jawing. Gabe and the cavalry all shot to their feet.

As soon as they rounded a bend in the path, Peter said, "Gals, looks like we got us some visitors."

"Really? Who?" April wiggled up beside him.

"United States Cavalry, miss," Captain Wood announced.

"You soldjer boys hungry?" Johnna asked.

"Yes'm." The enthusiasm behind that male chorus left everyone grinning.

"If you'll excuse us for a moment," Laurel said, "we'll freshen up and start cooking." She slipped into the tent.

Gabe walked to his saddlebag, then headed toward the tent. "Laurel?"

She stuck her head out of the flap. After a day of hiking, her hairpins had all skidded around, leaving her bun loose. Wisps of dark hair spun in tiny curls, framing her face. "Yes?"

All of a sudden, Gabe felt ridiculous. He'd gotten up early this morning and ridden clear to Wawona and back to buy these for her. But she needed them. He shoved two bars of soap at her. "Here. Use this. It won't attract insects like your other stuff."

She reached out and accepted them. "Thank you." Looking down at them, she said, "Ivory. Oh—I've heard of this. It's supposed to be very mild! Thank you."

He nodded. "It floats." *Why did I say that? I'm blathering like an idiot.*

"How fascinating!"

April walked up. "Soon as we freshen up, we'll have dinner going. I already put on the rice to boil. Hey—Ivory soap! I heard those bars don't sink."

"Let's find out." Laurel's smile at him made the whole trip worthwhile.

"Thank you for your thoughtfulness."

"It was nothing."

"Mmm. That was something," one of the cavalrymen said.

"There's plenty more," April said. "Help yourself."

"Don't mind if I do." He rose.

The captain handed over his mess tin. "Seconds for me, too." He turned back to April and Kate. "Best order I've given all week."

"These women can cook." Gabe's arm brushed against Laurel's.

The contact made her want to lean closer—as if it were possible. They were all crowded around the campfire. An enormous pot of rice sat on the table next to two other pots—one was empty now; the other soon would be, by the way the men ate with such gusto.

"April gets the credit." Laurel set down her fork and patted her cousin. "She's amazing in the kitchen."

"You all worked on the meal," Gabe said.

"It was nothing." April stirred the food on her plate. "It all came from cans and boxes."

"Nothing we ever make turns out like this," one of the soldiers grumbled.

"It's just canned chicken, a box of dehydrated vegetables, and Borden's condensed milk." April shrugged.

"And broth and seasonings," Kate tacked on. "You just dump it over rice."

Gabe forked up a bite. "Sure beats beef jerky."

"Anything is better than that," Laurel agreed.

"Somethin' else is ticklin' my nose," one of the men said.

"Yeah. Here. Hang onto this, will ya?" Johnna shoved her plate into his hands and knelt by the fire. Using the hem of her skirt as a hot pad, she turned a Dutch oven halfway around.

"I'll get this one." Laurel rose, and Gabe reached out to take her plate. She smiled her thanks, handed it off, and rotated the second Dutch oven.

As she took her seat and accepted her plate, Gabe's brows rose in silent question. "Dessert."

The right corner of his mouth kicked up. "I figured that much out. You ladies wouldn't let us near the table while you prepared it, so we're all wondering what it is."

"I say, we let 'em wonder awhile longer," Johnna said. "Pa always put for the notion that a man ought to be happy with what's on his plate and trust the Lord for whate'er would come next."

"Your daddy must not have had to survive on his own cooking for any length of time," one of the cavalrymen shot back.

Johnna wrinkled her sunburned nose. "Actually, my pa and two uncles et their own cookin' for a handful of years."

"Then when he said he trusted the Lord for whatever came next—assuming their cooking was anything like mine," Gabe said, "he must have meant whether they'd wind up with food poisoning."

While the others laughed, Laurel turned to him. "Your cooking is that abysmal?"

"Worse. I even manage to burn oatmeal and corn mush. I wouldn't mind learning a thing or two."

"I'd be happy to teach you."

"Great." He tilted his head toward the Dutch oven. "How about if we start with that stuff?"

"Mr. Rutlidge! Were you trying to play on my pity to make me reveal what's cooking?"

His eyes twinkled. "I'm wounded that you'd ask such a thing."

"He might be wounded, Sis," Pax said wryly, "but he's not denying it."

"I thought we were friends. Friends don't keep secrets."

Laurel couldn't hold back her giggles anymore. "Shame on you, Gabriel Rutlidge!"

"I'm shameless when it comes to good food. You have to take pity on me and all of these other men. We've been subsisting on our own cooking for so long, our taste buds went into hibernation. A grand meal like this jolted them awake."

April lifted both hands in surrender. "I can't stand it anymore. It's cobbler."

"Arghhh!" Johnna let her head drop back.

Kate clapped with glee. "I knew it!" She turned to Johnna. "Told you!"

Johnna nodded. "I'll do the dishes tonight."

"No, you won't." Gabe hefted another large bite. "You gals cooked up a feast. I'm willing to wash. Which of you men'll dry?"

"You're offering to wash dishes?" Laurel blinked in surprise.

"Sure. Why not?" He filled his mouth.

They managed to demolish all of supper and both apple cobblers. Laurel didn't know what to do with herself as men did the dishes. What was happening? Back home, the men never did dishes. For that matter, neither did the boys.

"Livin' on their own, I s'pose these men're used to takin' care of thangs," Johnna mused. "Shore is odd, seein' 'em do women's work."

Laurel nodded. "It makes me sad to think of them serving our country and eating so poorly. Let's plan a special breakfast."

Peter brought out his fiddle. One of the soldiers wheeled around. "A dance!"

Laurel and Johnna exchanged surprised looks. Before either could respond, Gabe barked, "No."

Chapter 10

Paxton, Caleb, and Peter were only a breath behind in the denial.

Gabe cleared his throat. "These ladies don't dance, but they sing like angels. Perhaps you could ask them for a song."

"We'll have a sing around the campfire," Caleb announced.

At suppertime, the soldiers had all vied to sit beside the women. Laurel noticed how her brothers and cousins managed to elbow their ways into sitting next to their sisters now. She wished Gabe could sit beside her again, but she said nothing.

After the second song, he sauntered over. Though a large man, his gait was nearly silent—yet she sensed his presence. He slapped Packard on the shoulder.

Pack twisted around. "Done with the dishes?"

"Yep."

Pack stood up and wandered over to the other side of the fire. Gabe took his place. He looked over her head at Paxton and held his gaze for a long moment, then glanced down at her and smiled.

She stumbled over the lyrics of the song and recovered, but for the rest of the evening, Laurel could barely contain her elation. Because her uncle Titus loved to play guitar so much, they often sang in the evening back home—but with her mother and five aunts as well as the younger boy's high voices, the harmony stayed balanced. With twenty-odd men and only four girls, the air vibrated with deep notes. Gabe's voice carried a rich timbre that warmed her clear down to her toes.

They sang "Oh! Susannah!" and "I Dream of Jeannie with the Light Brown Hair," then "Laura Lee." Kate tossed a little chip of wood into the fire and said, "You can tell the girls are outnumbered here. The men all keep suggesting songs with girl's names. Let's sing a hymn."

Gabe winked at Laurel and cleared his throat. She got the feeling he was up to some kind of prank. "What about 'Beautiful Valley of Eden'?"

"Oh, I like that one." Kate beamed. "It's more than fitting for where we are, too."

One of the soldiers chuckled. "I have a sister named Eden."

"My aunt's name is Eden, too," Gabe confessed.

"You're a rascal." Laurel ruined her scold by laughing.

"We should make him pay a forfeit," April declared.

"I concur," Captain Wood said. "Discipline is vital. The punishment should fit the crime. I recommend he sing that hymn solo."

Gabe rose. Folding his arms across his chest, he widened his stance. "Laurel shares the guilt. She knew I was up to something."

Her jaw dropped at his audacity.

"Then they'll sing a duet," the captain declared.

Extending his hand to her, Gabe invited, "M'lady."

Paxton nudged her. "Get going, Sis."

"I'm protesting my innocence." She took Gabe's hand and stood.

"Methinks the lady doth protest too much," Ulysses called from the other side of the fire.

"Oh, you and your Shakespeare," she said back.

"Beautiful valley of Eden!" Gabe began singing. He squeezed her hand.

She joined in, *"Sweet is thy noontide calm. . ."*

Peter didn't accompany them; they sang the hymn a cappella. Gabe didn't turn loose of her hand, and Laurel didn't pull away. Somehow, it just felt right for her hand to be enclosed in his strong, warm grasp. The unity she felt with him went beyond the blending of their voices—they were sharing the love of God and His wondrous creation. So much else felt topsy-turvy in her world, but this felt as solid and secure as anything she'd ever known.

Gabe woke to the smells of fresh coffee and wood smoke and the hushed whispers of women's voices and swishing skirts. He lay in his bedroll and relished those simple things. All around him, the Chance men and the cavalry formed blanket-covered lumps on the ground. The warm summer night hadn't required a fire, so they'd scattered about and bedded down after last night's music.

Gabe noted the Chance men had all managed to plop down closer to the tent than they had in the past. To his knowledge, there hadn't been any discussion about it—but there hadn't been any last night, either, when the horseman suggested a dance. These men showed a protectiveness that pleased Gabe. He didn't want Laurel or her cousins to be in any danger.

Not that the soldiers were dangerous. It had been an innocent suggestion last night—but Gabe didn't want those men spinning the women around and wearing them out. Back home, plenty of churches frowned upon dancing. Gabe wasn't sure where the Chances stood on that issue. Even if they considered it harmless, he figured a woman ought to be well acquainted with a man before he took her in his arms. He'd not even taken Laurel's hand into his until last evening. There was no way he'd allow any other buck to sweep her around to music.

The Chance men aren't the only ones being protective. He lay there and identified his Laurel's sweet voice as she and April discussed the breakfast menu. *My Laurel?*

Mine? He heaved a sigh. *Who am I kidding? I'm not just being protective; I'm being possessive. That gal hasn't tried a single coy move, yet she's beguiled me.*

But I don't want to get roped into any woman's world. Yosemite is my refuge. I need to back off and let this be a friendship. I can appreciate her company and artwork. When she leaves, she'll go back to her well-ordered world, and I'll still be free to roam at will. It's for the best.

He rolled over onto his side and opened his eyes. Peter MacPherson lay on his side, facing him. He inhaled deeply and rasped, "Ain't nuthin' better'n the smell of coffee in the mornin'."

"I agree."

"Ma always wakes Pa up with a cup. One of these days, I'm gonna find me a good woman who'll do the same for me."

Gabe crooked a brow. "That's pretty specific. Do you have a mere mortal in mind?"

Peter chortled and sat up. "I might, but I'm not sayin'. In my family, a man learns to keep a few things to himself. If he don't, he'll niver live past the teasin'."

Gabe sat up, shook out his boots, and yanked them on. "To my way of thinking, I'm better off to wake up and make my own coffee."

"Good Book says 'tisn't good for man to be alone." Peter stomped his foot to make it fit into the boot.

"Yes, but then God made Eve for Adam—a perfect fit. Adam didn't hold a question in his mind that they were intended for one another. The rest of us men—we have lots of women to choose from, and we don't have that same assurance of finding the perfect fit."

Peter shrugged. "I reckon no couple is a perfect fit at the start—it takes years of bumpin' along to rub each other smooth."

Gabe rose and folded his bedroll. All around him, men were waking and rising. All of them offered an opinion on marriage—all but Caleb seemed to think it was something far off in the future.

"Shore, some of you bucks are too wet 'hind the ears to do any courtin'," Johnna said. "And you soldjer boys ain't home, so no gal's gonna want a man who's married to his saddle. Others of you—well, I'm thinkin' God'll have His way sooner'n you expect. I'm gonna have me a good laugh when you get moon-eyed over some purdy l'il gal and change yore tune."

"She's saying that because she has Trevor wrapped around her little finger," Peter said.

"Watch what yore sayin'," Johnna said. "Trevor's goin' o'er to our place and holpin' with some of yore chores so's you could come on this trip."

"She's got you there," Pax teased.

Ulysses snapped Peter with his blanket. "Face it: Trevor's doing it so your ma and pa'll find favor with him. He's buildin' up the nerve to ask for Johnna's hand and figures it's smart to get on their good side."

"Ma and Pa only have a good side." Johnna shook a long spoon at them. "And Trevor's got a helpful spirit. Hit ain't worthy of you to fix motives to him."

Peter brushed by Gabe and muttered, "See? Toldja in my family, a smart man keeps his mouth closed."

"It's not just in your family—it's a sound rule for any man."

Gabe's resolve to keep his mouth full of food and empty of words lasted only until breakfast was ready. Plate heaping with flapjacks and bacon, he sat in the same place he'd occupied last night. When one of the cavalrymen came over to take the seat beside him, Gabe clipped out, "Miss Laurel will be sitting there."

"Then I'll sit on her other side."

Gabe nodded curtly and shoveled a bite in his mouth.

Five minutes later, Laurel walked away from the serving table with a plate of flapjacks. The cavalryman called out, "Miss Laurel, we've been saving a place for you over here."

Gabe couldn't decide whether to be embarrassed or grateful for that outburst.

Laurel smiled as she sauntered over. "I thank you, but I'm not ready to eat yet. We made plenty of the flapjacks. Would you care for more?"

"Don't have to ask me twice." The man's plate shot out, and Laurel expertly flipped two sizable flapjacks onto it.

She looked at Gabe.

"They're great. Thanks." He held out his plate and accepted a pair. "But I don't feel right about eating when you haven't yet."

Laurel smiled. "I'm rarely hungry in the morning. I often skip breakfast and stay out sketching or painting." She wended her way past a few more men and soon emptied that plate. After refilling the plate, she continued to serve seconds.

Kate wandered along in her wake with a jug of maple syrup and poured it for whoever wanted more, and Johnna did the same with coffee. April stayed by the fire, continuing to cook.

Caleb strode over and straddled a log by Gabe. He bent over and seemingly checked out the frayed hem of his britches as he asked in a low tone, "Do you think the captain would be offended if we offered some of our provender? We have plenty to spare."

"I'm sure he'd be grateful."

"You going to travel with us awhile, or do the girls need to set aside some grub for you, too?"

I'll be leaving as soon as breakfast is over. The words were right on the tip of his tongue. Gabe couldn't make any other decision. Only the syrup made the answer stick to the roof of his mouth, and once he washed it down with a gulp of coffee, he heard himself said, "Where are you going next?"

~

"What do you have there?"

Laurel didn't turn at the sound of Gabe's voice. She'd sensed his presence a few minutes ago. In the past week while he'd been camping with them, he always showed his thoughtfulness for her work by waiting silently until her brush or charcoal lifted from the paper. As she dabbed a tiny splotch of dark green on a tree, she said, "Another landscape. I must have painted hundreds of them since I've been here."

"Every one of them is beautiful in its own way." He moved to stand beside her.

"Thank you. As the weeks have gone by, I'm noticing the colors I use are changing. I'm using more dark green instead of the lighter tones. It's been a subtle shift, but the difference is still there."

"I don't doubt it. Springtime green is more yellow-y." He looked into the distance, then back at her picture. "It's the same, but it's not. How do you decide when to leave out a clump of trees like you did right there?"

Tilting her head to the side, she thought for a moment. "I knew I was doing it, but I didn't give much thought as to why. Now that you ask, it's because the picture would feel lopsided with more over here." She indicated where the trees belonged with the wooden tip of her brush.

"So you balanced it out."

She nodded. A slight breeze lifted the edge of the paper.

Gabe reached over and whistled under his breath. "When did you do this?"

"First thing this morning." She waited a second for the watercolor to finish drying, then leafed back for him to see the whole piece. "They were so beautiful."

"So the doe had twins. From what I've seen, that's quite common."

"I was afraid they'd move before I could capture them." Laurel looked at the sketch. "I'd like to paint them when I get home."

"It'll make a stunning picture."

She touched up one spot on the sketch. "I didn't know twins were common in deer. They don't happen much with the horses on our ranch, and when they do, the men practically pull their hair out."

"The foals don't survive?" Gabe asked softly.

"Daddy counts it a blessing when the mare and one of the foals survive. I can only think of three sets of twins that made it through."

"That's a pity."

"Kate's mare was a twin. Neither the mare nor the other foal survived. Our neighbor brought her over in hopes that my father and uncles might be able to get another mare to accept her. None of them would, but Kate hand-fed that foal and pulled her through. The only time I've ever seen Kate cry was that Christmas when her mother and father told her they'd bought the horse so she could keep it."

"That must have been when she was twelve."

Laurel gave him a surprised look. "How did you guess?"

"You mentioned once that the kids in your family receive a horse when they're twelve."

"You have a good memory. They're breaking the rule this summer. Cole, my youngest brother, is eleven. He and three of the others who are ten and eleven are all getting a horse. The plan is for them to master their animal so they can ride them here to Yosemite next summer."

Gabe straightened up. "So you'll be returning next year?"

"No." She sighed. "I'd love to, but we made a deal. The group that came this year will stay home and run the ranch next year while our parents and the younger kids come."

"That's some arrangement. Do you think you'll all be capable of keeping the place going?"

"I've thought about that." She flipped the tablet to a new sheet. "Grandma and her sons started that ranch when the boys were our ages. If they could do it, we can. We also have the MacPhersons next door, and they'll bail us out if we run into anything we can't handle."

"You're not afraid of hard work."

"Why should I be? God's blessed us with health and meets our needs. My aunt Lovejoy says it's only right that we meet Him halfway by baking that daily bread."

Gabe shifted his stance and looked away for a moment. "I wondered how you're set for supplies. I'm thinking of riding to Wawona to send off mail."

"April's the one to ask. She's kept track of the food."

"I meant art supplies, Laurel."

"Oh."

"I can't have you run out. Bridal Veil is next."

Mixing water in with the paint to lighten the tone of blue for the sky, she frowned. "I looked all through that store and don't recall seeing any tablets or pencils."

"I called that to Hutchings's attention the last time I was there. It never occurred to him to keep them in stock, but once I mentioned it, he promised to get some in. So—what do you need, and do you have any mail you'd like to send out?"

"Would you mind waiting while I write a quick letter? I'm sure others would love to send word home, too."

"That all depends."

She started to swirl her brush in water to rinse it out. "On what?"

"Your definition of quick." He plucked the glass from the easel and handed it to her. "My mother's idea of a short letter is ten pages." Collapsing the easel, he tacked on, "If that's your plan, I'll already be halfway to Wawona."

"I thought your horse was named Nessie. To make that kind of distance, you'd have to be on Pegasus."

"You've never seen her in a full-out run."

"Who's running?" Tobias asked.

"I am." Gabe started back to camp. "I aim to go to Wawona today."

"Any special reason why?"

Laurel gawked at her cousin. "Tobias, don't pry."

"I don't mind." Gabe shrugged. "They have a telephone there. It's my mother's birthday. I thought I'd give her a call."

"They have a telephone here?" Tobias marveled.

Unable to contain her amazement, Laurel asked, "Your mother owns a telephone?"

Gabe hitched a shoulder as if it were nothing.

"We don't even have telephone lines going through Reliable yet. I saw a telephone when I went to San Francisco this spring, but that was in a huge mercantile."

"I'll bet they're a lot more common in the big cities back East," Tobias mused.

Gabe scanned their surroundings. "The government was wise to set aside this national park. I hope they're smart enough not to let the modern world intrude. It would spoil the natural beauty to have a tangle of telephone lines, paved roads, and electric lights here."

"I can't see that happening." Laurel shook head. "The big cities barely have a touch of those things. It wouldn't make sense to run those services out this far."

"I dunno." Tobias grinned. "I saw a string of those electric lights in Sacramento. They make for an astonishing sight."

Gabe leaned the easel against the tent. "I'll take starlight over Yosemite over Broadway's Great White Way any night of the year."

"You've been to New York City?" Laurel squeaked.

"I've done a considerable amount of traveling."

"Have ya now?" Johnna tilted her head. "Like where?"

"Today, I'm going to Wawona." Gabe grinned at her. "I told Laurel I'd be happy to mail off letters, but you only have a little while to write them. You'd best get busy."

Caleb perked up. "Someone gimme some paper. I want to write to Greta."

April handed over some paper and teased, "After you're done giving her all of your love, tell her I love her, too."

A few minutes later, Paxton and Packard sauntered up to Laurel. "Give Mom and Dad our love, Sis."

She leveled them with a glare. "Each of you sit down and write at least a few lines."

"Aw, Sis—"

Pax looked downright smug. "Didn't bring any paper."

"Aren't we lucky I have plenty." Laurel handed each of them a piece of her stationery.

Packard shoved it back at her. "I'm not writing on paper that's all girly."

"Me, neither."

Laurel accepted the violet-bedecked stationery. "Okay." She paused for a moment, then pasted on an oh-so-innocent smile. "You may each take a sheet of my art paper. It's plain as can be, so I'm sure it won't offend your masculine sensibilities."

Paxton huffed and headed for the tablet still hanging from the easel. Packard stayed put and gave her a taunting grin.

"Did you need something?" Laurel asked.

"Nope. Just remember what Mom always says: 'Be careful what you ask for.'"

"What is that supposed to mean?"

"You want me to write, I'll write. . .just a few lines." His gaze shot off toward Gabe, then back at her. "I'm sure Mom and Dad will be very interested." He shoved his hands in his pockets and whistled as he walked toward Paxton.

Laurel stared at her brother's back in horror. Packard could be teasing, but he could also be telling the truth. Only what his version of the truth would be. . . well, that was unpredictable. Pack accepted a sheet of paper from Paxton and said something.

Paxton threw back his head and bellowed out a laugh.

"Yore brothers are up to no good," Johnna said as she took a place across the table from Laurel.

"At times like this, I remember why I was so glad the Chance girls have their own cabin." Laurel stared at her stationery and tried to figure out what to write. She'd planned to mention Gabe in her letter—now, she'd have to be careful what she wrote. Not knowing what her brothers intended to say only made it worse.

"You gonna let yore folks know a handsome young buck's brought you a courtin' gift?"

"What?" Her head shot up.

"Gabe brung you that fancy soap. Made a special trip just to fetch it for you." Johnna bobbed her head. "You done turned his head. Night after night, he sits a-side you. I reckon yore brothers'll spill the beans iff'n you don't."

Laurel leaned across the table and whispered, "Soap is not a courting gift."

"Thank what you want." Johnna shrugged. "Mind iff'n I use one of them fancy sheets of paper you brung?"

"Here." Laurel passed her several and pored over her letter. She'd already waxed poetic about the beauty of Yosemite and remarked on how well she'd taken to camping. Mentioning how the boys all went on climbs and she'd been drawing and painting ought to have been enough—but now, it wasn't.

What should I say about Gabe? If I say too much, Mama will read between the lines. If the boys make this out to be a courtship and I barely give him mention, Mama's going to have a conniption.

Steeling herself with a deep breath, Laurel started to write again. *We met an interesting gentleman named Gabriel Rutlidge. He's spent considerable time in Yosemite and gave us invaluable information so we have been able to use our time wisely. One night, he brought the cavalry to camp with us! He's spent a little over a week in our company now, and I traded some of my drawings for his Kodak camera.*

There. She'd devoted a whole paragraph to him. Not that it said much. But she really couldn't find anything more to say that wouldn't cause problems. *The truth of the matter is, I don't know how to explain how I feel. I barely know the man. I don't know what he does for a living, but I know how much he loves nature and Yosemite. He likes art and horses—and I know deep in my heart he likes me. He's kind to the other girls, but he's different with me. It's thrilling. But it's scary, too. He's from a big city back East. I never want to live anywhere but Chance Ranch. Nowhere else could ever feel like home.*

Johnna tapped her pencil on the tabletop and sighed. "Tryin' to describe what we've seen is harder'n talkin' Pa outta the last piece of rhubarb pie."

"You can tell them it's all breathtakingly beautiful, and we've taken a lot of photographs."

Perking up, Johnna nodded. "That'll tickle 'em sommat fierce. We'll have genuine photographic pitchers to show 'em onc't they come back from gettin' developed. I'll say you're paintin' up a storm, too. Thataway, they cain see what we've seen, and I don't have to trouble myself o'er trying to put hit all into words."

"I don't mean to be rude, but I'm going to rush you folks." Gabe started to saddle Nessie. "I plan to set out for Wawona in just a few minutes."

Laurel quickly scribbled, *I can't thank you enough for my easel. It's been wonderful. Mama, you'll want to borrow it when you come here next year. I love you dearly and miss you. God be with you all.*

"Anyone have an envelope?" Caleb waved his letter to Greta in the air.

"I brought several," Kate called back. "Come and get 'em."

Peter walked over and peered over Johnna's shoulder. "Tell Ma and Pa that I love 'em."

She flipped the paper over. "Write it yoreself." She flashed a smile at Laurel. "Hit'll mean more iff'n it comes from his own hand."

Laurel nodded as she folded her sheets and slid them into the envelope.

"Lookie thar. You already put a stamp on the envelope."

Handing Johnna another stamped envelope, Laurel smiled. "I can't take credit for that. It was Mama's idea."

Peter finished scribbling a few lines and set down his pencil. "Yore ma's done a fair share of travelin'. I reckon hit's one of them things she learnt along the way."

"Your mother travels?" Gabe asked as he walked up.

"In her younger days." Mama was still sensitive about having been a gambler's daughter with the attending footloose lifestyle. Though Laurel loved her mother and was proud of her, she didn't mention the cause out of respect for Mama's feelings. "Now Mama is content to live on the ranch and tend her garden. The only time she leaves is to go to San Francisco for her art shows."

"You'll have to hold a show of your own," Gabe said as he accepted letters. "But I get first pick before anyone else touches your pieces."

"You've seen everything she's done since she's been here," April pointed out.

"The trip's not over yet." He looked about. "Any more letters, or is this it?"

"Here's mine." Kate galloped up and handed hers to him. "Laurel, do you know what your brothers did?"

Dread iced her spine. "What?"

Chapter 11

Aw, c'mon, Kate," Pack moaned.

Kate folded her arms akimbo. "You tell her, or I will."

"I don't want to know!" Laurel blurted out. After Packard's threat earlier, she couldn't imagine having him embarrass her in front of Gabe.

"I do," Ulysses said.

A chorus of "Me, too's!" sounded.

Pack and Pax exchanged a look. Laurel felt heat creeping from her bosom to her hairline. When slow, rascally smiles quirked their mouths, she wanted to dive under the table.

Pax cleared his throat. "We. . .uh. . .used your art paper, like you said we could."

"They used pictures, not blank pages," Kate snapped.

"Just little ones—like a picture postcard," Pack hastily added. "You know the old saying—a picture is worth a thousand words. So I just wrote, 'This is where we are. Having a good time.'"

Laurel slumped and let out a shaky sigh.

"You what?" Gabe thundered.

Pax shrugged. "She's got hundreds of pictures. She won't miss a few."

Brows knit and face dark, Gabe widened his stance. "Your sister has a gift. You respect it."

"Gabe, thank you for liking my work—but it's okay. Really." Laurel patted his arm. "I should have thought to include pictures. Mama and Daddy will love to get a peek at what we're seeing. I don't begrudge my brothers a few little pictures."

Pax nodded. "Chances share."

Laurel flashed Gabe a smile. "Since it's your mother's birthday, why don't you choose a picture and mail it to her?"

He didn't even blink. "How much for the one you did of the poppies?"

"It's a gift!"

"I'm giving it, so I'm buying it."

"The man could teach stubborn to a mule," Johnna declared.

"Well?" Gabe prodded.

"Eggs," April said. "They have to be expensive up here, and we're almost out."

"Yes." Laurel gave him an exultant smile. "A dozen eggs. Can you get them?"

"You sell yourself short."

"You've never tasted April's sticky buns. She needs eggs to make them."

"Whoa." Peter wound his arm around April's shoulders and gave her a squeeze. "You'd make sticky buns?"

"I will if Gabe pays for Laurel's poppy picture with eggs."

Peter looked at Gabe. "I'd take it as a personal favor if you'd agree."

Laurel popped up. "I'll go get that picture."

Gabe halted her by wrapping his hand around her wrist. "Only," he said as he looked at everyone, "if Laurel gets first pick of the sticky buns."

Paxton slapped him on the back. "Being around us is rubbing off. We just might make a Chance outta you."

"You're going to scare him off," Laurel said.

Gabe crooked a brow. "Not a chance."

Balancing the keg across his thighs, Gabe rode back to camp. This was the second time he'd brought back a load of eggs. Packing them in straw this time was a whole lot lighter; last time, cornmeal buffered the precious eggs.

While at Wawona, he'd run into the Kibbies, who lived in the far northwestern portion of the park. They were some of the few legal residents of the land. Mr. Kibbie saw Laurel's picture of the poppies and fell in love with it. Unwilling to part with it, Gabe asked Laurel to make another. He'd ridden north from their current campsite by El Capitan to exchange the picture for more eggs.

Yesterday, he'd climbed El Capitan with six of the men. Today, the others were climbing with Caleb and Tobias's guidance. He had to give the Chances and MacPhersons credit; they never left their sisters on their own, even when they ached to explore.

Since he'd joined up with them, Gabe had put himself into the rotation to stay with the girls. It was supposed to work out to be every third day—but in actuality, he often helped plan a day's events to include a ride or hike in which the women could participate.

As he approached the campsite, Gabe looked at all the clothes fluttering on the line. His own spare shirts and britches hung among them. Since coming to Yosemite, he'd taken to swimming in his clothes to wash them. That technique worked well enough; but after yesterday's climb, they were filthy. Laurel had turned a fetching shade of pink when she told him to be sure to leave his laundry in the pile with everyone else's.

"Hey, Gabe!" Kate called to him as he drew closer. "There are still a few good hours left. Want to go fishing?"

"No." April shaded her eyes and looked up at him. "We don't need fish for supper."

"No use catching what we don't need," Gabe agreed as he ducked under the clotheslines and came fully into view.

Johnna's eyes narrowed. "That's some git-up you've got on 'round your boots."

"Johnna!" Laurel set down the shirt she'd been mending.

"Well, it is. Take a gander."

"Better still, how about you ladies unstrap me?" Gabe glanced off to one side. "Mrs. Kibbie thought you might appreciate some fresh cream. I put a marble in each jar, thinking the ride here might agitate it enough to churn a little butter, too."

"That was clever." Laurel reached up to take the keg from him.

"I'll hang onto this. If I swing my leg over Nessie, we're liable to lose cream, so I'll have to ask you to unwind the strips holding the jars to me." He kicked out of the stirrups, and the marbles in the jars rattled.

Kate started in on his right calf; Laurel bowed her head and began to work on his left. Kate grew impatient with the knots, pulled a pocketknife from her apron, and cut the jar loose while Laurel patiently plied the knots and let the cloth come free. Frowning, Kate remarked, "Those are some of the finest boots I've ever seen, but you need to take care of them. They're awful sorry-looking. Want to use some of my saddle soap?"

"I suppose I ought to. I'll be wearing freshly-washed clothes, so I may as well get cleaned up from tip to toes." He dismounted and settled the keg on the table. "April, I'll gladly polish your saddle and shoes if you'll make more of those sticky buns. You have plenty of eggs here."

"They're best when made with cream." She cast a quick look at Laurel. "But I might have to fight with my cousin for that. She's started to freckle and was bemoaning the fact that we didn't have any buttermilk here to fade them."

"Ever hear of anything so silly?" Johnna pried the lid off the keg. "Kate 'n' me've got a bumper crop of freckles. Neither of us never did a thang to banish 'em."

"Freckled or not, you're all lovely women."

Johnna shrugged. "I reckon if God put 'em thar, they b'long."

Laurel wrinkled her nose. "You and Kate were made with freckles. I'll believe God put yours there. Mine? I can't hold God responsible because I didn't wear my sunbonnet."

April let out a theatrical moan and made a shooing motion with her hands. "Gabe, run while you can. They're about to get into a theological discussion about God doing things or allowing stuff to happen."

"You mean you all don't agree on everything?" He stepped back. "I'm not trying to poke fun. I'm just surprised."

"We agree on the foundational truths," Laurel said. "But when it comes to some of the details, we interpret things differently."

"Happens all the time," Johnna declared. "Parson Abe back home said we cain let those opinions tear apart our church or we cain respect how each of us follows the Lord accordin' to the dictates of our hearts."

"When you boil it all down, the important thing is that we all belong to the family of God through the redeeming blood of Christ Jesus," Laurel said.

"Good. Now that you agree on that, I'm sending you back to your mending, and I'm making sticky buns." April started to roll up her sleeves.

Gabe found a shady spot, accepted Kate's saddle soap, and set to work. The girls chattered as they mended, but he purposefully turned the other way. He had a lot of thinking to do.

Back home, everyone at church was alike. He'd never once heard anyone accept the possibility of someone believing in the same God but viewing Him differently. God was God—unchanging, all-powerful. That much made sense. *And Jesus came to be a peacemaker because men messed up. That's what Laurel meant about the foundation. I agree with all of that. But I'm still not like them. They believe it, and it makes a difference in their lives. Me? Those things are just facts.*

"I can't decide whether to love you or hate you." Ulysses plopped down.

Gabe looked up from the boot he'd been rubbing.

"You brought eggs, so we're getting sticky buns. You coulda stopped there. But since you're tending your leather, the girls all think the rest of us ought to, too."

"I see." Gabe worked on another deep scuff.

Tanner plopped down next to Gabe and yanked off his boots. "I hear it was your idea for us to polish our boots." He glowered at Gabe. "They're going to get messed up again as soon as we put 'em back on."

Peter joined them. "I reckon we could all jist go barefoot. Ever notice in Genesis, when Adam 'n' Eve figgur out they're nekked, they make clothes, but there ain't no mention of shoes?" He stretched his bare feet out and wiggled his toes. "I'm thankin' God loves us too much to 'spect us to cram our poor feet into boots all day, ev'ry day."

Ulysses whooped and tossed a rag at Gabe. "Don't look so s'prised. You seen us walking 'round the campsite barefoot."

"I thought you left your boots here to keep them dry when you went down to draw water or bathe."

"Nah. Think on it: Shoes oughtta be for protection. When we're workin' or climbin', it makes sense to wear 'em. 'Round the house, a body ain't got cause to box in his feet."

Tanner knocked the dirt off his shoes. "They're not kidding. The MacPherson kids wear shoes in the winter and to church and school, but until they're old enough to do barnyard chores, nobody makes them wear shoes. Go over any evening in the summer, and the whole clan is barefoot."

"Nothin' beats walking in fresh grass. Always makes me think on the Twenty-third Psalm 'bout God letting me lie down in green pastures and leadin' me a-side still waters."

Peter nodded to himself. "It restores my soul."

Caleb wandered over. "Talk about restoring your soul. Could you believe the view from the top of El Capitan?"

"So you're back." Gabe looked up at him. "How did today's climb go?"

"Great!" Caleb grinned. "I took 'em up the exact same route you led us on yesterday. I'd climb that every day of my life if I could, just to have five minutes of the view. Someday I'd like to bring Greta here and let her see it, too."

"I've spent my share of time, standing atop all sorts of places here." Gabe let out a long, slow breath. "Being up there does something inside—the majesty of this place never fails to move me."

"Same feeling as kneeling at the altar," Tobias said.

I don't see how that can be. But I've never knelt at the altar, either.

Chapter 12

April," Gabe called from the knot of men over on the edge of the campsite, "I'm ready for your shoes."

"They won't fit you," she called back.

"Don't bother her," Peter said. "She's making sticky buns."

"He knows she's making sticky buns," Laurel told him. "He brought the eggs for them and promised to polish her shoes and saddle if she made a batch."

"Well, now, that changes thangs." Peter grabbed Gabe and hauled him over to the cooking table. "April, give up yore boots, or we'll take 'em off of you."

"This has nothing to do with you, Peter MacPherson." April turned away from him.

He grabbed her waist, spun her around, and lifted her onto the table. "Guess again. I aim to do one of the boots and stake a claim on some of them sticky buns."

Caleb elbowed his way over. "Take your hands off of my sister." He tilted her face up to his. "I'm doing the saddle, and I get first pick. Now give up your shoes."

"I already promised Gabe first pick." April couldn't stop laughing.

Laurel stood back and watched as the men all put on a show about squabbling over April's shoes and saddle so they could have more of her sticky buns. Though sweet as could be, April never managed to attract men or be the center of attention—and for once, she'd landed in the middle of their interest. Even if it was just her brothers and cousins, her blush tattled about how much she enjoyed it. Laurel decided to add to the fun. "Nobody's going to want the sticky buns if she messes with her shoes. You'll have to take them off for her."

"Laurel!" April shrieked.

"Well, you have flour all over your hands," Laurel said.

"No use protestin' modesty, neither. We all seen yore feet when you went wading," Johnna added.

"You boys get on with it." Laurel pulled on her apron. "April needs to hurry up and finish with those so I can start supper."

Caleb untied one of her boots and handed it off to Peter. Peter held it up. "Where's the rest of this boot? Looky how dinky this thang is."

"Well, it won't take us long to polish them," Gabe decided.

"You brought the eggs. You did your share." Tobias grabbed for the other.

Laurel laughed at Gabe's nonplussed expression and explained, "There'll be enough for everyone to have two, but there are always a few extra."

Gabe snatched the boot from Tobias.

"Hey!"

"I've tasted April's sticky buns." Gabe clutched it to his chest. "They're enough to make any man greedy."

"You're getting dirt ground into that shirt. It's expensive material, too." Johnna shook her head. "You men jest don't know how much quality fabric costs."

Gabe glanced down. "This would be about eight cents a yard in the East; eight and a half cents a yard on this coast."

"How did you know that?" Laurel asked.

"You mean he's right?" Ulysses gawked at Gabe.

Gabe shrugged. "Family business."

"Well, that makes me feel a whole lot better," Kate blurted out. "I've been worried about you."

"Worried?" Gabe's brows rose.

"Well, we couldn't come out and ask you what you do. You said you'd been loafing about Yosemite since springtime." Kate cleared her throat. "I couldn't make it all add up."

"You never asked."

Caleb folded his arms. "We don't. Code of the West is that a man might have shrugged off his past and deserves a clean slate. No one pries."

"I see." Gabe's brows knit for a moment. "There are things I wish weren't part of my slate, but they're nothing I'm ashamed of. My family owns a textile business back in Boston."

"Who's running it if you're here?" Tobias wondered.

"My brother, Stanford. Actually, before I left, I sold my half of it to him."

"You left a family business? Why?" Paxton looked at him in disbelief.

"I grew to hate it. I didn't want to choke myself wearing a tie all day long while dealing with people who told bald-faced lies just to make a better bargain. Almost all of the people in the community judge one another based on their financial worth. Stanford finds the whole affair rather amusing; I didn't want to be a part of it."

"So yore startin' out with a clean slate out here." Johnna nodded. "I cain understand that. Now you menfolk git back to yore boots. Dinner ain't gonna make itself."

"What're we having?" Calvin asked.

"Ham and seven-bean soup." Laurel started draining the water off the beans she'd put on to soak that morning. "Biscuits and honey."

"You were going to teach me to cook," Gabe said.

"I already mixed and soaked the beans." Laurel plunked the cauldron onto the table. "If you add a gallon and a half of water to this, it'll be about right."

"But you can't touch a thing until you change your shirt. No dirt around our food," April said as she hopped down from the table and started to sprinkle cinnamon and sugar on the dough.

Half an hour later, Gabe gave Laurel a boyish grin. "Cutting out biscuits with a glass is fun. I never imagined it was this easy."

"You're great with a cup." She smothered a smile. "But I'm not going to praise you for how you handle a rolling pin."

"That contraption hated me."

"Well, you practically snapped it in half."

"I was showing it who's boss." He started arranging the biscuits in the bottom of the greased Dutch oven.

"Oh, is that what you were doing?" April asked in an oh-so-innocent tone.

Gabe surveyed the pans of sticky buns she uncovered and muttered, "I'd say that no one likes a show-off, but in this instance, I'd be lying."

"Hey, Gabe." Tanner sauntered over. "Looks like you're the new biscuit expert."

"Don't say that until they're done baking and you've tasted one."

"We voted and decided to pull up stakes in the morning and head for Bridal Veil." Tanner paused and surveyed the table, then gave Gabe a cat-that-swallowed-the-canary smile. "That means you need to bake tomorrow's biscuits tonight."

"I'll take care of that," Laurel hastened to say.

Gabe looked at Laurel. "*We* will. You measure, I'll mix. You roll, and I'll cut."

Kate turned around from stirring the soup. "Johnna's already taking clothes off the line. I'll go help her pack up our stuff. Do you want me to leave out anything special, Laurel?"

"Not that I can think of." She let out a sigh.

"What's wrong?"

She gazed up at Gabe. "I'm glad to go on to Bridal Veil. From what you've said, I've been anticipating it a lot. I just hate the whole production of packing and pulling up stakes. Everyone's short-tempered on those mornings."

He nodded sagely, then ordered, "Don't do anything with these biscuits. I'll be back in a minute." Striding over toward Paxton and Caleb, he announced, "I have an idea."

April looked over at the men. "Gabe's getting flour all over his sides from propping his hands on his hips."

Johnna's arms were full of laundry, but she halted by the girls. "Puts me of a mind when Pa used to dust the babes with talc. Ended up a-wearin' more'n they did." She smiled. "Gotta like a man who ain't afeared of holpin' with the kitchen or the kids."

"Sis!" Caleb called. "How long before you'll have the sticky buns ready?"

"Twenty-five minutes," April called back as she started to put the first pan over the fire. "Why?"

"Gabe came up with a plan."

Gabe bustled back over. "We need to rush these biscuits. The men are going to pack everything they can, and half will travel on ahead to Bridal Veil. They'll pitch the second tent and set up camp. With the sun setting so late, it'll work. The rest of you will follow tomorrow at a more leisurely pace."

"Where will you be?"

He smiled at Laurel. "I'll go ahead, then come back and meet you in the middle."

"Oh, your plan worked wonderfully." Laurel rode into the new campsite at Gabe's side. "It's so nice to arrive and have the fire ring set up."

He nodded. "Some of the more seasoned scouts do that for wagon trains." He nudged Nessie into Laurel's dappled gray to force her to turn to the side. All day long, he'd waited to see Laurel's reaction to the view he'd revealed.

She didn't move or make a sound. Nessie stepped forward, and Gabe peered under the brim of Laurel's sunbonnet. Eyes wide and shimmering like pools of gold, she stared at the waterfall. Her mouth changed from a perfect O into a beatific smile. Unable to tear her gaze away, she reached out, touched his arm and whispered, "I've never seen anything this splendid."

He looked at the delighted flush on her cheeks, the delightful freckles speckling the bridge of her nose, and agreed, "I've never seen anything this splendid, either."

"Laurel!" Johnna hollered. "Lookie thar! Ain't that purdy 'nuff to make the angels weep?"

Laurel nodded.

Gabe leaned toward her. "Where do the MacPhersons come from?"

"Next door," Laurel said in a vague voice.

He chuckled. He'd never seen anyone so enraptured.

She turned toward him. "What's so funny?"

"I'm glad to see you're not disappointed in Bridal Veil."

Kate pulled up. "I know, I know. She's besotted. Johnna and I'll cook dinner. Go ahead and get out your sketchbook."

Laurel turned to her cousin. "Thank you."

"If," Kate tacked on, "You promise to do a sketch for our cabin. Don't you think it would be wonderful to hang a picture of that view by our back window?"

"I'm not going to be a gentleman." Gabe looked at her. "You'll have to wait your turn because Laurel promised to paint a watercolor of this for me."

"You all plan to sit ahorse for the rest of the day?" Tobias called over.

Gabe slid out of his saddle and helped Laurel dismount. Kate didn't wait for assistance. He gathered the reins. "I'll tend the horses. You ladies take a few minutes to get your bearings."

In no time at all, Laurel set up her easel and went to work. Absorbed in her art, she seemed oblivious to everyone's actions. All around her, the Chances were pitching the second tent, cooking, and hanging provisions from the trees. Her focus remained on the waterfall and on her easel.

Laurel didn't join everyone for the meal. April fixed her a plate, and Gabe swept it from her hands. "I'll take supper to her." Staying away from Laurel had taken all of his resolve, but he didn't want anything to disturb her. He wanted this picture to reflect what she saw. By now, she'd be close to done. It always fascinated him to watch as she put the finishing touches on her pieces.

"Ready to eat?" he asked quietly.

"Just a minute." Her hand moved deftly. "Okay." She started to rinse her brush.

"Step aside, sweetheart. Let me see."

Laurel moved.

It was his turn to fall silent. Gabe studied the watercolor in the waning light and knew he'd never be able to part with it.

"If it's not what you had in mind for your mother, I'll—"

"I want it. For myself. I've never considered myself a greedy man, Laurel, but I'm keeping this for my own and asking you to do another for Mom."

"You admitted to being greedy yesterday when it came to April's sticky buns."

Gabe grinned at her. "I've lived a deprived life. Twenty-four years without the culinary or artistic masterpieces of the Chance women. You aren't going to hold it against me, are you?"

She took her plate from him. "I suppose it would be churlish for me to be that way when you brought me supper."

He picked up his own fork and ate a bite of beans. "What do you women do to these? My beans never taste like this."

"Do you add molasses?"

"No. Just a lump of brown sugar if I happen to have some."

"Molasses is what makes brown sugar brown." She smiled. "When we go, I'll be sure to leave you a jar."

Gabe scowled. "Are you eager to go?"

Chapter 13

Laurel gazed off at the distance. "I miss my family, but I'm not ready to leave here. Chance Ranch has always been home, yet in my heart, I feel—this may sound silly—but from the moment I saw this place, I felt as if I'd come home."

"It's not silly. I understand. Since I arrived, I've felt Yosemite is where I belong."

They finished eating in companionable silence. Once done, Gabe offered, "I'll carry your easel back to your tent."

"Thank you. Here. I'll take your plate."

The next four days were the happiest of Laurel's life. Gabe rarely left her side. He kept her company as she sketched and painted to her heart's content. They rode or walked to several vantage points and took picnic lunches along. When they were alone, he'd call her sweetheart, and at night, by the campfire, he'd hold her hand.

Her brothers and cousins cast her entertained looks. At night in the tent, the girls teased her—but Laurel didn't mind. Gabe spoke of coming to visit Chance Ranch. Her heart soared.

Nothing had been said yet, but when they would break camp tomorrow, she assumed Gabe would ride along with them as they traversed the remainder of the park on their way home. They wanted to spend every precious moment they could together.

"Ready?" he asked after breakfast as he led their horses up.

"Yes." She hung a bag filled with her pastels and a sketch pad on her saddle.

"Up you go." He gave her waist a quick squeeze before lifting her into the saddle.

They rode about a mile away—within sight of the camp. Gabe was always mindful of her reputation, and Laurel appreciated that he'd not tried to pull her behind a tree and kiss her as some of the boys back home had attempted. She'd always felt a kiss should be something special between an engaged couple, and he'd not yet asked Daddy for permission to court her.

From the way Gabe acted around her and her brothers, Laurel felt sure he was bound and determined to pursue her. Her brothers obviously approved of him. Mama and Daddy would, too. He was honorable enough not to profess his love for her—but his eyes and the way he attended to her testified to the depth of his devotion. Mama always said waiting for the right man would be well worth it—and she'd been right. Gabe made Laurel's heart sing.

"How's this spot?" He halted the horses near a patch of grass. "Or would you rather be in the shade?"

"This is lovely. I brought my hat, so the morning sun is fine." She accepted his help in dismounting and for a brief moment, he drew her to himself in a tender embrace.

"I don't want to let you go," he said.

"I don't want to go," she whispered back.

He sighed and turned loose of her. In no time at all, they sat together on a blanket. Laurel sketched the waterfall and surrounding landscape, then turned her attention on Gabe. Her pencil moved over the new sheet, forming his general outline and features.

"Hey, what are you doing?"

"Dabbling." She bit her lip and continued. Capturing the essence of a person always challenged her. The slightest tilt of the head, the crook of a smile—the very nuances that conveyed personality made all the difference in the outcome. Other portraits she'd done had been for fun, but this one mattered. She wanted a picture of Gabe. Very few photographs were left on the camera, and she'd only taken one of him.

"Stop drawing me and do a self-portrait. I need one of you."

"I have a hard enough time drawing others. Drawing myself would be impossible."

"Use a mirror."

"It doesn't work that way." She continued to work on her sketch of him. Concentrating on his eyes, she said, "A portrait has to reflect the personality of the subject. I notice the little details like the impish gleam in eyes or the odd habits like walking with fisted hands. It's what makes a portrait look authentic, and I don't notice those things about myself."

"I'd take whatever you drew."

"You're not very picky." She used her gum eraser and rubbed out the edge of one of his eyebrows. "I'm not good at portraits, anyway."

"I disagree. I've seen the ones you've done of your brothers and cousins."

Shaking her head, Laurel asserted, "I'm better at nature—landscapes, flowers, animals. When it comes to humans, I'm mediocre." She glanced up at him and smiled. "I try to console myself with the fact that God started out with nature and man was His greatest creation."

"So you'll get better with practice?"

She shook her head. "Not appreciably. It's one of those things where I decided that though I want to be as much like my heavenly Father as I can be, that's one of the areas where I'll simply bow to His majesty."

"How do you do that?"

Laurel shrugged, "I try to concentrate on the areas where He gave me talent."

"No, that's not what I meant." Gabe looked at her intently. "I mean, how do you figure out what He wants of you? How do you bow before His majesty?" His brow furrowed. "It's all so nebulous."

"It's not always easy to determine what His will is and follow it." She drew in the details of the collar of Gabe's shirt and the buttons.

"Laurel."

Something in the tone of his voice caused her to set aside her pad. "Yes?"

"You and your family talk about God differently. I don't get it."

"What's different?"

He shrugged. "I can't put my finger on it. I go to church. We say grace at mealtime."

"Those are things you *do*," she said slowly. The conversation took her completely off guard. "Anyone can behave that way—they're actions. When God calls us to *be* Christians, we're to have a change of heart that transforms us."

"How do you hear Him when He calls?"

Laurel stared at Gabe and tried to disguise her utter surprise. All along, she'd assumed he was a Christian. He knew all of the hymns by heart. He was respectful at prayer time.

"Is something wrong?"

Yes, her heart screamed. *I've fallen in love with you, but you're not a Christian!* Laurel moistened her lips and prayed for wisdom. Finally, she looked at Gabe and invited, "Why don't you tell me about your relationship with the Lord?"

Gabe tented one knee and propped his bent arm against it. He thought for a moment and heaved a sigh. "I don't know. I mean, I guess I'm a Christian. I go to church. The other day when you said it all boiled down to thinking Jesus saved mankind from sin, I figure it's right. As for all the things you say about God and creation—I never really stopped to think about Him being responsible, but it had to get here somehow. So since I agree with you about God being the Creator and Jesus being the Savior, then we see eye-to-eye on the foundational matters."

Laurel's heart ached as he spoke. *How can I explain to him that logic and reasoning aren't the same as faithful acceptance and obedience?*

"It's just that all of you act. . ." He shrugged. "I can't describe it."

"We each have a personal relationship with the Lord. It's not just rational acknowledgment of the fact that He exists; we've made heartfelt commitments."

Gabe studied her intently.

"God created us with a need to commune with Him. He walked with Adam each evening in the Garden of Eden. When we sin, we separate ourselves from Him. There's an empty space in us until we are reconciled to Him through Christ Jesus. I think what you sense as a difference is that those of us who have accepted Christ and allowed Him to redeem us no longer seek to fill the void in our lives—He fills it to overflowing."

"My life is full."

Looking at him, Laurel asked softly, "Is it really?"

"Yes." He nodded emphatically. "I've never been happier than I am now. Between coming to Yosemite and meeting you, my life couldn't be any better."

"I appreciate the compliment," she said sadly. "But that's not enough."

"That doesn't make sense, sweetheart." He looked thoroughly confused.

"You want to walk by sight; I live by faith. You're looking for rock-solid proof, and I listen to my heart."

He lifted his hand in a what's-the-difference gesture. "I don't see that as such a problem. Even you said folks can believe differently and still get along. Isn't there some verse somewhere about all the different parts of the body? I guess you're the heart and I'm the brain."

"But when you accept Christ as your Savior, there is a transformation that takes place. You put off the old man and are renewed in His spirit. What difference has He made in you?"

"Why should there be a big change? I grew up in a home that taught values. I know the Ten Commandments and abide by them. Not to sound proud, but I'm a good man, Laurel. I thought you believed that."

"You are a good man, Gabe. I've never met a man as honest and kind and capable "

"Then what's the big deal?"

She looked down at the sketch she'd made of him. Touching it, she said, "I can draw or paint something that looks just like the real thing."

"Yes, you can. I admire that to no end."

"But it's still lacking something—it doesn't truly have the dimension, the spark of life." She looked at him. "Until we do as Christ said, are born again in the Spirit, we are missing that spark. To have Him dwelling within us gives life a completely new dimension and depth."

Gabe stared at her, but she knew he didn't comprehend what she was saying.

"I can use all sorts of tricks—by shading and using different lighting and colors, I can make a picture appear to have depth. But those are just illusions. You can attend church and sing hymns, pray, and live a virtuous life, but those are just representations, like a piece of art."

He reached over and brushed the tears off her cheeks. "Why are you crying?"

"You're missing the most precious thing in life. It breaks my heart."

"Sweetheart, I'd do anything in my power to make you happy. I can't lie to you, though. All of this baffles me. If it's a matter of me promising to read a Bible or something, I'd do it; but you said it's not just something a person does."

"So shall my word be that goeth forth out of my mouth: it shall not return unto me void, but it shall accomplish that which I please, and it shall prosper in the thing whereto I sent it." The verse in Isaiah went through Laurel's mind. She grasped Gabe's hand. "If I leave my Bible with you, do you promise to read it each day?"

"I wouldn't know where to start, but if you give me some advice, I will."

"Okay." She thought for a few minutes. "What about starting with a Psalm each morning and reading through the New Testament at night?"

He shrugged. "Fine. Only I already know all of the stories."

Laurel squeezed his hand. "Don't read the Bible like it's a collection of stories, Gabe. Why don't you read it like you're trying to get to know Jesus? Study what He does and says as if you were. . .interviewing him to be a business partner?"

He grinned. "That's a novel approach. I can see how it would make me look at Him in a different light." He reached up with his free hand and cupped her jaw. "So is everything better now, princess?"

Reaching up, she curled her fingers around his wrist and pulled his hand back down. Holding both of his hands, she looked into his eyes and barely managed to whisper, "No."

Chapter 14

"No?" Gabe scowled. "What's wrong?"

Her beautiful eyes filled with tears again. "I. . .made a terrible mistake."

"What's that supposed to mean?"

"I let my feelings get ahead of me. You're so special, Gabriel."

"I feel that way about you, too, Laurel."

"But I can't let this go any further. We aren't supposed to judge one another, but I did just that. I watched you and assumed you were a believer. Until you give your heart and soul to Jesus, all I can give you is my friendship."

"Friendship?" The word tore from his chest in a low bellow. "I'm way past feeling like a friend to you. I—"

"No." She halted the words by pressing her shaking fingers to his lips. "We're going to be apart from one another. We both have a lot of thinking to do. I know deep in my heart what the Lord's will is. I trust you to do as you promised—to read the Bible and study the character of Christ."

"But what does that have to do with you and me—with us?" He laced his fingers with hers and held tight.

Laurel bowed her head. "We haven't spoken about a future. Forgive me if I misspeak, but there's more to love than just the blending of two hands and hearts." She seemed to struggle to find the right words. "For Christians, the blending of their souls is the most important thing of all. You and I—we couldn't ask God's blessing if we weren't of one accord."

"Hold on a minute. It's not like I'm one of those Chinese Buddhists or anything foreign like that. I told you: I agree about God and Jesus."

Laurel looked up at him. He couldn't interpret the emotions shimmering in her eyes. "You agree in your head. Let's see after you read the Bible if you agree in your heart."

He didn't want to let her slip away. Given time, Gabe felt sure he'd be able to allay her concerns. Rather than allow her to walk away and close off her heart completely, he grasped at the one chance she'd left open. "I'll read, princess. Every morning and evening."

That evening, she handed him her Bible. He studied the worn leather at the edges and gave her an amused look. "Well used, huh?"

She nodded.

"I'll make sure I keep up the tradition."

Laurel gave him the first smile she'd summoned since their discussion that afternoon. "Thank you."

"Hey, Sis!" Paxton hollered.

Laurel turned. "Yes?"

"April's begging to stop for a while tomorrow so she can wade in Bridal Veil Creek."

"I'll fish while we're there," Kate volunteered.

"We'll have to set out earlier than we planned to do that." Pax rested his hands on his hips. "So you need to pack up what you can now so we can load up some stuff tonight."

"And I thought he was going to ask us to make the biscuits tonight," Gabe murmured.

"I heard that," Johnna singsonged. She merrily announced, "Gabe just volunteered to help bake biscuits tonight!"

Rather than have their usual nighttime campfire, they all worked to get chores done in advance. Standing alongside Laurel and making biscuits was bittersweet—they did so well together, yet he sensed a gulf between them that he couldn't bridge. As Gabe fell asleep that night, a tune kept running through his mind. He told himself it was just that they hadn't had time to sing as they usually did, but the lyrics to "God Is My Strong Salvation" played over and over again.

At dawn, Gabe got up after a restless night. He took Laurel's Bible and stalked off for some privacy. She'd recommended he start reading in Psalms. *Psalms. I always liked them. David was quite a man. He loved nature the way I do.* Gabe settled down, leafed toward the middle of the Bible and located Psalms.

"Blessed is the man that walketh not in the counsel of the ungodly. . ."

Gabe jolted at the contents of that short chapter. It didn't mince any words. Flat-out, it compared the righteous and the unrighteous. Laurel was like the third verse—like a tree planted by water. Gabe got the prickly feeling he didn't quite measure up. The fifth verse said sinners shouldn't stand in the congregation of the righteous. *That's what Laurel was saying yesterday—that we don't belong together if I'm not standing right with the Lord.*

Gabe shut the Bible. Everyone at the campsite was already stirring. He went back, took care of his bedroll, and got his horses ready. They all paused briefly for hot coffee, cold biscuits, and a slab of ham. Gabe helped lift trunks and crates into the buckboards, then drew Laurel off to the side.

She wore her pale pink dress—his favorite. The silly thing was far too fancy for camping, but the ruffles and color suited her. Her sunbonnet hung down her back, and the ribbons pulled a little at her slender throat. Her brows winged upward over her eyes, showing slight surprise. She'd never been more beautiful.

Gabe couldn't resist reaching up and playing with one of the tiny curls that wisped by her temple. "Sweetheart, I'm going to leave you today."

Her eyes darkened with pain, and her mouth opened slightly, then shut. She bowed her head.

He tilted her face back up to his. Tears shimmered in her eyes, turning them to molten gold. The sight nearly brought him to his knees. "I read the Bible this morning."

The corners of her mouth bowed upward, but she was still blinking back tears.

"I'm going away on my own to do some reading and thinking." He cleared his throat. "Until I make some decisions, it's not right for us to be together. I can't help how I feel about you. I don't want to help how I feel about you. Believe me, doing the right thing hasn't ever been this hard."

"I–I'll pack you some food."

"No need. I have the supplies I originally rode in with."

To his everlasting surprise, Laurel went up on her tiptoes and brushed a fleeting kiss on his cheek. "God go with you."

"They're home!" Cole shouted over by the barn as the wagons pulled in.

Laurel wearily accepted Daddy's help to dismount and gave him a hug. Mama hurried over and enveloped her in a hug. "Oh, we missed you!"

"We missed you, too," Laurel said. All around her, brothers, cousins, aunts, and uncles were embracing and slapping one another on the shoulder. They'd always been a demonstrative family, and after such a prolonged absence, the emotions flowed freely. But Laurel tried hard to keep her emotions in check. The past five days had tested her to the limit.

"Sis!" Perry yanked on her skirt. "You've gotta come see my horse!"

Laurel smiled down at him. "Tell you what: I have one last picture on a real Kodak camera. I'll take your picture sitting on him."

"Wow!" He wheeled around and shouted, "Cole! My sister gots a camera. She's gonna take my picture on Siddy."

"I wanna pitcher of me on Quartz!" Cole yelled.

"City? What kind of name is that for a horse?" Pax asked as he grabbed their little brother and swung him in the air.

"His real name is Obsidian, but I call him Siddy. He's black."

Caleb finished giving everyone a hug, then mounted his horse again. "I'm going to see Greta."

Aunt Miriam yanked his sleeve. "Not until you wash up."

"Not till you see my horse," Cole protested.

Uncle Gideon looked up at his son. "Caleb, family comes first."

Obviously peeved, Caleb dismounted. "Greta is going to be family—even if you're making us wait forever."

Wanting to cover the awkward silence, Laurel reached into the basket in the buckboard to fetch the camera and said, "I only have one picture left. You young men will have to all line up together with your horses."

As the boys scrambled to comply, Laurel glanced around. Chance Ranch still looked the same, but it felt different. The little boys had turned into—well, not men, but they'd matured significantly. The ranch had always seemed so big, and as ranches went, it was; but compared to the enormous vistas of Yosemite, home felt. . .snug.

"I can hardly wait to see your drawings and paintings," Mama said. "The ones the boys sent home are enchanting."

Daddy nudged up on Laurel's other side. He dipped his head and rumbled, "But we want to hear more about this Rutlidge fellow."

Laurel almost dropped the camera. As soon as she took the picture, Daddy swiped the camera from her, shoved it into Packard's hands, and steered Laurel toward his cabin. Mama had hold of her other arm.

"What did Laurel do?" Craig asked loudly.

"Hush," someone said as her parents marched her up the porch and shut the door.

Laurel wilted into the nearest chair. Daddy paced until Mama stopped him. He turned and glowered at Laurel. "Did that scoundrel steal your heart?"

"He's not a scoundrel."

Mama's eyes narrowed. "But your heart—"

Knotting her hands in her lap Laurel said sadly, "I love him. He's a good man—just ask any of the boys."

"So you're just upset at leaving him behind," Mama said in a tentative tone.

Laurel shook her head. "He knows about God; he just doesn't know God. It's all a rational thing to him. He goes to church and sings the hymns, but—"

"Oh, Laurel," Mama groaned.

Daddy sighed. "Honey, you know better than to keep company with a man who isn't walking with the Lord."

She nodded. "As soon as I realized it, I drew a line." She paused and tried to swallow back the ball in her throat. Her nose and eyes stung from trying to hold back the tears. "But I was too late. I left my Bible with him. He promised to read it."

Daddy came close and pulled her to himself. Laurel rested her cheek against his shirt and gave in to the need to weep. When she finally calmed down, Daddy handed her his bandana. She wiped her face and held the soggy cloth in clenched fists.

"Honey, I know the pain you're enduring. Your mama didn't know the Lord when she came to Chance Ranch. Caring turned into love before I even realized what was happening—but God's Word is clear about His children being equally yoked."

"I know," Laurel said in a tight voice.

"I'll stand beside you in prayer. If Rutlidge seeks to find the truth, it's all right there in the Bible. We'll ask the Lord to open his eyes and heart." He stroked her back. "In the end, Rutlidge has to make his own decision."

Mama reached out and held Laurel's hand. "It wasn't until I lived among your daddy and Aunt Miriam and the others that I finally saw Christianity in action. Being exposed to those whose lives were dedicated to God made me see the lack in my own heart. Maybe the reason you all went to Yosemite was for the Lord to use you to set Gabriel Rutlidge on the path of salvation."

"He talked about coming here, but that was before I told him we could only be friends. I don't know what he'll do now."

Daddy chuckled.

"It's not funny, Daddy!" she wailed.

"Oh yes, it is." Daddy grinned at her. "Honey, no man in his right mind would let you go. He's going to pore over that Bible and show up here sooner than you think. When he does, he's bound to have a bunch of questions. Until the spiritual ones are answered, you and he aren't allowed to so much as take a walk together alone. A man who is seeking needs to keep his heart and mind on spiritual matters, and you make for one very pretty distraction."

A knock sounded on the door. Mama went to answer it. Every one of Laurel's aunts and uncles traipsed in. She knew from their expressions that they'd been told about her and Gabe.

Aunt Lovejoy bustled over and enveloped Laurel in a hug. "We love you and are so proud of you. Puttin' Jesus afore the romantic desires of yore heart—now that takes a mighty strong spirit."

"We've come to pray over Laurel," Uncle Gideon said.

Laurel looked up at her family and whispered, "I'd cherish your prayers, but Gabriel needs them more."

"God never limits our prayers," Aunt Miriam said.

"That's right. We'll pray for both of you," Uncle Titus declared.

Surrounded by their caring and wisdom, Laurel bowed her head.

Chapter 15

Seven days. Had it only been one week since he rode off and left Laurel? Gabe scalded his mouth with a taste of poorly brewed coffee and winced. Nothing was right. He couldn't fix a thing that tasted decent. The past two nights, he'd gotten rained on. Yosemite's beauty no longer stirred him. Loneliness swamped him. When he closed his eyes, he saw Laurel—her arms outstretched as she pressed her precious Bible into his hands. And that Bible. He couldn't ignore it.

How could one solitary object repel and yet draw a man all at the same time? Gabe told himself that he read the Good Book because it was important to Laurel. He'd promised her he'd read passages each morning and evening. Most of the time, he spent the better part of his day reading it, too—even though he didn't want to.

He'd decided to approach the New Testament as Laurel suggested: Instead of thinking of the Good Book as a collection of stories, he took it on as a way to conduct a job interview. Did he want to partner up with Jesus? Laurel told him Jesus would gladly accept him at any time.

Captain Wood rode up. "Rutlidge."

"Wood." He nodded.

"What've you got there? A Bible?" The captain nodded. "Lot of power and wisdom in those pages."

Gabe carefully closed the cover and rose. "How're things going?"

The captain crossed his wrists over his saddle horn and heaved a sigh. "I'm still fighting the sheep and folks who're trying to make a fast buck by starting up businesses. Some bears raided a tent restaurant last night. The idiots left food in crates right on the ground."

"That's just begging for trouble."

Captain Wood nodded. He squinted off at Gabe's horses, then back at Gabe. "One of our mounts broke a leg in a gopher hole yesterday. I don't have any spares."

"I know a heavy-handed hint when I hear one."

"How much do you want for yours?"

"Tennessee Walker's not for sale. The pack horse it just that—a pack horse."

"I've seen him." The captain cast another assessing glance at the gelding. "He still steps lively and keeps pace with your Walker. Might not exactly be up to our usual standards, but he'll more than do in a pinch."

"Better a pack horse than shanks' mare?"

"Exactly. Too bad those Chance folks aren't still here. They had plenty of fine horseflesh, and the U.S. Cavalry has an account with them. Would have solved my problems neatly."

"They left awhile back." Gabe didn't let on that he'd been counting the days.

Captain Wood eased back in his saddle. "I know. They stopped by our headquarters in Wawona and left food behind for my men."

Thinking aloud, Gabe said, "Not that I have all that much along with me, but I won't be able to carry it all on Nessie. Can you keep some gear for me at your headquarters until I come back with another pack horse?"

"You're going to go buy another?" Captain Wood leaned forward. "I could commission you to obtain a few mounts."

The request was reasonable enough. Gabe didn't mind pitching in and helping. "Sorry. I don't know how long I'll be." Once the words exited his mouth, he could scarcely credit he'd spoken them. Still, in his heart he knew they were right. He wasn't worth a plugged nickel here.

A slow smile spread across Wood's face. "Are you going after a horse, or are you chasing that comely Chance girl?"

The Bible felt strangely heavy in his hand. Gabe wanted to declare he was riding off to claim Laurel, but he couldn't. The weight in his hand didn't compare with the stone in his heart. He cleared his throat. "To be frank, I don't know what the future holds."

Chance Ranch, the sign over the gate proclaimed. Gabe let himself onto the property, then leaned over in the saddle to make sure he latched the gate securely. For as far as he could see, and as far as he'd ridden for the past hour, strong fencing stretched across the property line. Laurel and the rest of her group hadn't let on that the family business extended to such an expansive scope.

A wry smile twisted his face. He hadn't let on that his family possessed any great wealth, either. Some things shouldn't figure into friendships and love.

Way off in the distance, he could see several rooftops. Clicking his tongue, he urged Nessie in that direction. Gabe really wanted to take her to a full gallop and reach Laurel without waiting another moment. It took all of his self-control to keep going at a sedate pace.

A huge complex came into view. A barn, a pair of sizable stables, and multiple cabins reminded him of how Laurel said all of the Chances lived together on the ranch. The place was a hive of activity. Horses frolicked in the pasture; men gathered around a corral where boys were training mounts. Chickens pecked the ground. One clump of women worked a garden while the other busily hung laundry on the clothesline.

"Stop that!" Laurel's cry from a far porch captured his attention.

Two young men Gabe didn't recognize threw punches at one another. Laurel shouted at them again, but they ignored her and continued to brawl. She lifted a nearby bucket and doused them with water. They stopped cold, and she threw down the bucket. "Both of you go home. There was no excuse for this."

Gabe sat frozen in his saddle. Was Laurel allowing other men to pay her court? The very thought sickened him. At the same time, a visceral desire to pound the daylights out of both of those boys swamped him. Laurel was his.

She made a shooing motion. "You both need to grow up. Now saddle up. I don't want to see either of you again." Her words pleased Gabe. He knew her well enough to be certain she'd meant every bit of what she said. Dressed in her yellow dress, she practically shimmered in the sunlight. As if she could feel his gaze on her, she turned toward him and lifted her hand to shade her eyes. He knew the minute she spied him. Grabbing handfuls of her skirts, she ran toward him.

Gabe set Nessie into a gallop, then pulled her to a halt and vaulted from the saddle as he neared Laurel. Arms wide open, he met her in the middle of the road. Her eyes shimmered with joy as she cried, "You came!"

Gabe wrapped his arms about her and swung her in a circle. *Let those other young bucks witness this reunion. It's time they learned Laurel belongs to me.*

Her arms wound around his neck, and she repeated breathlessly, "You came!"

Having come from a sedate home, he'd never received such a greeting. His heart swelled. "Of course I did. Nothing could keep me away."

"I take it you're Gabriel Rutlidge," someone said.

Gabe tore his gaze away from Laurel and discovered a huge clan surrounding them. He wasn't sure who'd spoken. "I am."

Laurel wiggled free of his hold and laughed nervously. "Mama, Daddy, this is Gabe. Gabe, these are my parents, Delilah and Paul Chance."

Gabe accepted Paul's outstretched hand and shook it. "Sir." He smiled at Mrs. Chance. "Ma'am, now I know where Laurel got her beautiful eyes and hair from."

As the two callers saddled up and slinked off, Laurel proceeded to introduce him to all of her aunts and uncles. Gideon, the eldest, told him, "We don't expect you to remember all of our names for a while."

"Thank you, Mr. Chance. You're a sizable family."

"None of the mister or missus stuff, either. We all answer to Chance, so you'll confuse us. We don't figure you mean any disrespect by addressing us by our given names."

"You can bunk down with us guys," Caleb offered.

"Thank you."

"Your mare's a beauty," another man said. "I'll take her to the stable and settle her in while you get situated."

Laurel patted Gabe's arm. "Uncle Bryce is itching to take a closer look at Nessie."

"We haven't had any Tennessee Walkers on the ranch," Bryce grumbled. "Can't fault a man for wanting to appreciate fine horseflesh."

"Judging from the horses everyone rode in Yosemite, I'd say the Chances know plenty about fine horseflesh." Gabe cast a look about. "And from what I see, those mounts were only a small sample of what you have on hand."

"I gotta new horse—my very own!"

"This is Perry, my brother," Laurel said.

"Congratulations, little man." Gabe reached out to shake Perry's hand. The boy gaped for a second, then puffed out his scrawny chest and shook hands.

"I cain't decide whether he's congratulatin' Perry on his horse or about bein' Laurel's brother," one aunt said to the other.

"Both," Gabe said quickly. "I'd say Perry's a very fortunate young man."

"Man's got hisself a silver tongue." The woman shook her finger at Laurel. "Gotta beware of them charmin' ones. We're gonna let him haul his gear to the boy's cabin. You 'n' me and yore mama need to finish up in the garden, else we won't have beans or salad for supper."

"Mama and I can see to that, Aunt Daisy. We're almost done. I'm sure Aunt Lovejoy could use your help with her herbs."

"Now that's a fact." A birdlike woman laced her arm through Daisy's and started to hobble off.

Gideon frowned. "Dan, Lovejoy's limping again."

"I know." Daniel grimaced. "She made me promise not to go fetch Polly or Eric."

"Polly's his daughter, and Eric is her husband," Laurel murmured. "He's a doctor, and they live in town. Polly's a healer, too."

Gabe watched as the Chance men all exchanged looks. One rocked back and forth on his heels. "Dan, you keep your word. You shouldn't fetch your daughter or son-in-law. Me? Well, I'm of the notion I need to send Tanner into town on an errand."

Caleb grinned. "No, no. I'd be happy to go, Uncle Titus. While I'm there, I just might stop in to see Polly and Eric, then I can swing by and see Greta."

April whirled around. "Stop by the kitchen before you go! I'll have food ready!"

Everyone started to disperse, and Laurel laughed. "Caleb will send back either

Polly or Eric, but since neither of them can cook worth a hoot, we take mercy and send meals to them whenever someone goes to town. As much as Caleb spoke about Greta while we were gone, I presume you understand he's adept at making excuses to see her."

"This is quite some family." Gabe watched as Paxton and Caleb took his belongings off Nessie, and Bryce led the mare away.

"It is." A warm hand clamped down on his shoulder. Laurel's father nodded. "And we all take care of one another. Laurel, honey, you go back to the garden with your mama."

"Yes, Daddy." Laurel gave Gabe a shaky smile and walked away.

Paul Chance hadn't broken contact yet. He stared Gabe straight in the eyes. "Son, you're more than welcome here. Every single one of our young folks speaks highly of you. Feel free to stay as long as you want, but I'm going to have to speak frankly with you."

"I wouldn't have it any other way."

"Good. From the way my daughter raced into your arms and the way you look at her, it's plain to see feelings run deep. But that's a problem because I won't give my blessing for her to be with a man who isn't committed to walking with the Lord."

"Laurel's already made it clear to me." In the excitement of their reunion, Gabe had lost sight of that fact. Now the reality of the gulf between them loomed like an impossibility.

"She tells me you've attended church and are reading her Bible. Both are good things. I'd like to see you continue on with those. I'm not going to push or preach. None of us will. A man has to make his mind up about spiritual matters without being coaxed or coerced. Just know that if you have questions or concerns, you can come to any of us—well, anyone except Laurel."

"Are you saying I'm not to speak with her at all?"

"No. You're welcome to sit by her at the table, at devotions, and at church. If others are around, you can be, too."

Memories of the early mornings when they'd been off by themselves as she painted flashed through Gabe's mind. "When she's working on her art?"

"She and her mama often slip off together." Paul Chance didn't yield an inch. He let go and folded his arms across his chest. "I fell for my wife before she was a believer. I would have done anything to spare my daughter from being torn by the same predicament. It's too late now, but I'm going to guard her from further heartbreak as best I can."

Rooted to the ground, Gabe fought with himself. He wanted to be here; for Laurel's sake, it was best for him to leave. How could their love be wrong when they both felt it so strongly? She'd flown to him. Her own father acknowledged the depth of their feelings—but he'd also said this was breaking Laurel's heart, and Gabe remembered how Laurel had wept.

"Stay," Paul urged quietly, as if he'd sensed every thought running through Gabe's mind. "Leaving won't resolve anything. The answers you're seeking can be found. What you need is time."

"Laurel—"

A grin wide as Yosemite's meadows split across Paul's face. "Son, the fact that you're willing to put her needs above your own wants speaks volumes."

Caleb rode up. "I'm headed for town. Either of you need anything?"

Paul shook his head.

Gabe shoved his hand into his pocket and yanked out a wad of bills. He peeled off one and shoved it at Caleb. "Yeah. Laurel cherishes her Bible, and I want to give hers back to her. Could you get me a Bible of my own?"

Chapter 16

Gabe sat opposite Laurel at the breakfast table. Packard and Paxton bracketed him. While he turned to accept the platter of flapjacks, Pax stole the bacon from his plate. Four days ago, Laurel would have said something. Today she stayed silent and watched. Gabe had proven he could take care of himself.

Sure enough, a moment later when Paxton turned to help his little brother serve up the flapjacks, Gabe poured syrup into Paxton's coffee mug. He winked at Laurel and jerked the pitcher back to drizzle syrup on his own pancakes. A moment later, he lifted the coffeepot and filled Laurel's mug, Paxton's, Pack's, and his own. Laurel noticed it only took a small splash to fill Paxton's mug to the brim.

"Great bacon," Pax gloated as he ate a rasher. "Aunt Daisy, you sure know how to season and smoke a hog."

"Thankee." Aunt Daisy beamed at him.

"Great coffee," Gabe said after taking a big gulp.

"Yeah, our women sure can brew a fine cup," Pax agreed as he lifted his mug. He took a swig, and his eyes grew huge as he choked on it.

Gabe pounded Pax on the back. "Go down the wrong pipe?"

"Pax, how often have I told you to slow down?" Mama tsked. "Laurel, here. Pass the bacon on down to Gabe. He didn't get any."

Laurel turned to take the platter from Mama and tamped down a giggle. The sparkle in Mama's eyes proved she'd witnessed the whole exchange. Gabe grinned at them. "Thank you. Don't mind if I do have some, especially since Pax gave Daisy's bacon such a glowing endorsement."

Pax gave Gabe a wary look. "I thought you said you only have one brother."

"That's right." Gabe helped himself to the bacon. "Stanford. He was quite a rascal in his younger days. Kept me on my toes."

"I'm sure you gave as good as you got," Pax grumbled.

"Of course I did." Gabe paused to eat another bite of bacon with relish, then added smugly, "It was a matter of honor."

Laurel and her mother exchanged a look, and both of them lost their self-control. They burst into laughter.

Gabe elbowed Pax and feigned ignorance. "What got into them?"

Pax gave him a smirk. "Who knows?"

"Hey, Pax," Cole called from the end of the table, "pass me the syrup."

"Sure." Pax lifted his coffee mug and handed it to Gabe. "Cole wants this."

Packard swiped the mug from Gabe and sent it on down. "If you two don't quit goofing off, we'll be late for church."

Cole protested, "I want syrup, not coffee!"

Kate accepted the mug, glanced down the table at Laurel, who still couldn't quell her laughter. Kate peeped in the mug, took a long drink, then snickered as she upended the mug over Cole's plate. Syrup ran out onto his pancakes.

Uncle Titus grabbed the cup and held it up in a cheering motion toward Gabe before emptying the contents onto his own plate. "No use letting good food go to waste."

"And mighty good food it is," Gabe agreed.

"Speaking of food," Tobias called over from the next table, "today is picnic day. Somebody ought to tell Gabe about the MacPhersons' dishes."

Paxton perked up and hastily cut in, "You'll have to try everything they bring, Gabe. You've eaten Lovejoy's and Daisy's cooking. The MacPherson women come from Salt Lick Holler, too."

"I've eaten Johnna's meals in Yosemite." Gabe nodded.

"But—" Perry interrupted.

"But," Pax cut in neatly as Tanner elbowed Perry to silence him, "with us home, there's far more variety."

Laurel couldn't believe Paxton was setting Gabe up like this. The MacPhersons were good cooks—but they also had some strange notions as to what constituted food. Everyone knew to ask a discreet question or two about dishes before digging in—well, everyone except Gabe.

Beneath the table, a boot nudged her shin. Paxton gave her a sly grin. As he did so, Gabe swiped a piece of bacon off of his plate. Laurel burst out laughing again.

"What's so funny now?" Kate peered down the table at her.

"No telling," Daddy said. "Best you get finished with those giggles before we reach the sanctuary, honey."

"Yes, Daddy." Laurel blotted her mouth with her napkin.

"Oh, man," Kate moaned. "If you don't get over your giggles soon, you'd better go help in Sunday school instead of going to worship." Her face twisted into a pained expression. "Violet Greene is singing the solo today."

"There's really someone named Violet Greene?" Gabe looked to Laurel for confirmation.

As she nodded, Packard groaned loudly. "Gabe, she follows the biblical injunction to make a joyful *noise*."

"Packard Wilson Chance, if you can't say something nice," Mama began.

Everyone chimed in, "Don't say anything at all."

"I was saying something nice. I said she was following the Bible." His mouth twitched. "Besides, it's not fair to have Gabe sit in the pew and not warn him."

"It'll be like going to the opera," Gabe declared. "I listen to the lyrics, even if the music isn't always to my taste."

"You've been to an opera?" Laurel gawked at him.

"Sure." He sounded incredibly blasé as he added, "A few in New York. Once in Germany and another in Italy. Why go to Europe if you don't attend the opera?"

"I'd go to the Eiffel Tower and Rome," Caleb said.

"Of course," Gabe agreed. "In New York, I walked across the Brooklyn Bridge and climbed the Statue of Liberty, too. No use going someplace if you don't avail yourself of all it has to offer."

"Well, eat up," Daddy said as he started the platter with more flapjacks on it. "What Reliable has to offer is a big breakfast and church today."

Gabe stared across the table. Laurel's heart leapt as he said softly, "I think Reliable has plenty more to offer."

Gabe stood with everyone else as the preacher gave the benediction. Other than the solo that rivaled a screeching cat, church had been downright enjoyable. He made a mental note to thank Packard for warning him about that little interlude. To Laurel's credit, she'd acted with perfect decorum during even the worst notes. As giggly as she'd been at the breakfast table, that was saying plenty.

During the sermon, Gabe used the deep purple ribbon on his Bible to mark the passage Parson Abe used. He wanted to go back and read it again. The preacher had made several interesting comments and had excellent insights. Instead of being an esoteric dissertation on theological premises, the message dealt with applicable principles. Gabe couldn't recall having ever heard such a sermon.

As a wizened old woman played the piano, folks started to leave the sanctuary. Gabe didn't like it one bit that several young men flocked toward Laurel and tried to earn her attention. To his dismay, Paul hauled him the other direction and introduced him to seemingly half of the congregation. Exercising his manners, Gabe made small talk when what he wanted to do was plow over and yank Laurel away from those moon-eyed men.

Daniel paced over. "I spoke to the MacPhersons. I know we were due to go over to their place today, but with my Lovejoy's back acting up, they've consented to come our way."

Paul squeezed his brother's arm. "Good. I thought Lovejoy looked a tad better last evening."

"I'd rather she lie back instead of getting up, but she insists she needs sunshine and company."

Gabe folded his arms akimbo. "If you have canvas, we can take care of that."

"How?" the Chance brothers asked in unison.

"We could rig up a hammock for her."

"She does love sitting on the porch swing," Paul mused.

Daniel slapped Gabe on the back. "Let's get going!"

Gabe didn't want to leave Laurel behind. Then again, she'd be home soon. He resolved to stay glued to her side all afternoon and evening. Lovejoy deserved comfort. Helping Daniel was the least he could do.

They rode back to Chance Ranch using a shortcut through a field and over a fence. Daniel confessed, "We don't let the kids go this way. Too many rattlers and skunks through here. If your horse takes an exception to your lead, don't fight her."

"Thanks."

Gabe remembered where the ropes were kept in the stable. As he fetched them, Daniel stalked off to grab some canvas. They met in the barnyard and walked toward a nearby pasture. There, between a pair of trees, they rigged up a hammock. Daniel tested it to be sure it would sustain his wife's weight. Lying in their invention, he stacked his hands behind his head and declared, "I'm going to have to rig one of these up on my porch. Don't know why I never thought of it. My wife's going to love this."

"We could take some of that shorter length of canvas and hang a sling-style chair over a branch. That way, she could sit up to eat."

"What do you have in mind?"

"Why don't you go get your wife? I'll have it rigged by the time you carry her back here." Gabe set to work. As he finished his creation, Daniel approached, carrying his wife. Several of the young men followed behind, carrying sawhorses and planks. While Daniel settled his wife into the sling chair, the boys put up makeshift tables. In no time at all, the MacPhersons and Chances gathered together. One of the MacPherson men asked a blessing, then called out, "Okay ever'body. Dig in. We got us gracious plenty!"

Gabe swept Laurel ahead of himself in line. "Ladies first."

She smiled at him and helped herself to a spoonful of potato salad. By the time they were through the line, her plate carried a small sampling of about half of the dishes. Gabe simply figured it was due to the fact that she never seemed to have much of an appetite. He, on the other hand, took a healthy serving of just about everything.

Soon, everyone sat around on blankets in the grass and chattered as they ate. Gabe noticed how Caleb and Greta managed to carry a blanket to the very edge of the clearing and sat there alone. He envied them their privacy.

Laurel arranged her skirts and gave him a strange look. Pax scooted closer and couldn't wipe the smirk off his face. Gabe knew full well he was about to have some kind of stunt pulled on him.

"Ain't this a wondrous fine day?" one of the MacPherson women said.

Johnna nodded. "Shore is, Ma."

"Everything tastes delicious," Gabe said as he took another bite of meat.

"What've you got thar?" Johnna leaned closer.

"If it was on the table, I have some of it," Gabe confessed as he took another bite. "I'm making a pig of myself."

"You'll have to fight Pa for more of that," Johnna declared. "Ain't often we fry up a skunk."

"Skunk?" Gabe chuckled, but his chuckle died out as Paxton started whooping with delight. Turning to Laurel he raised his brows.

"Skunk," she confirmed.

Chapter 17

"Well." Gabe forked another bite and lifted it. "I didn't know skunk was edible. I certainly wouldn't have believed it could taste this tender."

"You're going to eat another bite?" Pax's jaw dropped.

Gabe popped the bite into his mouth. "Why not? You ought to try a taste. The flavor is excellent."

"No, thanks!"

"Don't bother tryin' to change his mind," Johnna said. "I seen bear traps looser than a stubborn man's hard head."

Laurel poked her fork into a thin strip of meat on Gabe's plate. He noticed she didn't have any of it on her plate—so he figured she was trying to give him fair warning as she said, "This is raccoon. It's one of Eunice's specialties."

"Raccoon," Gabe echoed. He covered Laurel's hand with his and bravely drew the bite up to his mouth. "Very interesting flavor. Do you have the recipe?"

"Not yet. Eunice? Gabe wants me to get the recipe for your raccoon."

"Gabe," Paxton muttered, "needs to be dragged to the nearest insane asylum."

Ulysses wolfed down a bite and shook his head. "You're missin' out, Pax. You decided what's good and right afore even testin' it out. In the end, yore cheatin' yoreself."

"My life is fine just as it is." Pax picked up a chicken leg and took a huge bite.

They spent an idyllic afternoon in the pasture. When the women started picking up all the dishes, Gabe walked over to Daniel and Lovejoy. "Lovejoy, Daniel thought you might like the hammock on your porch. How does that sound to you?"

"That'd suit me fine, thankee."

"I'll carry it back for you," Gabe told Daniel.

"Obliged." Daniel stooped over his wife. "Sweetheart, I aim to lift you. It might hurt a bit."

Lovejoy reached up and wrapped her arms around his neck. "You love me, Dan'l. You'd niver hurt me."

Gabe stood to the side and silently watched as Daniel lifted his wife and carried her off. As he started untying one side of the hammock, Paul Chance began to undo the other. Gabe kept his gaze trained at the knot he'd tied so securely as he said, "I remember learning a verse when I was a kid about love casting out fear. It never made sense to me till now."

"Yeah," Paul agreed. "The Bible is full of wisdom. Sometimes it takes time for the truth to seep into our hearts and minds. We're so set in our ways, we can be blind to the simplest truths."

The second knot gave way under Gabe's attention. *I wouldn't have ever tried that food today had I known what it was. I wouldn't have been any different than Paxton—but tasting it without any preconceived notions led to a surprising discovery. All of the notions I've had about God—how do I know if they're true or not? The Lord these people worshiped and praised in church today isn't anything like the aloof God the pastor back home preached about.*

"This hammock was a great idea. I don't know why we never came up with it." Paul jerked at the rope and freed his side. "I suppose a fresh outlook can be a good thing sometimes."

Gabe coiled up the rope and slung the hammock over his shoulder. "Yeah. Maybe so."

Laurel curled up in bed and hugged her pillow. Kate and April's whispers filled the loft of the girls' cabin, but Laurel didn't feel like joining in on the conversation. She felt. . . unsettled.

Home had never been like this. She'd grown up so sure all she wanted out of life was a man to love her and to stay here, where everything would remain comfortably the same. Only now, the predictability of life had been blown apart.

Boys from church came by the ten days she'd been home before Gabe arrived. Daddy had made her promise not to close the door to a possible future with any of those boys, and Laurel did her best to be polite—but they were all so. . . boring. Young. Immature. None of them cared about her love of art or asked her what she thought. Since the day Bobby and Nestor fought and witnessed how she greeted Gabe, not a single man in the community came to see her. That was more than fine by her. She didn't want to mislead any of them into believing she could ever feel more than Christian charity toward them.

On the other hand, she had a terrible time limiting herself to simple Christian charity toward Gabe. Her heart cried out to be with him. Oh—they spent plenty of time together, but everyone in the family made sure they were never alone. Before she left for Yosemite, she adored being surrounded by her family; now she wished they'd all go away and leave her alone with Gabe. Only they wouldn't. Laurel knew in her head that this was the right way to handle things. Still, deep down inside she wanted so much more.

Chance Ranch wasn't the same, either. The youngest members of the family weren't little children anymore. Her aunts and uncles weren't old—but time was marching on for them. Just as Polly had taken over most of the simple healing and midwifery for Aunt Lovejoy, soon Laurel's generation would assume the lion's share of responsibility for the ranch. Laurel felt competent to do all of the necessary chores—but what was the use of existing from day-to-day when love didn't lift her heart? Though she was happy for Caleb and Greta, seeing them happily courting still hurt because Laurel ached to be allowed to draw closer to Gabe.

God, I don't know what to do. Gabe is all I could ever want, but he doesn't know You. Tears seeped from her tightly shut eyes. *That isn't true, Lord. I do know what to do. I know I have to put him in Your hands. I've been doing that hour by hour for weeks now. There are people who never accept You. I couldn't stand knowing Gabe was one of them.*

"Laurel?" April pulled back the covers and climbed into bed with her. She wrapped her arms around Laurel and pulled her close. "Come here."

"Scoot over," Kate added as she crept into the other side of the bed. The three of them barely fit on the mattress, but they huddled together. Kate squirmed for a minute, then handed Laurel a hanky.

"What if Gabe never makes a decision to follow the Lord?" Laurel sniffled.

"Then God will take away the love you have for him," Kate said.

"I don't believe that." April sighed. "I keep asking God to take away my love for dessert, and it hasn't gotten any easier."

Laurel let out a watery laugh. "Oh, April. I'll love you no matter what size you are."

"And you keep loving Gabe, no matter where he stands with the Lord." April patted her. "Christ loves us unconditionally. Gabe needs that same example."

"But it's not the same," Kate argued.

"Oh, what do you know? You've never been in love," April said.

"Neither have you," Kate shot back. "And I'll tell you what I do know: The Bible says we're not supposed to marry up with a man who isn't a believer. We need to help Laurel guard her heart."

"It's too late, isn't it, Laurel?"

Laurel nodded. "I do love him."

"Of course you do," Kate said. "Any dimwit could see that. What I mean is, Laurel can't act as if Gabe is going to suddenly accept Christ. She has to steel herself for the long haul. That means you and I are going to keep making pests of ourselves when Gabe is around."

"What's new about that?" Laurel asked.

"We're going to be more persistent. If you're exasperated with us, you won't be able to concentrate so much on him." Kate wiggled again like a happy puppy. "I'll tell the boys to do the same thing."

Laurel moaned. "They're already pulling all sorts of pranks on Gabe."

"Yeah, well, if Gabe really does have a change of spirit, he's going to need to be able to cope with those dopey brothers of ours. It's good training for him."

"If he can put up with it." Laurel stared up at the ceiling.

"He's obviously planning to." Kate propped up on one elbow. "Uncle Bryce talked him into having Orion service that pretty Tennessee Walker. The first pony will belong to Gabe, and the second time, Chance Ranch keeps the pony."

Laurel shot up in bed. "You're talking more than a two-year commitment!"

"Lie down and stop stealing the covers," April commanded. She jerked the quilts back up to her chin, then declared, "Gabe Rutlidge is a man of his word. He won't go back on it."

"No, he wouldn't," Laurel agreed. "He promised me he'd read the Bible twice a day, and he has."

"If you ask me, any man who can't make up his mind about the Lord or the woman he loves in two years isn't worth his weight in sawdust." Kate yawned. "Laurel, we're going to pester you and Gabe for two years. It'll be a burden, but we love you, so we'll do it. By then, if he can't get his head screwed on straight, you'll have to let him go."

April giggled. "Two years of us pestering her is liable to make her crazy enough to start frying up skunk."

"She ought to thank us. I'd never want to kiss a man who ate skunk."

"What kind of floozy do you think I am? Gabe and I haven't kissed."

"It's a good thing you haven't," April said. Without taking a breath, she continued, "What kind of man do you want to kiss, Kate?"

Kate snorted. "What difference does it make? Polly caught the doctor. Every boy in the county has chased Laurel, and when we went away, the only guy we met latched on to her. You and I don't stand a chance of ever attracting a man until we get Laurel married off."

"You're right." April swiped more of the pillow and plopped her head down on it. "That settles the matter. Gabe is going to find salvation and marry you, Laurel."

"Oh? How did you come to that conclusion?"

"Because it all makes sense. Look at the facts. In First Corinthians, it says, 'Now abideth faith, hope, charity, these three; but the greatest of these is charity.' We all have faith, and you and Gabe feel mighty charitable toward one another. That leaves hope. That's the first part. The second fact is, our heavenly Father is merciful. He'd never leave all three of us without husbands. So if you put it all together, the final fact is plain to see. Since you have to be married and out of the way before Kate or I get a crack at finding a man, we all have hope to hold fast to."

"Her logic could make Parson Abe weep in frustration," Kate mumbled.

As Laurel's cousins both slipped off to sleep, she remained wedged between them. They'd done their best to comfort her. Though their effort counted as noble, the results fell far short of the mark. Laurel had been so caught up in her own troubles, she hadn't realized they both questioned their ability to find a mate. Tucking the quilt up around all of them, she whispered the prayer they'd all agreed upon from the first night they all started living in the cabin together: "God help us all."

Chapter 18

I'm sure Laurel wouldn't mind," Tobias said as he reached for the package.

"It's not for you to say." Gabe snatched the bundle from the counter in White's Emporium. "The camera is hers, as are the pictures. She ought to be the first to look at them."

"We all took photographs," Caleb said. "You know us Chances—we all share. If Laurel didn't get her nose outta joint when her brothers swiped some of her paintings to use as stationery, she certainly won't be upset if we take a peek at the pictures."

The brown paper rustled on the package as Gabe held it securely. "I'm not changing my mind."

Tobias gave him an exasperated look. "You lost your mind the day you decided to take a fancy to Laurel."

Mrs. White leaned on the counter. "Young man, don't you listen to these boys. That there is a piece of United States mail. Only person authorized to open it is the person to whom it's addressed."

"Yes, ma'am." Gabe set the package atop a good-sized crate and lifted the whole thing. He and a handful of the Chances had come to town. After dropping the crate into the buckboard and hauling the other one out, he'd head over to the doctor's office. Laurel was there, visiting with her cousin Polly.

Tobias and Caleb hefted the items they'd purchased for the ranch and tromped out to the buckboard, too. Tobias plunked down his burden, then shuffled through the mail. "Rutlidge—sure you don't wanna let us have at those pictures? I'll trade you a letter from Boston."

Boston—it had to be from his mother or brother. "Tempting as the offer is, I'll have to decline."

"Haven't you noticed by now that on Chance Ranch, men stick together?"

"Only," Gabe retorted, "because they're honorable men, so they see eye-to-eye."

"Ouch!" Caleb slapped a hand over his heart as if he'd been shot. "Nothing like being wounded with the weapon you own."

Gabe chuckled. "Tell you what: We'll swing by and grab everyone. I'll spring for lunch at the diner, and Laurel can spread all of the pictures across the table."

"That's more like it!"

They took the largest table in the diner, but Gabe bristled when April took the seat next to Laurel. He understood why Polly sat on Laurel's other side—they missed each other and relished the opportunity to be together. But April shared the same cabin with Laurel. Surely, she could have allowed him—

"Let's see if I get it right," the waitress said as she approached the table. "Doc, Tobias, and April are going to want the pot roast. Caleb, a full pound rib eye. Laurel and Pax'll go for the blue plate—it's chicken-fried steak. Polly, it's either egg salad or corn bread and cold chicken."

"Corn bread and chicken, please."

The waitress nodded, then wrinkled her nose. "Only one I can't anticipate is you, Mr. Rutlidge."

"He's a Yankee, from Boston. Of course he'll have pot roast," Pax declared.

"Sounds good to me." Gabe set the package on the table and gave it a light push. "Laurel, here are your pictures."

Gabe suspected she would have torn open the wrapping had she been alone, but since her brother was rushing her, she took her sweet time carefully unwinding the twine and paper. Inside the pasteboard box lay the camera and a sizable stack of photographs. Laurel removed the camera. "See, Polly? Isn't it interesting?"

"Aw, c'mon, Sis," Pax growled as he grabbed for the box.

Laurel gave him a slap on the hand. "You sit tight, Paxton. In fact, you go wash up. I don't want you touching my pictures with hands like that. Mama would have a conniption if she knew you came to the table that filthy."

Pax slinked away, and Gabe tamped down a chuckle. Laurel handled her brother with a mixture of good humor and firmness. She'd make a good mother. Just as quickly as the thought flashed through his mind, Gabe winced. He wanted her to be his wife and the mother of his children, but a wall stood between them. *And I'm the one who keeps that wall up.*

Eric turned the camera over and gave it back to Laurel. He shot Gabe a lopsided grin. "I'm always intrigued by new inventions."

"His office is full of neat stuff," Caleb attested. "Now let's look at the pictures!"

"All right. Here we go." Laurel opened the box again. One at a time, she'd remove a photograph, then tell Polly and Eric a little something about where it was taken; then it would be passed all around the table.

He loved the animation in her voice. Other than himself, Gabe knew no one else who loved Yosemite as much. He could scarcely take his gaze off of her long enough to glance at each picture.

"I took this one." April turned toward her. "May I keep it?"

"Of course."

"Then I'm keeping the one of El Capitan that I took," Caleb declared. "I've told Greta all about it, but a picture will really let her understand what the place looks like."

When the picture Gabe had taken of Laurel came around, he smiled at her and carefully slid it into his pocket. She blushed and quietly slid the photo she'd taken of him into the box.

"Hey. What's going on?" Tobias protested.

Polly pinned him with a stare. "There are one hundred pictures here. Don't tell me you're going to have a hissy fit if you don't see a couple of them."

"I need you to clear room. Food's ready."

Everyone scrambled to protect the pictures. Laurel tucked them back into the box as Eric said, "Having a camera there was a magnificent idea. Since Polly and I can't get away, it's almost as if we were able to see Yosemite for ourselves."

"Gabe traded it for some of Laurel's art," Pax said.

"I got the better end of the bargain." Gabe inclined his head toward Laurel. "That young lady has a rare talent."

"Now that I think of it, Gabe," Caleb leaned to the side so the waitress could set down his plate, "what's in those big old crates you got shipped here?"

"A variety of things." He tried to sound offhanded, but the truth of the matter was, he wanted to sort through everything alone. Most of the time, he enjoyed the camaraderie of the huge Chance clan; the past few days, he'd been feeling a need for an opportunity to be alone. "Could I please have the pepper?"

After the meal, Eric said, "I think I'll ride out to the ranch and check on Lovejoy."

"I'll come, too!" Polly hopped up from the table. "I can see Mama and Daddy and look at the rest of the photographs."

Eric chortled softly. "Translated, that means we'd better grab what we need to spend the night."

Once back at the ranch, Gabe took advantage of the fact that between chores and the pictures, everyone was busy. He slipped into the boy's cabin and read the letter from home. Everything was fine, and his mother adored Laurel's paintings. Friends had come to tea and admired the pieces so much, they wanted to acquire drawings and watercolors for themselves.

Smiling at that news, Gabe pried the lid off the first crate. Stanford had followed his instructions perfectly—the whole thing contained length after length of cloth. A rainbow of hues lay stacked there, all of them the finest Rutlidge Enterprises had to offer. Gabe turned aside to the other box. The lid groaned loudly as the nails gave way.

The contents of the box had gotten jumbled during shipping. He pushed past several spools of ribbon, drew out his best Sunday suit, and stopped cold. A small box lay nestled atop other paper-wrapped bundles. Gabe slowly reached in and opened it to find his grandmother's wedding ring. Curled inside lay a little note. "I can tell she's stolen your heart, son. I wish you a happy life together."

The remaining bundles held another camera with a note, "Please send me pictures of the wedding!" as well as heavy white satin and lace along with a sealed envelope labeled, "To my dear daughter-in-law-to-be." Gabe slammed the lid on the box and pounded the nails in again to seal it. Every blow it took to do so matched the leaden beat of his heart.

As everyone took a seat for supper, Polly and Eric remained standing. Eric wound his arm around her waist and cleared his throat. "We have an announcement to make."

Laurel inhaled sharply.

"Come the first of the year, the first of the next generation is due to arrive."

After the ensuing din finally quieted down, Eric said, "We'd covet your prayers for a healthy time for Polly and the baby. There's nothing more important to us than dedicating this child back to the Lord who has blessed us with this miracle."

Uncle Gideon stood and said grace for the meal, then asked a special blessing for Eric, Polly, and the baby. Touched by the absolute sweetness of the news and the presence of the Lord, Laurel wiped her eyes as she lifted her head.

Gabe stared at her. A tiny muscle in his jaw twitched. Throughout supper, he barely said a word. As it was her turn to dry the dishes, Laurel couldn't keep track of him after supper, and he didn't show up when the whole family gathered for bedtime devotions.

Laurel couldn't sleep. Long after April and Kate went to bed, she stayed up. By the light of a single lamp, she cut tiny garments out of soft white cotton and started stitching them. Sewing and art always calmed her—only tonight, it didn't work.

She'd seen the bleakness in Gabe's eyes at supper.

Her Bible sat open on the table to the Fifty-first Psalm. Each day, she'd read the same psalm Gabe was supposed to be reading. This one, though, she knew was aimed at her. Long ago, she'd memorized the passage starting at the tenth verse. Now it pierced her heart with every stitch she took:

Create in me a clean heart, O God;
and renew a right spirit within me.
Cast me not away from thy presence;
and take not thy holy spirit from me.
Restore unto me the joy of thy salvation;
and uphold me with thy free spirit.

Laurel knew she'd done the right thing by telling Gabe their relationship wasn't acceptable in the sight of God. The truth of the matter was, she'd still been in the wrong. Instead of releasing her dreams and desires and letting the Lord direct her path, she'd had a stubborn spirit. Facing that fact struck her to the depths of her soul.

Lord, I was wrong. Help me to remember the joy of my salvation and give me the strength to follow Your will. You'll have to do this work in my heart and soul, Father. I won't ever to be ready to be a good wife and mother if I don't keep You first in my life. It hurts to let go, Lord. Please help me.

Tears wet the little gown in her lap.

Chapter 19

Gabe sat out on a split rail fence, staring up at the sky. He'd walked away from the supper table, but he couldn't escape the sight of the tears glistening in Laurel's eyes. She'd make a wonderful wife and spectacular mother—but he denied her both of those dreams. Oh, she'd smiled at him, a bittersweet smile that reflected how much she longed to be his wife and the mother of his babies. He knew she'd not given her heart lightly when they fell in love. *But what kind of man am I to bind her heart and make her settle for nothing in return?*

"Sittin' on the fence, huh?"

Gabe glanced over his shoulder. Paul Chance stood a few yards away. "Are you speaking literally or figuratively?"

"Take it whichever way you choose."

Smacking his hand down on the fence, Gabe offered a silent invitation to join him.

Paul sauntered over and shot Gabe a grin. "We're both big men and some of these slats are brittle. Might break if we put too big of a burden on 'em." After banging against the fence, he hitched up beside Gabe. "I've spent my share of time sitting off on my own, staring off into the distance, and trying to settle matters."

"Is that so?"

"Yup. Fact is, I didn't know you were out here. I came to do some thinking and praying. Seems you like the same spot I do."

Gabe started into motion to leave, but Paul stilled him. "I reckon since you were the subject of my thoughts and prayers, maybe you're meant to stay."

"You were thinking and praying for me?"

Paul nodded. "Of course I am. Son, you're a fine man—intelligent, hardworking, and kind. I've put myself square in front of what you want so badly, but you've respected my limits instead of resenting me."

"You've stood on your principles, and I honor that. I can't help wondering, though, whether there's room for compromise. If I vow to take Laurel to church each week, read the Bible, and pray, isn't that enough?"

"No," Paul said baldly. "Marriage blends two souls into one, but if you don't belong to the Lord, that bond can't be what it was meant to be. A man is the spiritual head of a home. If your head and heart aren't right with God, how can my daughter and grandchildren rely on your decisions and leadership?"

Gabe gritted his molars and shifted his weight.

"Son, I'm not pushing you to make any decisions. Having you here is a joy. Every last Chance on this ranch likes and cares for you. When you first arrived, I told you to take all the time you need. What I am going to say is, I think you're focusing on the wrong thing. Instead of trying to patch up a way you and Laurel can wed, you need to concentrate on the restlessness you feel deep inside."

"I never said I was restless."

"Didn't need to. You left your family. Wandered all over Yosemite on your lonesome. Stare off into the fire during devotions. Trust me—I've got brothers, sons, and nephews. I've seen the same struggle more than a dozen times. Only one thing solves it."

Gabe gave him a crooked smile. "Laurel sort of said the same thing. She said man was made with a void only God fills—that's why Adam walked with God in the Garden of Eden."

"Yep. I'm sure she mentioned sin separates us from God. Being without the Father leaves us restless. We keep trying to find something to fill up the empty spot, but nothing works."

"So your advice is to pay attention to myself instead of Laurel?"

"Did you notice how I tested the fence before I sat on it?"

"Yeah." Gabe wondered why he'd asked such a bizarre question.

"That's because my brothers and I put up this fence a long time ago. It was solid as could be. Able to carry a burden and do the job. But time passes. Weathering and wear take their toll. What once was reliable can crumble under a heavy burden."

Gabe listened. He wasn't sure where this was going.

"Son, men build fences for a reason. I'm not talking about a fence like the one we're sitting on. Inside, men build fences so they feel strong and capable of handling everything on their own. We're prideful, and keeping busy gives us a sense of accomplishment. Only in the dead quiet of night is the truth clear: Those fences only serve to keep out God and the ones we love. In the end, life wears us down. Either we have the Lord to rely on, or we fall apart."

"I've known prideful Christian men."

"I wouldn't dream to deny that." Paul chuckled. "We still sin, but the good news is that we're granted forgiveness when we ask for it. Just talk to Eric. Fine Christian. Came here to Reliable wanting to serve the Lord with his doctoring. His pride sure got bruised when Polly and Lovejoy kept treating folks and delivering the babies. When he finally set aside that pride, God did a mighty work. Now he and Polly heal the sick and are expecting a miracle of their own. It wasn't until Eric yielded that God moved in, though."

Laurel's father pushed off the fence. "I didn't come here to preach. I could tell you stories all night, but in the end, each man has to wrestle with his own heart. If you want someone to pray with you or answer questions, I'm available—so are any of my brothers or Parson Abe. It's the biggest decision any of us makes, so consider carefully. I respect that you've not made any pretenses or snap judgments."

"Thank you." Gabe stayed on the fence and watched Paul walk off. In a very short conversation, Laurel's father had managed to say quite a bit. Gabe needed time to think things through.

He wasn't wrong. I've been concentrating so much on finding a way to have Laurel be mine, I've ignored the root of the problem.

Laurel had urged him to read the scriptures as a means to get to know Christ. Gabe started thinking of the Gospels he'd read, and Christ's character traits seemed like such an unlikely combination. For being such a charismatic leader, Jesus had been astonishingly humble. He'd possessed undeniable power—the miracles He wrought testified to that—but He used His abilities only to serve. Compassion and mercy flowed from Him, yet He'd also stood firm for His convictions.

Gabe trudged back toward the boys' cabin. Lying in the dark, he couldn't stop the confusing whirl of thoughts. Rustling made him roll over. Tobias was sitting on the edge of his own bed, leaning across the space between their bunks.

"Can't sleep?" Gabe asked.

"Neither can you." Tobias drummed his fingers on his knee, then said, "You left your Bible open on your bunk this morning. I wondered all day whether you did it on purpose so someone would ask if you wanted to discuss what you'd read."

Gabe sat up. "I don't recall leaving it open."

Tanner grumbled from the other side of the cabin, "Take it outside. Some of us wanna get some shut-eye."

"No pressure. Just an offer." Tobias didn't move at all.

Gabe shrugged into his shirt. As they exited the cabin, he noticed Tobias had grabbed the Bible.

"Barn's probably the best place for us to go," Tobias ventured. "We can light a lantern."

Soon they sat on bales of hay that formed a V by the post from which a lantern hung. Tobias bowed his head. Gabe assumed he was praying, so he sat quietly. After a few moments, he flipped through the Bible, and the pages parted where Gabe had placed the ribbon that morning.

"I notice you have the ribbon and Laurel's picture as a bookmark in there," Tobias said.

"I promised Laurel I'd read a Psalm each morning and the New Testament at night." He didn't mention how he'd used the picture as his bookmark so Laurel's face was the last thing he saw each night. "I haven't gotten to tonight's stuff yet."

"What part of the New Testament are you reading?"

"I started at the beginning. I've read Matthew, Mark, and Luke. I got started in John last night. Jesus told Nicodemus that he had to be born again. I stopped reading when I hit John 3:16. It was sort of like being a kid in Sunday school—I remember memorizing that verse."

Tobias grinned. "I remember that one, too. Dad almost choked to death on the popcorn he was eating when I recited it for him because I said God so loved the world, he gave His only *forgotten* Son."

Gabe chuckled. "My brother, Stanford, thought the Israelites all had to eat *eleven* bread."

"It's easy to see how kids get stuff like that mixed up. Fact of the matter is, I think adults also get mixed up. We think we have a grasp of what the Bible or preacher says, but when it comes to getting through life, we don't always have the facts straight."

"Until you folks came to Yosemite, I thought I had a handle on everything."

"Do you?"

Gabe sat in silence. Finally he shrugged. "Part of me wants to say I do. The other part is calling me a liar."

"What's right in your life?" Tobias eased into a more comfortable position.

"My mom and brother are fine. I've got more than enough money to see me through. I've got free rein in Yosemite."

"Now the other side of the coin—what's not right?"

Gabe shifted uncomfortably. "Laurel. I'm breaking her heart, and it's killing me. Her dad told me tonight to stop paying attention to her feelings and to focus on myself. I'm trying, but it's hard. He said the restlessness I feel is because I lack peace in my soul."

"Do his words ring true to you?"

"I never even paid attention to my soul until Laurel pointed out that I lacked any personal commitment. Being around you Chances—I see you're different."

"Is it a difference that you want for yourself?"

Gabe leaned forward and rested his elbows on his knees. "I've read the Bible before—it was like a big collection of stories. Sort of like mythology and fairy tales. In my head, I figured they were basically true. Now I'm reading it with the intent of figuring out if Jesus is someone I'd want as a partner."

Tobias didn't say anything.

Gabe rested his chin on his palm. "To begin with, I'm not sure I want a partner. I like controlling my own life. So far I've done a good job of it. It may sound proud, but I've been honest and moral. The other thing is, I don't cotton to the notion of having God tell me what to do."

"If you're already living an honest, moral life, why would you expect God to direct you to do something outside of what your heart would lead you to do?"

Gabe let out a rueful chuckle. "Can't say I ever thought of it like that."

Tobias hitched a shoulder. "To take it a step further, we're only flesh and blood. We slip up. There are times we don't make the right choices. Christians still sin. When that's the case, I figure we deserve to be chastened, to confess, and to ask for forgiveness. God grants that grace to us through the blood of Jesus."

"But what kind of partnership is that? Jesus is perfect, but He pays the price. Man messes up and keeps getting the benefits."

"It's the most lopsided deal of all time. The truth is, we have a choice: We can be proud and live life on our own, or we can yield and accept."

"No in-between ground, huh?"

"Nope." Tobias shook his head. "We have nothing to bargain with. Man can't earn his way into eternity."

"That woman at church last Sunday testified all about feeling God calling her. What if He's not calling me? I don't hear or feel anything."

"The Holy Spirit works in different ways. Some people make their decision to follow God based on an emotional tug. Me?" Tobias spread his hands wide. "Practicality always wins out. I came to the point where I realized I had no call to be proud—Christ did more than I ever could. For me, in my life, I wanted Him to take charge and lead the way."

"I can't believe you ever did anything very sinful."

Tobias rubbed the toe of his boot on the calf of his jeans. "Growing up in a family like mine, I had plenty of people keeping an eye on me. I've never gotten drunk, had relations with a woman, or murdered someone. But I've been mean to my brothers and cousins. I've shaded the truth and shirked my chores."

Gabe made a scoffing sound. "Those are ordinary things. Everyone does them."

"They're still sins." Tobias looked him in the eyes. "Everyone does them because everyone sins. We all do. It's why we're all separated from God. Man tries to justify those actions by pointing to the fact that other wrongs are worse—but sin is sin."

"I've always figured humans are entitled to slip up. I didn't think of it as sin."

"Where do you draw the line? When is it merely a 'slip up' and when is it a sin? First John says, 'If we say that we have no sin, we deceive ourselves, and the truth is not in us. If we confess our sins, he is faithful and just to forgive us our sins, and to cleanse us from all unrighteousness.'"

Gabe winced. "That doesn't pull any punches. It condemns me because any wrong I've done is sin."

"No matter how 'good' we are, we still fail. God loves us and sent Christ to redeem us."

Gabe sat in silence. Memories assailed him. All along, he'd considered himself an upstanding man; but by this measuring stick, he was nothing but a sinner. He buried his face in his hands.

Tobias reached over and took the Bible. He read aloud the first verses from the Fifty-first Psalm that Gabe had read that morning. " 'Have mercy upon me, O God, according to thy lovingkindness: according unto the multitude of thy tender mercies blot out my transgressions. Wash me throughly from mine iniquity, and cleanse me from my sin. For I acknowledge my transgressions: and my sin is ever before me.' " He paused, then quietly added, "God's forgiveness is there. All you have to do is confess and ask Him into your life."

Gabe nodded. "I need to do that."

They knelt by the bales of hay. Tobias wrapped his arm around Gabe's shoulders. "Do as the verse said. Confess that you've been a sinner and claim salvation through the merciful blood of Christ."

For all the times he'd bowed his head, Gabe had never felt like this. Throat tight, heart pounding, he rasped, "God, I used to think I was good enough; but I'm not. My heart was full of pride, and I've sinned." Tears seeped from his tightly shut eyes, and his voice died out.

Tobias squeezed him.

"I'm asking You, Lord, to forgive me. It's only through Jesus' death on the cross that I can beg that of you. Change me, God. Help me be the man You would have me be. Amen."

Gabe couldn't wait. He strode across the barnyard and rapped on the door.

"Just a minute," a sleep-husky voice called. A few seconds later that same person grumbled, "This better be important."

Gabe grinned as Paul Chance opened the door. "Yeah, it's important. I know you've been praying for me. Thought you might want to move your attention to a different soul who's lost since I'm found."

Paul let out a whoop and yanked him inside. " 'Lilah!"

Delilah knotted the sash of her robe as she came into view. "What's wrong?"

"Not a thing." Paul wrapped his arm around Gabe's shoulder and pulled him close. "Tell her, son."

"I asked Christ into my heart tonight."

Laurel's mother burst into tears as she dashed across the room and enfolded him into a hug. "How wondrous!"

"It is," Gabe agreed. "I figure I have a lot to learn about living as a man of God. I was hoping I could ask for some guidance."

"I'm honored you've asked. I'd be happy to disciple you."

Delilah wiped her eyes. "You couldn't ask a better man. I've been blessed to have Paul as my husband."

"Speaking of husbands. . ." Gabe straightened his shoulders. "I'd like to ask the two of you to allow me the honor of being Laurel's husband."

Paul and Delilah exchanged a look Gabe couldn't interpret. Paul then turned to him and said, "There's a problem."

Chapter 20

Do you know what's going on?" Kate asked Laurel as they prepared breakfast.

"No." Laurel cast a worried look through the window, over at the bend in the creek. All of the Chance adults sat in a circle there. They'd called a meeting.

"This is Caleb's first time to get to vote," April said. "As soon as they're done, I'll see if I can worm any information out of him. I know just how to convince my brother to talk." She waggled her brows and set aside a sticky bun.

Laurel didn't laugh. She couldn't. Gabe sat in the circle with her parents, aunts, and uncles. His presence at that meeting constituted a complete departure from family tradition.

"This is so odd," Kate said as she cracked eggs into a bowl. "Tobias is strutting around today with the biggest smile you ever saw, but he's not saying a word. He's never like that."

"What do you mean? Tobias hardly ever says much," April disagreed.

"Well, he's only three months from his twenty-first birthday. I figured he'd be put out that they didn't ask him to be part of the vote."

Laurel dropped the rasher of bacon she'd lifted to turn. "They're voting? On what?"

"I don't know. I just assumed they were voting." April grimaced. "I shouldn't have said anything—not when they asked Gabe to be there. Oh. Wow! Caleb's hot about something."

Laurel and Kate gawked out the window and watched as Caleb stood, gestured emphatically, and stalked off. A few moments later, he rode away.

"Oh! The bacon's burning!" Kate cried.

Laurel ran back over and hastily saved most of it. A few rashers were like strips of black leather. She dumped them into the swill bucket for the hogs as April and Kate both opened the doors to get rid of the smoke. Tears ran down Laurel's cheeks. She hoped her cousins would attribute them to the smoke.

Lord, prepare my heart for what's going to happen. I'm so afraid. They're going to send Gabe away. I put this all in Your hands last night, but it's so hard to leave it there.

"Laurel?" Gabe's voice stopped her cold. "I'd like to speak with you."

"Let me wash my hands." She kept her back to him and tried to gather her courage. After washing up and taking off her apron, she turned around.

Gabe held out his hand. "Let's go for a walk."

She closed her eyes to block out the sight of that potent temptation. "I can't. You know I'm not allowed to be alone with you."

He drew closer, and his hand closed around hers. "Your father gave us permission. Come on."

She couldn't bear to look up into the face of the man she still loved. Laurel dipped her head and nodded. He squeezed her hand and led her out the back door. As she passed by her cousins, April silently shoved a hanky into her hand.

Gabe didn't say anything as they walked along the dusty path toward a stand of trees. Once under their canopy, he halted and leaned back into one of them. Reaching down, he took Laurel's other hand in his. "I need to tell you something."

Laurel braced herself.

"Look at me," he commanded in a gruff tone.

Trying her hardest to look composed, Laurel tilted her head back.

"Much better," he said. The smile on his face took her off guard. "I asked Christ to be my Lord and Master last night."

It took a moment for his words to sink in. When they did, Laurel squealed his name in delight.

He chortled and pulled her close. Hugging her, he whispered into her hair, "Princess, I wouldn't have ever known I needed Him if you hadn't taken a stand."

"I'm so happy for you."

He tipped her face up to his. "I'm happy for me, too. But there's something else. I'm happy for *us*. Your father gave us his blessing."

Laurel burst into tears.

Gabe clasped her to his chest as she soaked the hanky and his shirt. Finally, he said, "I'd hoped that would make you happy."

"It does." She sniffled. "You don't know how much it does. Last night, I decided I needed to trust God instead of telling Him what I wanted. Today, when they had the meeting, I was afraid they were going to tell you to leave."

"You can't get rid of me that easily." He stroked her cheek. "We had to work out a little problem, though."

Laurel's heart skipped a beat.

"I'll get to that in a minute." He smiled at her tenderly. "I love you, Laurel."

Finally free to confess it, she whispered, "I love you, too, Gabriel."

Gabe pulled her out to a small patch of sunlight, lifted her by her waist, and spun her around as he let out a laugh. Once he set her down, he went down on one knee. "Laurel, my love, will you marry me?"

"Yes!" She couldn't believe he'd asked. Through tear-sheened eyes, she watched as he drew a ring from his pocket.

"This was my grandmother's ring. I'd like you to wear it as a symbol of our pledge to wed."

"Gabe, I'm honored."

"Rutlidge tradition holds that I grace your hand with an additional ring on the day we marry." He slid it onto her finger and rose. "Now about that little problem."

"Nothing could be a problem on a day like today."

"Yes, it could." He crooked a brow. "I've been informed that before you all left for Yosemite, it was with the understanding that no one would get married until autumn of next year."

"Oh, no." Laurel covered her mouth in horror as she recalled the agreement. She hung her head. "I forgot all about that. We all thought it was just a way to make Caleb and Greta wait awhile longer. I'm sorry, Gabe. I had no right to make a promise when I wasn't speaking just for myself."

He chuckled. "I'm going to have to plead guilty to the same crime."

"There's nothing funny about this." She looked up at him.

"Yes, there is. Or at least I hope you'll see it that way. They took a vote. Your parents, aunts, uncles, Polly, Eric, and Caleb all agreed to release you and Caleb from that pledge on one condition."

"What?"

"Actually, it's two conditions." Gabe's eyes sparkled.

"Don't you dare keep me wondering. Tell me!"

"First, Greta has to accept Caleb's proposal."

Laurel let out a laugh. "I'm sure she will."

"The other thing—well, Caleb and I made a pledge." He paused. "I spoke for both of us without consulting you. I won't make a practice of it, Laurel, but under the circumstances, I hope you'll understand. I know women are touchy about things like this."

She couldn't stand it. "Just tell me."

"Caleb and I told them if we could get married in three weeks, we'd talk you girls into a double wedding."

"Three weeks!" she gasped.

"And I thought you were going to be upset about a double wedding."

"Why would I? We've told you time and again, Chances share."

"You won't be a Chance much longer, princess." He pulled her close and dipped his head. "But right about now, how about if we share a kiss?"

"Where's my shirt?" Gabe looked around the cabin in a panic. "I can't find my shirt!"

"It's gotta be around here," Caleb muttered as he yanked a comb through his hair.

"Caleb, I have your shirt here," Miriam called from the other side of the door.

Gabe and Caleb both stared at the shirt Caleb was wearing and burst out laughing. Gabe opened the door, grabbed the shirt, and said, "Thanks!" as he shut it again. As he shrugged into the freshly-ironed shirt, he said, "You Chances—your policy for sharing is going to make me crazy."

"Don't you dare let on about this." Caleb craned his neck as he knotted his tie. "We'd never hear the end of it—not after the way we've teased the women the past three weeks."

The day he'd proposed, Gabe had given Laurel the bridal satin and lace. He'd also given the crate with all the other fabric to her family. They'd been delighted with the material and each claimed a length for a dress to wear to the wedding. Since then, the women had spent every moment they could in the girls' cabin. Discussions about sewing, the plans for the wedding, and countless details filled their conversation. The men all sat back and found the whole thing amusing.

Caleb announced just one week into the preparations, "I don't know what the fuss is all about. Greta's seen me in dusty, ripped jeans, and I've seen her looking like a drowned rat after a downpour. Our marriage would be just as strong if I dragged her to the altar this Sunday and we said our 'I do's.'"

Gabe counted himself fortunate that he'd not opened his mouth. Every woman on the ranch scolded Caleb. He'd been called "unromantic," and they'd listed all of the essential preparations that included everything from gowns to trousseaus, flowers, cakes, and any number of other details. Gabe nodded solemnly, as if those things actually mattered. The way Laurel beamed at him made him feel dishonest, so he leaned over and confessed, "Princess, I want our wedding day to be all you ever dreamed of. None of this matters to me—but I know it's important to you."

Only now, as he and Caleb got ready to go to the church, did Gabe realize he and Caleb were both less than collected and calm. He'd never tell a soul that he'd crammed his right foot into his left shoe. Finally dressed, combed, and ready, he turned to Caleb. "Well, let's get this done."

Polly met Laurel's wagon at the church. "I pinned the boutonnieres on the grooms' lapels after they both tried and managed to stab themselves."

Daddy carried Laurel into the back of the church so her hem wouldn't get dusty. Before setting her on her feet, he whispered, "Your mama and I prayed for the right man for you. We're sure God's listened to our prayers."

"Thank you, Daddy."

Greta and her family arrived. Soon the pianist started the processional, and Greta's sisters and Laurel's cousins walked in to serve as bridesmaids. Rather than have the "Bridal March" played twice, Greta and Laurel had decided to have their fathers escort them down the side aisles of the church simultaneously. Clutching her flowers and her father's arm, Laurel walked along as if in a dream.

Last night, after telling her he loved her, Gabe had promised, "I'll meet you in the middle tomorrow."

Now he did just that. Daddy led her around the edge, up to the middle of the front of the church and placed her hand in Gabriel's. They spoke their sacred vows and shared communion. Parson Abe invited Gabe to greet his bride. Laurel shivered in anticipation as Gabe reached for the edge of her veil. Their kiss held the promise of a blessed future.

Later, as they all ate at the wedding feast, someone asked, "Are you going on a honeymoon?"

Gabe nodded. "I'm taking my bride to Wawona."

Paxton laughed. "I think that's called returning to the scene of the crime."

Johnna poked him. "You be nice. Yosemite's beautiful. I'll bet nothin's purdier than Bridal Veil in the early autumn."

Gabe turned to Laurel and dipped his head. He whispered in her ear, "Almost nothing. I've discovered a different bridal veil on a unique beauty. She stole my heart."

Laurel turned toward him. "Heart and soul—now we can be one."

"Hooo-ooo-ey. Lookit the lovebirds," one of the MacPhersons shouted out. "Go on, give yore gal a kiss."

"Don't mind if I do," Caleb said loudly.

Gabe reached up and kissed his fingertips as Laurel did the same. Their fingers then met in the middle as their laughter carried the anticipation of many years of happiness.

No Buttons or Beaux

Dedication

To my dear friend, Deb Boone,
who loves the Lord and others with every fiber of her being.

Chapter 1

Autumn 1892
Chance Ranch, just outside of San Francisco

Black smoke poured from the kitchen. "Oh no!" April Chance ran through the doorway toward the oven, grabbing the corners of her apron to use as hot pads. The acrid smell of smoke nearly overpowered her. One quick yank, and the oven's cast-iron door clunked open. She pulled out two loaf pans and stared in dismay at the charred bricks inside them. Scalding heat burned through her apron. By the time she made her way back to the door, both hands were unbearably hot. Flinging the loaf pans, she squealed, "Ouch!"

"Ouch!" a deep voice echoed.

April waved one of her tingling hands to disperse the smoke. Peter MacPherson approached from barely a yard away. A big, black rectangle of soot marked the front of his faded golden shirt. "Oh no! Peter, I'm sorry."

He reached out and encircled her wrists. Looking at her bright red fingertips, he frowned. "Let's soak yore hands straight away. Here. Sit down."

"I can't. I need to open the other door and make biscuits in a hurry. Otherwise, lunch will be ruined."

"You have yoreself a sit-down. I'll open the door and fetch you a bucket so's you cain cool off the burn." Somehow, Peter managed to make her sit on the back porch step. "Where's Kate? She cain fix the biscuits."

April shook her head. "No, she can't. She's in the barn, trying her hardest to finish making her gifts for everyone. They're bound to be back in just a few more days."

"Then what about Greta?"

"She's over at her sister's for the next week or so."

"Makes sense. Betty Lou's got her hands full. Heard tell this was gonna be another set of twins. What will that make?"

"Seven children in five years." April didn't have to think about it for even a second. *All around me, girls I went to school with—some even younger—are marrying and having babies.*

Peter strode into the cabin, opened the far door, and pumped water into a mixing bowl. He returned to her side, set the bowl in her lap, and calmly slipped

April's hands into the cool water. "There." He looked down at her, his red hair wind-ruffled and his blue eyes steady as always. A smile creased his face. "Ever' time I've come a-callin' this summer, the quiet here astounds me."

"It's odd, isn't it?" She looked around. Mama, Daddy, all four sets of her aunts and uncles, and the younger children had gone to Yosemite for a seven-week adventure.

"Yeah, but they'll all be back, noisy as always. Iff'n yore missin' the hullabaloo, you cain come o'er to my place. An hour there'll make you rush right home and hit yore knees to thank the Almighty for this peace and quiet."

April bowed her head and wiggled her stinging fingers in the water. "I don't think I'd ever feel that way. Nothing brings me more joy than being. . . surrounded. . .by. . .family." The last words came out choppily as she fought tears.

"Hey, there." Peter hunkered down in front of her. Cupping her jaw in his rough hands, he tilted her face up to his. "What's a-wrong?"

"Everything!"

He glanced over his shoulder at one of the loaf pans lying in the dirt. The huge lump of charcoal that was supposed to be bread rested beside it. "A coupla burnt loaves ain't worth yore tears, April."

"It's not just that."

"Hmm. Havin' a bad day all 'round?"

She nodded. "I broke a button off my boot this morning. Kate didn't rinse the laundry enough, so we're all rashy. I lost count while measuring the coffee. One pot was so strong, it could've dissolved a pitchfork, and the other was so weak, the boys said it tasted like bathwater."

Peter made a funny face. "How do they know what bathwater tastes like?"

April let out a feeble laugh that slid back into tears. "I've burned the bread, and I'm almost out of yeast. Then, I almost killed you by flinging the pans across the yard."

"Now I'm going to take offense at that." He sat down and bumped her shoulder with his in a friendly gesture. "D'you thank I'm such a weakling, a single loaf of bread would knock me into the hereafter?"

Staring at the mess, she tried to rein in her wild emotions. "It's more like a rock than a loaf!" Just then, her right wrist rested more heavily on the rim of the bowl so the water sloshed out and soaked her skirts. "Oh!"

"No use cryin' over spilt water. It'll dry." He wrapped his arm around her shoulder, and April soaked his shirt with her tears. "None of them thangs is 'nuff to upset you. Why don't you tell me what's a-really wrong?"

Embarrassed, she shook her head.

"Hey, it's just me. Peter. C'mon, little April."

"That's just it," she wailed. "I'm not little. I'm twenty-one, and I'm fat. Nobody wants me. I'll never have a family."

"Now hold on a minute, here."

Once the floodgate opened, she just kept talking. "Polly is a healer. Two years ago, she met Eric, and they got married. Laurel is an artist. Last summer, when our group went to Yosemite—"

"She met Gabe," Peter said.

"And now they're married. I've been foolish enough to hope that since I was the next oldest Chance girl, this summer would be my turn. But it wasn't. It'll never be. Nobody wants a no-talent, fat girl."

"Nobody? No talent? Fat?" Peter half-pushed her away, then held her shoulders and gave her a gentle shake. "You stop right thar, April. God made someone extry special when He made you. You got a heart for servin' Him and carin' for ever'body 'round you. As for talent—there ain't a woman in ten counties who cooks like you do."

"And there's not a woman in those ten counties whose waist measures what mine does, either." Horrified she'd admitted that shameful fact, April lifted her soggy apron and buried her face in it.

Peter yanked the fabric back down and snapped, "I've never heard such nonsense. I could name off lots of women who got meat on their bones. There's not a man alive who won't admit that the quickest way to his heart is through his stomach. Jist like some folks like different dishes, men have different tastes in women. Me? I don't wanna find me a bride who's wasp-waisted. A healthy one like you—that's what I want. The bitty ones look like a wallopin' hug'll break 'em in half. Not that I want you to thank I'm bein' coarse," he added, "but a man has to keep an eye out for a woman who'll be by his side for years and years to come. He wants a wife who'll give him plenty of strappin' young'uns. Scrawny women wear out fast. With yore cousin and Aunt Lovejoy midwivin' as they do, you ken that's the truth."

Letting out a sigh, April tried to regain her composure. It didn't work. She muttered, "If everything you say about my cooking and size is true, then it's got to be me. There's something about me that scares men off."

"What'd make you say that?" His brows furrowed.

"Because it has to be the reason. I have to be the only girl in all of Reliable who's never had a boy walk her home from school or ask her to take a Sunday afternoon stroll." Confessing that only made her feel worse. April started to bolt, but Peter yanked her back down.

"Now jist you hold on." He gave her a stern look. "You best better get yore head screwed on front-wise. Starin' back niver got a body where she wanted to go."

April couldn't help smiling a little. Peter. Dear Peter. A girl couldn't have a better cousin. They'd grown up as neighbors, and he'd always been extra special to her. No matter how much schooling he and all of the other children on the MacPherson spread had, they only used proper English while in the classroom. The rest of the time, they fell back into the colorful dialect their parents had imported from Salt Lick Holler, Kentucky.

"Better. Much better," he crooned. "Iff'n you reflect on it a spell, you'll realize some important thangs. First off, Polly didn't want to accept none of the attentions of the local boys. Hit took Doc Walcott comin' from afar-off to grab her fancy."

"But Laurel had suitors coming out of the woodwork."

"True 'nuff, she did. But if you pause and recollect, they wasn't really carin' 'bout her. They wanted to have a pretty gal on their arm so's they could strut about like peacocks. 'Twas vanity what kept them sniffin' 'round her; not true and deep love."

"You can say whatever you want, Peter, but the truth still stands. Something's wrong with me. Never once has a boy even looked my way."

"No accountin' for the foolish ways of others."

"It's not them. It's *me*." The admission cost her all of her nerve.

"Not that I agree, 'cuz I don't. But let's grant for the sake of this here discussion that yore right and hit's you. How's about us workin' together on the problem?"

"What do you mean?"

"Well," he drawled, "case you niver noticed, I'm a man."

"Don't be silly. That's not the problem. The problem's that no one thinks I'm a woman."

"And so me bein' a man is the answer. I'll start shadowin' you and watchin' what yore doin'. Then we'll meet up, and I cain give you pointers on how to act. Yore gonna practice on me." He nodded. "Yup. That's what we'll do."

"I don't know. . . ."

He gave her a stern look. "Just how much do you want to be hitched and startin' a nest full of your own chicks?"

More than anyone knows. Biting her lip, April studied him. His eyes remained steady. "You'd do that for me?"

"Yup." He stood up and pulled her to her feet. "I reckon there's nothin' I wouldn't do for you. Starting with me holpin' you bake biscuits for lunch. What're we havin', anyway?"

~

Up to his elbows in flour, Peter grinned at April. She sat across the table, her burned fingers slicked with butter. He'd applied the butter himself. It made for a good excuse to get to touch her—just like his noticing one of the pins holding her rich brown hair was sneaking free. He'd poked it back into place and relished just how soft her hair felt.

Chance Ranch usually buzzed with all of her aunts, her mother, and her cousin Kate, so he seldom managed to catch April alone. He'd been searching for an opportunity like this forever.

The Chance and MacPherson kids grew up calling each other cousins. About a year and a half ago, when he realized he loved April, Peter sat back and thought matters through. His uncle had married April's aunt's sister. He and April weren't related at all. Some of his cousins just happened to be cousins to one of her cousins. Both clans were big and loving. Somehow, they'd taken one slender kinship tie and wrapped themselves together into one big family—but they really weren't related.

The plan he'd come up with out on the back porch nearly had him giddy. He'd been biding his time now for what felt like an eternity. Finally, he'd be with April and get her to see herself how he saw her. Once he did, he'd pop the question.

He tore his gaze from her and looked out the front window. Chance Ranch boasted a big yard in the middle of a sprawling rectangle of cabins and a stable. Each of the five Chance men had his own family cabin. Another cabin bunked the eight oldest boys, who now operated the horse ranch. Nestled protectively between the buildings was one more—the one April shared with her cousin Kate. If he had his way, Kate would soon be alone there, and he'd be building a place for himself and sweet April over on the MacPherson spread.

"Are you daydreaming?" April sounded astonished.

"Yeah, guess I've been gatherin' some wool." He couldn't wipe the grin off his face. "Don't believe I've ever seen you jist sittin' still. Even at the table, yore always hoppin' up to grab sommat."

April smiled at him. "I was just thinking the same thing about you—you're always in motion. Between minding the livestock and crops and herding all of your siblings and cousins, the only time I see you relax is in the pew at church."

"I reckon that's why they call Sunday 'the day of rest.'" He flopped another biscuit onto the pan. "I niver guessed cookin' was this much fun."

"I love being in the kitchen." Just as soon as the words came out of her mouth, April groaned.

"Whoa. Now that thar's one of them times I can spot straight off that yore sabotaging yourself. 'Stead of making a big to-do, worryin' about what you thank the feller is thankin' 'bout what you said, jist tack on another comment to string the conversation where you'd like it to meander."

"Like what?"

Peter looked at the biscuits in the pan, then the mess all over the worktable. "Mayhap you could said, 'Cookin' is loads of fun. 'Tis the cleanin' up that vexes me.' Then again, you could say, 'Don't you love how good a kitchen smells? I 'specially like bakin' on account of the way cinnamon and vanilla tickle my nose.'

That sort of comment."

"I could do that!"

"Shore could." He grabbed the rolling pin and got ready to roll out the last bit of dough. Chuckling, he tilted the heavy utensil toward her. "Could be, you mention with all the knives and a rollin' pin, there's no safer place on earth for a woman. She's got herself a whole arsenal on hand."

April's laughter was ample reward for his nonsense. Peter sprinkled more flour on the table and started rolling the dough. "Next time someone sets a basket of biscuits afore me, I'm gonna have a new appreciation of them. You women make it all look so simple. Me? Some of my biscuits are thick and others are thin."

"You're doing great. When Gabe helped make biscuits the first time, he couldn't mix or roll them out. Laurel resorted to doing everything and just letting him cut them out with the glass. You're doing all of the steps on your own."

"I'm not 'zactly on my own. I've got you giving me directions." Peter glanced at her. "But what you jist did was good. A man niver tires of hearin' a word of praise."

"I don't want to be a liar, Peter. I can't tell somebody he's fabulous when he's just ordinary."

He halted. "Ain't nothing wrong with you appreciating how he pitches in and does the ordinary, April. Life jist flows along. Most days are much like the ones what came afore and the ones what'll come after. If you cain honestly tell a feller his daily effort is good, he cain walk back out and do the same work the next time with a warm feelin' in his heart."

Her brow furrowed. "I never thought of it that way."

"That's why you need me to holp you out. With me giving you a man's slant on matters, you'll understand what's important to us men." He emphasized his comment with a sage nod. "Yup. I'm gonna open them purdy sky-blue eyes of yourn and let you see thangs in a whole new light."

Lord, You ken I'm speakin' the gospel truth here. I aim to get my sweet little April to understand how special she is and how much I love her. Hit's kinda fun, like You and me are keepin' a pact all secret till we cain spring it as a big surprise.

"Peter?"

He raised his brows in silent inquiry.

"You won't tell anybody about this, will you?"

"About what?" Kate asked through the front screen door.

Chapter 2

Peter scrambled to think of a way to steer the conversation so April wouldn't be embarrassed. "Kate, c'mon in."

"I can't. I've got stain all over my hands. Come open the door."

April started to rise.

"You jist sit yoreself back down." Peter strode to the screen and bumped it open with his elbow.

Kate's eyes grew enormous, and she started to giggle. "And I thought my hands were a mess! What are you doing covered in flour? Wait—first tell me what we're not going to tell anybody."

April turned redder than Ma's pickled beets.

Peter held his hands aloft. "I'm holpin' April make biscuits on account of she burned herself."

"You burned yourself?" Kate's nose crinkled. "What else did you burn?"

"You're a smart one, Katie Chance. You done figgered it out for yoreself." Peter gave April a look, then shrugged. "Couldn't keep it a secret."

"Couldn't keep what secret?" someone asked from the back door. That screen opened, and April's oldest brother, Caleb, tromped in. "And why are you feeding the birds and squirrels outta the dishes?"

April shot Peter a wry look. "And you thought it was quiet and peaceful around here?"

He grinned back at her. It hadn't taken much time for her to pull herself together. "I might have to reconsider that opinion."

Kate heaved a theatrical sigh. "Oh, well. Caleb knows now. Yes, April's decided to feed the birds and squirrels. With all of the younger kids gone, not as much food's been falling from the tables when we eat outside."

Peter chimed in, "And you know what a soft heart April has."

Her brother groaned. "I've heard everything now. It's not like it's the dead of winter and the animals are snowed in without a single scrap to eat." He scowled at the pans of unbaked biscuits on the table. "And why are you feeding them before you make our lunch?"

"Believe me, you'd never eat what I fed them," April said. "It'll only take twelve minutes for the biscuits to bake. During that time, you can both wash up."

"Now wait a minute," Kate said as Peter quickly shoved the biscuits into the oven. "I'm trying to decide which color to stain everything. Which sample do you like the best?"

Caleb walked over to scrutinize the scrap of leather she held out. Peter gave April a sly wink as he passed her and went to give his opinion.

"The darkest brown is best for the men's belts," Caleb said.

"I agree." Still staring at the leather, Peter asked Kate, "What else are you making?"

"Knife sheaths for the boys and leather cases to hold the women's hair pins and jewelry."

"You've got five colors there," Peter observed. "Why don't you stain each of the cases a different color?"

"Do all the knife sheaths in this shade." Caleb jabbed the middle color. He then stared at Peter's chest. "What happened to your shirt?"

"I was holping April feed the birds and squirrels." Peter shrugged and said in a bland tone, "I stopped her from tossing the food too far away."

~

Kate lit the lantern and set it on her workbench. Since April had burned her hands, she couldn't very well wash dishes or cook today. Already feeling pressed for time, Kate had still stopped working on the gifts and pitched in. She'd never been one to wake up early, so staying up late to work suited her fine.

Frowning at the table, she tried to position the lantern so the leather pieces wouldn't be in shadow. Staining leather evenly took concentration and a careful touch. Attempting to do it in poor lighting guaranteed spots and streaks.

"Need another lamp?" Tobias asked.

Kate didn't even turn around at the sound of her oldest brother's question. "Yes, thank you. I want to get these done. I'm afraid everyone will come home before I finish."

Tobias lit another lantern and hung it on a bent nail. He sat and whittled as she started to stain a box. "How badly burned are April's fingers?"

"Not horrible, but not good. In about a week, she'll be back to the stove."

"Good thing," he chuckled. "If us boys have to start taking a turn at cooking, the chow's liable to turn out as tough as that leather you're working on."

Capturing her lower lip between her teeth, Kate concentrated on keeping the stain even. She'd started on the lightest one first, then would work her way clear down to the darkest color. That meant if she stayed up late, she might get three boxes and all of the sheaths stained tonight. That would leave two boxes and five belts for tomorrow.

"I've lost track of what day it is," she said.

"Wednesday. No, Thursday."

She laughed. "You don't sound any more sure than I am."

"Well, I'm trying to figure it out. We had church Sunday. Monday, we took delivery on the stallion. Tuesday, Tanner nearly got himself trampled by that horse. Yesterday, I had supper at Lucinda's."

"You're pretty sweet on her. Are you getting serious?"

"Can't say." He set down the clothespin he'd whittled on the edge of her workbench and started on another.

"Can't, or won't?"

"Don't be so pushy, Kate. It's none of your business unless I announce I'm planning to marry."

She shot him a saucy grin. "By then, it'll be too late for me to register any objections."

"Nothing objectionable about Lucinda." He shaved off a corner of the rectangular block of wood.

"It all depends on where you stand as to what you see." Kate rubbed one last spot on the box, then set it aside.

"Just what was that supposed to mean?"

Capping the lid on one can of stain and opening another, Kate mused, "Ever notice how Lucinda won't say much to any of our aunts or me?"

"Can't say as I have." He glowered at her. "She's polite as can be to Mom."

"Exactly. But only to Mama. If Lucinda were shy, I'd understand, but she's not. At first, I thought maybe it was me—that she thought my stained hands were dirty or something. And when she's been here for meals, it's cute how the two of you manage to sit side by side. But Tobias, she doesn't ever come in to help in the kitchen. She hasn't offered to clear the table or do dishes." Kate shot her brother a quick glance.

His brows were furrowed, but he continued to whittle. "When she's here, she's a guest."

"Maybe the first time or two. But the newness wears off."

"There are seven women in the kitchen. You don't need Lucinda."

"Aunt Lovejoy's back pains her too much to do any appreciable work, but she still sits there and enjoys our company and conversation." Kate knew she was treading on sensitive ground, but someone had to say something. Her brother needed to face the fact that Lucinda wasn't a good match for him. "Since everyone left, and April and I are doing all the women's work, a little help is in order."

"Is that what this is all about? You're feeling put upon, so Lucinda is to take the blame?"

Laughter bubbled out of her. "When have I ever been afraid of pitching in and working?"

"You're a Chance. Not a one of us could be lazy if we tried." His eyes narrowed as he rounded the end of the clothespin. "As for Lucinda spending time in the kitchen when everyone else is in Yosemite—she doesn't have all that much in common with either April or you."

"No, she doesn't." Kate dipped the corner of a fresh rag into the stain and started on the next box. "You might want to think about that. We're the same age, but Lucinda hasn't ever done a single chore. Maybe you need to start watching her. She's got a lively way about her and quick wit. Those qualities and being pretty make it easy for her to turn a man's head. I'm saying you might look at her from a different perspective."

"You wouldn't have brought it up unless something was weighing on your mind." His hands continued to move the knife across the wood in steady, sure strokes. "So why don't you go ahead and say what you intend to, instead of sidestepping all over the place?"

Kate took a steadying breath, then said, "Lucinda's mother orders her expensive gowns from back East. Their family has a cook, and servants do her laundry. Would someone like that survive on Chance Ranch?"

"She could learn how to cook and such."

"Yes, she could. But does she want to?"

Tobias snorted. "If we do marry, she'd have to."

"Not necessarily. I mean, you're right—she would. But I don't think she believes that."

"Why wouldn't she? Lucinda's been here a lot. She knows Chance women pitch in and do whatever needs doing."

Kate shook her head. "Everyone in Reliable knows Mama received a sizable inheritance. Don't get me wrong, Tobias. I think you're quite a catch, but I wonder if Lucinda thinks that if you and she get married, there's plenty of money to hire a housekeeper and cook so she won't have to work."

"You're reading far too much into this."

"You could be right." Carefully rubbing the leather so the stain worked its way into the floral pattern she'd impressed into it, Kate couldn't hold back one last comment. "When the time comes for any of us to marry, I'm hoping and praying we'll all be blessed like our parents. Regardless of how much or how little money they had, they've given their hearts to this family and been true helpmeets. A woman who worries more about keeping her hands soft than about standing by her man isn't cut out for ranch living."

"Sis, you're not exactly the person to dish out advice. You're only a year younger, but you have yet to even think about the future."

His words cut her deeply. "Who says I haven't?"

"Look at yourself." He waved his hand at her from head to toe. "Half of the time, I'm not sure you even bothered to brush your hair that day, and you're still tromping around in men's boots."

"Are you ashamed of me?"

"Don't go putting words in my mouth."

Not fooled by his evasive answer, Kate rubbed the stain in harder and faster. She dipped the cloth into the stain again and spread it with every scrap of concentration she could muster. Even then, she couldn't wipe away the painful knowledge that her big brother considered her a disgrace.

She finished that box and the next, then set to staining the knife sheaths. Six of them to do. . .five. . .four. . .three. Suddenly, each sheath represented how males dominated Chance Ranch. In her own generation alone, fourteen boys still lived here; with just her and Kate left, the girls were vastly outnumbered.

Two. Two sheaths for the very youngest Chance boys. Those boys would be allowed to run wild, get filthy, and holler to their hearts' content. No one would bat an eye at such behavior. No one would comment if a man's hair was a mess or inspect what he had on his feet.

"You're riled," Tobias said as he set his third clothespin on the worktable.

Kate bowed her head over the sheath and rubbed more furiously.

Tobias whistled. "*Hoo-ooo-ey.* You're so hot, it's a marvel there's not steam rising from the table."

Never in all of her hours of doing intricate leatherwork had she toiled so intently. *One more. I only have to stain this last one. Then I can walk away.*

"Sis." Tobias had the unmitigated gall to sound concerned. "Listen—"

Kate shook her head. "You've already said plenty tonight. I don't want to hear another thing from you."

"Aw, for cryin' in a bucket. How is it that you work leather like a man, gallop around like a hoyden, and suddenly get your nose out of joint because someone points out that you're not the picture of femininity?"

"My being a woman didn't stop you from asking me to repair your saddle last week."

"I knew it. I knew when you got all silent that I'd tweaked your pride."

She finished the last knife sheath, capped the stain, and tried to get the worst of the brown splotches off her hands with turpentine. *Why bother? I'll get them even darker when I finish staining the rest of the stuff tomorrow.*

Avoiding looking at her brother, Kate mumbled, "I'll see you in the morning."

Tobias reached out and grabbed her wrist. "You're not walking away yet. Ephesians 4:26."

" 'Be ye angry and sin not: let not the sun go down upon your wrath,' " she quoted. The verse had been drilled into all of them. There were times when two or three family members sat up a good portion of the night before settling an issue, but they didn't climb into bed until the matter was resolved.

He jerked his chin toward a stool, then turned loose of her.

Kate backed up a step. "I'm not angry. I'm hurt."

"Leave it to you to start acting like a woman about this. Everything else, you behave like a—"

"Like a what?" She folded her arms across her chest.

Tobias compressed his lips.

"I know what I am. I'm a woman. You might not think leatherwork is feminine, but it's what I do. It helps our ranch. It's never kept me away from doing my share of gardening, minding the younger kids, or washing piles of laundry. I mended that shirt you're wearing, and I made the supper you ate tonight. Tomorrow, I'll milk the cow, gather the eggs, and make your breakfast. Doing those things makes me happy because I love our family. Knowing you're ashamed of me—it hurts. A lot. I have hopes and dreams for the future. Know this, though: Any man who can't see past some stain on my hands isn't the type I want to marry."

Chapter 3

"Are you sure you'll be all right?" April stood out in the yard and studied Kate's face. She and her cousin shared a cabin. When Kate had crawled into bed the previous night, she'd been utterly silent. Usually, they'd chatter awhile up in their beds in the loft, but Kate had turned her back and pulled the covers over her head. This morning, Kate barely spoke a word.

"Of course I'll be okay." Kate made a shooing motion. "We need you to buy essentials before our mothers get home. They'll have a fit if we're out of anything."

"I could give Peter a list."

"Kate'll be fine." Tobias stepped up beside Kate and rested his hand on her shoulder. "We all love her chili. Tanner and I'll do the lunch dishes so she can finish staining the gifts."

"I'm using the very last of the yeast to bake bread. Don't forget to get more," Kate said.

"Then we're off." Peter curled his hands around April's waist and lifted her onto the buckboard. He rounded the front, gave each of the horses an affectionate pat, then climbed up. As he sat on the bench beside her, April tried to scoot over to give him a little more room. *Why do I have to be six axe handles wide?*

"You fixin' to fall out, first bump we hit?" Peter gave her a meaningful look. A sly smile lifted his lips as he tilted his head toward his left. "C'mon over here."

"See you later," Kate said over her shoulder as she went back into the house.

"Giddyup." Peter flicked the reins, and the buckboard started to move. Four crates and a pair of bushel baskets full of produce rattled in the back.

"It's uncommon for you to make a trip to town. Usually the MacPherson women go."

After glancing both directions, Peter looked back at her and winked. "Gotta make shore nobody's close 'nuff to hear us. Goin' to town made for a good excuse. You and me are gonna start in on our plan. I reckon this'll give us a time to start practicing."

"So what do I do?"

"Well, a buck don't want his gal perched so far away."

April said, "I scooted closer back home."

Peter chuckled. "You wiggled a mite, but if you got any closer to me, 'twas only a speck. 'Stead of actin' like I'm fixin' to bite you, you oughtta be close 'nuff for me to catch a whiff so's I cain 'preciate yore perfume."

"I don't wear perfume."

He thumbed back the brim of his hat and shook his head. "When I hefted you into the buckboard, I caught somethin' that smelled sweet."

Hefted? How mortifying. That's what he thinks?

"That's a right fetchin' shade of pink yore goin'. Hit's downright cute. Ain't nothin' a-wrong with a feller likin' his ladylove's scent."

"It's just the soap Polly makes for me."

"Iff'n she cain make it a soap, I'm shore she could make it into a perfume or lotion, too. Whilst we're in town, you cain drop in and ask her. You need to make it a habit to be dabbin' some on each day. A gal niver knows 'zactly when her beau might take a mind to drop in."

April nodded glumly. *No man's ever going to get close enough for perfume to matter. Peter's one of the strongest men around, and he has to "heft" me up.*

Coaxing the horses to take the right fork in the road, he said, "Speakin' of lotion, I'm countin' on you to remind me to get some of that lotion my ma's taken a shine to."

"Jergens. Aunt Lois likes Jergens. Aunt Eunice favors making her own concoction of Vaseline and mineral oil."

"Wish she wouldn't. It rubs off on ever'thang. Stuff's slicker'n spit on a glass doorknob."

April managed to laugh.

Peter smiled at her. "Now that was real good of you. Knowin' his gal thinks he's clever makes a man right proud. And you knowin' the likes and particulars of my kin—that tells me you care 'bout those I love. A feller wants his bride and family to get on real well."

"Of course, I love you all. The Chances and MacPhersons are like one big, happy family."

"Ain't that the beatenist thang? I always thought you were kin, but yore really not. Thank on it a spell. Yore aunt Lovejoy is Polly's stepmama. Since my aunt Tempy is Lovejoy's sis, that means Polly is a cousin by marriage to all of Tempy and Mike's children."

April's eyes widened. "I never gave it any thought."

"But 'tis the plain truth."

"I don't want it to be, though." April sighed. "I love all of you MacPhersons."

"Glad to know it."

She perked up. "Lovejoy says family's made by opening our hearts to others, not just by blood alone. I'm going to adopt you all."

"You shore you know what yore askin'?"

April laughed. "I most certainly do. My mind's made up."

When they reached town, Peter stopped in front of White's Mercantile. "Wait right here a moment," he ordered.

April sat up on the bench seat and stared down at her hands. They looked ugly. Blisters swelled on the pads of all ten fingers.

"Howdy, Mrs. White. I brung in fresh truck."

"Lovely!" the storekeeper said from the doorway. "I've been desperate for some."

Peter lifted the heavy crates and carried them inside. Farm work resulted in his strength—*strength he has to use to "heft" me.* April pretended to look back down at her hands.

"We'll be back in a bit, ma'am. We're gonna go pay our respects 'cross the street."

"I'll tally everything up and put it out to display." Mrs. White bustled back inside the mercantile.

April stood up and was ready to jump down.

"You hold it right thar," Peter boomed. "You tryin' to break an ankle atop already havin' burnt hands?"

"I. . .um. . ." *Don't want to break your back.*

"What's this about burned hands?" Eric Walcott asked as he stepped out of his office directly across the street.

"Howdy, Doc." Peter clamped his hands around April and swept her down. "April sorta burnt her hands yesternoon. Long as we're in town, seems like a good notion to have you take a look-see."

"Sure. Come on in."

Peter steered her across the street, up the steps, and into the office.

"Really, I'm fine."

"I'll be the judge of that." Eric took her by the wrists and turned her hands palm upward. "The blisters have to be tender. I don't want you to pop them, though. It invites infection."

"Got a salve for her?" Peter asked.

"That's not necessary." April pulled her hands back.

"Actually, I prefer burns of this nature to be kept clean and dry."

"Burns of what nature?" Polly walked in, cradling her daughter.

"April burnt her hands," Peter said.

"They're fussing over nothing." April walked over to her cousin. "How's our pretty little Ginny Mae?"

Peter stepped up and swiped the baby just before April took hold of her. "Yore in no shape to be totin' a young'un." He expertly popped the baby up by his shoulder and took to rocking her side-to-side.

"She's got a new trick," Polly said. "This week, Ginny Mae decided to sit up all on her own."

"She's bright-eyed as a bushy-tailed squirrel," Peter announced. "Polly, April's gonna need lotion for her hands. Cain you make her some?"

"I'll get on it right away."

"We're gonna go yonder to White's. We'll drop back in afore we hie home."

Steps sounded on the boardwalk. Someone entered the office. "Doc? I got me a carbuncle on my leg. Tried a drawing salve on it, but I'm hurting."

To April's surprise, Peter swiped a small towel, draped it over his shoulder, and switched Ginny Mae to that side. He patted the baby on the back as he said to Polly, "Looks like you and yore man got yore hands full. April and me—we'll carry little Ginny Mae on over to the mercantile with us."

"There aren't many men I'd trust with my baby," Polly started rolling up her sleeves. "But I've seen you with so many little ones in your arms, you probably have more experience than I do."

"Comes from bein' one of the eldest." Peter gazed down at Ginny Mae and smiled as he tenderly toyed with her darling baby curls. All told, the three MacPherson brothers had fathered thirty-four children. Twenty-five survived. "From the time I was knee-high to a grasshopper, I was holdin' or changin' a wee one."

"I'll hold her." April reached over.

Peter turned sideways so the baby was too far away for her to snag. "Nope. I'm gonna be stubborn here. Yore hands are tender. Not only that, but with Ginny Mae bein' the first Chance girl in twenty years, you all hog her to yoreselves. Hit's finally my turn to tote her, and that's that."

"Do you need anything from the mercantile?" April tore her gaze away from the sweet sight of a big, strong man doting over a bitty baby girl and looked at Polly.

"I went there earlier this morning."

"All right, then. Let's get outta their way." Peter took a step, then halted. "Polly? You gonna make that lotion smell good?"

Laughter bubbled out of Polly. "You still haven't forgiven me for using McLeans Volcanic Oil Liniment on you?"

"Truth be told, I'd ruther tangle with a skunk than have you put that on me again. I've forgiven you, but I ain't forgot. 'Twould be a cryin' shame for you to make little April sommat even a portion that stinky."

"I'll use calendula. It soothes skin and smells nice." Polly smiled. "I planned to make you more soap, April, but I've been busy."

"Don't push yourself," April said. "I still have almost a whole bar." As Peter walked her across the street, April fretted, "I should have brought food for Polly."

"This here babe is six months old. Polly's got her feet back on the ground."

April stopped and gave him a telling look.

Peter threw back his head and let out a belly laugh. Eyes twinkling, he leaned down and murmured, "I've suffered a few bellyaches from Polly's cookin'. I reckon she's given up and buys plenty of them fancy, canned vittles."

Shuddering, April whispered back, "She does."

"She and Doc look happy 'nuff." Peter took her arm and pulled her across the street. "Fact is, we et some of them canned vittles when we went to Yosemite last summer. Ever' last meal you made tasted grand. What you need to do is make shore when li'l Ginny Mae here comes to an age where she cain stand afore the stove, you teach her. Come the day she marries up, her man's gonna thank you from the bottom of his heart."

"Are you sure it won't be from the bottom of his stomach?"

Peter grinned. "April, I truly like that 'bout you. You've got yoreself a quick mind, but you niver speak words that cut."

April blinked.

"Now yore supposed to thank a buck when he pays you a compliment."

"Thank you," she said.

"Welcome." Peter continued to hold Ginny Mae against his shoulder as easily as could be and opened the door to the mercantile. When the bell rang, the baby let out a wail. "Now, don't you be cloudin' up and fixin' to rain." Peter shifted Ginny Mae and kissed her.

"Hello," Mrs. White called over from the produce display. Her face suddenly wrinkled in concern. "I didn't realize you'd brought in your aunt Tempy's baby! Oh, dear. And you went to see Doc. If you brought the baby, Tempy must be bad off and—"

"No, no," April hurriedly said. "It's Polly's little girl."

"All my kin are hale as horses." Peter turned so Mrs. White could see Ginny Mae. "Doc and Polly are busy, so we took the prize and ran."

Mrs. White let out a tense laugh. "You had me worried for a moment there."

Ginny Mae continued to fuss. April said, "Not many men would call a noisy baby a prize."

"As I said yesternoon, no accountin' for the foolish ways of others."

"I can hold her," April offered as she reached for Ginny Mae.

"Not with burnt hands, you won't. Grab us up one of them baskets. I'll tote it about whilst you fill it up with the stuff we need."

Mrs. White popped a cabbage onto the top of a pretty row. "If you brought a list, I could fill it for you."

April said, "Kate told me to ask if the rivets she wanted have arrived."

"I'll take a look in the back room. There's a crate of things I haven't unpacked yet."

"Thanks."

Peter rhythmically patted Ginny Mae. "We'll rustle up whate'er we need out here. April, how's about you fetching the basket?"

"The first thing we're getting is the Jergens for your mother."

"Gladdens me that you remembered." He followed her and swiped the basket she'd tried to hold. "Some of that Johnson & Johnson talc could help a bit if the lot of you are still rashy."

April's jaw dropped.

"Hot as it's been, might as well get a canister for you and Kate to share in your cabin and another for the boys." Calm as you please, he stood there, waiting for her to fill the basket.

She grabbed a canister of talc and the lotion, then shoved them into the basket.

Peter leaned down and stared her in the eye. "I ain't a-gonna budge from this spot till you get the boys some talc. Tanner was itchin' to beat the band at lunch yesterday."

April wanted to tell him the talc was for the boys, but she'd be lying. It was only merciful to get another. Putting a second one in the basket, she said brightly, "So what next?"

Chapter 4

"Johnna asked me to bring home some Mum."

Her face went burning hot. *Horses sweat, men perspire, women glow.* Her mother, having been a missionary who grew up wearing all of the proper clothing a true lady wore even in the brutal heat of the Hawaiian Islands, had quoted that phrase more than a few times. Buying a deodorant practically announced to all and sundry that a woman sweated like a draft horse.

Peter grinned. "C'mon, April. After we went camping in Yosemite last year, you spoilt ordinary livin' for us, totin' along all those extry little thangs."

"Like what?" She hoped to distract him from the fact that she was slipping two packages of Mum deodorant into the basket.

"Ulysses and me—we got the whole clan using Sheffield's Crème Dentifrice now 'stead of just dippin' into a box of bakin' soda. Ma's happy as a dog with two tails over it. That tube the cream comes in is right nifty, and we ain't swiping stuff from the kitchen that the womenfolk were countin' on."

"I'm surprised. I thought you were going to say you got started using Ivory soap, but Gabriel is the one who brought that to camp."

"Now that you mention it, I probably oughtta get a bar. Doc and Polly recommended Aunt Tempy use it on baby Artemis."

"The rivets are here," Mrs. White called out. "And Peter? Your mother and aunts always make new outfits for the kids to wear to school. Do they need anything? Buttons? Thread?"

"Yes, ma'am. The women shore have been stitchin' a heap to make all the little ones new duds. Thankee for remindin' me. They need more thread."

April walked over to the next aisle and reached for the gold. She didn't need to ask about the color. The entire MacPherson family wore golden yellow. Years back, Peter's uncles made that decision, and they'd stuck with it for the past decade. Once they determined to do something, the MacPherson men didn't waver in the least. "One spool or two?"

"Two. Iff'n they don't need two now, 'twon't go to waste in the future."

They moseyed around the store, filling the basket with embroidery floss, Semple's chewing gum, cinnamon, and salt. "How's about boot laces? I broke mine this mornin' and tied it together. Twine's a pain in the neck. Knots up and won't let go, so a body has to lace in a new length each day."

"Why don't you have Kate make you leather ones? She does it for all the Chance men."

"I hate botherin' her."

"Nonsense." April breezed by the laces and toward the ice box against the far wall. "I need to get some yeast."

"Best you toss in a few cakes of that Fleischmann's for us, too. With Tempy just birthin' Artemis, the women haven't been to town in a few weeks. I'm guessin' they're runnin' low and jist didn't thank to ask me to stock up."

"I'm taking all of the yeast, Mrs. White. Will that be a problem?"

"No, I'm due to get a new shipment in tomorrow at the latest. Peter, I ordered the sugar your mother said she wanted for canning. It'll be in day after tomorrow."

"Obliged."

"It's always fun to see what comes in." Mrs. White fussed with her lace collar. "You'd think they'd be accustomed to me asking for all of the bags to be yellow after making that request for years on end."

"I didn't get too excited last year. Most all of the sacks had posies all o'er 'em." Peter grimaced. "Hit took Ulysses and me two whole days to talk the women outta stitchin' us men shirts from that girly fabric."

"It's a shame it wasn't here for you today."

"I'm enjoyin' the trip to town. Mayhap in a day or two, me and April will come back to pick up the sacks."

Putting the yeast on the counter, April looked at the contents of the basket and the small packet of rivets. "What a shame that the sugar hasn't arrived. It's hard to imagine we made a trip to town for such a paltry collection of things."

"Thangs don't have to be big to be important." Peter lowered Ginny Mae onto the counter and grinned as she teetered a little before managing to sit up. "Do they, l'il darlin'?"

"Will there be anything else?" Mrs. White asked.

"I'd like three yards of yellow flannel, please."

"What is she doin', getting yeller?" Peter asked the baby, who promptly drooled all over the arm he used to steady her. "Don't she ken the yeller's for the MacPhersons?"

"I sure do." April smiled. "I thought I'd make a few gowns for Artemis."

"Now ain't that sweet."

Mrs. White took the new bolt from the shelf and started to unroll it. Clucking her tongue, she frowned at the fabric. "Shameful. Just shameful. Look at that." She unrolled more. "This flaw goes down the middle of the whole bolt!"

"Wouldn't be seen on a gallopin' goose," Peter said.

April leaned forward. Carefully inspecting the flaw, she said, "I could work around this."

"I can't charge you full price for spoiled goods. How about if you buy four yards and I sell it to you, two yards for a penny?"

After storing their purchases in the bed of the buckboard, Peter led April back into Polly and Eric's place. "Got yoreself a peachy babe here. Sweet tempered and smart."

Eric pressed a kiss on Polly's temple. "Yes, she is. I'm hoping Ginny Mae takes after her."

Peter laughed and slid the baby back into her mother's arms. *Someday, April and me—we'll have a passel of young'uns of our own. I'm bidin' my time, Lord, but 'twouldn't make me sad if You hurried things along a mite.*

"I made the lotion for you." Polly nodded toward her husband's desk. "There's some for Greta and Kate, too. Peter, I made a salve there for Tempy to use on Artemis's rash. That little baby has the most sensitive skin!"

"Thankee. Aunt Tempy's frettin' like Artemis is her first 'stead of her tenth baby."

"I'll try to get out to the ranch tomorrow or the next day." Polly smiled at April. "I'll help you wash your hair."

"I'd be grateful. Kate's too busy to do it. I'm not sure when Greta will come home. Caleb is moping around without her."

"You've got yore hands full already, Polly. Johnna cain traipse over to holp April. Fact is, Ma and Aunt Eunice are puttin' up tomatoes today. They plan to show up o'er at Chance Ranch to do the same tomorrow."

"But I—"

Peter pressed a finger against April's lips. "Now hush." Despite his desire to do otherwise, he broke contact. "Greta's away, and Kate cain't do it all on her own. With yore hands all burnt, them tomatoes would go to waste. We cain't abide seein' good food squandered. Plenty's the time you stood at the MacPherson stove in our times of need."

"If you expose those blisters to any heat, they'll worsen," Eric said. "Best thing for you is to use Polly's lotion three times a day."

"Here's a sugar sack for you to carry the things out to the buckboard." Polly smiled as she handed the small cloth bag to Peter. "Tell Eunice to use it to make Elvera a bodice or little skirt."

"Lookie thar. Hit's got yeller kittens all o'er." He chuckled. "It stretches my mind to believe Hezzie's a-gonna teach Elvera the difference 'twixt a kitty and a skunk."

"She was really cute," April said.

"Being cute didn't take off the stink."

"To hear Eunice tell the story," Polly said, "the juice from every last tomato in your garden didn't, either."

"I'm surprised they're canning tomatoes today." Eric grinned. "I didn't think you'd have any left."

"God gave us a bumper crop of 'em." Peter grinned. "Guess it proves how He knows our needs even afore we know 'bout them." He tucked the lotions and salve into the sack. "We'll be headin' out now."

When they reached the buckboard, April set a hand on the front wheel and started to put her foot on a spoke so she could climb up. Peter yanked her back and turned her around. "I'd be pleased to holp you up, miss."

Once they were seated and he'd headed out of town, he gave April an arch look. "You cain't be jumpin' outta the buckboard or scramblin' in like a schoolgirl in pigtails."

Quick as a bunny, she turned her head away.

Peter reached over and pressed against her right cheek, forcing her to face him. "What's got into you?"

"Nothing."

"I got me sisters and girl cousins. One thang I ken: when any of 'em say 'nothin,' it's sommat big. Suppose you level with me."

A mirthless laugh burst out of her. "Something big. That's me."

"You cain't be tellin' me yore afeared I cain't heft you into a buckboard!"

"*Heft.* That says it all." Her face felt hot as embers beneath his fingers, and she lowered her lashes to keep from looking him in the eyes.

"When sommat has a right feel in a man's hand, he says it's got a nice heft. When I wrap my hands 'round yore middle—hope you don't take offense at me speakin' plainly—you fill my hands real good." He nodded. "Yup. You do. Me sayin' *heft*—well, you oughta take that as a compliment."

April pulled away and covered her eyes and forehead with her palm. Fingers and thumb rubbed her temples as she muttered, "You've never had a sweetheart. What am I thinking, listening to your advice? This isn't going to work."

"Hold it thar just a minute."

She gave him a baleful glare.

Aware his plan was in jeopardy, Peter hurriedly said, "This bargain could benefit us both. Mayhap you could fill me in on a gal's view on matters."

"You have sisters."

"And you've got brothers. Fact is, it cain be dreadful embarrassin' to share yore innermost fears and failures with 'em."

April nodded.

"I didn't say 'haul,' so suppose you tell me what a gal would rather have a buck say."

"Lift." She gave him a timid, half-smile. "You *lift* a lady into a wagon."

"Okay." He smiled at her. "From now on, April, yore to wait for me to lift you in and out of the wagons. And yore s'posed to smile at me when I do. You got a smile that quickens a man's heart. Why, any buck watchin' is gonna be pea green with envy that I'm the one holping you."

"He's liable to be grateful he's not risking his back."

Peter heaved a loud sigh. "You gotta stop that. Any man who's afeared he cain't *lift* a woman oughtn't be courtin' at all. He should be visitin' Doc to figger out what ails him!"

He drove a little farther, then pulled back on the reins. "Whoa."

"Is something wrong? Why did we stop?"

"On account of it bein' lunchtime." He hopped down, went around to April, and raised his hands toward her.

"I need to get home, Peter."

"Horsefeathers."

"Truly, I do need to get home. I shouldn't have left in the first place."

"You cain tell a feller you ought to be home—that lets him know yore mindful of your obligations. But when you insist and he knows 'tisn't absolutely essential, he's gonna be insulted. Hit's like tellin' him you'd rather be scrapin' yore knuckles on a washboard 'stead of spendin' time with him."

"But we're just pretending."

"Cain't pretend when you don't do it." Peter grinned at her. "Now don't you be challenging what I jist said. You ken full well I meant iff'n you don't practice like yore out courtin' with some fine buck, then you'll like as not miss out on learning sommat important."

To his delight, she stood. Closing his hands around her waist, he ordered, "Now lay your hands atop my shoulders." She complied. He lifted a little, then drew her down. Instead of letting go, he rumbled, "Now don't turn loose of me quick. Wait a bit afore you draw back yore hands."

"How long?"

Forever. "Long 'nuff to look me in the eyes and whisper a sweet little thankee."

"Thank you." She broke contact, then gave him a funny look. "When do you let go?"

Never. "A man is a bit slow to turn loose 'cuz he's taken a shine to a gal. Iff'n a man keeps holt of you too long, you cain twist free or tromp on his toe to make him mind his manners."

"You still haven't let go."

He grinned. When April tried to twist, he held tight. Her eyes widened, then she chewed on her bottom lip. A second later, he chuckled. "Was that a mouse skitterin' 'cross my boot?"

She stepped a little harder, and he let go.

"There. I pretended."

"And you learnt sommat." He pivoted and pulled a blanket from the back of the buckboard.

"Peter!" She looked just as shocked as she sounded. Staring at the blanket, April stammered, "You said we were just pretending. We're not really going to plop down out here in the middle of nowhere and waste time!"

"Lookie how beautiful 'tis here. A field full of posies, a gentle breeze, and 'nuff shade to let you keep your ladylike complexion. A place like this ain't nowhere. 'Tis God's spread. Takin' the opportunity to 'preciate it—that ain't wastin' time." He grabbed the lunch Ma had packed for them and said, "Now you slide yore hand in the crook of my arm."

April balked. "That seems awfully. . .forward."

"Nah. What with women's shoes having them silly heels, and us bein' at a spot where the ground's uneven, hit's common sense for a woman to seek a steadying arm. Now iff'n you grabbed for my hand, that would be forward."

When he winged his elbow toward her, she slid her hand into the crook and sighed. "I don't know if I'll ever remember all of this."

"Don't expect you to, all at once. Practice makes perfect. We'll make shore we get together a bunch."

They spread out the blanket, then sat side by side. Curling his hand around hers, Peter said, "I'm tryin' to be mindful of yore fingers. When first you have picnics with other bucks, don't go lettin' 'em hold yore hand. Me? Well, both of our families practice linkin' hands for grace. Wouldn't seem right, us prayin' without doin' this."

"Even when there are just two of us?"

"Bible says where two or three are gathered, God's in the midst. Two's plenty." He bowed his head. "Dear lovin' Lord, thankee for April and givin' us time together. I ask Yore blessin' on our endeavors and on the food we eat. Be with our kin, where'er they be, amen."

"Amen." After emptying the buckets, April took one of the cloths and spread it across her lap.

"All you Chances—you got elegant table manners. What say you holp me learn some of 'em?"

"I'd be happy to. The first thing you do after prayer is spread a napkin across your lap."

"Why? Food ain't gonna drop till after you served up everything."

"It keeps everyone from grabbing."

"Seems easy 'nuff for a woman. Men don't 'zactly have a lap." He chose one thigh and draped the cloth over it. "And I'd thank a woman'd be gratified to see folks pouncin' on her food. Shows they like her cookin'."

April unwrapped a pair of sandwiches and served him one. "Oh, it's your mama's chicken salad! I don't know what she adds to it, but her chicken salad's the best I've ever tasted."

"Says hit's a secret. Johnna had to vow she'd not tell a soul other than her own daughter someday. I 'spect Ma'll share the ingredients with my bride." He waggled his brows. "How bad d'you wanna have that recipe?"

April laughed.

Honey pie, you don't know how serious I am.

Her laughter suddenly died out. "Peter! What did you tell your mother? She has to know something's up, or she wouldn't have made this lunch!"

"I tole her the truth—that yore a special gal and I wouldn't mind passin' more time with you."

"Peter! They're going to think—"

"I don't live my life frettin' o'er what other folks thank. Neither should you. Iff'n yore shore what you do is pleasin' to the Almighty, that's the only measure what counts."

"Yes, but—"

His heart twisted. "April, are you ashamed to have folks believe I've taken a shine to you?"

Chapter 5

Don't be ridiculous!" The immediacy of April's response made it clear that embarrassment wasn't the issue. "Peter, if folks think you're courting me, then you can't be free to follow your heart when the right girl comes along."

"You oughtta be more worried 'bout fellers who won't come callin' on you 'cuz I am."

"Have you taken leave of your senses? I've never caught the attention of anyone."

Peter snorted. "So you say. You hang onto yore hat, April Chance. Men always want what they cain't get. Soon as fellers see me 'round you, they'll be kickin' theirselves for not seeing you in a true light. I'm gonna make 'em jealous. Won't be long afore they beat a path to yore door."

"You're not making sense. In one breath, you tell me men won't come calling because we're seen together. In the next breath, you tell me they'll be beating a path out to the ranch."

"That's 'cuz you don't understand the plan yet." He took a big bite of his sandwich.

Looking completely disgruntled, April took a bite of hers.

"Here's how it works. Folks is gonna link yore name and mine. Soon 'nuff, the fellers'll take notice. You'll be yore friendly self to them, but I'll still have you on my arm. With me squirin' you about, they're gonna have to contend with me. Me? I'm gonna gloat aloud 'bout how wonderful them sticky buns are that you make." He lifted his sandwich, and just before taking a good-sized chomp out of it, he tacked on, "Yore gonna make me them sticky buns so I'm not bein' a liar, right?"

"I make them every Wednesday."

"But when you up and bake 'em any other day, yore kin are gonna take notice. Smack their hands away and tell 'em that whole batch is for me. Things like that make an impression. Won't be long afore someone on Chance Ranch goes to town and grumbles."

"I'm beginning to wonder if all of this is a ploy to get me to bake you a batch."

Peter set down his sandwich and looked at her. "Woman, I'm fixin' to give you a lecture, so pay me heed."

Her eyes widened.

"First off, I'm a straightforward kinda man. If all I wanted was yore sticky buns, I'd tromp up and tell you so. Second, I have no patience with a man who stoops to dally with a gal's heart. Most of all, yore worthy of love and respect jist for bein' you. 'Tis the truth. God gave you a special gift."

"Gift?"

"Gal, thank on this: Ever'body cain sing, but some got a special voice. Same is true 'bout cookin'. Most every woman—'cept for Polly—cain cook. But when you step into a kitchen, what comes out is a masterpiece. I'll be shore to praise yore talent, but don't you e'er make the mistake of thankin' yore only worth is a batch of sommat you pull outta the oven. Someday, like the Bible says, yore young'uns are gonna rise up and call you blessed, and a lucky man will value you far above rubies."

If he hadn't been sitting next to her, the longing in April's eyes would have knocked him to his knees. Peter said softly, "I believe it. Deep in my heart, I do."

"Peter?"

"Yeah?"

"You're an extraordinary man. Truly, you are. Why haven't you gone courting? Plenty of girls would be flattered to receive your attention."

He shook his head. "Not the right time yet. God's got someone special for me, and I'm fine with waitin' 'til He brings her along."

"You're not impatient?"

"At times, but most often not." He picked up what was left of his sandwich. "Shore was nice of you to speak well of me. I'm a simple farm boy, and I'm oddly spoken. My kin—we have all we need, but others prob'ly thank the MacPhersons are dirt poor."

"You're a hardworking man. Strong and handsome. As for your dialect—I find it charmingly expressive. In many ways, it resembles the phrasing of the King James language in our Bible."

"Niver thought of it thataway."

"Well, I have. When it comes to the MacPherson clan—you're all content with what God's given you. You're rich in the things that matter most: love, family, friends, and health. Any woman who can't appreciate that doesn't deserve you."

Peter stared at her. For so long, he'd wondered what she thought about those issues. She didn't have to search at all to come up with any of those fine words. The praise just flowed out of her, and he knew the sentiments were heartfelt. *If only she'd come to feel all of those things specially for me.*

He cleared his throat. "You shore said a mouthful."

"I meant every bit of it."

"Even though I don't tuck my napkin in my lap, first off?"

April laughed and yanked his hand from his mouth just before he licked his fingers. "Don't lick, Peter. Use the napkin! As for table manners—those can be learned in a trice. Character is developed over a lifetime. A woman would be a fool to choose a so-called gentleman with poor moral fiber over a rough man with integrity who's proven his devotion to God and family."

"Yore sweet words are better than dessert."

"I don't know. . . . We have grapes and Aunt Tempy's delicious cheese."

He looked into her lovely blue eyes. "The day couldn't get more perfect."

"The day couldn't get any worse." Matt Salter stared at the back of the buggy that carried away a weeping woman. "Her whole world has been destroyed."

"Bootleg moonshine." The San Francisco sheriff shook his head. "Killed her son and blinded her husband."

"Where's it coming from?"

Sheriff Charles S. Laumeister turned to go back inside the building. "Not sure."

"Anybody check orders for copper piping or large orders of sugar?"

Laumeister shot him a grin. "You'll be doing that. I'm putting two of you on special detail. Miller is canvassing south of here. You'll go east."

"Lot of land out there. Bootleggers could have multiple stills in operation."

"I expect they do." The sheriff sat behind his desk and shrugged. "I don't want you nabbing someone who's distilling a jug or two a week."

Matt didn't respond. It would be a waste of breath. Plenty of farmers and ranchers distilled small amounts of spirits for themselves. Rounding them up would be ludicrous.

"I want to put down the major source. There's a big operation out there somewhere. Pose as a man in need of work. You can drift from one area to the next. No one'll suspect a saddle tramp of being a lawman."

A wry smile tugged at the corner of Matt's mouth. "I was a saddle tramp before I became a deputy."

"Precisely why this case is suited to you."

"Folks are closed-mouthed. Finagling the necessary information means I'll have to earn their trust. That takes time."

Laumeister nodded. "I want a thorough job. Get to the heart of the operation. Keep in contact—once a week's fine."

"That's the fastest way to blow my cover. Places where there's a still, most of the locals know about it. Too risky for me to check in regularly."

"Do your best."

"That goes without saying. I'll have to give up my room at the boardinghouse."

"No loss. I've tasted Jenny's cooking. Burned baked beans'll be a treat by comparison. You can stow a trunk in the storage room here. Get going."

Matt strode out of the office, down the street, and into the boarding house. A wool blanket, one Sunday-go-to-meeting white shirt and string tie, a passably good pair of britches the color of charcoal, a pair of just-this-side-of-disreputable work shirts, and his Levis. . .that's about all a rover would have aside from his hat and saddle.

Matt changed into the red shirt and denims. A rodeo buckle he'd won a few years back gave the finishing touch. Rolling up the remainder, he realized he'd need a bandana. *Good. It gives me an excuse to mosey into a mercantile and pick up on gossip.* He picked up the roll and opened his door.

"Mr. Salter, whatever are you doing?" Miss Jenny asked from the hallway.

He looked at the homely old spinster. Bless her, she worked hard to earn an honest living. She couldn't cook worth two hoots, yet she tried her best. In the year and a half that he'd lived here, Matt had grown to respect her. He even paid for both room and board though he rarely ate any lunch or supper there. That way, she still had a tiny bit more in her pocket.

"Miss Jenny, you run a fine place. The bed's comfortable, and you wash sheets every week. I'm going to miss that, but—"

"You're leaving." Her lower lip trembled. "It's the cowboy in you, isn't it? You long to sleep out under the stars."

"It's been a long while since I have."

"You're a fine young man. I'll be praying for you. Would it be too forward of me to ask you to drop me a note every now and then? Just to make sure you haven't gotten murdered in your sleep by some nefarious bandit?"

She'd been reading too many dime novels. Then again, aside from working and studying her Bible, what did Miss Jenny have to fill her hours? Matt nodded. "I'll be sure to write you a line or two."

"I do appreciate that. I'll bake a going-away cake for you. We'll have it after supper tonight."

"Miss Jenny, that's as kind as can be, but I'm going to leave right after I pack the rest of my things." He dug in his pocket and pulled out a golden eagle. "This is for you."

"Oh no. I couldn't! Mr. Salter, that's ten dollars!"

"It might take you awhile to get a new boarder in. Since I didn't give you notice, it only seems fair."

She shook her head. "I can't take that. You're already paid clear through the end of next month. Truthfully, I ought to give you a refund."

"Let's not spoil our last few minutes together quibbling." He pressed the coin into her hand.

"God bless you, Mr. Salter."

"He does. May He bless you as well."

A scant hour later, Matt swung up into the saddle and headed east. At sunset, he reached the outskirts of a sleepy little town and spent the night outside. Hot as it was, he didn't need a fire—but his clothes lacked the smell of wood smoke and needed a touch of authentic ground-in grime. He'd bought a box supper right before leaving San Francisco. After eating the meal, he used the pasteboard box as tinder to start a fire.

By the time dawn arrived, he glanced down at his rumpled shirt and grinned. Roughing it for one night resulted in just the right disguise.

"Mornin'." He doffed his hat toward the old lady and gent at the counter of the mercantile of the nearby town.

"Never seen you before," the old man said.

"I'm just passing through. Lost my bandana."

The woman toddled out and beckoned him. "I have a whole stack of them over here."

Matt sauntered over and thumbed through the stack. "Nice ones. Sorta fancy." He gave her a crooked smile. "Last one I had was part of a sugar sack. Yellow. I was partial to that."

The old woman chortled softly. "You'll not find a yellow sugar sack on any shelf for miles around."

"Why?"

"Because the MacPhersons in Reliable buy all their sugar in yellow sacks."

"Is that a fact?"

The old woman's head bobbed.

He pretended to thumb through the rest of the stack and mused in a laconic voice, "Seems like a lot of sugar."

"Been like that for years. Those are first-rate bandanas. No skimping on the size. Edges done by machine with small stitches that won't give out under hard use."

"Yup." After patting the stack, he took the uppermost. "This'll do." He headed for the counter. As he was paying, his stomach growled.

"The diner's open across the street," the old man said.

"Now, Daddy," the old woman chided, "sending this young man over there's almost a crime." She waddled closer and clucked her tongue. "New folks from back East just bought it. Charging half again what the old prices were and serving smaller portions."

"Mama, it's their business. They can set whatever price they want."

"They won't stay in business long that way. When the diner doesn't draw folks to stop in, we won't have as many customers, either."

"We'll get more customers. Folks are bound to buy more groceries when they get a gander at the prices over yonder."

Matt gave the couple a curt nod, picked up the bandana, and walked out. Bickering irritated him. Instead of going to the diner, he rode toward the next town. Learning that the MacPhersons of Reliable used considerable quantities of sugar on a regular basis led him in that direction.

By midday, Matt reckoned even Miss Jenny's cooking would taste pretty good. He hitched his horse to the post outside of Joe's Eats. A burly man in a stained apron waved his arm toward the room. "Have a seat. Coffee?"

Matt nodded. He'd discovered if he let the other person start talking, they were more likely to give information as he subtly steered the conversation.

Thump. A mug hit the table. "I've got catfish, ham sandwiches, and ribs. Whaddya want?"

"How fresh is the catfish?"

"Billy there," the aproned man jabbed his thumb to the left, "caught a mess of'em this morning. I add cayenne pepper to the cornmeal to give 'em a kick, so if you've got a sissy-mouth, choose something else."

"I'll take catfish."

A slow smile lit the cook's face. "Double the cayenne?"

"Triple."

Billy leaned way back in his chair. "You don't know what you're asking for."

"The hotter, the better." Matt lifted the coffee mug and took a long, loud slurp. After enduring Miss Jenny's weak-as-dishwater coffee each morning, this stuff tasted strong. He nodded approvingly. "Cup of this could wake a dead man."

Chuckling as he headed toward the kitchen, the cook asked, "Staying around very long?"

"Don't know."

The man across from Billy shoved the last of a biscuit into his mouth and spoke around the food. "Itchy feet?"

"Show me a cowboy who doesn't have itchy feet," Billy shot back.

"Or a powerful thirst," the first man said.

Matt took another gulp, then set down the mug and twisted it slowly from side to side. "There's strong coffee; then there's strong whiskey."

Billy snorted. "Not around here. The Tankard waters down all of the liquor."

"Now that," Matt paused meaningfully, "is a crime." He'd spoken the truth. It was criminal to represent goods to a customer and purposefully give him less than he paid for. Nonetheless, Matt knew full well these men would take the comment in another light.

"A sorry circumstance," Bill agreed.

"Then the emporium—"

Billy scoffed. "The old coot at the mercantile won't sell spirits. Says it's the devil's brew. If a man here wants decent whiskey, he goes off to the city and brings himself back a supply."

"And he's got to reckon with his neighbors if he doesn't take an order from them." The other man smacked his hand on the table and bellowed, "More coffee!"

"Come get the pot yourself," the cook hollered.

"Some way to treat a paying customer," the man muttered as he rose.

Billy shoveled a heaping forkful of peas in, chewed all of twice, then swallowed. "Pennington's usually looking for another hand. Can't keep 'em long. Won't abide a man who takes a nip now and then. One of those holier-than-thou sorts. Everyone on his spread has to go to church. He's got no call, telling men what to do during the time they call their own."

"Can't keep the help for long, huh?"

"Nope. And his daughters are uglier than a mud-stuck fence." Billy shuddered. "Buck-toothed and horse-faced. A feller might turn a blind eye to that if he knew when the old man passed on, he'd get the ranch."

"But he won't?"

"He brought in a nephew last year. Greenhorn from back East."

Matt grimaced.

"I swear," Billy said, "there's more air between that Easterner's ears than there is under the crown of his ten-gallon hat."

The other man returned with the coffee pot. "Best you fill that cup of yours with milk, mister. Much cayenne as Sam put on your catfish, your mouth is gonna beg for mercy."

"I'll handle it." Matt knew the game. These men were taking his measure. It wouldn't hurt if he got a few folks talking about him. . .as long as it cast him in light of a tough, ready-to-work wrangler. He'd mentioned his experience. There was no way for these men to check it out, but by downing the punishingly hot catfish, he'd prove himself.

He lifted his mug and accepted the refill with a nod. "So Pennington is out. I'm looking for something short-term, but if I take a nip of who-hit-John, I don't want the job to be over. I leave on my terms, not theirs."

The cook came out with a plate. He placed it in front of Matt, then pulled out the chair directly across from him and took a seat. "Give 'er a taste."

"Don't mind if I do." He speared a chunk, popped it into his mouth, chomped a few times, and swallowed. "Now that's catfish!" He took another bite.

"Like it?" The cook gave him a sly look.

"It'll do. Don't mean to insult you, but do you have any Tabasco?"

As Matt doused the fish with Tabasco, he asked, "Any other spreads looking for help?"

"Could be the Berlews would hire you on. That kid's a skinflint, though. More than one cowboy's walked away with less in his pocket than Berlew promised."

"Is that a fact?" Matt mumbled that comment without intending it as a question. It would merely serve to keep the conversation going.

"He's got prime breeding stock and plenty of pasture. His granddaddy kicked the bucket and left the place to him. Won't come as no surprise if he runs it into the ground by the time he's thirty."

Matt washed down the last bite of fish with a long swallow of coffee. "Well, sounds like I'd better hit the road if I wanna find me work. Places hereabouts don't sound much to my liking."

The cook stared at Matt's empty plate with nothing short of admiration. "Somebody's gotta want a man like you."

Billy perked up. "Hey—d'ya only run cows, or will you work horses?"

"I'm not choosy."

"Next town east of here is Reliable. Chance Ranch puts out the best saddle horses you'll ever see."

The cook stood and wiped his hands down the front of his apron. "They hardly ever hire help."

Billy rapped his knuckles on the table. "Might be that they would. A bunch of the Chance men left for a while. Handful of young'uns are running the place."

Men leaving for a spell might mean they were up to something. If their horse ranch was so successful, few things would promise profits great enough to entice them away. Moonshining was lucrative. The facts added up to paint a suspicious picture. The MacPhersons who bought all that sugar were from Reliable, too. Either family or both could be involved. Matt mused, "Chance Ranch, huh?"

Chapter 6

Shoving back several damp curls that had escaped her precarious bun, Kate wilted onto a bench in the yard. "I'm beat."

April laughed. "Is that your way of saying you'd rather watch the kids the next time?"

"I'm going to write a letter to the Ball Mason company and ask them to make thirty-gallon jars." Kate grinned at her. "It would be a whole lot easier to can kids and watch vegetables."

"You have a point," April said. "I'm sorry I couldn't help."

Shaking her head, Kate turned toward her and said, "You're not the one who ought to apologize. I should. You've always helped with the canning. Most years, I either watched the kids or managed to be busy with some other project."

Peter sauntered up. "Well? Get a lot done?"

"I'm not sure," Kate confessed. "For all the work we did in the kitchen, it doesn't seem like all that much when I look at the results. How can it take that much work to fill up those quart jars?"

"It takes four jars to feed everyone just one supper."

"April," Kate moaned, "did you have to say that?"

Giving her a sweet smile, April said, "Well, it would only take two right now with half of the family gone."

Peter chuckled as he stepped to April's side and casually poked in a few of her hairpins as if they needed attention—even though they didn't. "But yore using fresh-picked truck right now. See how much work yore saving?"

Laughter bubbled out of Kate. "Only you would point that out. Are you staying for supper?"

"Will it be more work for you?"

Kate pretended to glower at him. "You know you're always welcome here. There's always plenty of food, too."

A stranger rounded the edge of one of the cabins. He yanked off his hat, revealing sable hair and deeply tanned features. A couple of days' worth of whiskers sandpapered his jaw. "Ladies, sir." He nodded, then rode his palomino a little closer before dismounting.

"Lose your way?" Peter asked as he stepped in front of Kate and April. Kate wanted to push him out of the way. Then again, she used the shield he created to reach up to swiftly tuck hairpins back into place and lift the corner of her apron to blot her face.

"Hope not. Sign at the entrance said Chance Ranch. I'm looking for work. I'm Matt Salter."

Peter stepped forward and shook hands. "Peter MacPherson. I'm the neighbor to the east."

Kate leaned to the side to see Mr. Salter's face. His smile robbed him of the disreputable look days in the saddle lent.

"MacPherson," Mr. Salter repeated. "You must belong to that buckboard that just went by me on the road."

Peter chuckled. "Were they all still singing at the top of their lungs?"

"Seemed like they were enjoying themselves." Mr. Salter's brown eyes sparkled as he tacked on, "Only time I ever saw that much yellow in one place was standing in front of the corncrib right after a husking."

Popping to her feet, Kate added, "I'd be willing to bet there were more children in the buckboard than there were ears of corn in the crib."

"Ma'am." Mr. Salter gave her a mannerly nod as he said, "I'd be hard pressed to disagree."

"It's *miss*," Kate said.

Peter cleared his throat loudly to drown out her words. "The Chance men'll be by directly. You'll need to talk with them."

"Thanks. Mind if I water my horse?"

"Please do." Kate couldn't get out another word before Peter took hold of her arm and pulled her around.

"Ladies, 'tisn't fittin' to leave Mr. Salter out here on his lonesome. I'll keep him company whilst you tend to the supper." Peter pulled April to her feet and prodded them toward the kitchen.

Kate didn't want to go back into the kitchen. She'd been there all day, canning beans, corn, beets, and tomatoes. Even with the doors open so the air would blow through the screens, the place still felt hot as could be.

April hooked her arm through Kate's. "We need to plan tomorrow's menu, anyway."

As soon as they got into the cabin, Kate pulled away from her cousin. "What was that all about? Any time a wrangler comes through, the least we do is invite him to stay to supper."

"Quiet down," April hissed. "We normally have five more men, five more women, and a half-dozen kids here, too. Peter's being cautious, and it's for our welfare."

"That man has honest eyes. Steady, deep brown, never-let-you-down eyes. He's taken good care of his mount, too. Uncle Bryce swears you can tell a lot about a man by how he cares for his horse."

"When the boys come in, they can decide whether he's staying for supper."

"I vote that he stays—for supper, and for a job."

"You're not old enough to vote," April reminded her. "You won't be twenty-one for almost a year yet."

Kate winced. The family's rule stood strong. Any member was given a vote on matters as soon as they reached their twenty-first birthday. "Caleb, Tobias, and you are the only ones who have votes. Well, Greta, too, but she's not here. So you have to vote in favor of him, April."

"Why are you taking on so?"

"We could use the help," Kate muttered. She turned toward the stove and grabbed a potholder. By keeping her back to April, she might manage to hide her feelings.

"Just yesterday, you were saying how well we've done on our own."

Kate opened the oven door and moved the huge roasters full of casserole around. They didn't necessarily require that action, but it kept her busy. "We have done well, but it would be good to hire a little help so we could accomplish a few extra projects before everyone gets home."

"We're expecting the family to get home any day now."

"See? That proves that we'd better grab this opportunity." Kate shut the oven door and turned around. "There's no telling when another man will be by."

April gave her a knowing grin. "I have a funny feeling there's something about this particular man that has you angling for him to stay."

"He's young and healthy, and he has fine manners." Kate stared at her cousin. "Not that you'd notice. You and Peter are so besotted with one another, it could rain pie tins and neither of you would notice."

Cheeks turning scarlet, April squeaked, "Kate!"

"Don't bother to deny it. Peter's hovering over you. He even fussed with your hairpins out there when they didn't need any attention at all." April looked ready to say something, so Kate plowed ahead, "Just now, Peter protected you from that stranger—even though no danger existed."

"Peter protected both of us. And you can't say for certain that Mr. Ummm. . ."

"Salter," Kate provided.

"Yes. Well, you can't vouch for Mr. Salter. Plenty of women have been beguiled and deceived by charming men."

"He was charming, wasn't he?" Kate stirred the peas.

"Add a pinch of sugar to that water. The peas always taste better if you do."

"So that's your secret!" Kate meant to put in a dab. Almost half a cup plopped into the boiling pot. "Oh no!"

April hopped up and grabbed the colander. "Dump them in this right away!"

She placed it in the sink as Kate snagged hot pan holders.

"Do you know how many peas I shelled to get this pot?"

"I have a pretty fair notion," April said wryly. "Now rinse them off. We'll cover them with water we dip out of the reservoir. It'll be hot enough to keep them warm till we slather them with butter."

As she rinsed off the peas then jumbled them back into the pot, Kate said, "You never slather peas with butter. You barely even dot them with it."

"Exactly." April winked. "This is a new recipe. We'll see how the men like it."

Kate dipped hot water from the stove reservoir and quickly covered the peas. "I never did get around to making dessert."

"Pull out two cake pans." April walked over to the far side of the room. April often measured out an extra set of the dry ingredients for a recipe she was making. She stored that set away in jars on the bottom shelf of the copper-punch-fronted pie safe.

"Oh, bless you!" Kate finished covering the peas with water, then reached for the cake pans.

April drew four, one-quart jars from the bottom shelf. Cradling them in her arms, she headed toward the table. "We need melted butter. While you do that, I'll measure out the vinegar, vanilla, and water."

"Ohhh," Kate breathed. "Crazy cake?"

Bobbing her head, April said, "I think I can manage to mix one while you do the other. You can take the casseroles out of the oven and pop in the cakes. By the time supper's over, the cakes will be done."

"As I recall, Peter loves your crazy cake," Kate said.

April didn't meet her eyes. She urged, "Hurry up and get to work. You can't go back out there looking like we stirred your hair with an egg beater."

"You're welcome to stay to supper." Caleb Chance smacked his leather work gloves against the side of his jeans, making dust fly.

Matt nodded. "Appreciate the invite. I'm hungry enough to eat the legs off a lizard."

"As for a job," Caleb warned, "I'll get back to you on that later this evening."

"Fair enough." A grin stretched across Matt's face. "Maybe better than fair. Decent food's been known to put men into a good frame of mind."

The blond gal with the cute freckles stepped onto the porch of a cabin. "Supper's ready. Tanner, go wash up."

"Awww, Kate—"

"Just 'cuz Mama's not here, that doesn't give you call to come to the table gritty as the path you rode today. You P's, come fetch the dishes. C's, you can carry out the food."

"P's and C's?" Matt looked to Caleb for an explanation.

"Brothers all have names starting with the same letter."

"Tanner is Kate's brother?"

"Yup. Girls got named whatever the mother fancied. April's my sis."

Matt murmured, "If MacPherson has his way, it won't be long before she's his wife."

Caleb's features darkened as he snarled, "They're cousins."

"My mistake." The sinking feeling that he'd ruined any opportunity to hire on assailed Matt. He shrugged. "Guess that's why I haven't gotten hitched. Never could figure out a woman."

In scant minutes, food and dishes appeared on the table. The women sat at the end of one of the two abutted tables. Matt made it a point to head toward the extreme other end.

"You jist lay yore hand atop mine," Peter told April. "That-away, I won't hurt yore burns none." When April complied, Peter's smile could put the moon out of business.

Cousins or not, that man's chasing that woman.

To Matt's astonishment, everyone linked hands. "I'll ask the blessing," one of the men offered. Matt bowed his head.

As prayers went, it was short and to the point. After the "amen," men yanked the napkins from the table, draped them in their laps, and grabbed for the nearest dish.

Not an hour ago, red-headed Peter MacPherson could have made a prosecuting attorney run for cover with all the questions he'd posed. Once the Chance men came from all parts of the property for supper, they'd been just as nosey. These men must not have heard of the Code of the West where a man's past was nobody's business but his own.

The way the Chances acted so guarded made Matt's suspicions rise. Added to that, the fact that a MacPherson happened to be here made the association between his two prime suspects all that more important. Matt refused to allow a brief prayer to fool him. The Chance men all had deep brown hair and blue eyes, but their features were dissimilar enough for Matt to tell them apart. He'd always been good with names—a skill that stood him in good stead since he'd met all eight of them in a matter of minutes.

Packard swiped the saltshaker from Tanner. "That foal looking any better?"

"Yup." Tanner shoveled in a huge bite and spoke around the food, "He's feelin' good enough to be ornery."

"Ohhh, man. Buttered sweet peas." The words escaped Matt's mouth. Feeling a little sheepish, he tacked on, "I haven't had these since I left home."

"Kate made them," April said. "They're a new recipe."

"Not bad, sis," one of the men said.

Kate beamed. The woman's whole face lit up when she smiled. She said, "April and I have crazy cake in the oven for dessert."

"I volunteer to go pull it outta the oven," Peter said.

Bellows of laughter met that comment. When they died down a little, Caleb said, "That's like having the fox mind the chicken coop."

"Cain't blame a feller for tryin'. Only thang better'n April's crazy cake is her sticky buns."

April blushed. "As soon as my hands are better, I'll bake a batch of them especially for you."

Every man around the table suddenly froze. Forks hung midair. Conversation halted mid-sentence. Matt pretended not to be entertained by the variety of expressions—some eyes widened in surprise, while others narrowed with anger.

Chapter 7

I thank yore brothers and cousins are het up o'er me claiming a batch all to myself."

"And who'd blame them?" Kate laughed. "You know Chances always share."

"Kate," Caleb gritted, "you stay outta this. Peter"—he jerked his thumb over his shoulder—"behind the stable."

"What's gotten into you, Caleb?" April looked down the table at her brother.

"Yore big brother thanks yore too young to court." Peter's voice held an entertained lilt.

"He started courting Greta when he was younger than I am."

Caleb stood. The muscles in his jaw twitched. "Behind the stable. Now."

Peter rose. "Kate, would you please make shore the cake don't burn? 'Twould be a dreadful pity iff'n this little misunderstandin' ruint dessert."

"Don't bother, Kate," Caleb said. "Peter won't be staying for dessert."

"Caleb, you sit right back down." Kate scooted off the end of the bench. "You're the eldest here, and April's your little sister. But you need to cool off."

"Kate—" Caleb snapped out her name.

"Hold it right there." Matt stood. "Whatever's wrong here can still be reckoned out peacefully, but nobody's going to talk to a woman in that tone of voice when I'm around."

"Mister, sit down, shut your mouth, and finish your meal." Caleb never turned his glower off Peter as he added, "You'll be leaving as soon as you're done."

"That does it, Caleb." Kate threw her napkin on the table. "We've all put up with you being cranky since Greta's at her sister's, but you're downright impossible anymore."

"She's right," one of the men muttered.

"I'm getting the cake out of the oven. When I come back out here, every last one of you had better be sitting here with a smile on his face, or I'm going to do the laundry all by myself again."

Kate left. Peter stared at Caleb. "Ain't gonna be no skin offa my nose if Kate don't rinse the lye outta the skivvies. None of my clothes hang on your clothesline."

"And they never will." Caleb's voice rivaled a thunderclap. "I'll put up with itchy clothes before I let you court my sister."

"I s'pose you cain object all you want, but it'd be mighty nice iff'n you had a decent reason."

"You're cousins!" one of the men shouted.

Peter shook his head. "Two thangs. First off, I'm not deaf. Second, and more importantly, April ain't my cousin."

"Of course, she's your cousin."

"Nope. Polly is a cousin to Tempy's children." Peter grinned as he drawled, "The rest of us ain't related at all."

April laughed. "When we said the Chances share, I guess we took it too far. We claimed aunts and uncles and cousins who actually aren't ours at all."

"Iff'n you still wanna meet me out back 'hind the stable, I'll be happy to oblige." Peter's brows rose. "Haven't e'er had a set-to so's I could whup you, Caleb, but April's more than worth a coupla skinned knuckles."

"He's right," one of the men marveled.

"Right about me whuppin' Caleb, or that April's the finest woman 'round these here parts?"

"We're not cousins," Caleb said slowly. He stepped over the bench, took three quick strides, and smacked Peter on the back. *"Hoo-ooo-ey!"*

Peter returned the hefty slap. "I could still take you on, level you out, and eat the whole cake afore you came to."

While the Chance men all palavered, Matt left the table and headed for his horse. He'd blown his opportunity to hire on here and keep watch on his prime suspects—but he'd find a way to continue surveillance. *I couldn't live with myself if I let a man treat a woman that way.*

"Hey!" A young man hustled over. "You're not going."

"Looks that way."

"You'll have to forgive Caleb. Between his wife being gone and him feeling protective of his sister, he overreacted. Me? I appreciated you sticking up for my sis. If I hadn't been so shocked about Peter and April, I would have pounded Caleb into the ground for snapping at Kate myself."

"Tobias!" Kate yelled from the porch of the kitchen cabin. "You can't send Mr. Salter away until we vote."

"Think hard before you speak," April called to Tobias. "Two crazy cakes hang in the balance."

Tobias rested his hands on his hips. "Caleb, Greta's not here. There's no telling what her opinion on this would be, so that leaves us down to three votes. April and I—we vote this man's staying on as a hired hand. Say what you will, but you're outvoted."

Caleb's chin rose a notch. "He's opinionated."

"Show me a man around here who isn't." Kate stayed on the porch and wiped her hands on the hem of her apron.

"He stuck his nose in where it didn't belong."

"Only to protect my sister." Tobias glared. "I would have called you out a heartbeat later if he hadn't spoken up. There's no excuse for being rude to a lady."

Caleb cleared his throat. "Kate, you have my apology. Peter, you do, too—though I think you were underhanded to sneak up on my sister without asking permission to court her. As for Salter, Tobias, you're wrong. I'm not outvoted. The vote is unanimous: He stays for now."

"Well, what do you think of that?" Kate called.

Tobias slugged Matt in the arm. "Guess it's time we ate dessert. It's crazy cake!"

Matt shook his head. "The cake's not the only thing crazy around here."

April closed her eyes and felt Peter gently glide a comb through her just-washed tresses. "Johnna was nice to come help again today."

"Sis reckoned Kate might need holp wringin' out the bedding. Ain't easy to do on yore lonesome."

Opening her eyes, April looked over at Kate and Johnna as they hung another sheet on the clothesline. "I feel so silly. I'm sure I could help out—"

"Hold it right there. Doc said you've gotta keep yore hands clean and dry for a week."

A buggy pulled into the yard, swirling dust all over the place and covering the freshly washed and hung laundry with a coat of grime. "Hello!" Merry laughter filled the air. "I can see I don't need to ask if anyone's home."

"Hi, Lucinda." April forced a smile. She ought to be hospitable, but it wasn't easy. Lucinda's thoughtlessness just made a lot more work for Kate and Johnna. Then, too, at the moment April knew full well she looked like a drowned rat. Lucinda's peach-colored silk dress spread about her on the buggy seat, giving her the appearance of a much-cherished china doll.

Lucinda daintily lifted a gloved hand to her mouth and gave April a wide-eyed look. "Why, I just cannot fathom what your mama would say if she saw you out here with your hair down, April."

"Her mama would stand here and comb it for her," Peter said as he continued to tease out a stubborn tangle. "Sun dries it right quick."

"My hands are burned," April explained.

"You poor thing. I've never suffered so." Lucinda's dimples deepened as she smiled. "Daddy insists Mama and I. . ." She drew in a dramatic breath. "He says a lady—well, never you mind." She surveyed the yard. "Isn't Tobias here?"

Kate dried her hands on her apron. "My brother is out working."

"Will he be back for luncheon?"

"Doubt it." Peter drew the comb through April's hair again. "Kate sent the boys out with sandwiches."

"Come on down from yore buggy," Johnna invited. "Plenty wants doin'."

"Like rinsing, wringing out, and rehanging the sheets," Kate tacked on.

"That's a fact." Johnna rubbed her cheekbone with the back of her wrist. "Another pair of hands would holp."

As if he sensed April's impulse to rise, Peter's hand curled around her shoulder. Carefully leashed strength held her in place.

Lucinda cast a look toward the clothesline and shrugged as if it were of no concern. "I can't stay. I just can't."

"Then why," Johnna asked, "did you ask if Tobias'd be home for lunch?"

Lucinda ignored the question and held a slip of paper aloft. "I only stopped by on my way home because a telegram came for you."

"Thanks for bringing it by." Kate reached for the message.

"Anything to help a neighbor." Lucinda handed over the telegram. "Oh, and please tell Tobias I'll be expecting him for Sunday supper."

"We've already arranged a picnic with the MacPhersons," Kate said.

"You all go right on ahead. There are so many of you, I'm sure Tobias won't be missed." Lucinda gave them a jaunty wave. "Bye-bye."

"Who's the telegraph from?" Johnna looked over Kate's shoulder.

"Uncle Gideon."

"Daddy!" April popped up. Peter's arm went about her waist.

"He says Yosemite's beautiful. The boys are having a great time. They're traveling slower than planned, and we can expect them to get back home late next week."

"Do you think Aunt Lovejoy's having trouble? Her back—"

"Don't go borrowin' worries," Peter said. "Lovejoy has trouble with her back, but with all the beautiful views, she's probably too busy gawkin' to pay much mind to those twinges."

Kate beamed. "We have a whole week to get extra things done. It's a good thing we hired Mr. Salter."

Johnna elbowed her. "Best we get back to work. No use in gettin' moon-eyed o'er a saddle tramp. Most don't stay more'n a month or so."

Watching the girls go back toward the laundry, April let out a sigh.

"Don't you fret yoreself none 'bout not holping with the wash."

"I'm not," she said glumly.

He drew the comb through her hair once again. "Lucinda has an air about her. 'Tisn't you, April. She prob'ly don't even know she comes 'cross as bein' biggety. Don't let her bother you."

"She doesn't. Her parents dote on her so much, I figure she expects everyone else is supposed to treat her with the same indulgence."

"See? You went and done it again. Plenty of folks would get gossipy and make catty comments. You practically bend o'er backwards to be nice." He set aside the comb and slid his fingers through her hair a time or two before dividing it into three segments.

"You know how to braid?" April turned her head a little to the side to look up at him.

"Nope. But I seen my sisters and cousins and ma plait hair day in and day out. Cain't be all that hard."

Minutes later, April tried not to laugh. Peter had twisted, knotted, and undone a variety of crazy attempts. "Peter, take the left section and put it over the middle one. Then take the right section and put it over the middle. Left, right, left, right. . ."

"So the middle ends up havin' a turn at bein' a side. Ain't that the beatenist?"

From the rhythmic way her hair swished, April could tell he'd achieved the technique. She started to relax a little.

"So iff'n the wash and Lucinda aren't nettlin' you, what is it?"

April tensed. She'd hoped they'd left that sore subject alone. "I think you have the plait long enough. Here's a ribbon to tie at the bottom."

He tied the thin lavender grosgrain ribbon near the end of her waist-length plait, then tickled her cheek with the edge of her braid. "You cain tell me, little April. I'm yore friend, and I wanna share yore woes as well as yore joys."

"I'm drowning in self-pity," April confessed sheepishly. "Lucinda and Tobias are courting. Johnna has Trevor. Last night, that new hand took up Kate's defense. This morning at breakfast, I caught them trading glances. I'm older than Kate, and I truly hoped maybe this summer when Daddy and all of my uncles were gone, one of the local boys would get up some nerve and come calling."

"I cain't say that yore wrong on most of what you said. Then again, any man who's ascairt of yore pa and uncles ain't man enough to come courtin'. Besides, is there anybody 'round these parts who you'd like to marry up with?"

"No," she admitted. After sucking in a quick breath, April added, "But it wouldn't hurt to at least have one man want to take a stroll with me."

"I'm that one." Peter stepped over the bench and straddled it. "You and me—we've been havin' ourselves a nice time, haven't we?"

She nodded.

"Far as I cain see, things is goin' jist as we planned. Betcha most of the folks at church will already have our names linked after last night. 'Stead of you a-sittin' in the Chance pew, yore gonna come sit by my side." He nodded. "Yup. That's where you b'long."

April smiled up at him. "You're such a dear friend, Peter. Truly, you are. I wasn't kidding last night when I promised you a batch of sticky buns. Once my burns have healed, it's the first thing I'll make."

He grinned. "A man couldn't ask much more than that."

"Hey, you two lovebirds!" Johnna walked up. "I do declare, I called you both twice. Yore so set on one another, you didn't hear a word I said!"

"So whaddya want, sis?" Peter didn't jump up or sound in the least flustered at being called lovebirds.

"Didn't seem right, Lucinda expectin' Tobias to turn his back on family plans. She trotted off ere we could say so. Kate and me—we reckon what's easiest is to send word back to the Youngbloods and tell 'em to meet us for Sunday picnic like we already had planned. Lucinda niver has managed to come to one."

"It seems passing strange she hasn't, what with us doin' our clan picnic so often." Peter tucked a small strand of April's hair behind her ear. "Don't you agree, honey pie?"

April nodded. She couldn't quite summon her voice. When she shoved her hair back or one of the Chance women helped with her hair, it didn't feel this way. Peter had taken to tucking in her hairpins, spiraling wayward tresses around his big, rough fingers, and giving her the shivers.

"Tell ya what. Me and April—we'll jaunt right on o'er to the Youngbloods and give 'em the invite. The mister and the missus, too."

"I reckoned you'd volunteer for that." Johnna laughed and shook her forefinger at them. "But you know the rules, Peter."

He gave his sister an affronted look. "Course I do."

"What rules?" April rose as Peter gently cupped her elbow.

He cleared his throat and turned a tad ruddy.

"Us MacPhersons got rules 'bout courtin'," Johnna said. "Hand-holdin's where it ends. No kisses 'til the buck asks for the gal's hand in marriage."

Heat rushed clear up to her hairline. April rasped, "We haven't kissed."

Peter looked her straight in the eyes and murmured, "Not yet."

"Soon, I'd warrant, from the way the both of you are actin'." Johnna sashayed off.

April couldn't look away from Peter and whispered, "I feel like a liar."

"You got no reason to. None atall. There ain't nothin' a-wrong with you and me passin' time together. What other folks make of it..." He shrugged and stepped over the bench. "I reckon I oughtta take it as a compliment that they suspect yore acceptin' my suit."

As he said those last words, he cupped April's waist and lifted her to the other side. "Peter!" she squealed.

Kate and Johnna's laughter filled the air.

Peter's smile broadened. "Unh-huh. I'm downright proud to squire you."

Chapter 8

"There's an elaborate rig." Matt straightened up and squinted toward the north.

"Yeah," Tanner scoffed. "Belongs to the Youngbloods. Looks like Lucinda took a mind to come pester Tobias."

"You could tell who was in the buggy?"

"Wasn't a matter of seeing. It's a matter of knowing. The Youngbloods are the only ones around these parts with such a fancy rig. Her pa favors his Tennessee Walker, and her ma sends servants to town."

"Mrs. Youngblood doesn't pay calls along with her daughter?"

Tanner shook his head. "On occasion, she invites someone over for tea. That's about it. Lucinda goes to town whenever she gets a notion to. That, and coming here to see Tobias. Otherwise, she doesn't gad about."

Matt shrugged. "No matter where I go, folks are always set on living life on their own terms. Guess it doesn't matter much, as long as they've got a roof, clothes, and food."

Tanner yanked the barbed wire taut. "To my way of thinking, they're missing out if that's all they have."

Matt hammered a staple over the wire and into the fencepost.

"Love of God and family—those are what truly make life worth living." Tanner looked up from the wire. "Man is more than flesh. His heart and soul have needs just as keen as his body."

"Far as I can tell, you've got yourself quite a family."

Tanner chuckled. "This is only a fraction of us Chances. Five sets of adults and six youngsters will be home any day now."

"Five? I only counted three sets of siblings. The C's, the P's, and the T's."

"Yup. Dan and Lovejoy have Polly—but she's the doctor's wife. They live in town. Bryce and Daisy—well, they had Jamie, but he passed on. Cute little guy. One of these years when I have a son of my own, I'm going to name him Jamie. Polly did something similar. Ginny Mae was her sister. Ginny and Jamie died at the same time—diphtheria. Polly's baby girl is named Ginny Mae, and it sorta soothed away the lingering sorrow."

"You just said you're a believer. Don't you think they're in heaven?"

"Absolutely." Tanner swatted at a bothersome fly. "In the depths of grief, that was our comfort. You talk like a man who's skeptical about the Lord."

It might actually help him make connections if he agreed, but Matt refused to. He'd never deny the Lord. He knocked on his chest. "Asked Christ into my heart when I was a schoolboy. Never once regretted it."

A big grin creased Tanner's sunburned face. "So you're a brother."

Matt chuckled. "You Chances really do claim a lot of family."

"You bet. I expect you'll wanna come to church."

Matt nodded and pulled out another staple. "Thanks for the invite."

As they continued to reinforce the stretches where the fence needed help, Matt fought with himself. He wanted to attend worship for all of the right reasons. At the back of his mind, though, he also cataloged how attending church could help his mission.

Almighty Father, You know my heart. My intent is to praise and worship You. Help me keep my priorities straight. I mean You no insult.

"You'll meet most of the folks from Reliable at church. Nearly everyone attends."

"You mean there are more people in this little town than all of the Chances and the MacPhersons?"

Tanned nodded. "You know about the Youngbloods. He shows up maybe once a month or so, but his wife and Lucinda are there every Sunday."

"Folks in town come out this way?"

"Yup. Way back when, the Chances reckoned the time had come for Reliable to have a real church building. Before then, folks came and worshipped in our yard if the weather was fair. On bad days, we held church in the barn. The plot of land where the road forks between our place and the MacPhersons' seemed logical."

"Are there as many MacPhersons as there are Chances?"

"More."

"Most every place I've been, there are a few big families that run the community." He held up one hand. "I didn't mean that in a bad way. Communities need leaders."

"Reliable isn't all that big, but plenty of folks step up when things need doing. The Dorseys' barn burned last year. Everyone pitched in, and a new one was up the next week."

"Turning tragedy into good."

Tanner shrugged. "Not that big of a disaster. Tragedy—well, the Walls' wagon overturned a year back. Lost all of 'em 'cept for the father. Don't see much of him these days."

Matt tried to sound casual as he asked, "Anyone know what started the barn fire?"

"Never know about those things."

Stills sometimes blew up. That could explain the fire. Feigning an absence of any real curiosity, Matt shrugged. "Dumb question. Accidents just happen—like that wagon flipping over."

Tanner's features tightened. "That accident shouldn't have ever happened."

Holding his hands up in front of himself, Matt shook his head. "Whoa. Sorry if I hit a nerve. Chance Ranch's horses are the finest I've ever seen. If the horse—"

"Wasn't the horse." Tanner's features twisted with disgust. "Thaddeus Walls was drunk as a skunk when it happened."

Matt whistled under his breath.

"The Good Book tells us not to judge. But it would be a far sight easier for me to pity Thad if I didn't remember his wife's weeping. Since our place was closest, they brought Etta here. Doc, Polly, and Aunt Lovejoy did their best. It wasn't enough. I've always reckoned Etta didn't want to live anymore—not without her children." Tanner looked away. "We've got this section done."

Understanding the topic had closed, Matt grinned. "Good. I'm hankering after those sandwiches Kate sent with us."

"Me, too. Sis is a fair cook."

"Fair? I've relished everything she's made."

Tanner smacked him on the back. "That's 'cuz you've been eating your own food too long."

"Anything beats my cooking." Matt opened the small knapsack and drew out a stack of sandwiches wrapped in a dishcloth. "But I know good cooking when I taste it."

"This is a disaster!" Kate slammed the lid back down on the roasting pan and resisted the urge to kick the stove. She wanted to impress Matthew Salter with her cooking; one look at this burned roast, and he was liable to hop on his horse and head for the hills.

"No, it's not." April motioned to her to lift the lid. "Plunk the roast down over here, then put on some rice to cook."

"Why?"

"Because," April smiled, "no one's going to know it got burnt. While the rice is boiling, you'll trim off the crispy edges of the roast, then chop the good meat into bite-sized pieces. We'll use the drippings to make gravy and—"

Kate stood stock-still in the middle of the kitchen, holding the roast precariously aloft with a big carving knife. "You mean the times you make beef and rice. . .it's because you. . ."

Her cousin winked. "Now let's get busy. I'll put the evidence in the slop bucket and cover it with a splash of milk."

"I can't believe it," Kate crowed about half an hour later. "Dinner's going to turn out fine."

Laughing, April nodded. "Plenty can go wrong in the kitchen. If the fire in the stove burns too hot or too cool, even the best recipe fails. The trick is learning how to recover from a disaster. Often what you make out of the mess is just as good, if not better, than what you started with."

"I haven't decided what to take for dessert to the picnic tomorrow." Kate set two bowls heaping with snap beans on the table. April promptly dabbed butter on them.

"What about taking—"

"Hey, sis!" Tobias hollered from outside. "I'm half-starved. Is supper ready?"

Normally, Kate would have yelled back her answer, but now that seemed. . . well, not very ladylike. She walked to the doorway, pushed open the screen, and stepped out onto the porch. "If you're only half-starved, you must've had a snack thirty minutes ago."

The Chance men all chuckled. Even so, Kate heard a deep, rumbling laugh that didn't belong to her brothers or cousins. She turned and spied Matthew Salter. Glee sparkled in his brown eyes. She smiled back at him. "Supper's ready. T's, grab the dishes. P's, take the food."

"Miss Chance, I'm an M." Matthew drew closer. "What's my chore?"

"Mr. Salter—"

"Looks like a mighty capable dishwasher to me!" Paxton declared, slapping the ranch hand on the back.

The opportunity to shuffle around the sink and cupboard with Mr. Salter sounded heavenly. Still, saddling a man with that chore didn't often happen around Chance Ranch. Kate opened her mouth, but Matt spoke first.

"On one condition. You call me Matt, not Mr. Salter."

Someone whooped in the kitchen, then bellowed, "Beef and rice!"

Kate shifted to the side to avoid being trampled.

Caleb started through the doorway. Tobias and Tanner pushed past him, exiting the cabin with heaping plates. Tanner yelled, "It's every man for himself!"

Matt shouldered through the line and grabbed their plates. "Ladies first, of course. Thanks for thinking of the gals. Miss Kate and Miss April, I'll set this food on the table for you."

Tanner and Tobias exchanged outraged looks, then plowed back toward the kitchen.

April came around the cabin holding a plate with a modest helping of supper and a pitcher full of gravy. "It's worse than a stampede in there. The men are so food-crazed, they've plumb forgotten the cabin has a back door they can use to exit!"

Looking at the two plates in Matt's hands, Kate's heart did a funny little flip. "Well, Mr.—I mean, Matt—it looks as if you've avoided the throng and still ended up with supper."

"Brings that saying to mind. 'All good things come to those who wait.'" He set a plate on the picnic table, then looked at her and said in a low voice, "Some things are especially worth waiting for."

All through supper, Kate told herself he'd been referring to the meal. *Maybe he meant me, too. How am I to know? Laurel would have known. She had suitors fighting over her.*

"Kate, what's wrong?" Packard frowned at her. "Are you sick?"

"No. Why?"

"You just poured gravy on your beans."

"It's my fault!" April half shouted.

All of the men stopped staring at Kate and turned toward her cousin. Blushing, April muttered, "I didn't put enough butter on them." She jerked her chin upward. "As a matter of fact, I'd like to put gravy on my beans, too."

Matt cleared his throat. "Best gravy I ever tasted. If there's any left, I wouldn't mind trying it on my beans, too."

Kate appreciated how her cousin spoke out. Bless her heart, April knew exactly how to divert the men's attention so they wouldn't figure out Kate was so enamored of the new ranch hand that she'd lost track of what she was doing. But Matt? Why had he chimed in? *Men. I've been surrounded by them all my life—outnumbered by them—but I don't understand them. Especially this new hand. . .but I'd like to figure him out!*

"Hey, sis." Tanner passed the gravy boat to Matt. "Barbed wire sprang back today. Ripped Matt's work glove. Think you can stitch it up?"

"I'd be happy to take a look at it."

Caleb leaned forward and demanded, "Neither of you got cut, did you?"

"Nah," Tanner said. "Woulda sliced my chest something awful if Matt didn't have such fast reflexes, though."

"You would have done the same for me," Matt said. He then looked at Kate. "It's kind of you to offer to take a look at my glove, but your sewing needles won't begin to pierce leather."

Packard burst out cackling.

Tanner grinned. "Kate does all of the leatherwork for Chance Ranch."

Matt's brow furrowed.

Kate's heart dropped. *Tobias told me it's not a ladylike pursuit. What is Matt going to think?*

Chapter 9

"Your parents named you Tanner, but you don't work leather?"

Tanner chuckled. "Never thought about it before."

Kate fought the urge to put down her fork and bury her stained hands in her lap.

"And you," Matt turned his gaze on her, "you made the belts your brothers and cousins wear?"

She nodded stiffly.

"Saddles, too," Caleb chimed in.

April giggled. "You don't wear saddles!"

"Some days, I think they ought to." Kate bit her lip once she'd blurted out that statement.

Tobias bumped her with his arm as he shrugged. "At least she didn't say muzzles."

While everyone else at the table chuckled, Matt didn't. He continued to stare at her. Kate couldn't read the look in his deep brown eyes. The rest of the meal, Matt didn't say much. Kate took a few more bites and set down her fork.

"Whats'a matter?" Tobias focused on her plate.

"I'm not hungry."

"Sure you're not turning sick?"

Lovesick. "I'm fine."

"We both tasted the food while cooking." April pushed her plate away. "I've had all I'm going to eat, too."

While their brothers swooped over and swiped the rest of their food, Kate gave April a smile of gratitude. *April knows I'm fond of Matt, and twice tonight she's kept me from making a fool of myself. Beef and rice is one of her favorites, and she's going hungry just to help me.*

A short while later, with bubbles surrounding his muscular forearms, Matt grinned at Kate as she dried a plate. "Not much to wash, really. Supper tasted so good, I fought the temptation to lick my plate. Your brothers and cousins scraped every last grain of rice off theirs, too."

"I'm glad you liked it." Kate shot April a look. "It's April's recipe. Compared to how she cooks, what I make is only fit for slopping the hogs."

"I haven't tasted Miss April's cooking, but I'm still going to disagree." He felt around in the bottom of the water and pulled out one last spoon. "Speaking of hog slop, do you add the dishwater to it?"

"I'll do it!" Kate set down the plate so fast, it almost cracked.

"Actually, I need to add a little cornmeal first." April bustled over and grabbed a scoop. "Especially since we didn't add any dinner scraps, the hogs'll need this. Kate, why don't you pour in that last bit of milk, then let Mr. Salter use the pitcher to dip out the dishwater?"

"Good idea."

Matt cleared his throat. "I mean no familiarity, but I'd rather be called Matt. It was part of the deal Miss Kate and I made when I offered to wash the dishes."

"It doesn't seem equitable for us to call you Matt and have you use 'Miss' in front of our given names." April kept stirring cornmeal into the slop and tacked on, "Don't you agree, Kate?"

"Absolutely."

Matt shook his head. "My mama drilled a few things into my thick head, and she'd be spinning in her grave if I lost my manners at all, especially around ladies. I'd be making a false promise if I said I'd address either of you in such a way. I reckon the only woman I'll ever call simply by her first name is the gal I'll wed."

Oh. He's just as much as said he's not interested in me. And why would he be? Tobias was right—men don't want women who are boisterous and disheveled.

"You can add in the milk and dishwater now." April stepped back. "By the way, Kate, Peter needs laces for his boots. Do you think you could make him a pair?"

Kate nodded.

Once Matt added the dishwater to the slop, he lifted the heavy bucket. "I spied the pigpen on the far side of the barn."

"I'll take this." Kate tried to pull on the handle.

"No, you won't. No reason for a woman to tote when a man's willing to help her out. Besides. . ." He paused, and a smile tugged at the right side of his mouth. "I'm trying to come up with an excuse to talk you into showing me your workshop."

"I already said I'd repair the tear in your glove."

"And I'd be much obliged. Now you turn loose of this slop bucket, Miss Kate."

"Kate isn't sure she ought to let you near Frenzy." April looked down at her hands and frowned at the blisters. "I'd be happy to do the chore, myself, but—"

"You wouldn't dare. Doc and Polly would have a fit!"

Matt chortled. "They'd have to stand in line behind Peter."

"But Frenzy," April said woefully. "She's been in a wicked temper for days now. She's our meanest sow. Kate, you'd better go along. Make sure the gate to the pen isn't loose. You know how the lock's slipped the last few days."

"You ladies oughtn't fret over such a thing. I'll be sure to repair that at once."

"Thank you." April looked entirely too pleased with herself. "Kate's workbench is in the stable, and the men keep all of the woodworking tools just to the right of her place."

Thousands of times, Kate had walked beside a man—her father, uncles, brothers, and cousins. But walking through the barnyard with Matt felt different. His loose-hipped gait testified to years spent in the saddle, and the square set of his shoulders showed confidence that he could handle whatever life threw his way. He switched the slop bucket to his left hand, away from her. Kate couldn't tell whether he'd done so to put the smelly thing farther away from her or if it was so Matt could walk a little closer.

He looked down at her, and his brows rose in silent query.

Kate didn't want to tell him what she'd been wondering, so she blurted out, "How did you know about giving the hogs dishwater?"

Matt hitched his shoulder. "I thought most everybody knew the lye in the water cured hogs of worms. Now that I think it over, I'm not sure when I learned about that fact. Growing up around animals, those bits of wisdom are passed on."

Whew. So he didn't think I'm crass for asking such a dumb question. "So you grew up around animals—farm or ranch?"

"A little horse ranch. Nothing near as splendid as this spread."

"Where?" She winced. "Sorry. I'm prying."

"Nothing wrong with asking simple questions. Wyoming. My dad was the foreman. Worked solid, made the place turn a profit for the widow-woman who owned the spread."

"Why leave a place like that?"

"The widow up and married. Her husband didn't want someone else giving orders." He stopped at the pen. "You'd best step back, Miss Kate. No use risking you getting splattered when I pour this into the trough."

"I'm already a wreck."

Matt looked her over from neckline to hem and back again. Shaking his head, he murmured, "I disagree. You look like a woman who's not afraid to work hard for her family."

"I—" Horrified, she stammered, "I wasn't fishing for a compliment, Matt."

"I know." He grinned. "Life's taught me women don't seek praise on their appearance unless they're dead certain every last bow and flounce is perfect."

She looked down at her smudged apron and the dust-covered hem of her rose calico dress, then forced a laugh. "Not a single bow." *Oh no! I hope he doesn't think I meant beau!*

"Some men admire gals who prance around like live fashion plates. Me? I'd rather see a woman whose smile warms a man to the toe of his boots and whose rumpled apron bespeaks a willingness to pitch in alongside her loved ones." He pivoted and poured the slop into the trough. "*Sooo-eeeEEE! Sooo-eeeEEE!* Pig, pig, pig, pig!"

The hogs squealed and trampled through the muck. Matt chuckled. "I didn't need to call them, did I?"

"No, but you might win a hog-calling contest. Your pitch is great." Kate giggled.

"What's so funny?"

"Promise you won't tell?"

He lifted one foot and rested his boot on the first slat of the pen. "I like to know what I'm giving my word about. If it's illegal or unethical, I couldn't agree."

"I was thinking. . ." She laughed again. "My brothers looked just like that, pushing into the kitchen for supper tonight!"

Amusement lit his eyes and lifted the corners of his mouth. "Can't say as I blame them. Had I known chow was that tasty, I might have jostled my way to the head of the line."

Giggles spilled out of Kate. They weren't the practiced twitters of young ladies who played coy. Hers were so honest and refreshing, Matt was thoroughly enchanted. He didn't want to walk her back to the house yet, so he decided to string the conversation along on a topic she could speak about with ease. "So you do leatherwork." Something flashed in Kate's eyes, but Matt didn't know how to read it. "Never seen such handsome belts. You do quality work."

"Thank you." She glanced over her shoulder.

"Nice diversionary tactic, that glance." Matt reached over and gently tugged on her sleeve. "But you don't have to hide your hands behind your back."

She let out a small sound of despair.

Curling his fingers around the cuff of her sleeve, he drew her hands out in the open. "It's just stain, isn't it?"

Kate nodded. "Yes." Her chin went up a notch. "I'm more splotched than not."

"I disagree." He flashed her a smile. "I'd say you're more not than splotched. Besides, what does that matter?"

"It's ugly. Not very ladylike, either."

That same fleeting look crossed her face, and Matt realized she'd just revealed her vulnerability. "I disagree. The stain on your hands is only skin-deep. The devotion you show to your family by doing that fine work is soul-deep. To my way of thinking, nothing's more beautiful than a woman who loves with all her heart."

Her eyes widened, and a flush of pleasure tinted her cheeks. Funny, how something so inconsequential mattered so much to women. But Matt was glad the truth he'd spoken made her feel good. He looked down at the empty pail. "I'll rinse this and set it out on the back porch."

"You don't need to do that."

"No reason why I shouldn't. No job is beneath a man's dignity—that's what my granddad always said."

"He sounds like a wise man."

"He never had more than two years' schooling, but Granddad was blessed with wisdom that came from the Lord."

"Kate?" They turned in tandem toward Paxton's voice. "When you make the bootlaces for Peter, make an extra length."

"How long?"

Not why, but how long? Matt noted how she just took it as a matter of course that the requested item was needed and didn't demand a reason.

"Not all that long. Maybe eight inches." Paxton scuffed the toe of his boots in the dirt as a guilty flush colored his cheeks. "I broke the loop on the fishing basket."

"You went fishing without me?"

Matt couldn't be sure whether Kate was outraged or teasing. She wasn't like any other woman he'd ever met.

Heaving a sigh, Paxton kicked the dirt. "Didn't go for long. It was a waste of time. Nothing was biting, unless you count mosquitoes."

"I have a scrap of leather that'll yield a thong long enough to do the repair. Here. Go rinse out the swill bucket and bring me the fishing basket."

"Salter—"

"Offered to fix the gate on the pigpen," Kate cut in. "I'll show him where the tools are since I'm heading toward my workbench."

Paxton accepted the smelly bucket. "Watch out for Frenzy. She's the runty-looking sow. Her name warns you of her temperament."

"Obliged for the warning."

Paxton stared at Kate and smirked. "Ever notice how the little ones are always the scrappiest?"

"Nothing wrong with having plenty of spark and spirit. Miss Kate, do I need to fetch a lantern from the kitchen for you so you'll have light to work by?"

She shook her head. "There's one on either end of my workbench. You can have one if you think it'll take long to fix the latch."

"Doubt that'll be necessary." He walked alongside her toward the far side of the barn. Kate's gait matched her personality—her zest for life showed not only in her bright eyes and friendly smile, but in her high-stepping prance that made her sway and bob as though she heard a lively march and couldn't resist matching the rhythm.

Sliding the barn door wide open, Matt asked, "Ever do custom pieces for neighbors and friends?"

She headed toward a cluttered table that had a pair of well-ordered shelves above it. "Sure. I've often made gifts for them."

He drew near and took the matches from her. She could have easily lit the lantern herself, but Matt didn't like a woman doing things for herself when he could do them—especially Kate. From the moment he'd arrived, she'd been in motion, always doing things for others. It wouldn't hurt for someone to show her the same kindness.

The match sizzled, then Matt held it to the wick as Kate held up the hurricane glass. The wick caught, and Kate settled the glass sleeve in place. Matt reached up and barely grazed her left cheekbone.

"It's not stain. Really, it isn't."

"I'm partial to freckles." He stepped back. What was it about Kate that had him acting this way? He'd never dallied with a gal's affection, and he wasn't about to—but this was different. Kate was different. *But I can't be completely honest with her. I'm on assignment, and I have a job to do. If the rest of the family is as forthright and upright as everyone I've already met, I'm going to need to move on to continue my search.*

I don't want to move on.

But I do. It would tear Kate apart to learn someone she loves is involved in bootlegging.

"Probably all you need are a nail or two and the hammer." She waved toward the nearby tool bench. "Just be careful. Pax wasn't kidding when he said Frenzy riles easily."

The latch on the pen turned out to be quite sturdy once Matt moved it up an inch. Someone else had reinforced it previously, so the nail holes were too large to anchor the latch in the same location. As he placed the hammer back into the spot he'd taken it from on the tool bench, Matt let out a low whistle.

Kate's hands stopped. "What?"

"You've already almost finished that lace?" He gazed at the long leather thong hanging from her fingers.

She hitched her left shoulder diffidently. "This is the second one. They don't take all that long. I cut a circle, then just keep cutting spiral-style into it."

"That knife has to be sharp. I'd massacre the leather and my hands."

"I've cut myself on occasion." She started working again and tacked on, "More often in the kitchen than by working leather."

"Beats me why you talk like that. Every last meal I've eaten here has tasted mighty fine, and you've been the cook."

Kate shrugged. "I can turn out a passable meal. Once you taste April's fare, you'll understand."

"Not that good food isn't high up in my estimation, but a meal is gone in a short while. The saddles and belts you make last for years."

"Ah, but the latch on the fishing basket didn't." She set down the bootlace, bent over a scrap of leather, and carefully scribed a circle on it.

He didn't want to leave. Talking with Kate counted as a pure pleasure. Then, too, he hoped to glean some information from her. Matt leaned against her workbench. "I've seen the stuff you've made here on Chance Ranch. Tell me about what you've made for neighbors."

"Mrs. Dorsey had me make her husband a saddle to replace the one he lost in their barn fire. My family voted to give them all of the spare halters, leads, and the like that we had on hand."

"That's the second time you've mentioned voting."

"It's a family rule: Anyone in the family who's twenty-one is given the right to vote on issues."

"I don't mean to be indelicate, but you're not of voting age—at least, that's what I gathered when Caleb, Tanner, and April were speaking the other night."

"I'm not." She tilted her head to the side and continued to cut the leather thong.

"So everyone older than you voted to give away the work you'd done."

"Never thought of it that way. Chances share. It would be miserly of us to keep halters and such that we don't even use when a neighbor is in need."

"I agree. So tell me about your other neighbors."

"You've already met Peter and Johnna. They're from the MacPherson spread. Tomorrow, we'll have a family picnic after church. You—"

"Sis?" Tanner moseyed into the workshop and shoved his hands into his pockets. "What're you doing?"

"Making bootlaces for Peter. Why?"

"Just wondered." Tanner pulled his hands back out of his pockets and pulled a knife from his belt sheath. "Reckoned I ought to make more clothespins. I don't think we have nearly enough."

"Probably not." She turned her attention back to Matt. "Anyway, you're welcome to go to church with us tomorrow; then we have the picnic afterward."

"I already asked him."

"Appreciate the invitation. It'll be good to worship." Though he felt strongly about the necessity of Christian fellowship, Matt wished Tanner would saunter off. At the present, spending time with Kate—only Kate—sounded far more appealing.

"MacPhersons are coming here for the picnic," Kate said as she finished the piece she'd started.

"We swap." Tanner examined the small block of wood he'd picked up, then dragged a stool over closer to the lantern. "Once or twice a month we have a family get-together."

"Judging from how Peter and April act, I'd say the family ties are going to grow stronger."

Kate flashed him a smile. "Isn't it wonderful? I'm so happy for her."

"I'm not." Tanner smirked as he hiked up his pantleg and slid onto the stool. "Well, I am, but I don't think we ought to let her marry and move away until she teaches you more of her special recipes."

"Kate'll move away when she marries, too."

Tanner let out a snort. "No danger of that."

Chapter 10

Kate blushed so deeply, her freckles completely disappeared.

Matt lounged against her worktable. "You might be right. A man could get lost in her pretty blue eyes and decide to marry her and stay right here on Chance Ranch."

Tanner's head flew up, but the surprised look on his face immediately changed. "Ouch!"

Kate slipped off her stool and fished a hanky from her apron pocket. "Here."

Matt marveled that Kate ignored her brother's ridicule and tended his cut. Most people would have gloated and said it served him right.

"No use in getting that bloodstained." Tanner plucked a bandana from his pocket.

"Oh no." Kate yanked the bandana away and shoved it onto her worktable. "That has to be dirtier than Methuselah's tent."

"Methuselah's tent?" Matt echoed, thoroughly entertained by her choice of words.

Kate held her hanky against Tanner's finger. "If that amuses you, you're going to have fun tomorrow."

"Yeah, he will."

"Why?"

"The MacPherson brothers hail from Hawk's Fall, Kentucky. They got so lonely, so they went to a neighboring place in Kentucky called Salt Lake Holler for brides. Tempy's sister Lovejoy came as the brides' chaperone. Our uncle Daniel snagged her for himself. All of that being said, they brought a rich heritage and delightfully colorful speech with them."

Many of those Appalachian men are adept at brewing moonshine. It's part of their culture, and the land there isn't rich enough to support a family. More than a few of those people earn their living by operating a still.

Kate slowly peeled away the handkerchief, then pressed it back around her brother's finger. "You need to go wash this with lye soap."

"No need to fuss over it." Tanner scowled at her.

Kate pretended not to hear him. "After you do, sprinkle some styptic powder over it."

"Hey, what's going on in here?" Tobias came in, carrying the fishing basket.

He set it on Kate's worktable. "Pax said this needs fixing."

"Tanner's going to go take care of his finger. He cut it. I'm going to fix the basket."

"It's nothing." Tanner curled his hand around the reddening hanky. "Just a little slice."

Tobias's brows knit. "How'd you—"

"Whittling."

"Go take care of that." Tobias bumped his brother off the stool, then took the perch for himself and picked up the same block of wood. "I'll take care of this."

This? Matt hooked one boot heel on the workbench's crossbar. *The clothespins are just an excuse to stick around out here so Kate isn't alone with me. It's no wonder no one's courted and married her—she has half an army of brothers and cousins to be sure a man can't get close to her.*

Unwilling to be put off, Matt grabbed another block of wood. "What kind of clothespins are we making?"

Tobias chuckled softly. He stood and reached for a large tin bucket on Kate's upper shelf. As he set it down, dozens upon dozens of homemade clothespins rattled inside. Flipping one to Matt, Tobias said, "This kind."

Matt ran his thumb along the wooden piece. "I didn't know anyone still whittled these. You can buy factory-made ones for a song."

"Aunt Lovejoy believes if you can't make something for yourself, you don't need it." Tobias shaved off a corner of the wood.

That explained why. Still, Matt didn't understand why they were making more. "Not to dismiss the virtue of work, but it looks to me like you've already made plenty."

"Gifts should always be from the heart." As soon as the words slipped out of her mouth, Kate bit her lip and cast a questioning look at her older brother.

Intrigued by the small mystery, Matt prodded, "So the clothespins are gifts?"

"You've let the cat out of the bag," Tobias muttered.

"I'm sorry." She bowed her head.

"It's not a big deal. No use getting upset over it." Tobias looked at Matt. "On his ninth birthday, every Chance is given a knife. He's taught to whittle—mostly little animals and toys. Same with the MacPhersons."

"So you exchange gifts?"

Tobias shook his head. "Not those things."

Matt knew when someone was trying to deflect questions by redirecting the conversation. He'd learned to string them along as though he was fooled, then when they let down their guard, he'd go right back and discover what they were trying to hide. "Then where do the toys go?"

Some of the tension in Kate's shoulders and in Tobias's jaw eased. Kate said, "They go to children who wouldn't otherwise have toys."

He took up a knife and started on one of the rectangular wooden blocks. "There's a wonderful orphanage in San Francisco. If you don't have anyone or any place specific in mind, I'm sure they'd appreciate having toys for the little ones."

Kate concentrated as she repaired the fishing basket. "We could keep that in mind, couldn't we, Tobias?"

"Reckon we could—but there have to be at least a couple of orphanages in such a big city."

"The one I have in mind is unique. It's an enormous old mansion. Most of the younger children are adopted quite quickly, and the older ones receive educations or training in keeping with their talents so they can be self-reliant when they leave."

Squinting at the wood in his hands, Tobias said, "Our mother grew up in an orphanage."

"She must be a special woman to have married into this family and reared you as she has."

"Mama is very special." Kate straightened up and patted the fishing basket. "There. Good as new."

Knowing he had to press for answers or lose this opportunity, Matt's gaze went from Kate to her brother and back. "The two of you are dodging my question as to what happens to the clothespins."

Kate's shoulders drooped. "You know how in the Bible it exhorts us to give without the other hand knowing? It's one of those situations."

"I can respect that."

"Good." Tobias's curt tone made it clear he thought the discussion was over.

"I've seen some that were all painted and decorated to serve as Christmas ornaments." Matt held his up toward the light and pretended to squint along the side to see if it was smooth. Though Kate didn't make a sound, he sensed her sudden inhalation. *So that's why they're sensitive.* "I reckon there aren't all that many things you can do with clothespins." He went back to whittling. "If you're worried I'm opposed to Christmas trees, I'm not. I figure Christ is like an evergreen—His beauty refreshes us and gives us life. Then, too, it never depends on the seasons of life—His love endures even through the coldest, darkest times."

"That's quite a testimonial." Tobias grinned. "So are you coming to church with us tomorrow?"

Kate laughed. "Tanner invited him, then I invited him. Now you did."

"And they also invited me to go to the picnic."

Looking at his sister, Tobias asked, "Did you tell him about the MacPhersons' dishes?"

"Not yet."

"Don't." An impish smile tugged at the corners of Tobias's mouth.

"I overheard Johnna saying something to Peter about cat-head biscuits. If that's the kind of food they bring, I'm going to make a pig of myself."

"You did that at supper tonight." Tobias's grin bloomed.

"It's Kate's fault. She cooks better food than I've ever eaten."

"I've told him to wait until April is back at the stove."

"You've been whippin' up some decent meals on your own, sis. What're you making for the picnic?"

"I've already made Aunt Miriam's coleslaw. It's hanging in the well along with egg salad, and I boiled potatoes for potato salad. While I make that tonight, I'll bake some shoofly pie. I have some lemons that need to be used up. Maybe I'll do a lemon meringue, too."

"Now you've done it." Matt gave her a baleful look.

"What did I do?"

"Lemon pie. I'll lie in bed thinking about it, and come morning, when there's not a trace left of that lemon pie, I'll be fired. Instead of going to church, I'll be heading down the road, searching for a new job."

Kate's eyes sparkled with merriment. "You could still go to church. It's the perfect place for sinners to repent."

"Now there's the problem. I couldn't say I was one bit sorry for what I'd done."

"Better make a couple lemon meringues." Tobias stretched. "I might have to supervise our new hand if he takes to wandering around at night."

"If you eat that much, when folks talk about the Chance spread, no one will know whether they're discussing you or the ranch."

"I have a long way to go before I look like Mr. Roland."

Matt jumped on the opportunity. "Roland. Now there's a neighbor you haven't mentioned yet. So what does he do?"

"Eat," Tobias said succinctly.

"He's turned his cattle operation over to his son and his son-in-law." Kate opened and shut the basket lid a few times to assure herself everything lined up easily. "Gout's made it hard for him to get around much. I can understand why he's thickened in the middle a bit."

"Must be a huge holding if he's got two men running it."

"Just average-sized, but Sam and Hector are doing something right because it appears they're turning a tidy profit."

So they might have found another way to make money—and moonshining is lucrative.

"Speaking of the picnic. . ." Kate methodically put away the few tools she'd used. "I was so busy with supper, I forgot to tell you that April and Peter invited the Youngbloods to come."

"Great!" Tobias deftly started creating the center notch in his clothespin. "Guess that means we'll have to leave that lemon pie alone tonight, Salter. Lucinda's real fond of them."

"You men can stay here and whittle to your hearts' content. I need to get back to the kitchen."

Matt regretted that Kate had to leave—even more than he regretted her big brother barging in and playing chaperon. *I'll manage to spend time with her tomorrow at the picnic. Meantime, maybe I can get Tobias to tell me more about the folks around here.*

"Tanner said just about everyone attends church. That's good to hear. Most towns have a couple of skeptics or black sheep. . . ."

"No. No thank you." Lucinda looked up at Tobias and batted her eyes. "You're a big man. You eat it for me."

Peter tossed a pickle onto his plate. Lucinda made a big to-do over what she'd eat. For coming here without a single dish to share, it seemed mighty wrong for her to be so finicky. Then again, her mother had taken one look at the womenfolk putting out the huge spread of food and suddenly declared she felt poorly. Mr. Youngblood took her on home.

Peter plopped down close to April. "Here. Have a bite." He held the sandwich up for her. He'd used the excuse of her sore hands to make them eat off the same plate.

"Oh! It's your mama's chicken salad!"

Mama beamed. "I made it special, jist for you, lamb."

April took a bite, closed her eyes as she relished the flavor, and swallowed. "Magnificent! Thank you for making it."

"Thangs keep a-headin' where they are betwixt you and my son, I'll wind up sharin' my secret recipe with you right soon."

Turning the same shade as the inside of a ripe watermelon, April swiped a pickle off the plate and took a big bite. Her face twisted in dismay.

Lord, ever'body else knows we're a good match. Why's April actin' like this?

She dropped the rest of the pickle back onto the plate and shook her hand in the air. A small sound of distress curled in her throat.

"Peter, pour yore water o'er her fingers. That salty brine's hurtin' her dreadful."

He emptied his cup over April's hand, then accepted Matt Salter's. After pouring it slowly over the blisters that had opened, Peter yanked a bandana from his pocket and gently dried her fingers. "That any better, honey pie?"

A choppy sigh accompanied a tiny bob of her head.

"Best you go on a-feedin' her," Pa declared.

Johnna chimed in, "Yep. Hit'll be good practice for when you give her a bite from yore weddin' cake."

Still red as could be, April called back over to his sister, "Don't go rushing things. You and Trevor have been courting well over a year. If anyone's due to marry, it's you!"

"He's fixin' to ask her," one of his little cousins shouted.

"Hush," Mama chided.

"But I'm only tellin' the truth. I heard Trevor talkin' to Uncle Obie. He asked—"

Aunt Eunice clapped her hand over her son's mouth. "You done said more'n 'nuff."

Trevor chortled. Fishing something out of his shirt pocket, he shifted onto his knees. "Johnna, I planned to take you off on a walk all alone, but since I'm getting so much help, I'll ask you here and now." He pulled out a ring. "I love you. Will you marry me?"

While they kissed, everyone cheered.

Matt Salter frowned. "Shouldn't she give him her answer?"

"Already did," Peter declared. "MacPhersons don't kiss unless they're bespoken."

"Hey, Peter!" Trevor called over. He shot a meaningful look at April. "Jump on in. The water's fine!"

Caleb shouted back, "Not a chance!"

Paxton let out a whoop. "That's right. April won't be a Chance anymore."

Peter looked at April. A fetching blush stained her cheeks, and she bit her lower lip—something she rarely did. *Nothing would make me happier than to propose here and now, but she's not ready yet. She deserves a full courtship and to know how deep my love flows ere I ask her.* Peter lifted his chin and gave her a slow, audacious wink.

Caleb cleared his throat loudly. "Nobody's doing any proposing to anyone until our folks get home."

"That's only proper," Kate agreed. She smiled and tacked on, "Our folks are due home late this week."

"That gladdens my heart," Aunt Tempy said. "I've missed my sister more than words can tell."

"I'm sure Aunt Lovejoy's missed you every bit as much." April sighed. "I've worried about her."

"Frettin' ne'er yields good." Ma caught little Matilda as she toddled by and started to tie her shoe. "We'll all hold our Lovejoy up to Jesus."

"Thank you, Aunt Lois." April gave Peter's mother a tender smile. "I've been thinking about you all going to Yosemite the next few summers. While you're praying, I want you to ask the Lord about leaving Matilda in my care. Aunt Eunice, I'd keep Elvera for you, too. That way, you'd all be able to enjoy yourselves more."

"Ain't that kind of you!" Aunt Eunice said as she poked a tomato wedge into Elvera's mouth.

Ma gave Matilda a hug, and Matilda gave her a sloppy baby kiss before pushing away and coming straight to Peter. She curled her chubby little fingers around the other part of the pickle. "Pees?"

April pulled his tiny sister down into her lap. "Yes, but you have to sit down here to eat. No running around with food in yore mouth."

"I can watch the young'uns," Johnna said. "I already went to Yosemite."

"Nope." Trevor nestled her close. "I aim to go see Yosemite. I want my bride by my side."

A deep longing speared through Peter. *I want the woman by my side to be my bride.*

"Kate?" April tugged on her cousin's sash. "Don't you think Johnna ought to come to our cabin to make her wedding gown?"

Kate bobbed her head. "We have plenty of room, and it can be left out instead of being tucked away when you can't work on it."

Ma sighed. "I always reckoned my daughters would wear my weddin' dress. But yore a whole hand taller. I checked the hem last night, and it's not deep 'nuff to let down for you, Johnna."

"Lambkins, could be one of the others'll still wear it." Pa patted Ma's shoulder. "I'll send Peter to San Francisco to fetch a dress length of fine satin. That way, that gal of ourn cain stitch a purdy dress she cain pass on to her own daughter someday."

Matilda twisted and held up the end of the pickle she'd been gnawing on for April to have a bite. April pretended to nibble on it. "Mmm-mmm! Thank you!" She turned to Peter. "Laurel and Gabe are in Boston, visiting his family."

Lucinda fluffed up row upon row of ruffles in her skirts. "Mama has all of my clothes made back East."

"No daughter of mine's gonna walk down the aisle in a ready-made gown." Ma shook her head. "I won't have it."

Lucinda spluttered. "My dresses are not ready made!"

"Yore right purdy in that frock, Lucy." Ma reached for her mug of water.

Peter was glad she did, because she missed seeing Lucinda's scowl. He didn't know whether Tobias's sweetheart didn't accept the heartfelt compliment or if she objected to Ma's habit of granting folks nicknames. Either way, the gal oughtn't be so disrespectful to her elders.

Ma kept on talking. "Yes, you are a sight to behold. But ever' stitch in a weddin' gown ought to be made with hope and prayer, not by a machine. Machines don't carry a thread of love."

"Making Polly and Laurel's dresses was so much fun," Kate said.

"Plenty of love and joy filled the hours we spent." April looked at Peter. "We could send a telegram and have Laurel ship material to San Francisco."

"Won't that be expensive?" Lucinda stared at her plate and scooted the food around.

Peter bristled. *She'd best mind her tongue. Just 'cuz we MacPhersons ain't wealthy don't mean we don't do right by our own.*

"It won't be expensive at all." April beamed. Bless her heart, it never occurred to her that someone might be unkind. "Laurel and Gabe took a list from us before they left. Laurel already told me she planned to send back fabric for the MacPherson clan. We didn't ask what you'd like—"

"Because you always wear golden yellow," Kate said.

Johnna burst out, "I don't want a yeller weddin' dress."

"But you'd look gorgeous carrying yellow flowers." April lovingly rubbed her cheek against Matilda's mop of russet curls.

Peter's heart swelled. April cherished his kin. Here she was, natural as breathing, lovin' on his sisters. Everyone in both families knew for certain that he'd fallen head-over-heels in love with her—everyone but her. *Someday soon, she'll see the truth.*

"I'd never carry yellow roses." Lucinda stuck her nose in the air. "They represent infidelity."

The friendly chatter came to a dead halt.

Trevor curled his arm tightly around Johnna. "Johnna and me—our love is stronger than that sort of nonsense."

"Some of those customs have no meaning here," Tobias told Lucinda.

"That's right." Johnna smoothed her hand down her yellow gown. "I reckon I wouldn't much feel like myself iff'n I didn't have yeller somewheres on my weddin' day."

"It doesn't matter what you hold in your hand," April said. "It's what you hold in your heart. We all know how devoted you are to one another."

Matt Salter rose. "Anyone need anything?"

"I couldn't possibly eat another morsel." Lucinda's gaze shifted toward April. "Gluttony is a sin."

Chapter 11

"Pride's a sin," Peter half-growled.

"And sloth," Kate chimed in.

"That leaves greed, envy, wrath, and. . ." Tanner's brows knit.

"Lust," Pa finished. "Mr. Salter, iff'n yore headin' to the table, I'd appreciate you toting back some of that Heinz ketchup."

Matt nodded. "Sure will. I'm getting more of that noodle stuff if any's left."

Tanner chortled. "You like it, huh?"

"Delicious."

"Coupla rattlers got bold and slithered into the henhouse," Pa said.

Ma nodded. "Eunice skinned them snakes and boiled up a mess of noodles."

"So you've been eating rattler!" Tanner's eyes danced with mirth.

Lucinda shoved her plate to the side and started gagging. She scrambled off the blanket and raced toward a clump of trees.

Salter shrugged. "Isn't the first time I've had rattler. Hope it's not the last. I'd rather eat snake than have one take a bite of me any day."

Kate started to get up. "I suppose I ought to go see if Lucinda needs any help."

"Thanks, sis." Tobias handed her his bandana.

"Bring over a cup of water in a few minutes."

"Here, honey pie." Peter held the sandwich to April's mouth. He couldn't fathom why Lucinda acted so catty, but he wasn't going to let April think for one second that he agreed.

Tears glossed April's eyes as she shook her head. "I've had enough."

"You've only had one bite."

"Bite!" Matilda opened her little mouth wide.

"Shore." Peter gave his baby sister a bite, then took one himself. He held the sandwich back up to April's mouth. Talking around the food, he said, "See? It's yore turn now."

Matilda twisted around and bobbed her head. "Turns. Share. Good!"

April pasted on a smile and took the tiniest bite possible.

Tobias stood and looked at everyone. "I'm sorry if feathers got ruffled. Lucinda was nervous."

Peter stared up at his friend. "There's nervous, and then there's wicked mean."

"Iff'n any of mine got that fresh-mouthed, they'd be tasting a cake of lye soap." Aunt Eunice folded her arms across her chest. "A hickory switch iff'n they'd show half that much—"

Pa cut in, " 'Cept for Caleb, Tobias, yore the eldest Chance here. 'Tisn't my place to tell you what to do, but I'm more'n riled. Mayhap you oughtta take Miz Youngblood home to her folks."

Tobias left.

Pa turned to Peter. "Hit'll take three days or so for the material to get there onc't we send a telegram. Not to say that we don't 'preciate all yore hard work, but with so many of the Chances gone and you bein' there to holp with the horses and court April, we've managed to get along. I'm of a mind to send you to San Francisco with yore sis."

Johnna laughed delightedly. "Thank you, Pa! April, you could come with us!"

"O'er my dead body." Ma shook her head. "Wouldn't be seemly, what with them courtin'. 'Sides, absence makes the heart grow fonder."

"Don't know about that," Peter said. "I'm already right fond of this here beauty. If anything, I'm afeared some other buck's gonna try to steal her away whilst I'm gone."

"Have a safe trip." April passed a box to Peter. The MacPhersons needed all of their wagons, and with some of the Chances still gone, Caleb offered to have Peter and Johnna borrow one for their trip to San Francisco.

"Now you jist hang on a minute." He set the box on the porch railing. "First thangs first. Honey pie, I'm startin' to miss you, and I ain't even left yet."

"Don't you even want to know what's in the box?"

He tugged her into his arms. Dipping his head, his breath tickling her ear, Peter murmured, "You're more interestin' than anything in the whole wide world."

She shivered. *Dear Mercy, Peter's my friend. I can't have feelings for him this way.* April did her best to sound lighthearted. "You wouldn't be saying that if you knew I got up early this morning to bake you the sticky buns I've been promising."

"Yore sweeter'n any old sticky buns. Still, thankee for makin' them. I'll relish ever' last one."

"You'd better." Caleb tugged her away from Peter, and April suddenly felt very lonely. Her brother groused, "It's Wednesday. April always makes those sticky buns for us. Not today. She boxed them up and threatened if we so much as opened the lid, she'd never make them again."

"That's right." A spurt of joy filled her when Peter snatched up the box.

Johnna giggled from the wagon bench. "You Chance boys are just outta luck. Chances might always share, but Peter's a MacPherson."

Caleb poked Peter in the chest. "If you won't share, I won't either."

"You don't have anything he wants," April shot back.

As Caleb's arm wrapped around her, Peter shook his head. "Honey pie, that's where yore wrong as wrong cain be. Yore brother has you."

"You don't have to give me the whole box." Caleb smiled audaciously. "You can keep one bun for yourself."

By now, all of her brothers and cousins had lined up. "That's right," Cole said. "And once Caleb gets the box, he'll share with the rest of us."

"Now jist a minute." Johnna scowled. "I aim to have one, too!"

"I shouldn't have bothered to put them in a box," April muttered as Peter handed over the buns.

Kate, the egg basket hanging from her arm, came toward them. "So help me, if you boys are trying to steal those sticky buns from Peter, I'm not going to cook a lick of food for you for a week."

"April's cooking again," Caleb called back.

"I might be, but then again, I might not." April tilted her chin upward.

"She won't if you steal away the courting gift she's made for Peter." Kate sailed past them and into the kitchen cabin.

"Aww, man." Caleb grimaced. "Sis, are those sticky buns a courting gift?"

"What else would they be?" The jubilant look on Peter's face started April into a fit of giggles.

Matt Salter came over to see what the commotion was about. "What's going on?" He sniffed, and his eyes lit up. "What's that I smell?"

"We've got to be headin' out." Peter dared to lean down and rest his forehead against hers. "Don't you forget what I've been tellin' you."

Her heart plummeted. He'd been advising her on how to go about catching another man's interest. *I'm such a fool.* Unable to speak, she stepped back and nodded.

Caleb shoved the box into Peter's arms.

"You mean he's taking away whatever it is that smells so good?" Matt sounded outraged.

"April and I are going to go bake another batch." Kate came back out and slipped her hand into April's. "Peter, there's something in that box for your sister. Make sure she gets it."

"I'll be shore she gets one of these buns."

"That, too." Kate tugged on April's hand. "We'll end up standing here all day if I don't tear the two of you apart. Come on into the kitchen."

Once the screen door shut behind them, Kate let out a sigh. "I'm so glad you didn't ask what I put in the box. I didn't have a chance to tell you, but I wrote a little note and told Johnna we wanted her to buy some pretty things for herself.

I signed it from both of us and put in a double eagle."

"Twenty dollars!" April gaped at her cousin.

Merry laughter bubbled out of Kate. "Mama left me more than that in case something came up. Now we'd better start a batch of sticky buns, or the boys are going to get ugly."

The only ugly one around here is me. April reached around and retied her apron. "May as well get busy."

~

As April pulled the second dozen from the oven, Kate went to the porch and barely hit the huge iron triangle they used to call everyone to supper. She raced back inside. "Watch out. We've got a stampede headed our way."

The back door opened. "I ah. . .remembered how they all came in the front when you made the beef and rice." Matt stood there with his hat in his hands.

"No need to be sheepish. You're smart!" Kate nudged him toward the table. April noticed how Kate stayed beside him.

Caleb barreled through the doorway. "Jeff Borley's here. Wants to buy another horse."

"I've never seen a man buy a horse at the kitchen table," Packard grumbled, reaching for a bun and scowling as Jeff entered the kitchen.

Jeff took a sticky bun. After the first bite, he straightened up. "Feed me more of these, and you could talk me into buying both of those mares!"

"Hear that, sis?" Caleb grinned.

"So these are the sticky buns Peter MacPherson was bragging about." Jeff reached down and greedily helped himself to a second bun, even though he hadn't finished the first. "I'm going to have to come pay my respects to you, April."

"Too late," Kate said. "Peter's been coming by all summer."

"It's not too late." Jeff smacked his lips. "There's no ring on her finger."

April pretended she didn't hear him. Jeff never so much as once traded a greeting with her at church or in town. Peter's words echoed in her mind. *Don't you e'er make the mistake of thankin' your only worth is a batch of sommat you pull outta the oven.* Clearly, Jeff felt otherwise.

The kitchen grew noisy with all eight of her brothers and cousins, Matt, Kate, and Jeff. April scooted past them and onto the porch. She started turning the handle on the Daisy butter churn.

"You're industrious." Jeff's voice came from just a few feet away.

April shrugged. "We've had extra milk all summer. No use letting it go to waste."

He hitched a pantleg and perched on the porch railing. "That doesn't smell. When my mom and sis make butter, it stinks."

"I'm making sweet cream butter. My father likes it better."

Jeff hooked his thumbs into belt hoops. "Way to a man's heart is through his stomach."

"I wouldn't know. Daddy loved me long before I was old enough to cook."

"Time'll come when your father's not the one you'll stand in front of the stove for. Are you going to use the buttermilk to make biscuits for dinner?"

She shook her head. "I'm planning to make flapjacks for breakfast tomorrow." *So you can stop angling for an invitation to stay to lunch.*

Caleb came outside. "So what's it going to be, Jeff—the bay or the mustang?"

"See you around." Jeff slapped his hat on his head and walked toward the stable with her brother. April couldn't remember ever feeling so relieved to see a man saunter away.

Sleep wouldn't come. Kate blew out a resigned breath. "Are you asleep?"

"No."

Turning over and propping her chin in her hand, Kate squinted across the dark loft at April. "It must feel wonderful, having men stop by to pay their respects to you."

"Not a one has stopped by to pay his respects."

"Could have fooled me. In three days, you've had Jeff, Grayson, Horace, Enoch, and Everett come see you."

"Peter's talked about my cooking, and Jeff happened by and got a taste of my sticky buns. Men talk about animals, weather, and food. Folks didn't pay much attention to what Peter said about my cooking since the MacPhersons are famous for liking odd dishes. Once Jeff said something, they all got curious. They don't respect me. They respect my cooking. There's a world of difference."

Kate absently ran her finger along the stitch line of her quilt. "You can't be sure of that."

"Oh, I'm dead sure. Not a one discussed anything but my ability to cook and sew."

"Men think more practically."

"Which is why each of them managed to show up at mealtime." April huffed. "They wanted to taste my cooking, but none of them bothered to try to sit by me."

"Give it a chance. It takes time."

"I don't want to," April said. "They've ignored me forever, and now they're reckoning even a short, dumpy woman like me is worth considering because I'd ease his life by being a housekeeper and cook."

"You're not dumpy! You don't eat any more than the rest of us. I've seen pictures of your grandma and her mama. You're shaped just like them—like a happy little chickadee!"

April snorted. "So now I'm a bird brain. Well, I still have enough sense to send those so-called suitors packing. Enoch talked about me the same way he talks about a horse he wants to buy. I'm surprised he didn't ask to see my teeth."

After her giggles died down, Kate figured this was as good a time as any to say something. She gathered her courage. "April, I need you to do me a favor."

"What?"

"I've been keeping the boys away while your suitors come. I need you to do the same for me. My brothers won't let me have a minute alone with Matt."

April sat bolt upright and squeaked, "You've been leaving me alone with them on purpose?"

"Of course I have."

"Don't!"

"How was I to know that's what you wanted? For four years now, you've been mooning and moping over men. You've even cried over not having swains seek you out. Now that they're swarming, you're not happy getting what you wanted."

"I don't want any of them!" April flopped back down, turned on her tummy, and started sobbing into her pillow. "I've made such a mess of things!"

Chapter 12

Kate climbed out of bed and went over to April. "You haven't made a mess of anything." She slid in next to her cousin and petted her hair.

April turned toward her. Tears continued to pour down her face as she wailed, "I've been living a lie, but now it's the truth. I don't know what to do."

"You? A lie?" Kate couldn't hide the surprise in her voice.

April nodded. "It's been a secret between Peter and me. He's pretended to like me so I could practice how to act with a suitor. Only now, I don't want any of those other men. I want Peter!"

Kate couldn't believe her ears. Ever since last year's trip to Yosemite, she'd known Peter loved her cousin. Part of her wanted to tell April so, but something kept her from doing that. Slowly, she said, "I don't know that you've been living a lie. Deep down, your heart knew what your head didn't. You and Peter have always been close."

Mournfully shaking her head, April wailed, "It's ruined now. Before he left, he told me to remember what he's taught me. He's ready to move on and find a wife. I can't stay here and watch that. I can't!"

Kate wrapped her arms around her cousin and held tight. "You're not going anywhere. We're going to pray about this."

"I've been praying. I have for years. I kept begging God to give me the right man. You know I have."

"We both have." Kate scooted closer still. "It's not easy to see God's will. I want more time alone with Matt because—well, because deep down, I think he's the one for me."

"I'd be so happy for you if he is."

Kate sighed. *Sweet April—here she is, afraid of losing Peter, and I'm telling her that I've found my man. I'm an idiot for saying anything at all, but this was the worst time I could have told her how I feel. Her heart's breaking.*

April rubbed her cheek on the pillow to wipe away her tears. "Matt fits in. It's like he's always been here. And that first night, he stood up for you even though he thought it would cost him his job. I wish Peter loved me like that."

I still think he does. The words were on the tip of Kate's tongue, but they wouldn't come out. Instead, she turned the conversation in a different direction. "Just a year ago, you and I were comforting Laurel about whether she'd ever marry

Gabe. Back then, you said we had to have faith—that God wouldn't let us all be without husbands."

"He won't. He's already given Laurel Gabe, and it's looking like you and Matt are a good match. Maybe I'm supposed to be a spinster. I've been so busy telling God to give me a husband, I didn't ask if He wanted me to have one."

Aching silence filled the loft. Finally, Kate quietly admitted, "I've been doing the same thing."

Isn't that just like me, God? I'm always running full tilt at whatever catches my attention without thinking ahead. How many times have Daddy and Mama told me to stop and think? I've been so busy letting my head and heart rule me, I didn't seek Your will. I sort of figured since Matt is a good Christian, the soul part was taken care of.

April wiggled and rested her head on Kate's shoulder. "Remember what we always say when we get into fixes like this?"

"You mean before we pray?"

In unison, they whispered, "God help us all."

Kate went on, "Lord, we need Your help and direction. . . ."

Matt stifled a yawn. The steady cadence of pushing and pulling the two-man saw with Tanner demanded physical effort, but he let his mind wander. The middle-of-the-night explorations were catching up with him. So far, he'd inspected the entire Chance Ranch and found no evidence of a still.

Lord, these are salt-of-the-earth, God-fearing people, and it bothers me to be here under false pretenses. I'm trying to do right. Early as it is to say, I'm even feeling like You brought me here to meet Kate. She's something else. But how will she feel when I tell her I've come here pretending to be a saddle tramp?

The saw paused while both men wiped away sweat with their sleeves. Tanner raised his brows. "Wish you would have stayed back helping Cole and Paxton with the horses?"

"I can muck out stalls any day. This is a good change."

Tanner nodded and squinted in the distance. "Caleb and Tobias said they marked one more tree. We don't want to overtimber."

Matt nodded. "Someone got too rambunctious on the spread over that-a-way."

"Dorseys." Tanner wrapped his hands around the wooden saw handle. "Yep. Only good thing about that cutting was that when their barn burned, there wasn't much else to go up in flames."

"Probably saved your spread from going up." Matt grabbed his side of the saw and got back into the push-pull rhythm. One quick survey of the Dorseys' holding told him the truth. They'd cut down so much of the timber, it would be impossible to hide a still anywhere on the property.

Thaddeus Walls, even though he'd lost his family due to drunkenness, proved to be completely incapable of being any part of an illegal operation. He'd been in a drunken stupor both nights when Matt went to spy on him. The bottles littering his property showed he bought the cheapest rotgut available. Anyone owning a still or being part of the operation would save the bottles to refill or have jugs or a keg instead.

The MacPhersons still remained suspect. Matt yawned again as he recalled skulking around part of the MacPherson place the last two nights. The first time, he'd seen some activity far off toward a treeline. The second time, he'd riled a few dogs and had to leave before someone in that huge clan discovered his presence. *The best way to check them out is for me to have an excuse to be on their property.*

"Hey!" Tanner shouted.

Matt halted and looked around the tree trunk at him.

"We've gone deep enough." He grinned. "Only time I've ever seen men lose track of the work they're doing is when they've started falling in love. You've been doting on Kate. Are you thinking of her?"

"Might be." Matt shrugged. "It's none of your business, though."

"She's my sister. Of course it's my business!"

"Let's shove over this tree." Matt moved the saw and stepped to the far side. "All clear?"

"Yep." Tanner hollered, "Timber!" and the two thrust their weight against the tree. The tree groaned loudly, then the air whistled through the limbs as it began to tilt. "Got it!" Tanner and Matt scrambled backward and off to the side so they'd be out of danger if the trunk bounced.

Soon, several of the Chance men worked on the fallen tree. Some cut off limbs while others hitched the severed pieces to a team of horses and dragged them off a ways.

Pausing a moment, Packard called to no one in particular, "Our folks are going to be glad they stayed gone awhile longer."

Chuckles met that observation.

"Dunno about that!" someone on the far side of the tree shouted back. "Uncle Dan likes working his problems out with an axe."

Tobias smacked Matt on the back. "Ready to go cut down the other one?"

"Hey. Matt and I are a team." Tanner scowled at his brother.

"You *were* a team. The next tree is mine."

Matt shrugged and hiked after Tobias. Tobias picked up the saw and gave him a piercing look. "Dad'll be home in a day or so. Between now and then, I'm the head of our family. My sis might seem tough and capable, but she's got a tender heart. I don't want you breaking it."

"Kate is capable. She's smart, too. I don't believe in dallying with a woman's heart. I enjoy her company and get the notion that she could like me—but it's sorta hard to tell. You and Tanner act like a couple of watch dogs."

"We take care of our women."

"If the day comes where what's between Kate and me gets serious, you can be sure I'll take care of her."

"That's what worries me—you said *if.* You're not sure how you feel. She's already getting her heart set on you. You being underfoot all of the time makes it easy for her to plan out a future."

"I don't know what my future holds. I have to leave it in God's hands. If He gives me Kate as my wife, I'd be a very blessed man."

"Gals are just like birds. Doesn't matter how fancy or drab they are, they still wanna nest. It's in their nature."

"If you're trying to compare Lucinda to Kate, don't." Matt stared at Tobias. "I don't know anything more about Lucinda than what I saw at the picnic. I am positive, however, Kate wouldn't ever cut down another person—not even on her worst day."

Tobias winced. "I didn't mean to make a comparison, but I can see how you thought I did. I've never seen Lucinda act like that."

That admission hadn't come easy. Matt chose to move on. "Kate tried to hide her hands from me. I don't know where she got the ridiculous notion that dabs of stain would matter to a man. She's beautiful, inside and out."

They came to the other tree Caleb had marked. Just as they set the saw against the tree, the dinner triangle jangled.

Tobias's brow wrinkled. "It can't be lunch."

The jangling didn't stop. "Something's wrong!"

Chapter 13

Matt and Tobias simultaneously let go of the two-handled saw and ran for their horses. The other men dropped their axes and joined them. Those whose horses were hitched to branches hurried to release them, but Matt didn't wait. He vaulted onto his mount and raced toward the cabins.

"Don't see any smoke!" Packard shouted.

Kate. Matt urged his horse on.

"Cole better not have tried to break that stallion." Distress and anger tainted Tobias's voice. "I shouldn't have left him there. I knew he was tempted."

"Ringing stopped." Packard rode on Matt's other side. "Someone's hurt. Kate and April must be busy trying to help."

Lord, I don't want anyone harmed, but please—especially not Kate.

Their horses skidded to an abrupt halt in the barnyard. Relief flooded Matt when he spied Kate standing on the porch clutching the striker that belonged to the triangle.

The men bolted from their saddles. "Where?" Caleb demanded at the same time Tobias yelled, "Who?"

"Everyone is okay!" Kate called back.

April stood by her side and yelled, "Nothing's wrong!"

"Then what did you think you were doing?" Caleb bellowed as he started toward her.

Matt jumped in front of him. He wasn't sure whether to fight Caleb or shake Kate until her teeth rattled. She'd given him a fright.

Lucinda pushed between the Chance girls and stepped forward. Her lower lip poked out in a pout, she said, "That's what I asked them, too."

"Kate?" Matt's tone demanded an explanation. Relief continued to pour through him at the sight of her.

"Forget it." Cole strode over from the stables. "Lucinda came over and couldn't find anyone."

"So I rang the triangle." Lucinda didn't seem apologetic at all. "At least that made folks show up."

The rest of the men tore around the corner and came to a dead halt. "Everything's all right!" Tobias yelled.

"Then who set out the alarm?"

"Since you men are here," April said, "we may as well put lunch on the table."

"Go ahead and wash up." Kate turned toward the door. "I'll get the dishes."

Matt wasn't going to let her out of his sight until he reassured himself that she was all right. He rushed to open the door for her. "Sure everything's okay?" he asked quietly.

Her gaze darted over to Lucinda. Tobias stood close to her and was speaking in a hushed, forceful tone. Kate looked back up at Matt. "I guess the important thing is that no one's hurt."

Several more horses thundered into the yard. Matt hadn't seen the riders before, but he knew in an instant they were Kate's father and uncles. "What's wrong?"

"Nothing's wrong, Dad." Tobias let out a beleaguered sigh. "It's all a misunderstanding. Welcome home."

A tall man with silver at his temples hopped off his horse straight onto the porch. "Are you okay, Katie Louise?"

"I'm fine, Daddy." She stood on tiptoe and kissed his cheek.

"Good." He turned and glowered at Matt. "Who are you, and why are you holding my daughter's hand?"

Just then, a bunch of MacPhersons arrived, demanding to know what the emergency was. Matt ignored them. He stuck out his hand. "I'm Matthew Salter, sir."

"Our new hired hand, Daddy. He's a hard worker."

Matt didn't for an instant mistake the possessive spark in Kate's father's eyes. Something even more possessive flared inside him. "As for holding your daughter's hand, well, I've never seen a more lovely one."

"It's got stain on it."

Matt shook his head. "Better look again. Those are beauty marks."

April wound her arms around Mama. "I'm so glad you're home!"

"It's good to be home."

"Daniel, put me down," Aunt Lovejoy said. When he refused, she reached over and cupped April's cheek. "April-mine, we went past the MacPhersons'. My sister tole me about you and Peter. Hit's about time. Two of you b'long to one another."

Guilt churned inside, and April blinked back tears.

"Why are you crying, honey?" Mama asked.

"They're happy tears," Kate said. "But she misses Peter. He and Johnna went to San Francisco."

Uncle Obie snorted. "April ain't the onliest one missin' that son of mine. He's a hard worker."

Uncle Titus folded his arms across his chest. "With all of us back, we'll do just fine. I understand our new hand, Salter, isn't a stranger to work. We'll loan him to you."

Kate gasped, "Daddy!"

"I don't mind, Kate." The corner of Matt's mouth kicked upward. "After all, you've told me on more than one occasion that Chances share."

"Won't be for long." Obie combed his fingers through his beard. "I reckon Peter and Johnna'll be home in two more days."

Mama gave April a tender smile. "Quicker than that if he's missing April half as much as she's missing him."

"Don't mean to rush you folks, but I need to tuck Lovejoy into bed."

"I'll do that!" April chased after Uncle Daniel. "You go on ahead and eat lunch. I'd love to visit with her and hear what she liked best in Yosemite."

"That's a grand plan." Lovejoy patted Daniel. "You jist tole me how hungry you are." April rushed forward to open the door to their cabin and turn down their sheets. Uncle Dan gave his wife a kiss and gently settled her on the bed. "Stop frettin', Dan'l. Get on out thar and eat hearty."

For the past week, Kate and April had been putting a fresh pitcher of water in all of the cabins just in case their family got home. Now she poured water into the basin and dampened a washcloth. All at once, doubts assailed her. *I can't believe I volunteered to come in here. I was afraid Mama would figure out something's wrong, but Aunt Lovejoy knows me just as well.*

Daniel left, and April pasted on a smile as she turned around.

Aunt Lovejoy let out a sigh. "Darlin', I don't mean you no offense, but I'm plumb wore out. All I want is to lie down and take a nap like I'm ninety years old."

"The day we came home, I was at least ninety. You have to be ninety-nine." She gently washed her aunt's face and hands.

"Ahhh. Nothin' feels finer than comin' clean."

It took no time at all to slip her aunt out of her dusty clothes and into a fresh nightgown. April tucked her into bed and brushed a kiss on her pain-etched face. "Welcome home."

"It's good to be home. Onliest thang that don't feel complete is my Polly and baby Ginny Mae aren't here."

As soon as Lovejoy drifted off to sleep, April walked the long way around to the stable so she could avoid everyone. She saddled up her mustang and rode to town. Lovejoy deserved to see Polly and her grandbaby. Besides, April had to think.

Lord, I don't know what to do. It's all such a mess. I don't feel good about asking You to fix this when it's my fault. The people I care about the most are going to be disappointed in me. I've used Peter to reach my selfish goals, and I've misled everyone else.

I know I have to pay the consequences, Father, but could You please work things out so no one else does?"

When she reached town, April headed straight for the doctor's office. Old Mrs. Greene hobbled out of Eric's office and smiled at her. "Doc Walcott's in. You here to see him or visit Polly and that cute little baby of theirs?"

"I'm hoping they're not busy. Everyone got home from Yosemite, and Lovejoy wants to see them."

"I heard that!" Polly sang out.

April laughed and let herself in. Polly enveloped her in a hug.

"Eric's seeing a patient; then he needs to go pay a visit on the pastor's kids. Ginny Mae finally got down for her nap. I can pack for us, and we'll come spend the night."

"Need some help?"

Polly's eyes lit with humor. "Actually, what we really need are some sourballs. Eric's out, and he always gives his pediatric patients a sourball. Would you mind running over to White's and grabbing them?"

"I don't mind at all."

Mrs. White was busy measuring out yardage for Mrs. Dorsey, so April took the lid off the big jar of sourballs and started filling a quart jar when the bell over the door rang.

"April!" Peter's voice rang through the mercantile. "What're you doin' here?"

"Getting sourballs," Mrs. Dorsey said.

April wanted to crawl into the corner and hide. Everyone in the place was going to think she was buying sweets for herself.

Peter hadn't stopped in the doorway. He strode straight to her. "Put 'em down, honey pie. I aim to claim a hug."

"Here?"

Mrs. White bustled over. "Young love. It's so sweet. April, hand me that little jar. I'll fill it for Doc. Peter's looking impatient, and I don't want these candies to roll all over the floor."

Being in his arms felt right. April allowed herself a second to relish his closeness one last time before she ended things and set him free to find a girl he could love.

"Missed me?"

She nodded.

The bell rang again. Johnna said, "Peter, you said you were jist gonna pick up the mail. What's—oh. Hi, April! I want to hurry home so I cain still see Trevor afore it goes dark."

"We ain't hurrying anywhere with those big crates full of material Gabe sent."

April tried to sound casual. "Johnna, you're welcome to borrow my horse. I'm sure Peter can get me home."

"Oh, thankee!" Johnna wheeled around, but the door no more than shut when it opened and jangled the bell again. "Where's yore horse?"

"In front of Eric and Polly's."

Peter chuckled. "Well that proves that love is blind. Eric and Polly are right across the street!"

They collected the mail, delivered the sourballs, then Peter curled his hands around her waist and lifted her into the buckboard. He looked her in the eyes. "I'm glad you sent my sister on ahead. I sorely need to talk with you."

April felt sure her heart had dropped right out of her chest and Peter had run it over with the buckboard. It took every bit of her courage to stay on the seat beside him. As soon as they'd gotten out of town, she blurted out, "Everyone's home."

"Is that a fact?"

"Yes. Peter, you're right we need to talk. I've gotten us into a horrible mess."

Chapter 14

Horrible mess?" April's words cut deeply. Peter had decided he had to come clean and confess his love to her.

"I've prayed for years for the man God intended to be my husband. Instead of waiting patiently for God to prepare me, I roped you into getting me ready. I should have known better and trusted in His timing. Instead, now everyone thinks we're in love. It's the very first thing Mama and Aunt Lovejoy said to me."

"Afore you go blaming yoreself any further, you need to recollect 'twas my idea to come calling and teach you thangs you needed to know."

"Only after I cried all over your shirt."

"I ain't never once felt anything but honored to spend time with you. I've tole you afore, I'm here to share yore joys and sorrows."

"I was afraid you were going to do that—be all honorable."

He gave her an exasperated look. "Most gals would be afeared a buck wouldn't be honorable."

"I'll have to confess to our families. It's my fault."

The horses knew the way home, so he focused his attention fully on her. "Are you miserable o'er having to swaller yore pride and tell them, or are you upset on account of how you might feel deep down inside?"

Pain flashed across her face. "Don't ask me that!"

He cupped her face between his hands. "I gotta ask. Time's come for truth, April. You ain't been o'er my spread on account of havin' so much extry to do back home with so many gone. I cleared a spot, and we've all been spending time putting up a cabin. That cabin is for me and my true love."

She closed her eyes and swallowed hard. In a tight voice, she whispered, "I hope she makes you happy."

"Yore the one who makes me happy."

Tears seeped out as she scrunched her eyes even tighter. "You're being noble. I was afraid of this."

"Noble?" He snorted. "Gal, I been crazy in love with you for over a year now. I been a-waitin' for you to fall in love with me. All this business 'bout me holpin' you catch a man was jist an excuse for me to be 'round you more."

Her eyes opened, but he couldn't interpret what she was thinking. "The whole time I've been gone, I near worried myself sick, thankin' on how other bucks would come a-callin'."

Her eyes dilated.

"They have!"

He heaved a deep breath and let go of her face, only to grab both of her hands. "I knew onc't they realized how special you are, I'd have to wrastle for your love. But I ain't a-gonna let you go. 'Member what I tole you afore I left?"

"You told me to remember everything you'd said." Her voice went ragged. "How to build a man up, to make him feel special—"

"No, no! Not that. I meant about how you got a heart full of tenderness and sweet words trip off yore tongue. Not to let a man jist look at you as the gal who makes tasty food. Yore value is far above rubies."

Not sure she was convinced, Peter halted the wagon and looked around. He hopped down, pulled April down, and didn't turn loose of her. She waited a second, then tilted her head up to give him a startled look. He yanked her into a hug. "I ain't a-turnin' loose of you."

"You stopped in the middle of the road to give me a hug?"

"Ain't no better reason." He grinned.

For an instant, one of her beautiful smiles burst through, but it dimmed just as quickly. "I don't suppose you noticed there's less of me. I've been trying—"

He pressed his fingers over her lips. "Shhh." He looked around and ordered, "Go yonder to that shady spot. I'll be there in a jiffy."

He rummaged in the boxes and crates, then went over to kneel by April's side. Carefully setting two candles on a flat rock, he looked at her. He lit the short, round pillar first, then the tall, narrow taper. Sitting back on his heels, he whispered a prayer. "Tell me, honey pie. Which candle gives the most light?"

"It doesn't make any difference."

" 'Zactly. God don't make His children all alike. Some folks are tall and skinny like that taper; others are stocky. Our Creator sets fire to our souls, and we're to be His light. How could you thank I'd care 'bout somethin' that don't matter one whit?"

April's gaze dropped from his, back to the candles. "Lucinda is right. Gluttony is a sin."

"That's 'tween you and God. Ain't nobody else's business to judge."

"But they do."

"Most sins are hidden in the heart. Folks cain foster greed, lust, envy, or wrath in secret or jist show that side of their character to one other person. Sloth—well, folks don't show that flaw in public. Gluttony's the onliest one that shows on the outside.

"Gluttony is eatin' and drinkin' to excess. That bein' said, I cain't honestly say

I've e'er seen you eat more'n anybody else. Kate's remarked on that, too. My uncle Mike—well, he's downright runty and scrawny compared to my pa or my uncle Hezzie."

A smile flickered across her face.

Heartened by that fleeting smile, Peter winked. "Don't you niver tell him I said so. But 'tis the truth, and we both know it's so. Anyhow, Uncle Mike—I cain't recollect a single meal where he didn't eat as much or more'n his brothers. Anybody jist a-lookin' at him might assume he eats less, but appearances and actuality—well, they're worlds apart. Could be, God fashioned you to be short and round to begin with. Whether you added on a little more, only you and He know."

He took her hand in his. "Not a one of us is perfect. God holps us, works with us to be more like Him. You and me—we both yearn to be what God wants us to be. We gotta harken to His voice and follow His will. Philippians says, 'Being confident of this very thing, that he which hath begun a good work in you will perform it until the day of Jesus Christ.' We cain be confident He'll lead us aright."

"That's talking about our relationship with Him. What about other people?"

"He don't compare us to anybody. He loves us jist 'cuz we're His. We get ourselves into trouble when we compare. Iff'n a thin person starts makin' comparisons, then Lucifer has a high old time lettin' pride seep in. Lucinda sat there, preening and actin' all superior when she decided to judge you. 'Twas a stingy heart she showed that day, but you cain't let yoreself believe that ever'body who's lanky feels the way she does."

She twitched him a smile. "That's true."

He paused and tucked a wisp of hair back behind her ear.

"April, iff'n you compare yoreself to a gal who cinches herself 'til she's got a fourteen-inch waist, yore takin' yore eyes off God. Lets the devil have a chance to make you feel defeated."

She nodded slowly. "I do feel beaten down."

"That saddens me no end. April, yore the most beautiful gal I've e'er seen. I reckon I could tell you how yore fine brown hair sparkles in the sunshine and when 'tis silvered with age I'll love you all the more, but that ain't what you need to know most."

She chewed on her lower lip.

Lord, holp me here. I don't wanna be vulgar. Peter's gaze swept across her and back to her eyes. "In the Bible, in the Song of Solomon, when that feller tells his gal how he feels—I feel that way 'bout you. Yore generous—in heart and of body. I cain't holp thanking how much a man would be blessed to come home each night to you. Yore body was made to cuddle a man and cradle babes. Nothin' would please me more than to be that man."

Pink tinted her cheeks, and her eyes widened—but she didn't look away from him.

He reached over and pinched out the flame on the taper and lifted the pillar. "You already let yore light shine, April. My heart warms by it's glow. I'm askin' you to become my wife."

"Oh, Peter. I love you. Nothing would make me happier."

An almost sickening sweetness hovered in the air. Matt inhaled and looked around. *If the moonshiner is using sweet mash instead of sour mash, it might smell like this. But the wind's blowing from over by the MacPhersons' cabins. I've managed a glimpse inside all of them, and none holds a still.*

He'd been at the MacPherson spread for a full week and a half. They might be as simple and straightforward as they seemed, but with so many of them going different ways, he hadn't been able to determine whether they managed to have a few members slip off and run a still. They sort of rotated through certain chores, but Matt couldn't see a pattern emerge.

"Bet you never thought you'd be lumberjackin' instead of cowboyin'," Peter teased.

Together, they heaved another log onto the pile. "It's for a good cause."

"I want this cabin to look jist like the one April's leavin'. The loft'll give us plenty of room for young'uns."

"Why don't you all just halt everything and spend a day to erect it?"

Yanking a splinter from his palm Peter shrugged. "We got too many thangs happenin' already. Harvest hits the same time the women are cannin', and the younger ones gotta get fixed up for school. Add two weddings to that."

A bell clanged. "Lunch." Peter dusted some tree bark from his shirt.

"I'm so hungry, I could eat just about anything." Matt chuckled at the look Peter shot at him. "The 'possum pie, porcupine stew and dumplings, and rabbit were all excellent." He tactfully left out fried lizard.

"This time of year, we always give the boys the job of wrastlin' up meat. Don't normally eat such a variety in the space of a week; but with everyone busy, it lets them shoulder a responsibility."

"They're all good kids. I get a kick out of how accurate they are with those slingshots."

"Slingshot ain't no match for a badger. We're all grateful you was out takin' a hike last night. Octavius and Reggie woulda gotten catawamptuously chewed up iff'n you hadn't been thar. Hey! Lookie!" He started jogging.

Matt kept pace. The Chance women and young children had come to call. *I hope Kate came.*

Peter swept April up and spun her around in a circle before setting her down. Matt spied Kate sitting off to the side, laughing. He beelined for her. "Hi."

"Matt!" She looked up from her work. Delight danced across her features. "How are you doing over here?"

"Fine. I've whittled some clothespins. Make sure I give them to you. What're you doing?"

"Shining up a few pairs of shoes."

A little girl jumped from one bare foot to the other. "Kate's gonna turn mine red!"

Matt rested his hands on his knees and bent over so he could look into her eyes. "Won't you be a sight in pretty red shoes!"

When she nodded, the little girl's braids jumped from behind her shoulders to the front and back again. "I'll be bee-you-tea-ful!"

Kate set aside the pair of shoes she had repaired. "Okay, Birdie. Bring me yours now."

Matt chuckled as the child hopped away. "Her name sure fits!"

Kate shot him a conspiratorial look and patted the space beside her. Glad of the invitation, he sat down. In a low tone, she said, "Her real name is Birdella. Eunice and Hezzie saddle their children with odd names."

Matt poked his tongue into the pocket of his cheek, thought a second, then said, "So they weren't kidding when they called one of the little fellows 'Lastun'?"

"That's really his name. Eunice was wrong, though. She had Elvera after him."

"I'm still trying to sort out who's who."

"And who's whose?"

"Yep. There's an army of kids here."

She dusted tiny slivers of leather from her apron. "It'll take time, but you'll manage."

"Is that your way of saying Chance Ranch doesn't need me anymore?"

Before she could reply, two women walked up. "Matthew Salter," Tempy MacPherson said, "words cain't say how grateful I am that you rescued Octavius—"

"And my Register—" Eunice added.

"Yestereve. Badgers are fearsome fighters."

Eunice shoved a bowl into his hands. "But they make a fine stew! Cain't thankee 'nuff and wanna honor you by givin' you the first bowl."

Chapter 15

"Thank you, ladies," Matt said. "I'm just glad the boys are okay. You know, I've never eaten badger."

"Neither have I." Kate's eyes sparkled with mischief.

"My mother would spin in her grave if I ate before a lady, Miss Kate." Matt slid the bowl to her before she could respond.

"Ain't it nice to see a man with such fine manners?" Eunice patted him on the shoulder. "Don't you worry none. I'll bring another for you now."

"Wait!" Kate used her free hand to grab Tempy. "Aunt Tempy, everyone knows how thick and meaty your stews are. One badger can't have made enough stew for all of us. Since Mama brought over beef stew, why don't we just let Mr. Salter have this? I'll have the other."

"I wouldn't want any of you feeling I didn't appreciate good cooking. Why don't I come over and get a bowl of the beef stew, then Kate and I can switch halfway through our bowls?" Matt nodded his head once to indicate it was a done deal.

"Now ain't they the most thoughtful young'uns?" Eunice beamed at them. "Nothin' like that uppity Lucin—"

"We wouldn't want to gossip," Tempy interrupted.

Eunice gave her sister-in-law a confused look. "Hit ain't gossipin' in the least. We was all thar and saw for ourselves—"

"I guess," Kate said, "it just goes to show how blessed we are to have friends and family who try to find the best in others."

"Yore right. I oughtta be ashamed of myself, standing here a-ditherin' whilst Mr. Salter's powerful hungry and wantin' his lunch."

"Why don't the both of you come sit at the table?"

Kate's laughter floated on the breeze. "If I do, you'll never pry me free. After the vat of marmalade you've made and been jarring all morning, I'll either stick to the bench from the sugar or stay there because I can't resist tasting it."

"Best you stay put. Hey! Homer, don't you dare show up to the table with that much grime on you!" Tempy scurried toward one of her many children.

Matt rose and accompanied Eunice to the tables. "Not counting weddings or church picnics, other than the MacPhersons and the Chances, the only time I've ever seen so many people gathered along tables like this was at an orphanage."

Kate's mother jerked around and stared at him. "Did you grow up in an orphanage?"

"No, ma'am, I didn't. While I was in San Francisco, I—" He caught himself before he admitted having to take an abandoned child to the orphanage. He cleared his throat. "I dropped a little something off."

"I hope the children were all happy and well cared for."

"It sure looked that way to me, ma'am. The children had plenty of good food to eat. The girls even wore ribbons in their hair. They weren't expecting anyone to drop by, so it wasn't as if someone put on a show. I was told a wealthy benefactor provides funds to keep the place operating."

"Here you go, Mr. Salter." Eunice shoved a hot bowl into his hands. "Grab yoreself a spoon and be shore you get a taste of the badger stew, too."

"Thank you, ma'am." He strode back to Kate. "I must have missed when someone asked the blessing."

"Uncle Obie did."

Matt sat down, bowed his head for a quick prayer since he'd not heard Obie's, then said, "Did my ears deceive me, or did Eunice call her son Register?"

Kate grinned. "We call him Reggie. Vinnie and Benny are girls—their nicknames are acts of mercy. No little girl ought ever be called Vinetta or Benefit."

"I agree." He waved his spoon at her bowl. "So how does it taste?"

"I was waiting for you."

"Don't let me hold you up."

Stirring the stew with her spoon, Kate said, "We have an agreement, right? We'll trade bowls?"

"Fair's fair." He took a bite of the beef stew. "Then again, this is awfully tasty. I might not want to give it up."

Kate muttered under her breath, "Here goes nothing," and lifted her spoon. As soon as she swallowed the first bite, she gave his bowl a sideways glance.

"We don't swap until halfway." He dipped his spoon and brought up another big bite. "Your mama sure makes a flavorful stew."

He ate faster than she. Matt figured it was because Kate wasn't fond of how badger tasted. He didn't much blame her, either. In a low tone, he said, "You don't have to eat all of your half."

"I will." Resolve vibrated in her low tone.

"I appreciate a woman who sticks to her word." He cocked his head to the side and surveyed two rows of shoes all lined up in the dirt about a yard away. "Some of those shoes look pretty battered."

"Kids are hard on shoes. Simple polishing and new laces will perk most of those. Since Birdie is getting Octavius's hand-me-downs, I'll die them red so they take on a girlish look."

"That's clever of you. Is that why the pair on the end are sporting yellow leather bows?"

"Yes. The next pair to the right will be Meldona's." He raised his brows, and she nodded. "Yes, she's Eunice and Hezzie's. Melly's shoes have been passed down twice—but both times, they were girls'. I'll put some pretty new buttons on them once I banish the scuffs. They'll see her through Christmas."

"Your talent serves both clans exceedingly well."

"Your boots look like they could use a little help."

Matt lifted his empty spoon and shook it at her. "No buttons or bows for me."

Her laughter stopped abruptly when he tried to take the badger stew. "I'll finish this, Matt. You said the beef is tasty. Go ahead and enjoy it."

"Nope. I honor my word." He switched bowls, looked down at the chunks of badger meat, and consoled himself with the fact that he didn't have to eat a whole bowl all on his own. Kate watched him avidly as he lifted the spoon to his mouth.

"This is wonderful!"

"I was just as surprised as you are." She looked down at the bowl she now held. "I love my mother's stew. I didn't think anything could compare."

"So now you can have two favorites."

"I don't mean to gossip, Matt, but I think you should know something. Tobias isn't courting Lucinda anymore."

He swallowed his bite. "Appreciate knowing that so I don't go putting my foot in my mouth. Your brother's a steady man, so a big change like that had to come after a lot of soul searching."

"I'd be lying to say I'm sad, but it's hard to see him hurting." She ate a little. "On the other hand, Caleb's wife, Greta, is home again. Her sister had twins, so she was over helping out. You might not recognize Caleb—he's found his smile again."

"I don't mean to boast, but I'm pretty good with remembering names and faces."

Kate's eyes sparkled. "But I'm telling you, Caleb's face looks entirely different. It's amazing what a smile can do."

It sure is. Your smile makes you glow. Matt tore his gaze from her. "I'll take your word for it. Seeing a new woman sitting among the Chances in the church pew will help me figure out which man is Caleb."

"Not for certain. I don't think you've met my cousin Polly. Her husband is the doctor—they live in town. Last Saturday, some men got rambunctious at the Nugget and had a gunfight. She and Eric missed church because they were still in surgery."

He whistled softly. "Either someone got hit bad, or it must've involved quite a few men."

"There's talk about the town needing to hire a sheriff. Until recently, Reliable was small enough and quiet most of the time." She let out a sigh. "I rather doubt it will happen. Folks have talked about needing someone to come reopen the boardinghouse, too. Neither has ever materialized."

Boardinghouse. His promise to drop a line to Miss Jenny flashed through Matt's mind. Later that evening, he wrote her a short note that said he was keeping busy. *Fact is, Miss Jenny, I'm seeing all those stars you knew I'd been missing. . . .* It was the truth. He'd been investigating the area during the night. *I've been eating well and met some good, God-fearing people.* He wished her God's blessings and signed the bottom, then stuffed the paper into an envelope.

Then next morning, he rode to worship along with the MacPherson men. The women and smaller children filled three buckboards. As they pulled into the churchyard, April called from the wagon she was driving, "We didn't plan a picnic, but it's a beautiful day. Are you folks interested?"

Lois looked at her husband, then nodded. "Johnna an' me—we were fixin' to look through the feedsacks and decide on what to use for the next quilt. Y'all cain come and holp. Delilah, yore always good at choosing colors that look fine together."

"That shouldn't be hard," a woman said from the church steps. "You MacPhersons always have yellow ones!"

"Reba White, 'tis mostly the sugar sacks that're yeller." Lois laughed. "Cain't manage to get the man at the feed and lumber to keep a supply of yeller feedsacks."

A man nearby let out a booming laugh. "Lois, I keep telling you, God makes all your leghorn chicks yellow, so the color of the sack doesn't matter!"

Lois pulled Matilda down from the wagon. "Bill, yore always glad to get my eggs and eat my chicken salad. Why cain't you humor me and bring in yeller sacks?"

"Because the rest of us have wives who want other colors!"

"I cain't be shore who said that, but I'll hold charity in my heart for you. Everyone as wants, come on o'er today for a picnic. 'Twould be a pity to waste a fine day like this."

"I already have a roast in the oven at home," one lady said. "Why don't we make it tomorrow? It'll let us ladies quilt!"

April's father clapped his hands. "I'll go tomorrow on one condition."

"What's that?" Pastor Abe asked.

"We men help finish the cabin Peter is building. I'd like to announce that my daughter, April, accepted his proposal. Chance Ranch will be roasting a steer, so bring your appetites along with your tools!"

The Youngbloods stood over by their buggy. Lucinda's father rumbled,

"Tomorrow's a workday. I'm not stopping everything just to be fed beef. I've got plenty of my own."

"Guess he's sore angered at Tobias Chance," Johnna whispered from behind Matt. "Tobias told Lucinda they'd come to a partin' of the ways. I s'pose her daddy's got call to be a mite hot under the collar. Pa would splavocate if Trevor did that to me."

"Weren't no promise nor proposal," Tempy murmured. " 'Twas wise, Tobias calling a halt to the courtship soon as he realized 'twouldn't work out."

Looking remarkably unperturbed, Gideon Chance nodded at Lucinda's father. "It's short notice, and it's a busy time. No one's under any obligation."

"Jist you watch," Eunice said in a hushed tone. "Folks're gonna come through. Makes me glad I come out to Reliable to be Hezzie's bride. People pitch in."

"You all stopped everything when my barn burnt down to help me get back on my feet." Dorsey squared his shoulders. "It's not about what we get fed. It's about helping a neighbor."

Soon pledges of help and promises to bring food filled the churchyard. Mrs. White and Bill decided since everyone was going to be at the cabin raising, they might as well close the mercantile and feedstore.

Pastor Abe stood on the church steps. "Folks, the sermon today was entitled 'Who is My Neighbor?' I could say plenty, but you've demonstrated the heart of the concept here and now. The sanctuary windows are open, but it's far cooler out here. Why don't we gather on the lawn and have a time of prayer and worship?"

While people moved their rigs and horses to free up shady spots, Matt noticed two of the MacPhersons slip away. So did two Chance men—Daniel, who was married to Tempy MacPherson's sister, and Kate's father.

Lord, I want to stay and worship You. This time is precious, holy. I don't want to believe that these men could be guilty—especially not Kate's father. It would break her heart. I can't reconcile the Christian values they've instilled in their children or the character they've displayed with the possibility that they may be making moonshine. But it's so suspicious that these men are slinking away. I ought to follow them.

"You won't need to move yore horse," Peter said. "What say the both of us go into the church and bring out a bench or two? Sitting on the ground'll be too hard on some of our elders."

"I didn't see benches in there—just pews."

"We keep one in each of the coatrooms." Peter started to stride away. "Follow me."

I'm stepping out in faith, Lord. My mind tells me to trail the others, but my heart tells me to follow Peter.

When they exited the church, Peter paused a moment. "Now ain't that a sight to fill yore heart?"

Kate and April sat on either side of their frail Aunt Lovejoy. Little children from the congregation had flocked over and sat pressed close together. Their sweet high voices hovered in the air as they sang the hymn, "Who Is Thy Neighbor?"

As they sang, a few quilts appeared—probably from wagon beds. The women of the congregation spread them out until the grass looked like a giant patchwork quilt. Men came back from moving their rigs and joined their wives.

Pastor Abe motioned to Peter and Matt. "Good, good. Why don't you young men bring one of those up front here?"

"I thought we'd put them off to the side or in back for the elders," Matt said to Peter.

"Go on ahead and do that. I'll tote this one up by the parson. Jist you wait and see. We're in for a treat."

Matt carried the bench over near Kate. Of everyone in the congregation, her aunt looked the most frail. He went down on one knee behind her. "Ma'am, I'd be honored to help you up and onto that bench."

Kate's eyes sparkled with gratitude. "How nice!"

"You must be that Salter buck."

"Yes, ma'am, I am."

"I'd 'preciate the holp, but I'd take it kindly iff'n you'd get me up t'other bench instead."

Matt gently gathered her in his arms and lifted. He no more than took two steps before April's father stopped him. "I'll take her."

Lovejoy patted Matt's chest and whispered, "Don't you be takin' that as a slight to yore strength. Gideon's a-tryin' to give you a fair excuse to slide into my spot and sit yourself down aside Kate."

"That wasn't my intent," Gideon rumbled.

"Good thang you Chance boys are strong and handsome. At times yore a tad dense." Lovejoy reached over and wound her arms around her brother-in-law as Matt slid her into his arms. "Thankee, Mr. Salter, for heftin' me up. I'd a-been stuck thar like a tip-turned turtle."

"We couldn't have that," Matt whispered. "One of the MacPhersons might make soup out of you!"

Gideon Chance chuckled.

Lovejoy grinned. "If that ain't a fact, I'm a 'possum."

Matt shot back, "Eunice and Lois make a tasty 'possum pie."

April's father threw back his head and let out a belly laugh. He laughed the whole way up to the front and while he seated Lovejoy on the bench.

Matt sat down beside Kate. She turned to him. "What's so funny?"

"Not a thing." He lifted a pair of kids, straightened out his legs, then plopped them back down. Two more kids popped up and promptly sat across his shins.

Kate took in the sight. "You're not going anywhere for a while."

Matt looked at how a little tyke climbed into Kate's lap, squirmed into a comfortable position, and started sucking his thumb. "Neither are you. I wouldn't change things one bit."

Discordant twangs and pings made Matt look up. Tempy and Johnna each held a mandolin, Lovejoy had a dulcimer, Titus Chance was tuning his guitar, and Peter drew his bow across a fiddle. A quick glance around showed the MacPhersons and Chances who'd left earlier were all back. Relief flooded Matt. He settled in for a time of worship.

"Since Pastor wanted today to be about neighbors, why don't we do the one. . .you know. . . ." Mrs. White began to sing, *"Ye neighbors, and friends of Jesus, draw near."*

Members of the congregation joined in, and as soon as that hymn ended, the pastor stood and prayed. He scanned the people seated across the lawn. "The Spirit is here among us. Let's continue to worship in word and song. If anyone wants to give a word of praise or thanksgiving, needs prayer, or wants to request a hymn, please feel free."

Lovejoy looked at Tempy. Matt couldn't hear what she said, but they both started to play "O Praise Our God Today."

April and Kate immediately raised their voices, *"His constant mercy bless."* At the end of the hymn, Kate said, "That's Aunt Tempy's favorite."

Peter started to speak. His gaze rested on April. "A man cain't be blessed more'n God givin' him a woman whose value is far 'bove rubies. Y'all heard April's to be my wife, and my heart near bursts with love for her and for a Lord who brung her to me. 'Tis hard to sing and play a fiddle at the same time, but 'Now Thank We All Our God,' shore suits me today."

After a few testimonies, prayers, and hymns, the pastor rose again. "Almighty Father, we thank Thee for being with us always—not just on Sunday mornings, but each hour of every day of the week. How wonderful it is to be surrounded by a great church family that practices Thy commandment to love our neighbors! Bless and keep us all in the center of Thy will. Amen."

During the worship, little Matilda had crawled into April's lap. She had fallen asleep, as had the boy sitting on Kate's lap. Parents came over and claimed the children perched on Matt's legs, but he wasn't in a hurry to get up. He reached over and traced the whorls of curls on the little boy's head.

Stooping in front of April, Peter scooped up his baby sister. He rose, then extended a hand to help April rise. Tobias bumped past them and pulled what had to be the youngest Chance kid from the blanket. "Come on, Perry." He tilted him upside down and shook him just for fun.

Kate laughed. Abruptly, her laughter stopped and she went tense.

Matt followed her gaze and shot to his feet.

Chapter 16

Matt took a few steps forward and stuck out his hand. "Youngblood. Matt Salter. It's good to see your wife's feeling better. Sorry she took sick last Sunday."

Tobias turned Perry right side up and shoved him behind his back.

Mr. Youngblood's eyes narrowed; then he bobbed his head as he shook Matt's hand. "Yes, she was better once I got her in out of the sun."

Kate patted her little cousin and ordered, "Off to the wagon." *This isn't the place or time, Lord. Please don't let things get ugly.* She wanted to nudge Tobias to silently urge him to make a tactful getaway. Matt had been clever enough to stall for him, but Tobias didn't budge.

Mr. Youngblood turned to Peter. "I was harsh earlier. My wife and I wish you every happiness. I'll send a man or two over tomorrow to help."

Peter shook his hand. "Thankee, sir."

Mr. Youngblood strode off.

April wilted into Peter's side, and Tobias's features eased.

"You're the only Chance gal who isn't spoken for," Mr. Greene said as he claimed his little son.

Heat filled Kate's cheeks. Mr. Greene was a fine blacksmith, but he had no talent for exercising tact. *He's just saying aloud what everyone else is thinking.*

Tobias slapped Greene on the back. "Kate's like Aunt Lovejoy. Children adore her. Bet it won't take long before someone snaps her up."

Kate started to get up. Tobias and Matt both reached to help her at the same time. She accepted both hands and rose. "Thank you, gentlemen."

"Peter."

Peter and April turned to face Tobias.

In a muted voice, he said, "We'll still have a picnic at your place today. Give us time to go home and change into work clothes. You'll need more logs for the cabin raising tomorrow, and the ox is in the ditch."

"I'd appreciate that."

Matt nodded his head sagely, but he couldn't suppress his grin. "That has to be the first time I've heard someone refer to the scripture that allows hard work on the Lord's Day. Most men quote how it's supposed to be a day of rest."

"Reckon I've only heard it onc't or twice in my life, but shore seems fittin' to me." Peter elbowed Matt. "Won't even mention April's daddy pushed the ox into that ditch."

Tobias, April, and Peter all sauntered off. Kate stooped down to gather the quilt they'd been sitting on.

"Miss Kate, I'll help you shake that out."

"Thanks." They held the corners and flapped the colorful quilt in the slight breeze. Bits of grass fluttered away. Matt looked across the quilt and coordinated folding the ends together and folding the quilt again lengthwise.

"Things went better than I expected with Youngblood," Matt said as he approached her. Kate took the corners, and he bent to lift the fold to double the quilt again.

"I guess it doesn't say much about my faith in my fellow man or in God, but I was sure Mr. Youngblood planned to get ugly."

"I don't have any room to talk." Matt folded his arms across his chest. "I thought the same thing. He took me by surprise." The corners of his mouth lifted. "So I'll see you at lunch?"

A thrill shot through her. Kate nodded.

"Just a word of advice: A couple of the MacPhersons gigged for frogs last night."

"Cold frog legs?"

"That, too." Matt lowered his voice. "The women saved the skins and were rolling bacon and grits into them today."

Giggles spilled out of her. Matt looked at her as if she'd lost her mind, so she tried to control herself long enough to say, "A special dish like that ought to be reserved for the engaged couples, don't you think?"

"Absolutely."

"What's so funny over there?" April called.

"We were both saying how wonderful it is, knowing how much you and Peter love one another and that you're going to be married."

"Johnna and Trevor, too," Matt tacked on.

~

"We got us a tradition," Peter's father announced to the crowd as he opened the door to the just-finished cabin. "Started back when Hezzie, Mike, and me got those pretty brides of ourn. Onc't the cabin's done, the groom takes one last gander 'round the inside; then he don't get to see it again till his bride's fixed the house into a home."

"The first thing I'm going to do," April said in a merry tone, "is hang curtains so Peter can't peek!"

Peter chuckled and beckoned her.

Uncle Gideon grabbed her. "Young man, the day my daughter becomes your wife, you can carry her over the threshold. Until then, she's mine!"

"Honey pie, how long is it gonna take you to get ever'thang ready?"

"Until Thanksgiving," Johnna declared. "Me and April decided 'twould be fun to have us a double weddin'."

Kate clapped with everyone else, but her joy for her cousin was tinged with sadness. After the Chance clan held a double wedding last year for Laurel and Gabe and Caleb and Greta, Kate had secretly thought it would be lovely if she and April would be able to do the same thing.

"Folks, thar's still gracious plenty on that steer and on the tables." Aunt Lois wiped her hands on the hem of her apron. "Take a look at what all yore hard work got done, then amble on back and fill yore bellies."

Kate waited until most of the others had gone in the front door and exited the back before she stepped onto the porch. Mr. Dorsey unexpectedly turned around and bumped into her. Someone caught her before she fell.

"Whoa. Are you all right, Miss Kate?" Matt set her down and gazed at her with steady brown eyes.

"I'm fine. Just clumsy, that's all."

"It was my fault." Mr. Dorsey gave her an apologetic smile. "I'd say I was weak from lack of food, but you'd laugh me clean out of town. I can't believe Lois thinks any of us can stuff in even one more bite."

"I'm never too full for good chow." Matt grinned. "As soon as we've gone through the cabin, I aim to pile enough food on my plate to feed a bear for winter."

"One plate isn't enough," Kate told him.

"Good thing no one here minds if I go back for seconds."

April ran up and gave Kate a hug. "I can't think of a better place to ask you. I want you by my side at the wedding. You'll be my maid of honor, won't you?"

Birdie tugged on Kate's skirt. "Tell her no. 'Tisn't a good thing, being the old maid. You lose the game on account of bein' the last one."

The last one. That's me.

Matt chortled softly. "Birdie, there's a difference. Old Maid is a card game. Being the maid of honor is a special job."

"But she still don't getta be the married one."

"Not this time," April said.

"But," Matt said as he leaned down and whispered very loudly, "everybody knows the best is always last because she's worth waiting for!"

Kate's heart skipped a beat, then soared. *I've been hoping he felt something for me, Lord. You know how I've tried not to throw myself at him. Thank You for the way Matt seems to understand me and how he says what my heart needs to hear.*

They walked through the cabin, and Kate commented as they exited the back door, "I know they said it's exactly the same as the cabin we share, April, but without anything inside, it feels so big and empty."

"Doesn't it? I already have some ideas. Let's talk over some plans tonight."

"Okay." Kate turned toward Matt. "Ready to eat?"

"Always."

Mrs. White came over. "Oh, dear. Mr. Salter, I feel terrible. Just terrible. You gave me that letter to mail for you, and it's not in my pocket anymore. I've asked everyone to look for it."

"I'm sure it'll turn up."

"But I've never misplaced a single piece of mail. This is—"

"A minor mishap," he soothed. "If we can't find it, I'll write a replacement letter."

"I found it!" One of the Greene's boys ran up and skidded to a dusty stop. "I found it."

"Thanks." Matt accepted the letter and handed it to Mrs. White. "See? Things worked out fine."

Kate felt anything but fine. Her throat constricted, and it hurt to breathe. She could only see part of the address, but even that was too much. Matt was sending a letter to a Miss Jenny Something-or-other.

Chapter 17

Kate went so white, every last freckle stood out in stark relief. Matt braced her arm. "Miss Kate, are you okay?"

Her head nodded woodenly.

April and he traded concerned looks. "Why don't you sit down here with your cousin? I'll go grab a cup of lemonade for you."

"No. I'm fine. Really. Excuse me." Kate headed off toward the trees.

"I don't like how she looked. No, I don't." Mrs. White made a shooing motion. "April, go on after your cousin, and make sure she's all right."

The envelope in her hand crackled with the action. Matt noticed the address on it. *Kate thinks I'm stringing her along when I already have a sweetheart!* He turned to April, "Miss April, today's a special day for you and Peter. Go on and enjoy yourself. I'll fetch Kate and bring her over so we can all eat a little more of that barbecue."

Matt didn't ask to be excused or wait for a response. He hiked to the edge of the wooded area where Kate had fled. *I have to find her. I can't let a silly misunderstanding come between us. I won't.* Following her didn't take much skill. At first, she'd stayed on the path, but then she'd struck out into an unmarked area. He'd done a fair amount of tracking in the past, and she'd been upset enough to leave a trail. She'd headed deeper into the woods than was wise—a mark of how upset she was. He followed the path she'd left behind and rounded a big pine.

Kate stood in a small clearing and held up a dandelion. Pursing her lips, she gently blew, sending all of the minuscule pieces of fluff into a flurry in the air.

I love her. How could I have done this? I've hurt the woman I love. Those two realizations hit with a double punch. Matt stood there, suddenly aware of just how deeply his feelings ran and what he stood to lose.

"Kate—"

She startled. "What are you doing here?"

"I came to talk with you."

"I'd rather be alone."

Matt approached her slowly. When he got closer, he bent and picked another dandelion. "When I was a boy, my mother said these were like candles on a birthday cake. If you blow it all gone in a single breath, your wish is supposed to come true."

"The nonsense of youth."

"It's not nonsense at all. There's nothing wrong with wishes and dreams." He blew the fluff off his stalk. "See? Now I'm entitled to hope my wish comes true. Know what I was wishing?"

"I'd rather not. I need to get back."

"Kate, I was hoping you'd give me a moment. That letter is going to the lady who ran a boardinghouse I stayed at. She's—"

"It's none of my business." She looked poised to bolt.

He hurriedly said, "Miss Jenny is at least twice my age and reads dime novels. She's worried nefarious bandits are going to bushwhack me, so I promised I'd drop her a line now and then so she wouldn't worry."

"You don't owe me an explanation."

"I might not owe you one, but I want to. Kate, I know we've only recently met, but you're unlike any woman I've ever known."

"I'm different." Her lips twisted wryly. "Yes. I know."

"You're wonderful. Intriguing. Clever and fun to be around." *It's too soon to tell her I love her.* "I hoped maybe you were feeling as comfortable with me as I felt with you."

She compressed her lips and turned away.

"I wouldn't hurt you for anything. You have to trust me on that. Trust your heart, too." He waited as seconds stretched in silence.

Finally, Kate said in a tentative voice, "Nefarious bandits?"

"That's a direct quote. On my wildest day, I couldn't concoct such a phrase. I didn't have the audacity to ask Miss Jenny if there was any other kind of bandit. It might make her self-conscious, and then she'd give up those novels she relishes so much."

"My little brothers and cousins are enamored of Deadwood Dick. If you say anything bad about those novels, the boys might gang up on you."

"Ah. There." He eased one step closer. "See? I blew on the dandelion, and my wish came true. Not only did you stay and hear me out, but you even gave me one of your pretty smiles."

"That's nonsense, and you know it."

"I'll tell you what I know. You're a beautiful young woman. We're alone in the woods, and your daddy's very protective. If I aim to keep life and limb, I'd best escort you out of here and over to the tables."

"I'm not hungry."

"Not even for something small?"

She hitched her shoulder. "It would have to be really little."

"I have just the thing in mind: Eunice's frog-skin-and-grits roll."

Kate's laughter let him know things between them were settled. Matt reached over and took her hand. "Come on. You got pretty far off the path. I don't want you to get lost."

"What path?" She shook her head. "It's gone by now."

"What do you mean?"

"Halfway through these woods, the land changes hands. When the Phillips lived on the other side, they didn't bother to fence in this part of the property. The MacPherson kids would cut through as a shortcut to school."

"But they don't anymore?"

Kate shook her head as he led her.

"Who lives there now?"

"The Youngbloods. He put up a barbed wired fence so he'd keep his cattle out of the MacPhersons' crops. Most folks would split the cost, but Mr. Youngblood paid for it. He said that arrangement was only fair since it made the kids take a longer route."

"Seems mighty generous."

"Unh-huh. Sometimes he comes off as standoffish or gruff, but he's also done some kind things—like apologizing to Peter and sending a couple of workmen."

"Careful. Log's rotten." Matt turned loose of her hand and lifted her over the log.

"This isn't the way I came in." Her gaze darted around.

"The MacPherson kids aren't the only ones who like shortcuts." He kept a light tone, but Matt wanted Kate out of those woods as fast as possible. The path wasn't overgrown as it ought to have been after a few years of neglect. Someone was using it regularly, and he aimed to find out who.

~

Matt silently entered the cabin and sneaked back into bed. He wouldn't be able to sleep, but he could use the time to formulate a plan.

"You wanna tell us where you've been?" Peter lit a lantern. His father and uncles all glowered at him.

Sitting up slowly, Matt realized he didn't have time to concoct a plan. He stared at the MacPherson men. "I've been in the woods."

"Ain't the onliest place you've been. Ever' night you've been here, you've snuck out." Peter raised his chin. "I might be plainspoken, but I ain't dumb."

"No one could ever mistake you for being dumb. Yes, I've gone out every night."

Obie's eyes narrowed, and he leaned forward. "You ain't meetin' a gal, are you?"

"No." Matt decided these men were honest. He'd have to trust them. Even warn them. "Someone's been making bootleg whiskey."

Mike nodded. "Yup. That'd be the Youngbloods."

"You knew?" Matt gawked at him.

Mike's brothers sat on either side of him. Their heads cranked toward him, and they said in unison, "How come you didn't tell us?"

"Tempy."

Matt reeled from that reply. "Your wife is involved?"

"Course not!" Mike shook his head. "Tempy's real name—'tis Temperance on account of her ma namin' all her daughters after the fruits of the Spirit. But her ma skipped a few names and stuck my beloved with that handle as a message to her man. Old man Linden had a still. I didn't want nobody upsettin' Tempy by rakin' up sommat painful in her past."

"You coulda told us. We woulda put a stop to it!"

"Hezzie, you and Obie couldn't keep a secret if your lives depended on it." Mike tapped his boot on the floor.

"So yore the excise man," Hezzie said.

"Not exactly. I've been working as a deputy in San Francisco. Moonshine's been a huge problem, and we've had folks die or go blind from bad batches. I was assigned to locate and shut down the still."

"Niver knowed a deputy who could down trees worth a hoot," Peter's father mumbled.

"You niver knowed a deputy at all," Obie shot back.

Peter ignored them. He stared at Matt. "We're going to put an end to that still. Once we do, you're going to have to reckon with us."

"The Chances, too." Hezzie shook his grizzled head. "I seen their lil' Kate a-lookin' up at you like you done hung the moon. They ain't gonna be happy one bit 'bout how you've played them false."

Matt stood. "Keep Kate out of this."

"Cain't." Obie rose. "We's a-gonna holp you shut down Youngblood's moonshine still, but we ain't a-gonna stand for you breakin' her heart. That gal's like a daughter to us."

Between the MacPherson men and the Chance men, Matt had more than enough help to take Youngblood into custody and dismantle the still. The men all worked together well, carrying the mission with grim determination and near silence. By morning, however, there was no jubilation over their success. Tobias made the discovery that Lucinda was just as deeply involved as her father. That alone was enough to leave the men subdued—but Matt knew the problem ran even deeper than that.

"We don't have a jail. I'll go send a telegram," Caleb said.

"Send it to Sheriff Laumeister in San Francisco." Matt scanned the men. "I've worked alongside you, but it was under false pretenses. When I came here, we didn't know who was involved."

"Don't bother," Kate's father ground out. "You had a job to do, and you did it. That much, we understand. You messed with my little girl, though."

"I didn't plan on falling in love." He stared her father in the eye. "I didn't mess with Kate's heart. She's a special woman, and as soon as I get this matter wrapped up, I aim to come back and court her."

"No, you're not." Her father's declaration would have been easier to take if he'd roared it. Instead, he'd said the words in a low growl.

"Thinking you've found the person God has for you, then discovering they're not what they seem—" Tobias broke off and shook his head. "No. There's no fixing that. You stay away from my sister."

Chapter 18

"I don't know what to say to her," April said to Peter as they walked along the stream. "Kate's barely talking to any of us. When we came home the night of the cabin raising, she was so excited. Matt had confessed he cared for her."

"For what it's worth, I thank he was tellin' her the truth. When her pa and brother tole Matt to stay 'way from Kate, Matt looked lower'n a snake's belly in a wagon rut."

"You know how much I love you."

"Sure do, honey pie."

"It's hard, though, for Johnna and me to work on our wedding dresses right there in the cabin under Kate's nose. She tries to paste on a smile and even helped baste the skirts, but she's hurting."

"That's gotta be tough. Johnna said Kate's taken it hard. Tobias don't look any better. Him breakin' thangs off with Lucinda—'twasn't an easy decision. But findin' out she was up to her eyebrows in brewin' whiskey—that shook him bad."

"Aunt Lovejoy! It's so nice to see you out here."

" 'Tis always a joy to bask in God's sunshine. Makes a body feel all warm and right inside and out." Lovejoy's gaze went from April to Peter and back. "But I look at the both of you, and neither one of you's wearin' a smile."

April sat next to her aunt on the bench Uncle Dan built for Lovejoy back when he was courting her. "I don't know what to do about Kate," April confessed.

"I reckoned this would come up. A wound niver heals when it's left to fester. Ever'body's tippytoin' 'round and pretendin' nothin's amiss. That's gotta come to an end. Ain't no reason she cain't have herself a good stormy cry, jist like there's no call for the both of you to be robbed of the joy you ought to be sharin' in yore sweetheart days."

Peter nodded.

"Peter, fetch me a little rock from the crick." He did as she bade, and Lovejoy held the wet pebble and rubbed her thumb over it. Pressing it into April's hand, she said, "That rock weren't smooth a long time back. It had rough edges. God put that rock in the path of water, and that water wore down the sharp spots till it turned into a right purdy lil' pebble.

"We cain't say why God sent Matt here. The memory of him's like water, rushing over Kate and wearing her down. Don't know iff'n the dear Lord plans a different man for her—or any man atall, for that matter. Certain as we sit here, God's niver gonna let His children suffer for naught. Someday down the line, we'll look back and see how He directed the currents of life. We all love Kate and wanna protect her from the pain, but if we take her outta the river, then we remove her from where God intended her to be. Iff'n 'twas her life or limb that were at risk, then we'd hop right to it, but when it comes to matters of the heart—well, interfering ain't right. Best thang we cain do is stand 'longside her. Kate's got to trust God that whate'er betides her'll turn out aright as long as she lives in the center of His will."

"That's not just true for Kate." Peter accepted the pebble April handed to him. "It's true for all of us."

"Yup. There ain't no doubt our lovin' heavenly Father wants the both of you to leave and cleave. Don't be so worried o'er something else that you forget what's important: Aside from yore relationship with Him, you each gotta be concerned more for one another than anybody else."

"April comes first," Peter declared.

The rapidity and certainty in his response thrilled April. "I feel that way about you, too."

"And God's gonna bless you abundantly. Now go on and moon o'er one another as you finish yore stroll. I aim to be talkin' to the Lord as I sit out here."

"See you later." April gave her aunt a kiss, then placed her hand in Peter's as they started to walk off.

Uncle Daniel came stomping out. "Lovejoy? We've got a problem."

"What's a-wrong?"

"Matthew Salter just took over the Youngblood place and applied to be Reliable's sheriff."

Matt accepted the dipper and gulped down the cool well water. "Thanks, Miss Jenny. How're things looking up at the house?"

"I'm going a room at a time. The two bedrooms were in fine shape, and so were the parlor and kitchen. I can't for the life of me imagine how they allowed the rest of the house to fall into such disrepair!"

"Don't work too hard. We've got nothing but time. Let me know if there's anything else you need." He lifted the pad of paper and started scribbling on it again.

"Salter."

Matt looked up. "Tobias."

"What're you doing here?" Kate's brother didn't bother to dismount.

"I'm setting down roots because I aim to spend my life here."

"Any place else'll do. We don't want you here."

Matt rested his hands on his hips. "I'm not in the least bit surprised."

"Good. Then get—"

"Son." Titus Chance's voice cut through the air. He rode up slowly. In a matter of minutes, so did Kate's uncles, Caleb, and four of the MacPherson men.

Matt stood his ground and said nothing. The verse he'd read that morning in the first chapter of Joshua ran through his mind: *"Have not I commanded thee? Be strong and of a good courage; be not afraid, neither be thou dismayed: for the Lord thy God is with thee whithersoever thou goest."*

Obie MacPherson called over, "Titus, Kate's yore daughter. Whaddya wanna do 'bout this?"

Kate's dad stared down at him. "Every man's entitled to have a say. You've got one minute, Salter."

"That's more than fair. I did hide my original purpose in coming to Reliable. It's plain to see that gave you cause to distrust me. That's understandable, but you need to know I never told a lie about who I am or how I feel.

"I'm a brother in Christ. Character and integrity matter to me, and that's one of the reasons I became a lawman—to protect the innocent. I appreciate your motive is to protect Kate. I fell in love with her. I make no apologies for any of that, and I'd never knowingly hurt her.

"You told me to keep away from her. I know that's what you want; I don't know if that's what she wants. Kate's an exceptional woman, and God will have to heal the rift between us, but I believe He can. She's worth waiting for.

"I've prayed long and hard. As a result, I'm putting down roots because I'm acting on faith. I want to rear our children here where they'll have grandparents and uncles and aunts and cousins. I'd far rather we all live in harmony."

Silence hovered thick in the air.

"Mr. Salter?" a soft voice called from over by the house.

Obie MacPherson's eyes bulged. "You brung a woman with you!"

Matt elbowed his way past the circle of horses. "Yes, Miss Jenny?"

"You told me to mention anything I need. I can't seem to find a stepladder, and one of the windows in the kitchen is cracked."

"I'll see to those things. Thank you, Miss Jenny."

She began to wring her hands. "I'm sorry I don't have any refreshments ready to offer your friends. If you give me a little time—"

"The gentlemen didn't plan to stay long. Don't worry about that."

Matt watched her until she went back into the house, then he turned back around.

Obie muttered, "I seen buzzards what'd look purdy compared to her."

"Miss Jenny is beautiful on the inside."

"She yore kin?" Hezzie surmised.

"No. She's going to be my housekeeper. I'll definitely hire a cook." Matt gave them a wry look. "You men should thank me for sparing you from eating her food."

"We're taking a vote," Daniel Chance said.

"Us MacPhersons is gonna be in on this here vote," Obie declared.

"The women will have a fit if they find out we didn't include them," one of Kate's uncles said.

"Then we jist won't tell 'em." Peter grinned.

Gideon looked around at the men. "Anyone want to weigh in on the matter before discussion is closed?"

"Yep." Peter pulled a pebble from his pocket. "Dan, yore wife jist gave this to April and me. She's a wise woman."

The men bobbed their heads in silent agreement.

"She said God smooths us with the currents of life. We all love Kate and wanna protect her, but Lovejoy says it ain't right to interfere when 'tis a matter of the heart. We oughtn't to remove Kate from where God intended her to be. Whate'er betides, Kate'll turn out aright as long as she lives in the center of His will. Our place is to stand by her and pray."

"Anyone else?"

Silence.

"Caleb and Tobias are old enough to vote. Peter—"

"If he's old enough to marry my daughter," Gideon said, "he's entitled to vote."

Hezzie scratched his head. " 'Zactly what're we votin' on?"

"Cain't make him move." Mike MacPherson mused. "I reckon whether we're gonna let him be near Kate."

"It's not a voting issue. Kate is my daughter." Titus Chance stared down at Matt. "You said some things that bear consideration. In the end, I want my daughter to be happy. Before Peter spoke, I wanted you as far away from my Katie Louise as possible. But that's probably the worst thing that could happen. She has to work through this for herself. I don't want you to go to her, and I'm asking you to give your word that you won't approach her. If she seeks you out, that's her decision."

A wave of relief washed over Matt.

Kate's father continued. "You're on a mighty short rope, Salter. Never thought I'd see the day that one little rock would sway my intent."

"Sir, it's not the size of the rock. We're standing on the Solid Rock together. I wouldn't want to base my life any other way."

Chapter 19

No matter where she turned, Kate couldn't escape the pain. She went to church, but Matt Salter attended, too. She went to town, and he was walking down the boardwalk, wearing the sheriff's badge. He doffed his hat to her, but then he turned and went the other direction. She wanted to duck into her cabin and be alone, but April and Johnna were there, sewing wedding gowns.

Craving privacy, she went into her workshop. Laying out a tanned skin, she tried to occupy her mind on how best to use the leather.

"Kate?"

"Oh. Hi, Mama."

Her mother pulled out a stool and perched on it. "I've wanted to have some time alone with you. It seems as if everyone's hovering over and crowding you."

"I can hardly breathe."

Mama nodded. "I've tried to give you some time to think matters through. You've always been like that—you need a chance to let everything settle before you make a decision. What are you making?"

"I don't know. I haven't settled on what's the most important thing. I always decide on that before I cut anything out." A rueful laugh bubbled out of her. "At least I'm predictable."

"Matthew Salter has to hold very strong feelings for you, or he wouldn't have come back."

"But how can I trust him? He lied to me."

"Did he lie? From what Caleb and Tobias say, they hired him to do a fair day's work, and he did more than any hand we've ever had."

"But he deceived me. He acted like he was an ordinary citizen. How can I ever trust that he won't mislead me again?"

"I don't have an answer to that. Have you been praying?"

Kate sniffled and nodded. "I don't have an answer. I keep begging God to show me the way, but He's silent."

"That's a hard place to live. You know we're all praying for you."

"Thank you, Mama."

Mama leaned forward and ran her hand over the leather. "Your Daddy's Bible is about worn through, but he loves it so much, he says he won't use another. Do you think you could make a new cover for it?"

"Sure."

"I thought I heard you in here." Aunt Delilah came in. "I've run out of clothespins, Kate. Do you have more in the basket for me?"

"Yes." Kate went up on tiptoe to reach the pail.

"Good. Laurel sent some pictures for me to take to the gallery. Between her pieces and mine, we'll have enough for a big show."

"Here." Kate set down the bucket.

Aunt Delilah's eyes widened. "I never imagined! With the rest of us gone in Yosemite, I thought the boys would be too busy to whittle much."

Kate leaned over and pretended to examine a spot on the leather.

"Honey," Mama asked, "how did we end up with so many?"

Kate didn't want to answer. She cleared her throat to buy time, but it didn't help. In a tight voice she said, "Matt made a lot of them."

"That was nice of him. I'll have to thank him."

"You don't need to, Aunt Delilah. We didn't tell him about you painting them and giving them away as a thanks to people who sponsor the older orphans' education."

"I take it he doesn't know that our family sponsors the orphanage," Mama said.

"He's aware the family takes wooden toys to the orphanage for Christmas. We've all agreed nobody needs to know you gave that mansion away to be an orphanage, Mama, and the family's support is a case of the left hand not knowing what the right hand is doing."

Dumping the clothespins from the pail into her apron, Aunt Delilah said, "It's okay to keep some things to yourself."

"I know. Those are all things where I wouldn't just be speaking for myself. I'd feel wrong divulging a confidence that I held for others."

Delilah left, and Mama quietly slipped away to get Daddy's Bible. When she came back, she didn't say a word. She set it down on the workbench and walked back out.

Lifting Daddy's Bible, Kate felt the cover on it shift ominously. It was so precarious. *If I make a new cover, maybe we can take this to a bindery in San Francisco and have them repair it. He'd have to make do without it for a while, but in the end, he'll have something that'll last his lifetime.*

Try as she might, Kate couldn't remember the measurements she took so she could cut the leather. After the third time, she grew exasperated with herself. *What's wrong with me?*

She stared at the Bible, then at the clothespin pail. *I feel just as empty as that pail, Lord. What am I going to do?*

Suddenly, I feel guilty. Like I did something wrong. But I didn't. Aunt Delilah even said it was okay to keep some secrets. She leafed through the Bible. It opened to

Luke—which came as no surprise. That was Daddy's favorite book of the Bible. Christ's words jumped out at her: "And why beholdest thou the mote that is in thy brother's eye, but perceivest not the beam that is in thine own eye?"

Conviction poured through her. *I felt justified in keeping information back; how can I fault Matt for doing the same thing?*

She tore off her apron and rushed to the stable. The few minutes it took to saddle her mustang felt like an eternity.

"What's got into you?" Tobias asked.

"The truth. I'll be back later."

"Where are you going?"

"Pray for me. I'm hoping to meet my future."

"Sheriff?"

Matt set aside the WANTED posters he'd been studying and rose. "Yes, Mrs. Walcott?"

"Could you please come over to the office?"

The doctor's wife looked a tad flushed and held her baby tight to her bosom. Matt nodded and took his hat off the peg behind his desk. "Is there a problem?"

"Yes, but I think you'll be able to solve it. I think it would be best if I take Ginny Mae and wait over at White's Mercantile."

"Is your husband at risk?"

"No. But please go over and straight into his exam room. You're the only one who can handle this, so you're expected."

Matt figured she'd said as much as she could. He'd learned Polly was a healer, and she and Doc were laudably closed-mouthed about their patients. He headed down the boardwalk with ground-eating strides, considering all of the possible situations he might encounter.

Dr. Walcott's place smelled of lye soap and carbolic acid. Matt veered to the left as soon as he entered and pushed his way through the curtain.

"Kate!"

She stood on the opposite side of the exam table. "I didn't know where to find you. Your housekeeper thought you might be in town. I didn't want to interrupt if you were in the middle of something important, so I asked Polly to see if you were available."

She'd said all of that in one breath. Matt knew because he hadn't taken a breath, either.

"I was upset because you said you cared, but you kept a big secret from me."

"I know. I'm sorry—"

She held up one hand. "But I had no room to judge. I'd been keeping secrets from you, too. Aunt Delilah and my cousin Laurel are successful artists. Each

Christmas, they paint clothespin ornaments and give a dozen as a thank-you to each sponsor who funds the education of one of the older kids at the orphanage. And the orphanage—the one you've mentioned. Mama inherited that mansion. She gave it up to become the new location because the old orphanage was falling apart. And my family—we don't want folks to know that we fund the orphanage."

Matt rounded the table. "Why are you telling me these things?"

"Because I don't ever want dishonesty between us." Tears filled her eyes.

"I don't want that, either." He slowly took her hand in his. "But with my kind of job, there are bound to be times when I can't tell you what's going on."

"I know. I understand now."

"If it'll bother you, I'll give it up in an instant. I bought the Youngblood place. I could farm or ranch."

"Between the Chances and MacPhersons, there are plenty of those already. They'd gladly rent the land from you."

Matt shook his head slowly. "No, Kate. That's not really what I hoped for."

A stricken look flashed across her face.

He slowly trailed a fingertip across the freckles on her cheek. "I told you that night we did dishes together that I reckoned the only woman I'd call simply by her given name would be my wife. That day I sought you out in the woods, you might not have noticed, but I stopped calling you Miss Kate. I did that because I realized I'd fallen in love with you and wanted you to be mine. What I've been hoping for, praying for, was to have you as my wife."

At first, she gaped. Then the very tip of her tongue slipped out to moisten her lips.

"I'm not the most patient man, but I'll wait until you figure out your feelings. I know where I stand, and if it takes seven years to court you, I'll do it, just like Jacob waited for Rachel in the Bible."

"It took him fourteen years." Her voice sounded low and shaky.

That reminder didn't please him, but Matt tamped down his feelings. Kate's feelings were what counted. "If it takes twice that long, I'll wait. I love you, Kate. Nothing's going to change that."

"I love you, too."

Her admission nearly knocked him out of his boots.

"But Matt?"

"Yes?"

"There's a problem."

"Darlin', nothing is going to stand in our way. Look how far God's brought us."

"I met Miss Jenny. She insisted on giving me a cookie and a glass of lemonade. She's a nice lady, but we'll both be seeing God a lot sooner than we imagined if we keep her as our cook."

Epilogue

Folks packed the pews in church. Johnna squeezed April tight. " 'Tis a joy to be sharin' today, ain't it?"

"Yes!" April then whispered, "Kate told me Miss Jenny made potato salad."

"Thanks for warnin' me. Last thang I want is to wind up ailin' from our weddin' supper. I s'pose I ought to mention that you'll want to thank Aunt Eunice for doing sommat special. She took a mind to fancify the deviled eggs. They're a right purdy color on account of her addin' Tabasco to the yolks."

"I'll be sure to pass the word on."

"You gals best save your talkin' for the words what matter most down at the altar," Uncle Obie said.

Tobias and Caleb opened the doors from the narthex to the sanctuary, and the organist began to play the "Wedding March." Johnna held her father's arm and a sheaf of yellow roses as she walked down the aisle.

Trevor could barely wait for her. Uncle Obie's normally booming voice had a catch to it when he said, "I ain't a-gonna give up my little girl till she gives me one last kiss."

Johnna calmly handed her roses to Trevor, lifted her veil, and bussed her pa.

"Ain't easy. I'm marryin' off my two eldest today. But, Trevor, ain't a better man for my Johnna, so I'm a-givin' her to you."

Trevor handed back Johnna's flowers. "I'll love her forever."

"I aim to go sit by my Lois so's we cain share the sight of my son's bride a-walking down this aisle." Uncle Obie tugged Lois out into the aisle, stepped in, and tugged her to his side. "You cain't see past me, sugar. Here you are."

The organist took her cue and began playing again. Gideon Chance stood in front of April, blocking everyone's view of her. He lit the white pillar candle she held. "You're beautiful, sweetheart. Mama and I love you and trust God to bless you and Peter."

"I love you, too, Daddy." She peeked around him as Peter stepped to the front of the church. April let out a delighted laugh. "Oh, Daddy—I asked him not to wear a white shirt, and he didn't! The only thing more golden than that shirt is his heart."

Gideon Chance stepped to the side, and April slid her hand into the crook of his elbow. Joy lit Peter's face as soon as he saw his bride.

Tobias continued to hold the door open and looked at Kate. "Take off those gloves, sis. Matt loves you just as you are."

Kate hastily tugged off the gloves, and Tobias shoved them into his pocket. Her father smiled as he pressed his newly covered Bible into her hands. "You look just as pretty as your mama did in that gown, Katie."

"Thank you, Daddy."

"Dad," Tobias hissed. "The music's started up again. Get going!"

Titus Chance shot his eldest a reproving look. "Salter knows my daughter is worth waiting for."

"He's patient, Daddy," Kate agreed. "But I'm not. If you don't give me your arm, I'm going to gallop down the aisle all by myself."

He threaded her arm through his and chuckled. "You'll always be my little girl."

"Yes, Daddy, I will." Kate looked ahead at her bridegroom. "But even more, I'll be Matt's wife."

All three couples stood at the altar. Pastor Abe smiled at them. "God's home is always full of hope and love. Today, an extra measure of both has been poured out upon us because three of our young couples are here to pledge their hearts in holy matrimony."

Sacred vows were exchanged, communion was shared, then each couple sealed their promises with a kiss.

The pastor looked at Johnna and Trevor, then April and Peter, and finally at Kate and Matt. "It's my privilege to pronounce these three couples as man and wife. Surely we can all say our cup runneth over with love."

If you enjoyed this story collection,
you may enjoy

California
CHANCES

Kentucky
CHANCES